First published in 2014 by Endeavour Press Ltd.

This edition published in 2018 by Sharpe Books.

Sword of Empire:
The Complete Campaigns

Richard Foreman

Table of Contents

Sword of Empire: Praetorian

1.

Rome. 171AD.

"He's dead," the stabbed figure overheard as he lay upon the sofa in the triclinium. Blood soaked the scrawny youth's tunic. His usually pale face was now ashen. Junius Arrian had been attacked in his own home. A dozen or so drunks had made their way up from the Subura carrying torches and grudges. The mob had discovered that Arrian was the son of a German tribal chief. And Rome was at war with the German tribes.

Over the past year Arrian had been anxious about being outed as a German, even though he considered himself a Roman, having lived and been educated in the city from the age of eleven. He had been sent to the capital, along with his older sister, on the suggestion of the governor of a neighbouring province. It was not uncommon for Rome to educate the sons of its potential enemies – in order to win future allies.

The eighteen year old could not find the strength to open his eyes. His thoughts wandered, as if in a dream.

The attack was a blur. The men had broken in with a couple of axes. Half sought out the owner whilst the rest sought out his valuables and the wine cellar. The bookish youth had frozen in terror upon encountering the intruders, fearful both for himself and his sister, Aurelia. Two wild-eyed men approached him, spitting out curses and cackling. One called him a barbarian and the other judged him to be a spy. Arrian could not remember which one had slid the short blade beneath his ribs. He lay on the floor, bleeding, vainly stretching out his hand, as they took a screaming and tear-soaked Aurelia with them out into the night.

Two slaves, Clarus and Tiro, did their best to attend to their master. Arrian had drifted in and out of consciousness over the next couple of hours. He thought he heard and saw a couple of members of the Praetorian Guard, but again the scene felt like a dream and he couldn't be sure. Clarus had lit a fire and covered his young master with a blanket but Arrian grew increasingly cold.

He understood why he had been targeted. Rome was at war with the Marcomanni and various other northern tribes. The Germans had crossed the Danube and drew first blood in a series of devastating and brutal raids. Twenty thousand Romans had perished, and twice that number had been sold into slavery. Rome had finally mustered sufficient forces to go on the offensive, over a year later, but the war had not gone well for them so far. The Emperor Marcus Aurelius had suffered a series of defeats. Farmhands, firstborns, foreigners and even gladiators, much to the anger of the audiences in the arena, had all been conscripted. Famine had struck and the Tiber had burst its banks in the past few years creating discord. Christians were a growing political and religious force, who looked to serve their God rather than the Emperor. The plague and high taxes were also laying siege to Rome. Marcus Aurelius' co-emperor, Lucius Verus, had recently died. Germans and Christians were, as the Jews might describe them, scapegoats. Romans could and did blame their ills upon the enemy within – and equally they were willing to sacrifice them.

Arrian flicked through the pages of his mind, looking to select a quote from his philosophical studies to help console him at his end. *It is possible to provide security against other ills, but as far as death is concerned, we men live in a city without walls.* Epicurus. *The day which we fear as our last is but the birthday of eternity.* Seneca. He also wanted his last thoughts and prayers to be for Aurelia. She was one of the most virtuous people he knew – at least she had been before finding religion.

14

The youth winced and arched his back in pain as he re-lived the knife penetrating into his side. He thought that there was nothing he could have done to save himself, or Aurelia. Like the Emperor he had spent his time in the company of philosophy – rather than fencing – tutors. You don't have to fight on the frontline to be a casualty of war, Arrian sadly concluded.

Sweat glazed his countenance. His breathing grew shallow. His dazed thoughts grew even dimmer. Would the afterlife be akin to the forests and grasslands of Germany, or the porticoes and marble of Rome? Arrian wished for the latter. He had made the diverse and wondrous (but far from perfect) city his home. He had embraced his Roman name and lifestyle. Literature, laws, philosophy, civilised conversation – all these would make the afterlife worth living. Ironically his death, at the hands of Romans, could help cause the downfall of the civilisation he so admired. On hearing the news of his passing his father might side with the Marcomanni and their King Balomar – and take up arms against Rome.

The German youth drifted in and out of consciousness again. When he woke he heard Clarus mournfully remark to Tiro, "Get some coins for the ferryman."

Arrian deliriously wondered, had he died and was now hearing these words as a ghost?

2.

A thick layer of sawdust soaked up the wine, spit and various other bodily fluids which stained the floor of the tavern, *The Ambrosial Fountain*. Although it was the dead of night the establishment was still home to a dozen or so patrons. The smell of alcohol, sweat and cheap perfume filled the air. Oil lamps hanging from the ceiling flickered. In the half-light one could still make out the large mural on the wall, depicting certain carnal acts that might have made even Caligula blush.

A couple of haggard-looking whores on a bench turned their heads towards the two praetorian guards who had just entered. Their eyes were bloodshot with drink and the drabs appeared too tired to raise a smile for the soldiers, let alone anything else.

The larger of the two men, a centurion, stepped forward into the centre of the chamber, the studs of his boots sounding across the stone floor. For the first time that night everyone stopped drinking – and took in the soldier. Gaius Oppius Maximus. He wore a red tunic, grieves and breastplate. A gladius hung from his belt. A broad brow hung over dark brown eyes. His short black hair was flecked with grey, his face dusted with stubble. A number of patrons eyed him with suspicion. Maximus returned their stares with a look of thinly veiled contempt, the way a gardener might look upon weeds which needed cutting down.

The centurion's optio, Rufus Flavius Atticus, moved into the centre of the room too. His blue eyes were bright with wit and intelligence and in contrast to his colleague the young man appeared amused, rather than angry. A wry half-smile lined his handsome features as the optio scanned the various faces gazing back at him. Although born to an aristocratic family, Atticus had spent many an evening in similar drinking holes to this during his late teens. The former philosophy student had often closed his books early to seek out wine truth. The tavern, as much as the Forum, was the face of Rome, Atticus judged. The Senate would be wise not to ignore all the grievances spouted out during drinking sessions in such places, although they would be equally wise not to listen to all the bile and ill-informed opinions spewed out from the Subura too.

The Ambrosial Fountain was the third tavern the soldiers had visited that evening, passing by scrawny dogs and scrawnier beggars whilst walking the narrow streets. The servant, Clarus, had given Maximus a description of the ring leader of the gang who had abducted the girl. Maximus' orders had come via a letter from the Emperor himself, to retrieve the brother and sister and escort them to his base at Aquileia. The centurion put his confusion and disappointment to the side when he reached the house. It was not worth ruing the fact that if only they had got to the house earlier, then they could have prevented the tragedy. "We are where we are," Maximus had stoically remarked. He sent for a doctor to attend to the brother and interviewed the servant about the intruders, figuring that they would take the sister back to a tavern.

Maximus spied his quarry. From his leathery, weather-beaten features and the tattoo of Neptune on his neck Sinius (as the servant Clarus named him) had been a sailor, the centurion surmised. His body was still knotted with muscle. His red hair was doubtless as fiery as his temperament.

Sinius met the soldier's challenging gaze and smiled, or rather sneered – revealing a set of teeth more crooked than a tax collector. His nose was out of shape too, having been broken more times than a poet's heart.

"Give me the girl and that will be an end to it," Maximus said, his voice as hard, flat and direct as a Roman road.

A short silence ensued. Sinius continued to sneer at the centurion. Three of his fellow gang members were still around the table. The rest of the mob who had attacked the house had slithered off into the night. The men were part of a carpentry gild. They worked together, drank together and fought together.

"The Praetorian Guard. We used to call you toy soldiers when we served in the navy. Ceremonial puppets, who spent more time polishing their swords than using them. You think you can make or break an Emperor, put a Claudius on the throne and take a Nero off it? In this tavern we're the ones who make or break people. Now fuck off, before I shove your sword up your arse. Although being a praetorian, you might like that sort of thing," Sinius announced. The trio around the table chuckled in support.

The rest of the patrons in the tavern slowly but surely slunk into the corners, cradling their cups. They would be content for blood to be spilled during a fight, but they did not want any brawlers knocking over their wine. One man carried his bowl of stew over to the opposite corner where Sinius was sitting. He happily left his chunk of bread on the table though; he had half-joked to the landlord earlier that the loaf was so hard that it could hammer a nail into the wall.

Maximus pursed his lips and rolled his eyes at his antagonist, seemingly bored rather than annoyed by his response.

"He has a lovely way with words," Atticus drily remarked to his friend, his half-smile widening into a grin.

Sinius grew even more irate. He had inspired boredom and amusement in the arrogant soldiers, rather than fear.

"I have a lovely way with women too. But I won't be shoving my sword up that German bitch's arse later. It'll be something else. Eh lads?" The group once again gave out a drunken, or sycophantic, laugh. Sinius here stood up, revealing the extent of his brawny frame. Maximus sized up the rest of the group sitting around the table. An equally well built brute sat next to Sinius on the side of the table closest to him. His bulk – and the copious amount of alcohol he had drunk – would slow him in a fight, but he still would prove a fearsome opponent. He looked like a man who had taken part in many a wrestling bout, although how many times he had been victorious was a different matter. A lank-haired, rat-faced looking man sat opposite from Sinius and fingered the handle of a long-bladed knife. Small dark eyes and a sadistic smirk suggested that the cretin would just as rather put a knife in a man's back as his front, Maximus thought. The final member of the gang, sitting in the far corner, was by far the youngest in the group. He looked about as brave and threatening as a Gallic cavalry officer – and would retreat as quickly as one too. The centurion fancied that he could probably pay the whores on the bench to best the teenager.

"Give me the girl and that will be an end to it," the soldier remarked again, his voice even deader than before.

"I heard you the first time. I'm not deaf, although if seems you may be dumb. What do you want with her anyway? We're at war with the godless barbarians. A good German is a dead German. Her brother is most likely a spy. You should be thanking us, buying me a drink. Can't you see? We got rid of a snake in our midst."

As Sinius spoke he walked forward and fronted up to the officer, looking to intimidate him. Maximus could smell the wine and garum on his breath.

"The only unwelcome creature I can see in our midst at the moment is an ass," the centurion replied matter-of-factly.

Sinius' face folded itself up in rage. He went to draw his dagger from his belt but before the blade was freed from its scabbard

Maximus whipped his forearm around and slammed his elbow into his opponent's nose. The landlord winced as he heard bone and cartilage break. *The Ambrosial Fountain* gushed with blood.

Atticus quickly drew his knife, as he saw the rat-faced gang member grab his blade from the table and rise to attack Maximus. With a well-practised flick of his wrist the soldier's dagger zipped through the air and buried itself into the man's thigh. Surprise and pain shaped the man's features – turning to shock as he looked up to witness the optio's fist swinging into his jaw.

Sinius fell to the floor, half concussed. He jolted back to life however when the centurion brought his boot down upon his left ankle, shattering the bone in two places. Sinius snapped his head back and screamed in pain. At the same time the brutal looking drunk who had been sitting next to the gang leader bellowed in anger. Maximus saw a cudgel swinging towards him. Whether it was a reflex action, or deliberate, the centurion raised his forearm. His greave duly deflected the blow of the short wooden club. In reply Maximus butted the pugilist – and then kneed him in the groin (twice) – leaving the brute doubled over and writhing on the floor like a child having a tantrum.

The remaining member of the gang, in the far corner, retreated rather than attacked. His eyes were wide with fear rather than fury. The youth had nowhere to run or hide.

"Where's the girl?" Maximus asked.

"In the back room there," the frightened youth nodded and pointed (repeatedly) in the direction of the door. If he could have told the praetorian in any other way, to appease him more, he doubtless would have.

3.

"Rather than give those coins to the ferryman, I suggest you put them aside for his medical treatment."

Clarus watched, his eyes and mouth wide open, as the smartly dressed doctor entered the room, accompanied by an attendant. His tone had been haughty, aristocratic. His features were slim and sharp, although the doctor would have argued that his intellect and wit were even sharper. Clarus thought that the physician looked more Greek than Roman. His beard was as grey as it was black but the doctor moved with the energy and purpose of a man half his age.

Galen of Pergamum, the Emperor's personal physician, ushered the slave out of the way with a wave of his hand and set about examining his new patient. Friends called the polymath confident; his detractors condemned him as being arrogant. Rather than being something in between, he was both. The Emperor had called Galen "the first and only physician in the Empire." It was a judgement that the doctor and philosopher did not feel the need to dispute.

"Our master is lost. Only the gods can save him now," the slave sorrowfully replied, reverently looking skywards as if he had already started to supplicate Jupiter and Alcipius.

"Well by all means offer up your prayers to save your master, but forgive me if I utilise more scientific methods to cure him. I warrant however that your prayers may well prove more effective than some of the medical practices that my error-filled contemporaries have been known to employ."

The doctor emitted a snort of derision as he thought of some of his contemporaries, who had at one point also been his critics and persecutors. Such had been the whispering campaign – and open

21

abuse – against the freethinking physician that he had been driven out of Rome. Yet he had bravely returned to the capital and gained the patronage of Marcus Aurelius himself. Scientists and lay people alike flocked to attend his public lectures. As well as being engaged by the spectacle of the renowned doctor cutting up all manner of animals (pigs, goats, dogs, elephants), the audience also enjoyed Galen's commentary during which he dissected the practices and philosophies of his rivals. His barbs could cut as deeply as his scalpels.

"He has lost too much blood!" Clarus bemoaned, half burying his master already.

"I dare say that you could set up a practice with such a lack of medical knowledge. All is not lost. The injury need not be fatal. I've treated gladiators who would consider such a wound a mere scratch. Your master may not possess the hardiest frame and constitution, but I can detect a strong enough pulse. As Cicero used to say, where there's life there's hope."

"And do you think that there is any hope that my master's sister will return?" Clarus asked, nervously chewing his nails whilst watching the calm and methodical doctor attend to his patient.

"Yes, both your master and mistress are in safe hands. There are scarce a dozen men in the Empire who the Emperor trusts more than Gaius Maximus. If it is in his power to bring the girl back, he will. Indeed you might rather feel sorry for the men who abducted her. For a score of physicians might need to be called out to attend to the injured, should the gang give Maximus any trouble."

As Galen commenced to clean the patient's wound he thought about the centurion who the Emperor spoke so highly of. Rumour had it that Maximus was a descendant of Lucius Oppius, the famed *Sword of Rome* who had served both Julius and Augustus Caesar. Oppius had a child with a lover, a political agent named Livia. Galen did not know any more about his descendants. He was, however, aware of what had happened to Maximus' immediate family. His wife and children had been victims of the plague. They perished within the space of two months. As well as pitying the centurion for his tragic loss – the Emperor mentioned how much Maximus had genuinely loved his wife – the doctor also admired the soldier. Unlike many of the officers serving in the Praetorian Guard, Maximus did not behave like a martinet. Nor did he serve in the army with an eye for political or financial gain. Galen recalled a story that Rufus Atticus once told him: a corrupt treasury official once tried to bribe Maximus – the centurion's response was to break all of the bureaucrat's fingers and arrange for the official to be removed from his post.

The doctor broke off his thoughts concerning the praetorian when he noticed his patient regain consciousness.

"Am I still alive? Or am I a ghost?" Arrian semi-deliriously asked, staring up at the serene and sagacious physician as if he were a god in the afterlife.

"I suspect you are still alive, but if you are a ghost I would be grateful if I could write you up as a case study. Dissection of an incorporeal being may prove somewhat tricky though," Galen drily replied.

Arrian managed a feeble smile. As he came round further the youth realised who was attending to him, having spent many an hour at his public lectures. Arrian had far more questions than answers, but his first was perhaps the most pertinent.

"Will I live?"

"I believe so. Just let me work – and then rest and recuperate. Time heals most wounds."

As he spoke these words Galen once more thought of Maximus and wondered if time would ever cure the widower of his grief.

4.

"If you've harmed the girl in the slightest then I'll cut off your thumbs. If you've done worse to her I will cut off your bollocks – and then kill you," Maximus vowed, as he stood over the still prostrate Sinius. Those who overheard the centurion were left in little doubt that he would make good on his threat. Sinius moved his jaw up and down to respond, but he could only emit rasping groans of pain.

"He's got an even lovelier way with words now," Atticus sardonically remarked, standing next to his friend.

"I'll fetch the girl, if you keep an eye on things here."

The optio nodded and then turned to face the still resolutely fretful owner of the tavern.

"Landlord, make it a large one. I think I've earned it. These ceremonial puppets can put on quite a show, no? On second thoughts, let me buy a round of drinks for everyone, except of course for our friends here who already look somewhat worse for wear," an amused looking Atticus announced, handing over a sum of money that made the evening a memorable one for the tavern owner, for the right reason.

Light sliced into the dank storeroom as Maximus opened the creaking door.

They may take this body but they will not besmirch my soul, Aurelia forcefully told herself.

The young woman in her early twenties was bound by rope to a pole in the centre of the room. Strands of black hair clung to her tear-stained cheeks but there was a look of defiance in her luminous green eyes. Her dress was expensive, made of Chinese silk. The evening's events had sullied the pattern of the garment, but it hadn't been ripped open. Thankfully Maximus had reached the girl in time, before Sinius could have his way with her.

Aurelia took in the figure of the stolidly built praetorian. Had the vile gang sold her to some soldiers? Legionaries often ogled her and made suggestive comments when she went to the market. They were all Godless brutes, the spirited woman thought to herself, whether they were German or Roman.

"Aurelia? Please don't be alarmed. I'm here to take you back to your brother's house," Maximus gently remarked, his tone dramatically different to that of how he had addressed the gang leader.

"Who are you?" the young woman replied haughtily.

"My name is Gaius, Gaius Maximus."

For a second or so the soldier thought he saw that the woman appeared to recognise the name and she stared at him differently, intently. Time stood still. But the fires of distrust and disdain soon re-forged themselves into her expression.

Not wishing to startle the woman by drawing his sword and cutting her loose, Maximus untied her. As he stood close to Aurelia, Maximus breathed in her perfume, which scented the air over the odours of the mouldy cheese and stale wine polluting the storeroom. The girl was wearing the same perfume that his wife Julia had used. The fragrance brought back the memory of the campaign against the Parthians, when Maximus would sit in his tent and read over her scented letters. He had closed his eyes and breathed in the perfume, imagining she was there with him. Even now he would sometimes unlock the chest he kept Julia's correspondence in and read her letters. He never wanted her fragrance, or his memories, to fade. A wave of both fondness and sorrow buffeted him whilst Maximus continued to free the woman.

"Have you seen my brother? Is he alive?" Aurelia asked desperately.

"You'll see him soon," Maximus answered in earnest. If Galen had been unable to save the brother then at least he had not, technically, deceived the girl. She would indeed see him soon, alive or dead.

Aurelia did not want to waste any time in getting back to Arrian. She quickly dusted down and straightened her dress. She tucked her long black hair behind her ears, revealing a pale but attractive heart-shaped face, and walked out of the storeroom. The soldier initially admired her fortitude in the face of the trauma she had just experienced, but then considered that the woman may just be in delayed shock.

Her abductors received a withering look of scorn as she passed by them in the tavern. As Aurelia gazed at the youth, however, who had been party to the attack on her home, her expression was one of shame and disappointment – as if he were a lost sheep.

"Drink up," Maximus said to his optio.

Atticus nodded – or tutted – and swiftly drained his cup of wine, wincing after doing so. He didn't know which year the wine was – he just knew that it wasn't a good one. Atticus smiled at the woman as she marched by him but he too received a less than friendly look. He wondered whether she was unimpressed by his drinking, or whether she was chastising him for potentially delaying her. Perhaps it was both. Not even his own mother looked at him with such moral disapproval, Atticus wryly thought to himself – and she knew about his affairs with married women, his gambling, cynicism, wasted academic potential and general profligacy.

Slate grey clouds tessellated together and rain peppered the air as Maximus and Atticus walked ahead of Aurelia and they made their way out of the Subura. The optio glanced back to check on the woman. She still wore a proud, pinched expression on her face. Atticus was unsure whether she was turning her nose up at the

26

stench which pervaded the streets of the Subura, or if she was disdainful of the company she was in. Perhaps it was both.

"Let's hope that the brother's alive when she gets back. The girl's frosty now. She'll be positively glacial if Galen is unable to save him," Atticus whispered to his centurion, under the shush of the wind.

"She'll still need to accompany us to the Danube to meet the Emperor, whether he's alive or dead." Maximus had grieved for his wife whilst still fulfilling his duties to his Emperor. The girl could mourn for her brother in transit too if needed, he concluded.

"She seems like a woman more used to giving orders than taking them."

"Perhaps I should have kept the length of rope from the storeroom that they used to tie her up with."

Atticus tilted his head back and let out a burst of laughter, not knowing, however, if his friend was entirely joking or not.

Aurelia barely heard the laughter of the soldier in front of her, absorbed as she was in her own thoughts. Rain fell down her cheeks, masking the tears. Her expression was pinched, due to the revulsion she felt at reliving her ordeal. Images stung her inner eye and turned her stomach. She recalled the scene – and scream – when they stabbed her brother. She could still smell the sour wine on their breath and the rancid odour of garum on the hand that had been clasped over her mouth as they took her back to the tavern. A pock-marked Spaniard had pawed her, saying how much he enjoyed stroking silk. The gang's vile leader had called her a "spoil of war," one which they would all have the opportunity to enjoy. She hated them. All of them. If the authorities did not punish them in this life then they would be damned in the next.

Tears had streamed from her eyes in despair in the murky storeroom. She had prayed to God to save her. Yet rather than the

Holy Spirit, Aurelia had been rescued by a ghost from her past – a demon rather than angel, she believed.

5.

The centurion felt somewhat like a captain, whose ship had been becalmed upon the sea. Two weeks had gone by and still they were in Rome, as opposed to journeying north and fulfilling his orders. As keen as Maximus was to deliver the brother and sister to the Emperor he duly deferred to the advice of the physician and allowed time for Arrian to recover his strength.

Maximus assigned Atticus – and a handful of legionaries – to guard the house whilst the adolescent recuperated. He did so partly out of precaution in case the house was attacked again, and partly he wanted the guards there to prevent the brother and sister from escaping.

The officer visited the property every few days to check upon Arrian's progress. After speaking to the youth Maximus realised why his Emperor wanted him to escort the Germans to the Danube. They were the son and daughter of the chieftain of the Arivisto tribe. The Arivisto were still to ally themselves with Rome, or the Marcomanni, in the war. Marcus Aurelius would ask Arrian to appeal to his father to side with the Empire – and hopefully tip the balance of power in Rome's favour within the region.

"I would be willing to speak to my father, but I'm not sure how much weight my opinion will carry. I'm not sure I've grown up to be the type of son he wished for. He wanted a warrior, but he's ended up with a philosophy student," Arrian said, with both a flicker of humour and sadness on his pallid face.

"Well, as we will need you to deploy words, rather than arms, you will be well suited to the task at hand," Maximus replied, in an attempt to boost the youth's spirits. He had grown to more than tolerate the boy. Although he wasn't entirely physically developed, the youth was thoughtful and good natured.

Whereas Arrian grew to be at ease in the centurion's company Aurelia would often absent herself from the room whenever the soldier looked in on the brother and sister. Or she would silently gaze upon him with a look of intrigue, or resentment, in her expression. But the praetorian was inured to such behaviour.

"If looks could kill then I would have died a thousand deaths before now," Maximus said to his optio whilst discussing the brother and frosty sister. "It's her father that we need to compel her to speak to, not me."

"You should consider yourself fortunate. The girl responds to me with something far more galling than scorn. She treats me with indifference," Atticus had wryly replied.

*

In order to give Atticus an evening off from guarding the Germans – so he could attend a party hosted by his father, a prominent senator – Maximus came to the house at dusk to relieve him. He encountered Galen upon entering, who had just finished attending to his patient.

"What the prognosis?" the centurion asked. The words had been like a refrain to Galen over the past couple of weeks.

"You will be pleased to hear that he will be fit to travel in a day or so. He should not be over extended in the journey, however. The boy did not possess the most robust of constitutions even before his injury."

"Thank you, Doctor. Now are you sure that we cannot pay you a fee for your time?"

"I'm sure. My motivation is medicine, not money. If ever you call upon me again though try to make the case a more a challenging one, in a less odorous neighbourhood," Galen tartly replied, his beak of a nose still smelling the sewage in the air from a nearby drain.

"I'll bear that in mind. Are you attending the party this evening too? Atticus tells me his father has invited you."

"Spend an evening with senators, talking about politics? I would rather spend an evening attending to lepers. No. The politicians there will ignore me for not being sufficiently important enough for them to speak to – and their wives will carp on about their imaginary health problems. I would doubtless end up wishing certain diseases on the irksome creatures, after discussing the ones that they think they have. Suffice it to say I have declined the invitation. I'm content enough to spend the evening with a good book. I also have to start preparations for our journey together. The elephant that I was due to dissect in a public lecture in a week's time is far more ecstatic about my leaving Rome than I am, but there you are. As many challenging cases as I might find in a warzone, I'm far from enamoured about joining you on your campaign.

"However, it will be a pleasure, rather than a duty, to see the Emperor again. I share your fondness and admiration for him, Maximus. Julius Caesar was great, in regards to his achievements rather than morals perhaps. We may deem Augustus great, too. Vespasian was a great pragmatist and Antinous was wise in that by doing very little he did much. But Marcus Aurelius is rarer than them all. For, more than great, he is a good man. But I now worry that I am starting to sound more garrulous than a politician. Or worse still, a politician's wife. Or worse still, his mistress. I will leave you to your duties," the doctor remarked, with a cursorily polite smile and nod of his head, his mind already focused on some scientific or philosophical problem as opposed to his exchange with the soldier.

31

Shortly afterwards Maximus found himself at the entrance to the house again, bidding a farewell to Atticus. The blood-red horizon was darkening by the minute. Tendrils of smoke began to spiral up into the air from a phalanx of nearby chimneys. The smell was – Galen was right – odorous.

"Enjoy the party."

"I may well enjoy the wines and food tonight but I cannot vouch that I'll enjoy the company. My father's friends talk endlessly well of themselves – and endlessly ill of everyone else."

"It won't be all that bad, I'm sure. You said that wives had been invited too. You might get lucky."

"Lucky would have been avoiding the invite in the first place. But my mother insisted. She used her own version of an officer's vine stick to coerce me – guilt. But enjoy your evening too my friend. Try not to stand too close to the sister. You might freeze to death."

The two men shook hands and Atticus took his leave.

The wine, the news that they would be leaving soon, and Atticus' joke brought a rare smile to the centurion's usually flint-like expression. The smile soon fell from his face when he turned to find Aurelia standing before him, carrying a book. Her dress was plain, her dislike of Maximus plainer. Atticus had said that – should she allow herself to be – the sister could be fiercely attractive. Instead she was just fierce looking, especially in the presence of the officer.

"I want you to know that I am willing to travel back home, not because your Emperor has asked me to, but because my brother has," the woman coldly stated, peering down her nose at the praetorian.

"I've stood in front of thousands of bloodthirsty Persians on a battlefield, all wishing to kill me. How much do you think I'm a-feared or bothered about you standing before me now, wishing to have a tantrum or futile war of words?"

Aurelia stood slightly aghast that the soldier had spoken to her in such a manner in her own house. But before she could muster a reply he had already walked by her, heading towards the wine cellar. She called him a brute in her mind, and remembered Julia again. How could she have loved him as much as she said she did? He was coarse, violent, a non-believer. Aurelia missed her friend dearly, especially given their parting – but thought little about how "the brute" would be grieving for her too.

6.

Music played in the background. Tired and gaunt looking slaves held up lanterns in the garden, providing light and heat for the party guests. Silk dresses shimmered in the moonlight, as the women inside them shivered a little. The low murmur of conversation was occasionally punctuated by the sound of unaffected – and affected – laughter. Around fifty people populated Pollio Atticus' lawn. Merchants lobbied politicians. Salacious gossip and discreet favours were traded. Everyone had an opinion in regards to the war against the Marcomanni, with those who were ignorant of the situation expounding on things all the more.

Rufus Atticus, speaking to his sister Claudia, overheard snatches of a discussion between two elderly, waspish senators.

"...Pius brought Aurelius up to wrestle with philosophical problems, rather than battle barbarians...Taxes are up, the number of desertions is up – and the conscription rates have risen too. The only thing that's down is morale... Aurelius may be a hardworking legislator, but what we need now is a Caesar who is willing to pay the blood price in defeating our enemies... Soldiers are there to be sacrificed for the greater good, that's what we pay them for..."

Atticus (having shaved, washed his hair and changed into a toga) rolled his eyes and wondered how Maximus would have reacted to hearing such criticisms of Marcus Aurelius. He would have made them eat their words he suspected – and may well have knocked their teeth out beforehand. Atticus soon turned his attention to his sister again. Claudia was cynical, sarcastic and pleasure-loving; but it was because of these traits, rather than in spite of them, that he enjoyed her company so much. Other women at the party may have possessed better figures and finer features, but few possessed a greater intellect or caustic sense of humour, Atticus thought. Claudia shared her brother's same intelligent, amused expression. She was the only person in the family who he genuinely admired, or who even half understood him.

"So it seems you will be off to the frontline again soon. I'll miss your company. As you can see, the jewels my girlfriends own sparkle far more than their conversation," Claudia issued, pursing her lips in disappointed resignation as she re-pinned her hair up in a slightly different position.

"I fully intend to come back from the war, although there is of course the ongoing danger of my dying of boredom at this party before the night is out," Atticus countered, whilst nodding in thanks to a slave who filled up his cup.

"You will not be the only one venturing to the front soon, if Cornelius Sulla has anything to do with it. Our local pederast made a speech today, calling for further troops and resources to be put at the Emperor's disposal. He said that he was willing to help oversee the conscription of the young recruits personally, which raised several eyebrows and a number of sniggers in the crowd. But the senator was as bellicose as a Spartan, although given the length of his speech he was not quite as laconic as one. You should have seen it. A vein throbbed in his head and he pounded his fist on his pigeon chest at least half a dozen times to convince his audience of his convictions. He said that he was not one for speechifying, but he felt that the hand of history was upon him."

"If the hand of history was there, I hope that it would have had the good sense to give Cornelius a slap. I'm sure that his patriotic fervour had nothing to do with him being a shareholder in a tin mine which supplies the military."

Atticus could not decide whether he should smile or scowl at the thought of the odious, self-serving senator. Claudia saved him from any decision however as she changed the topic of conversation.

"But tell me more of your campaigns, so to speak, on the home front. I hear that the social lioness, Lucilla Domitia, invited you to dinner the other evening. Did the lioness get to devour her prey?"

"I declined the invitation. Some vintages are best left on the shelf."

"And what about young Portia? She's far from vintage, indeed she's probably just ripe enough to be plucked off the vine," Claudia remarked with a suggestive glint in her eye, remembering the virginal girl's doe-eyed expression when she spoke about her brother.

"Annoyingly she seemed far more interested in trying to engage me on an intellectual level. She's still in a phase where she wants to talk about poetry or, worse, love. So I'm seeing her mother. She's now a much more happily married woman I dare say, due to the affair. But how is married life treating *you*?" Atticus again gave a nod of thanks to the attentive slave who re-filled his cup.

"Fronto is barely at home nowadays. And when he is there he no longer feels any desire to sleep with me. His life is centred on his business interests. He spends money, rather than time, on me. He doesn't even care that I'm having an affair. In short, married life is bliss at the moment," Claudia replied, eyeing up her father's new bodyguard over Atticus' shoulder – Chen. His broad chest and biceps filled out his tunic nicely. The Chinaman seemed to always wear a sour, disgruntled expression but Claudia believed that she could put a smile upon savage looking features. She had never had a Chinese before and was mildly intrigued as to how he might perform. He had largely been speechless in her presence so far, but perhaps he would open up to her more, in regards to her father's plans, during pillow talk.

"But tell me, how is the widower's life treating Maximus? You must allow me to invite you both to dinner before you head off to save the Empire. You will of course be welcome to depart early, to leave him alone with me."

"You would still end up sleeping alone for the evening. Maximus is still devoted to Julia, for good or ill." Atticus replied.

"The ghost of his wife cannot keep his bed warm at night though."

Claudia grinned and tried to sound glib, but she had more than once thought about being with Maximus, burying her head in his chest and having his muscular arms cradle her. She always felt safe with him – and he brought out the best in her. She liked herself when she was with him. Atticus had introduced the centurion to her some years back. Maximus was a good man, refreshingly untainted by ambition and pretension. She had envied Julia for her marriage to the soldier – and desired Maximus even more for still being devoted to his wife. Too many men were solely devoted to themselves.

Before Atticus could reply he spotted his father making his way towards him from the other side of the garden. He quickly downed his cup of wine and beckoned for another, arming himself for the inevitable, but needless, encounter with the host. At least the slave would make it in good time, before his father could reach him. Pollio Atticus, an influential senator and soon to be candidate for a consulship, laughed, smiled, shook hands and nodded in appreciation and agreement with any and all of his guests as he made his way through the crowd. Despite his silver hair and wrinkle-filled face, Pollio Atticus still possessed an air of vigour and virility (he still bedded two different women a week, neither of which were his wife). The "Augur", as he was titled in certain circles (for knowing – and shaping – which way the political wind would blow), was a man to be courted rather than crossed. He was "corrupt and corrupting" as Atticus had once explained to Maximus. The well-groomed statesman was a man used to getting his own way, either through charm or more forceful means. Pollio Atticus was ever conscious of being in command of himself – and of those around him. He was a man used to being listened to – and obeyed. Despite his will to dominate, the senator never displayed anger, or any unseemly emotion, in public. "I get even, rather than angry," he would icily state. Many a guest at the party could testify to the extent of how the would-be consul could ruin a rival both politically and financially. "He is Crassus, Seneca and Agrippina all rolled into one," one guest could be heard to whisper, in either admiration or condemnation, during the party.

"Evening. Claudia, would you be a dear and go see your mother? She wants to introduce you to someone, Marcus Dio," Pollio Atticus remarked warmly.

Claudia clasped her brother on the arm and smiled.

"Duty calls," she said to him, suspecting that the "someone" would be a person of influence who her father wanted her to seduce "in the interests of the family," as he often explained.

"Seems you may be about to die of boredom at this party too. Take care."

"Do visit before you leave Rome."

"I will," Atticus replied, offering his sister a reassuring smile – letting her know that he would indeed visit her and that he would be fine in dealing with their father. Claudia hugged her brother one last time, kissed him on the cheek and moved off in the direction of her mother – before her father could offer her a reproving look for keeping his guest waiting too long.

"I'm pleased that you could attend the party this evening, Rufus. It must have been a struggle to tear yourself away from another night in the barracks. At least the company is a tad more civilised here," Pollio Atticus said, offering his son a quick, sharp smile like a snake darting out his tongue.

"More civilised perhaps, but not necessarily more enjoyable – or honest."

For all intents and purposes it looked as though the father and son were engaged in polite conversation as they each nodded and smiled at one another. But years of mutual antagonism, bitterness and disapproval festered in every sentence spoken by the two men. Atticus had defied his father by joining the army. At first the statesman believed that his son would come crawling back to him, after experiencing the realities of the service. But his son proved him wrong and continued to defy him, crimes which Pollio Atticus refused to forgive. The two men had barely spoken a word to each other in the past five years.

"Your mother tells me that you are venturing off to the front again. Do you not think that it's about time you gave up this nonsense of playing the soldier? I still can't quite figure it out. Are you being stubborn? Is it because you think that women like a man in uniform? I can say with some authority that they also like a man in power. I shall laugh if you try to tell me that you have served this long out of a sense of duty. The Rufus Atticus I know has only ever had a sense of duty towards himself," Pollio Atticus derisorily remarked and laughed, whilst his eyes flitted about behind his son, checking to make sure that his guests were being attended to and to see if anyone else of importance had arrived.

The soldier's laughter was louder – and genuine – as he replied however, "Is the great Pollio Atticus attempting now to warn of the dangers of being selfish? I should inform all the lexicologists working in the libraries at Athens and Alexandria. I have discovered a new definition of irony. I'm pleased to say also that the Rufus Atticus you know is not the one I'm familiar with."

39

"Well, should you enjoy irony, you may be interested to know, believe it or not, that I partly arranged this gathering for your benefit. You should make some connections here. You still have the time and opportunity to make something of yourself and venture into politics."

"I'm not quite sure that those two things are as strongly related to one another as you might think."

Pollio Atticus made a sound – somewhere between a snort of contempt and an exasperated sigh. His son had been his greatest failure, when he had hoped that he would be his greatest success.

"There is a storm coming, Rufus. The plague, the war with the Marcomanni and the rise in numbers of Christian dissidents – all these problems demand strong leadership, leadership which Aurelius is not providing. The people are scared and resentful. They want someone to cure our society's ills. Cornelius Sulla was right today to call for a larger, more powerful army. I will back his proposals."

"Is it not rather the case that he is backing your proposals? Aren't you a little too old to be getting into bed with Sulla? I didn't think you were his type," Atticus wryly replied, smiling into his wine. He soon gazed at his father with a sense of wariness and sobriety though, over the rim of the cup. He knew that his father also had investments in tin mines and with other military contractors, but was far more concerned with power than money. He had even been willing to prostitute his own wife in the past – as he was doing now with his daughter – to win influence. How serious had he been in predicting, or providing, opposition to the Emperor? How much did he know of his father – and what he was capable of?

The music stopped. Rain spotted the air. The women were the first to retreat inside, holding their hands over their various hairstyles, attempting to keep them dry. The men followed them into the large triclinium, which looked out onto the garden. Several of the guests wondered why their host and his son remained outside, still in conversation, in the ever worsening shower.

Pollio Atticus shook his head and screwed up his face, looking at his son as if he were further estranged, or disowned.

"Your jokes won't save Rome, Rufus. A powerful army will, which can be kept on a leash but set loose accordingly by its master. You are about to head off to the frontline, but you may find yourself involved in a different type of conflict soon. And, as with any fight, you will have to choose a side."

Pollio Atticus' tone sounded as ominous as the thunderous night sky. He may have lost his son's love over the years, but he hoped that Rufus was still wise enough to fear him. Anyone who was not an ally he would look upon as an enemy. Politics eclipsed life.

"I've already chosen," Atticus replied – and walked off to join the rest of the party inside.

7.

Maximus drained his cup of wine and re-filled it, again. Some people drink to feel alive. Maximus drank to deaden himself, to forget. He stared into the writhing flames of the fire, his expression as cold and fixed as the bust of Aristotle which Arrian kept in the triclinium. He remained seated and staring into the fire even when he heard the young German come up beside him.

"I couldn't sleep," Arrian remarked tiredly, wincing slightly in discomfort from his wound as he sat across from the centurion.

"Wine?"

Arrian shook his head. It was either too late, or too early, to start drinking. Although the adolescent would have an occasional cup of a fine vintage with his dinner, wine didn't agree with him.

"I'm not a big wine drinker."

"Well you might have to get used to the taste of it soon if we stay on the frontline in the north. Wine – and cheap wine at that – is often all there is to drink. Acetum lubricates the army."

"Germans love their wine, too. I'm an exception that doesn't disprove the rule. I'm also an exception that doesn't disprove the rule in regards to my people being a warrior race. War is in their blood, as much as wine. I'm not sure I'll ever live up to my people, though. You cannot put in what the gods have left out. This conflict could last for years. The wines will become vintages by the end. I can only see war, not peace," Arrian remarked, wincing now at the thought of the suffering the conflict would cause on both sides.

"Rome demands victory, not peace. You are a student of our history. Whether it be a contest against the Carthaginians, Pyrrhus, the Persians or the Marcomanni, Rome will endure and will not stop until it's defeated its enemy."

"The irony is I believe that this war has been caused by our similarities rather than differences. I am not the only German who aspires to be more Roman than barbarian. Trade – and cultural exchanges – have brought our two peoples together over the past decades. We have grown as a civilisation, to such an extent that the northern tribes now want to be considered as an equal rather than as an inferior. Rome has wanted my people to be prosperous, but not too prosperous it seems; to be armed – and able to defeat Rome's enemies – but not too powerful. We want to grow economically, within a free market without trade restrictions and an oppressive bureaucracy. But Rome dictates the area of the free market. It sets unfair taxes and implements unfair subsidies. An autocratic political elite in Rome decides the fate of Germany – one which we have no power to elect in or vote out. And also, my people just want more living space."

Arrian made an impassioned argument, but Maximus remained impassive.

"Aye, so much so that they are willing to kill for it. But they will also die for it. The Marcomanni have sowed the wind. Now they must reap the whirlwind. They drew first blood, but we'll draw the last. Balomar must pay for his duplicity and war crimes."

The soldier drained his cup, again – sneering either at the sourness of the wine or at the mention of the German king. Yet Maximus had no desire to argue with his new young friend. He appreciated Arrian trying to defend his people, but rather than debate the causes of the war the soldier wanted to discuss how Rome could win it. The student shared his thoughts – feeling slightly conflicted as he did so as if he were betraying his homeland. Yet he also realised how, ultimately, he believed in the character and cause of Marcus Aurelius over the Marcomanni.

"...There is no capital to sack or pour salt into the soil of in the north. There is also no Hannibal to defeat with a single pitched battle to fight and win the war. If you cut off Balomar's head then, Hydra-like, two may grow in its place. We possess few archers and also swords, but every German is practised in using his spear. The warriors of the Marcomanni and other tribes will lack the discipline of the legions, but they do not lack courage or honour. Indeed be it through pride, or stupidity, the warriors will look to break the Roman line in the centre where it appears strongest... Our women can and will fight too."

"Atticus mentioned this. He also said that we should consider sending Roman wives and mother-in-laws to the front – so that they can nag our opponents to death." Rather than smiling though Maximus frowned, as he remembered Julia again. She would have laughed at the joke and enjoyed Atticus' company, he thought. He missed her laughter so much. He still occasionally woke and expected his wife to be next to him, his two children to be sleeping in the next room. Those few mistaken moments were the best part of his day – and the rest of his day was the worst part. Maximus drained his cup once more, hoping to wash away the painful, seductive memories – Siren songs.

The flames ceased to writhe, as if they were too fatigued to do so. The wine became medicinal and helped the soldier drift off to sleep.

8.

"Romans may well know how to construct straight, flat roads but their ability to engineer carriages with effective suspension is somewhat lacking," a pinch-faced Galen expressed, unable to hear himself think over the loud rattle of the coach as it travelled along the road to Aquileia.

Accompanying the physician in the coach were Arrian and Aurelia. Galen added, "Apparently this coach once belonged to Lucius Verus. I'm surprised that the curtains were not permanently set to being drawn across, given his love of travelling with actresses – whose talents were far more apparent off stage I warrant. If Verus did previously use the coach to escort his mistresses across the empire then that would explain the well-worn suspension."

Arrian covered his mouth with his hand and grinned, either at the physician's joke or at his priggishness.

"Would you like another cushion?" Aurelia remarked, kindly removing one of her own pillows from behind her back.

"No, my dear. But thank you. I will just duly suffer in silence," Galen stoically replied.

Arrian's grin widened and he shared a look with his sister. The good, fusty doctor had barely stopped complaining ever since they had left the capital. The landscape was featureless and colourless compared to the area surrounding his home in Pergamum. The language of the small attachments of legionaries guarding the party was as filthy as a sewer. And if the lunch he had was pork, he wanted the chicken. And if it was chicken, he wanted the pork.

It was not before long that the physician sighed in exasperation again – and his head came up from peering behind a book, which

45

he could scarce read due to the jarring movements of the carriage. Unable to work, he turned his attention to his travelling companions.

"So, tell me, are you both looking forward to returning to your homeland?"

"I call Rome my home now. My village may well seem strange or backward should I go there. And we will appear alien to the tribe," Arrian replied, wistfully gazing out of the window, thinking more about what he was leaving behind rather than travelling towards. He missed his studies, books, the theatre and his tutors.

"And what about you, Aurelia? Has Rome captured your heart like young Arrian here? Are you glad the Emperor has summoned you back to the north?"

"I love and respect my brother – and I am glad that he feels at home in the capital. But he knows how I am far from enamoured with Rome. I am looking forward to seeing my father and my village again. I do not feel altogether comfortable however in being used by the Emperor to win his war. We are unwittingly on the side of the Roman army – an army which is married to the causes of death and destruction," the woman answered forthrightly, her head raised up high as if she were giving a formal speech – or sermon.

"And also one which executes Christians," the doctor posited.

The gimlet-eyed, knowing look which accompanied Galen's statement probed as much as any of the physician's surgical instruments. Arrian crimsoned, as Aurelia blanched. Revealing his sister's secret could mean the death of both of them, Arrian worried. Indeed Galen's words hammered into him like nails upon a crucifix. The shock was akin to being stabbed again. Was Marcus Aurelius' physician merely fishing, or did he know Aurelia served a different god to that of the divine Emperor? Arrian's glance towards his sister contained a plea to let Galen's words pass, but her expression was already imbued with pride and defiance. She did not want to dishonour so many fallen martyrs who had suffered under Nero and other tyrants by denying her faith.

"How did you know?" Aurelia asked.

"I am a scientist. I come to evidence-based conclusions," Galen answered, matter-of-factly. Over the course of attending to her brother he had observed the woman reading certain books, heard her quote from certain texts in her conversation. She paraphrased Paul as much as her brother paraphrased Aristotle. She had also, on more than one occasion, passionately condemned the Empire's treatment of Christians, too.

"I cannot, nor will not, renounce my Christian faith."

The carriage jolted up and down once more and Arrian felt like his sister's declaration had hammered another nail into his being. Many in Rome despised Christians more than Germans. They blamed the superstitious cult for all manner of ills – the plague, bad harvests and even rainy days. The new religion, which believed in one god (as opposed to the plethora of Roman, pagan gods) was also politically divisive. One's service to God should be sovereign over the service one owed to Rome and Caesar. For years the unofficial policy had been not to hunt Christians down and persecute them. Only those who became too militant – and who did not renounce their belief – were punished. But hostilities had grown towards the cult under the rule of Marcus Aurelius, an Emperor who was, ironically, lauded for his sense of tolerance and forgiveness. But the traditions, laws, religion and social institutions of the Empire were in direct conflict with Christianity. The Emperor was as much at war with an ideology as he was with the Marcomanni. Romans, Greeks, barbarians and Jews derided Christians – denouncing and attacking them. The appetite for persecuting Christians was as great as it had ever been – and as a result the lions in the arena had been well fed.

"Her belief is of a private rather than public nature now. She no longer sees her congregation even," Arrian said quickly to defend his sister – and mark her out as not being an enemy of the state. Aurelia stared at her brother with a storm in her eyes, but Galen spoke before she could reply how she no longer saw her congregation because the Praetorian Guard had arrested and executed them.

"Your secret is safe with me, do not worry. My job is to cure people, not send them to their deaths. Albeit you wouldn't think that all the doctors in Rome could claim to do no harm. The thoughtless quacks! But I am fine with you practising any religion you wish, just so long as you do no harm whilst doing so. People have often tried to pin certain beliefs on me. I've been called a stoic, empiricist, logician and all manner of things. The only being I see worth wholeheartedly believing in is myself however. I'm a Galenist. I'm jesting of course."

Arrian smiled in relief, rather than at the physician's joke. He concluded that doctor would not betray his sister's confidence. It was as if she were his patient – and indeed the philosophy student sometimes believed that Christianity was an illness that needed to be cured when it came to Aurelia. Christianity was as irrational as paganism. One should only have faith in scepticism, he reasoned. Arrian had hoped that it was just her congregation who were infecting her with the religion in the past, but her commitment and devotion waned not after their demise. If anything it increased. But as much as Arrian could have argued that his sister's faith now stemmed from a form of pride or conceit, he also knew that it brought a genuine sense of consolation and purpose to her life.

"Thank you for your understanding and discretion," Aurelia remarked. She squeezed the doctor's hand and smiled, gratefully, sweetly. Her aspect hardened again however as she mentioned how saddening it was that his friend, the Emperor, could not similarly be as tolerant and enlightened.

"Do not be too harsh on the Emperor, my dear. Marcus Aurelius is far more tolerant and enlightened than you give him credit for. Indeed, he is the best man I know. You may now laugh at this, but he is in some ways the most Christian man I know also. Please do not let his views on religion colour everything you see. I dare say Marcus can appreciate how spiritually nourishing your beliefs are, but politically they may be considered poisonous. People who believe in a spiritual world still have to live in the real world, too. Not all Christians are terribly Christian. They desire a vengeful rather than merciful God. They even applaud the plague – and see it as God's way of punishing Rome for its sins. Some are political, rather than divine, souls; self-interested revolutionaries, who crave a holy war. Aye, I have encountered many a Christian over the years Aurelia – and too many of them proved to be over zealous, overbearing and under sexed."

Aurelia appeared thoughtful and morose – recognising the wisdom in some of the things Galen had said.

*

Fingers of sunlight poked down through the ambling flocks of clouds. Half a dozen legionaries marched behind the carriage whilst another two, accompanied by Maximus and Atticus on their horses, walked in front of it. The road was flanked on both sides by woodland. Previously they had passed through farmland – which had appeared barren in contrast to when Maximus had last ventured north. The land needed to be tended to – but farmhands had been conscripted into the army during Rome's last recruitment drive.

Maximus patted and stroked the neck of his sorrel mare, in order to soothe the creature whilst a host of insects buzzed around its ears, and continued his discussion with his friend.

"Unfortunately any accusation made against your father will probably fall on deaf ears, or land you in trouble. He will be able to refute any allegation against him – it'll be your word against his. You'll be painted as a wilful son, trying to get revenge on his father for a personal slight. Your father has been a faithful servant of Rome over the years, as much as it now seems that he would like Rome to serve him. Hopefully we will have nothing to worry about. Ever since I've served in the army Rome has always had some form of a conspiracy or prospective coup that the gossip mongers have chewed upon. It may well have been that your father was just trying to reach out to you, attempt a reconciliation."

"In my experience the only thing that my father reaches out to is power. But perhaps I should give him the benefit of the doubt," Atticus replied, not entirely doubting his suspicions. But he was willing to change the subject. "I couldn't help but notice how my sister looked to reach out to you, so to speak, during our parting at the city gates. Claudia embraced you for so long that I thought you may have both been modelling for a sculptor. She seemed to whisper something in your ear, too."

"You'll start to see conspiracies in the way the wind blows or in the cawing of crows soon. Your sister just asked me to look after you. She also invited me to dinner when we return to Rome, though the gods only know when that will be."

"Hmm, I certainly don't need the cawing of any crows to tell me that my sister would love to take advantage of you. I may well have to look after you at that dinner," Atticus said with a smirk and shake of his head, thinking of his wilful – and wily – sister.

"Claudia will have to get in the queue. The army and tax man already take advantage of me – although I'm all for her trying to get to my heart through my stomach."

"If I know my sister, it won't be your heart that she'll look to get to – but rather a different part of your anatomy."

The two friends shared a good humoured look and would have laughed together – but for the ambush.

9.

Men and horses appeared from out of the forest on both sides, like ghosts, with barely a broken branch or rustle of leaves. The bandits were well armed and well trained. The small group of legionaries behind the coach quickly snapped into a defensive position, but they were equally quickly surrounded by a superior number of brigands, each carrying a spear or sword and small round shield.

Maximus and Atticus found themselves similarly outnumbered. Half a dozen bandits had run out from the tree line, accompanied by a trio of horsemen. The arrowheads, glinting in the sunlight, aimed at their chests, and checked any impulse the centurion and optio might have had to attack. A couple of the bandits behind the carriage howled in triumph and expectation.

Maximus remained calm and took in the scene and strength of the enemy. He then turned his attention to the leader of the group of brigands. The head of the gang sat upon a black cavalry charger in front of the officer. He was dressed in a bright blue tunic with yellow trim, over which he wore an ornate silver breastplate. His ears, fingers and neck dripped with gold jewellery, no doubt fruits of his labour from previous robberies. He was tall, wiry and looked as he if came from Spain or North Africa. Black, oily hair ran down past his shoulders. A smile, revealing a set of sharp yellow teeth, came out from beneath a well-kept forked beard. The two men, positioned either side of him on horseback, relaxed their bow arms – but still sat ready to release their shafts into the centurion and optio should the order be given.

"I am Sextus Bulla, you may have heard of me. My name should have sounded all the way back to Rome by now," the leader remarked, speaking in a charming tone, as if they were all at a dinner party.

"Rome may have problems hearing your name over the sound of your loud dress sense," Atticus drily replied.

Although Atticus pretended not to he had indeed heard of the brigand. He headed up one of a number of criminal gangs who terrorised the arteries of the Empire. They targeted wealthy travellers and merchants. In order to win the affection and loyalty of the regions they operated in, the thieves would share part of their spoils with the local people. He had been nicknamed "The Gentleman Bandit," due to his reputation for high fashion and good manners. But as well as wearing gold on his fingers, Sextus Bulla had blood on his hands. His gang robbed, raped and murdered on a weekly basis. They also extorted as much money out of small businesses as the tax collector (well maybe not quite that much). The gang was also renowned for recruiting deserters to its lawless campaigns. They would escape from the armies serving along the Danube and Bulla would welcome them with open arms.

"You will do well to keep your jokes to yourself, unless you want to die laughing," the bandit replied. The mask of charm slipped from his face and Bulla spoke in a more guttural accent, but he soon regained his composure. "My quarrel is not with you centurion. We just want to unburden your carriage of its valuables and those passengers we can ransom. This can all be over quickly and painlessly – if you cooperate," Bulla said and nodded to a brace of men nearby him, instructing them to check out the carriage.

The two men ordered the passengers to get out of the carriage. They licked their lips and leered at Aurelia as she did so. Sextus Bulla smiled in satisfaction too.

"Don't worry. Everything will be fine," Maximus turned and remarked to the brother and sister as they huddled together, after being man-handled by their captors. For once Galen was short of something to say. He was used to metaphorical knives being drawn against him. They all looked scared and for once even Maximus appeared a little anxious.

"You're probably now thinking about playing the hero, but at best you'd be a tragic one, praetorian. My men are well trained. Indeed you may have even been responsible for training some of them yourself. They're former legionaries. They grew tired of having empty bellies and empty purses. They also grew tired of serving under sadistic centurions and optios – and wouldn't think twice about killing an officer in cold blood. I hope you're not a sadistic officer of that ilk."

"Hopefully you'll soon get the chance to find out how sadistic I am," the centurion replied.

"Ha! I admire your spirit. But I'm still content to let you and your soldiers continue on your journey. If nothing else you can all go back to Rome and tell a story about how you encountered Sextus Bulla and, how like Julius Caesar, he displayed clemency. I'll even let you keep the old man. But your valuables and the Germans will be staying with me. And a good German is a dead German after all, no?"

Maximus and Atticus shared a fleeting look. Both now realised how the ambush had not just been bad luck, for how could Bulla know that the travellers were German?

The centurion turned his head and pensively gazed out into the forest, as if pausing for thought before making his decision. He sighed, either in a spirit of despair or fatalism. Arrian and Aurelia clasped each other's hand and stared at the officer with a mixture of hope and forlornness – for even if he defied the bandit and refused to hand them over, it was unlikely that the troops could defeat the enemy. The praetorian would give in to the brigand's favourable terms and spare his men. Rome looked after its own, Aurelia thought.

Maximus gave a nod of his head, as if assenting to the bandit's offer. For half a second Aurelia's heart sank and she cursed the centurion – and Rome – under her breath. She remembered what she had said to Julia, that "all soldiers were the same."

Bulla fingered one of his gold chains and grinned in triumph. All had gone to plan. He may have even permitted himself to laugh – but for the ambush.

10.

The arrow flew in at an angle from the treeline, but struck Bulla between his shoulder blades. The bandit let out a breathless scream as it punctured his lung. A few other arrows zipped in, striking either horses or men. The centurion had ordered a quartet of legionaries, who were skilled with a bow, to retreat into the woods and screen the party as soon as they had entered bandit country. Maximus had waited until his men were in position before giving the order to attack. Everyone froze in shock and confusion, except Maximus and Atticus. Before the brigand slumped forward and fell from his charger the optio drew his knives and took out the threat of the two archers on horseback in front of him. He then drew his sword and waded in to the enemy standing nearest to him, ordering the two legionaries behind him to do so also.

Maximus quickly wheeled his horse around and charged the two bandits who were guarding the Germans. One of the men had pulled his arm back and was about to stab Arrian, as he pushed himself in front of his sister. Before the enemy could strike, however, Maximus slashed him across the face with his gladius, whilst mowing his comrade down with his horse. The blood-curdling scream from the wounded bandit was soon silenced as the centurion plunged his sword through his upper chest. Blood spat through the air.

"Go back into the carriage. Arrian, pick up that sword. If anyone attempts to get inside then call out for help – whilst stabbing the bastards. Understand?"

The youth nodded, though understanding his task and being able to carry it out were two separate things.

The sound of arrows continued to hiss through the air behind him. The familiar noises of battle cries, death rattles and swords crashing onto shields also swirled around the praetorian. Maximus felt alive again, at home. He'd been organising the guard rotations at the imperial palace for far too long. He noticed how the legionaries behind the coach had put themselves on the front foot even without his orders. They moved towards the enemy in two well-disciplined lines with their shields up and spears pointing outwards. The intimidating sight caused a number of the enemy to return to type and desert. A group of brigands were starting to form their own line on one side of the road though, which would be long enough to wrap around his soldiers and perhaps encircle them. Maximus decided to even out the odds. He kicked his heels into his horse and attacked his enemy's flank, hacking away at the line of bandits as if he were a forester cutting a path through the woodland. Seeing the line in disarray the legionaries broke formation, launched their javelins and then ran to engage the enemy with their swords.

The sight of blood soon accompanied the familiar sounds of battle. Gore smeared their tunics and skin. A few of the enemy were able to retreat back into the forest, but most were put to the sword. Once the skirmish was over Maximus returned to the coach. He shared a look with his optio and friend which communicated gratitude, relief and praise. Atticus was helping a still shaken Aurelia down from the carriage, as Galen and Arrian stood beside him. The woman looked up at the centurion, her face pale and her lips still quivering. Tears, either of gratitude or despair, welled in her almond-shaped eyes. Maximus removed his cloak and placed it around her shoulders, smiling in a comforting manner as he did so. He then tenderly cupped his hand upon her arm. She didn't recoil – indeed she missed the sensation once the touch was gone. She wanted to say thank you – for saving her again – but was somehow unable to do so. Her usual icy expression melted away though – and Aurelia remembered her friend's reply, when she had condemned all soldiers: "No, he's different."

Maximus took the physician aside and asked if he could give the woman something to calm her nerves or help her sleep.

"I also want you to try and save that bastard Bulla over there, so I can torture him," the officer said. But even Galen failed to find a pulse. Maximus shot out a curse at hearing of the bandit leader's death, frustrated that he would not be able to find out any answers as to who had ordered the attack. He soon regained his composure though and asked Galen to attend to any injured legionaries.

Whilst Galen saw to the wounded Maximus went around and thanked and praised each soldier personally for the manner in which they had conducted themselves during the attack. The centurion took additional time out for the young legionary who had fired the arrow that had brought down the leader of the gang. The soldier was barely much older than Arrian. His brown hair was cropped short and there was an impish gleam in his expression. His bow and kit were in good order and his broad chest was puffed out, pleased and proud to be commended by his officer.

"That was a fine shot earlier. Was it a lucky one, too? The best answer is the honest one. I'll know you're lying before you do, soldier," Maximus asked, remembering with mixed fondness how his former centurions had spoken to him in such a way.

"The harder you practise the luckier you get," the legionary replied confidently.

Maximus paused in thought for a moment, trying to remember where he had heard the phrase before. It was a good, if unoriginal, answer.

"What's your name?"

"Cassius Bursus. But most of the men call me Apollo, Sir," he remarked, holding up his bow by way of an explanation.

"The rest doubtless call you something far less complimentary. But here, take this. Have a drink or three tonight to celebrate," the centurion said, retrieving a silver coin and tossing it to the fresh-faced recruit.

"Forgive me, Sir, but what am I supposed to be celebrating?" Apollo replied, squinting from both the light and in slight confusion.

"You've just joined the Praetorian Guard."

11.

The inn they stayed in that evening was much like any other. It met their needs but there was a lot left to be desired in regards to the establishment and its amenities. Most of the rooms were as filthy as the jokes the legionaries shared over dinner, and the innkeeper had a list of extra charges that would have made even a quartermaster blush. But the wine wasn't watered-down (that much), the food was fresh-ish and most importantly the serving girls were willing to work overtime through the night, servicing the soldiers. A number of the girls worked overtime throughout dinner too, hoping to catch the eye of the attractive, well-spoken optio. But unfortunately for them – and him – Maximus had other plans for Atticus. In light of the attack that afternoon the centurion arranged for his optio to provide close protection for Arrian and Aurelia.

"There have been a couple of occasions when I've been in the same room as a husband and wife, hiding beneath the bed, but this will be the first time that I've been in the same room with a brother and sister," Atticus remarked to Maximus over the dinner table.

"Well you're always saying how much you crave new experiences, to help fight off boredom."

"I warrant that boredom may well prove victorious this evening still. I'm just pleased that you trust me enough to share a room with the woman."

"I don't trust you. But I do trust her. It could be worse. Young Apollo over there will be spending half the night posted outside the door of the room. Let's just hope that he's as attentive to his duties as he is to that brunette serving him up his main course."

"I'm not sure which he's salivating over more."

"I am," the centurion replied with a hint of a smile, remembering his days as a new recruit and enjoying the charms of serving girls who knew what they were doing in the kitchen – and bedroom.

"Shall we buy an hour or two of her time as a reward for his promotion?"

"He'll only need an hour, at most. I've just paid for his food and drinks for the evening though. You can his pay for the dessert."

*

A couple of extra braziers (which they would be charged extra for) lighted and heated the musty, low-ceilinged room. Arrian and Aurelia sat, leaning forward, perched upon two chairs, listening to the optio. Atticus encouraged his audience to have a measure or two of wine – at the very least, it would help them sleep, he argued. After discussing the Parthian campaign, Arrian asked the optio why he had given up his studies to become a soldier. Was it not true that he was an accomplished poet in his youth?

"Soldiers make more money than poets. And women like a man in uniform," Atticus argued, winking at the German student as he did so. Arrian grinned, whilst Aurelia rolled her eyes. Rather than Atticus, Aurelia wanted to now know more about the optio's superior officer – and she steered the conversation towards the subject of Maximus accordingly.

"Your centurion displayed a great deal of courage today to fight for us. No one would have thought less of him I suspect if he would have handed over two Germans to save the lives of twenty Romans," Aurelia said, whilst watering down the wine some more.

"He would have thought less of himself," Atticus replied, inwardly sighing at the woman for turning wine into water. He also thought how Maximus sometimes acted as if the ghost of Julia was standing by him, as if he didn't want her to think less of him. The optio had only met his centurion's wife on a few occasions, but she still made a favourable impression. Atticus thought her

61

intelligent, without being conceited; she was attractive, without being vain. She was not without cynicism, but more memorably she was not without compassion. Most of all he remembered how Julia, more than anyone else, could make Maximus laugh. She had the dry and black humour of a soldier, but still remained wonderfully sweet. As far as Atticus knew his centurion remained faithful to his wife whilst they were married. Atticus recalled how, drinking the night away after winning an engagement against the Parthians, Maximus confessed to him that he was happy because he had been fortunate enough to marry his best friend.

The optio paused in his thoughts due to hearing increasingly audible sounds come from the neighbouring room. The bed began to knock against the wall. A woman's voice could be heard to impatiently utter, "Hurry up". Arrian appeared slightly embarrassed, Aurelia pursed her lips in disapproval, and Atticus raised a corner of his mouth in a half-smile as he heard the soldier emit a groan (although he was unable to determine whether the groan was borne from fatigue, drunkenness or ecstasy).

*

The braziers murmured and half a dozen insects buzzed above her head. The bed was hard and rickety on the creaking floor. But there were other reasons why Aurelia was unable to drift off to sleep. She grieved for her friend, again. Julia had been a Christian and, for a time, Aurelia's closest companion. The two women had met by accident one afternoon, both finding shelter from the rain beneath the same awning in the market. They soon began to shop and attend the theatre together. They swapped recipes, as Aurelia improved her friend's culinary skills. In return Julia improved Aurelia in other ways. She introduced her to new people and also new authors, as they swapped not just cookery books – but plays, history books and philosophical texts. Aurelia made a leap of faith one evening and confessed her devotion to the Christian religion to her friend. Julia, curious about the religion and wishing to support her companion, attended a few gatherings. Although Julia was hesitant about wholly committing herself to joining Aurelia's congregation she found meaning and purpose in the Gospels. She started to believe. Aurelia wanted her friend to give more of herself however.

"You should marry yourself to God," she argued, brimming with religious fervour.

"But I already have a husband and as far as I know he doesn't want a divorce quite yet, despite my cooking," Julia replied, jokingly. But Aurelia failed to laugh at the comment.

"He is a soldier, part of Satan's army," Aurelia declared, quoting from a sermon that she had attended the previous week.

"Gaius is a good man. You'll see. I'd love you to have dinner with us both when he returns from the front." Julia was tempted to add how her husband was a better man than most in regards to those in the congregation, especially the religious scribes who failed to practice what they preached. They acted as though they were the key holders to the Kingdom of God. She was also tempted to say how much she worried that Aurelia was changing. She was losing her sense of humour and sense of perspective, being blinded by the teachings of her church – which were not always in harmony with the teachings of Christ.

When Maximus came back to Rome Julia spent less time with Aurelia. Aurelia grew resentful and jealous of the soldier – even though she had never met him – for stealing her best friend. At the time Aurelia felt increasingly isolated as her congregation discovered that she was the daughter of a German chieftain – and the war with the Marcomanni had commenced. People distanced themselves from her. *Not all Christians are terribly Christian.*

Aurelia confronted her friend after the praetorians arrested a number of worshipers in her congregation. The charge was that they had been conspiring against the state. She called Maximus the enemy and urged Julia to leave him. She told her how the soldier had been present at the trial and execution of their friends, although she was only sure that he had been in attendance at the former.

"In the same way that Man cannot serve both God and Mammon, you cannot serve God whilst being married to such a sinner."

"I love my husband," Julia had replied, with a gentleness and wisdom that was in stark contrast to the ire of her shrill friend. They were the last words that Aurelia ever heard her say. Shortly after their argument Julia and her children fell ill. Aurelia wanted to visit the house, to help in any way she could. But she didn't. She wanted to apologise. But she didn't.

Tears glistened in Aurelia's eyes as she lay upon her side and curled up in a ball on the bed. The feelings of guilt and grief which knotted her stomach were as palpable as the feelings of hunger in a beggar. She silently prayed to God for strength and forgiveness – again – and tried to take some consolation from Julia being in a better place.

"I love my husband."

Aurelia recalled her friend's words once more and for the first time could appreciate why she had said them. *Perhaps he is a good man.*

12.

The afternoon sun burnt through the clouds like wax. Sweat glazed the limbs of the marching legionaries. The party would reach Aquileia by nightfall.

The autumnal russets and browns of the north had replaced the vernal greens of Italy. The forests were denser and pungent with the smell of peaty soil, verdure and swampland. Trees – oaks, ferns, willows and birches – towered over them. Shrubs, mushrooms and blackberries sprouted up everywhere. Occasionally one could hear the distant howl of a wolf, or the rough snort of a wild-boar. All manner of birdsong, entwined like myrtle, whistled out from the trees. Yet as they grew closer to the front and the wilds of his homeland Arrian saw evidence of civilisation increase rather than diminish. Instead of the muddy tracks and wattle and daub dwellings he remembered from childhood, he saw now Roman-built stone houses and forts. Wide all-weather roads serviced soldiers, local people and tradesman alike.

Arrian had claimed a bandit's horse. He rode up alongside Maximus and his optio. He rode uneasily, shifting uncomfortably in the saddle and out of tune with the rhythms of his mount. Muscles ached that, before the morning, the student scarce knew he possessed. Atticus had put him through his paces that morning, in terms of a conditioning and fencing session. Having felt so helpless during the attack on his house – and the carriage – Arrian asked Maximus if he could give him some rudimentary training so as to be able to defend himself – and his sister – should they be put in peril again. The centurion admired the young man's intentions, if not his abilities, and asked his optio to commence the training sessions. It was perhaps out of a sense of amusement, rather than duty, that Atticus spent so long with the German. Arrian had to constantly pause to catch his breath – and Atticus had known blind men who could wield a gladius more effectively.

"So do you think that we will see the Emperor late this evening or tomorrow?" Arrian asked, nervous and excited about meeting with the revered Marcus Aurelius.

"Probably. Our Caesar is a night owl rather than a lark," Maximus answered.

"How well do you know the Emperor? What's he like?" Arrian posed, leaning forward, eager to hear the reply and trying to find a more comfortable position on his horse.

The centurion thought how he knew the Emperor more than most, but at the same time he barely knew him at all. Thankfully Aurelius was more a son of Pius than Hadrian. Traits such as rapaciousness, paranoia, cruelty, depravity and weak-mindedness filled out the history books in regards to describing past Emperors – but a young Aurelius had studied history in order to try to avoid repeating the mistakes of others. At the same time as there being a constancy and equanimity to his temper, Aurelius once confessed to Maximus that he sometimes felt like a walking contradiction – with the duties and mind-sets of being both an Emperor and a philosopher pulling him in opposing directions. The centurion recalled how, late one night, shortly after hearing about the Marcomanni's incursion across the Danube, Aurelius had buried his head in his hands and confessed, "If I wasn't so worried about being succeeded by a Nero or Tiberius I would be tempted to abdicate and spend the rest of my days studying. But, as you know only too well Maximus, duty calls – and it shouts so loudly sometimes that we cannot turn a deaf ear to the sound... To find peace may be considered to be the aim of a philosopher, but as Emperor I must go to war..."

Despite considering himself a walking contradiction Maximus believed that Aurelius had found a balance, harmony, in his soul. He was content in his sorrow, as though melancholy was the apogee of wisdom; if Aurelius didn't feel sorrowful then he was somehow not being true to himself. Similarly Maximus often believed that if he was somehow not feeling grief then he was not being true to himself, or Julia.

But sorrow seldom turned into bitterness or enmity. Maximus had never known the Emperor to raise his voice, lose his temper or allow his passions to overrule his judgement. Many criticised the Emperor behind his back for his lack of warmth or affection, but for Maximus it was far more important that Aurelius was never cold or vindictive. He just sometimes seemed detached from the world, as though the realm of abstract thought was the real world – to which he was a devoted citizen. Unlike many of his predecessors Aurelius did not lack a sense of modesty and humility either. He would cut short any flattery if ever he was unjustly (or justly) praised, or direct the praise onto another. For those who believed Aurelius lacked for warmth or affection, they should have heard him talk of his fondness and admiration for Antonius Pius.

"How well do I know the Emperor? Well enough."

Before the praetorian could say anything else he was distracted by the sight of Aurelia trotting towards him on Bulla's black charger. Unlike her brother she rode well, perfectly poised and in control whilst riding side saddle (albeit Aurelia wished she was dressed differently and able to sit astride her mount). She had, quite literally, let down her hair. Her glossy tresses blew as freely in the breeze as her horse's mane. There was a contented smile on her face and colour in her cheeks. Finally she's stopped trying to look like a Vestal Virgin, Atticus mused.

Maximus, his optio and even Arrian all remained stunned, their mouths slightly agape. Finally Aurelia broke the silence.

"I became bored with the conversation in the carriage. It consisted of Galen talking to himself – about himself." There was good humour, rather than haughtiness, in her voice. The men all laughed – and even a couple of the horses whinnied, as if laughing too. Aurelia flicked her reins and rather than trot up beside her brother, she positioned herself next to the still somewhat bewildered centurion. He gazed at the woman, his head slightly cocked, as if she were a stranger. Arrian recognised her however as his amiable and witty sister of old.

"Do you think that we will get to Aquileia before the end of the day?"

"I hope so. Atticus may well mutiny if not. He's never been this long without a fine vintage in front of him at dinner before," the centurion wryly replied, in earshot of his friend.

The optio smirked and thought how he was not only pining for a decent vintage.

"Abstinence does not make the heart grow fonder," Atticus remarked, thinking of how he was missing his dessert, as well as his wine, at dinner each night.

"And what do you think will happen to us once we reach the Emperor?" Aurelia asked – and then gently closed her eyes, letting the rays of the sun and a cool breeze wash over her skin.

"I suspect that he will ask you to carry on your journey, talk to your father – and petition for him to side with Rome against its enemies. Or at the very least remain neutral."

"And will you continue to act as our escort?"

"I'm not sure. I'll duly find out after I have spoken to the Emperor."

"I hope you will remain by our side. You never know, I may even make a request for you to accompany us," Aurelia said, smiling slightly after witnessing the soldier's startled reaction.

Atticus coughed, as the gulp of water went down the wrong hole in his throat on hearing Aurelia's comment and witnessing the light in her eyes. She could perhaps even teach Claudia a thing or two about flirting, the optio jokingly thought.

"And will you do so out of a sense of a reward, or punishment, for us?" Maximus queried, arching his eyebrows in amusement – and amazement.

"You will find out, after I have spoken to the Emperor," Aurelia answered, unable to suppress an attractive, unaffected grin. For the first time she looked upon the soldier as a potential friend rather than enemy, and it felt good.

13.

"They can kill me, but they cannot hurt me," a tired looking Marcus Aurelius philosophically stated, as much to himself as to Maximus, in reply to the centurion's report. "The events in Rome and on your journey here do indeed add up to the sum of a conspiracy."

The room was modestly furnished, merely containing a desk and several bulging bookcases. A large map of the region also covered one whole wall in the room. The house was modest, too. The governor of Aquileia had offered his Emperor the use of his own residence but Marcus Aurelius had replied that although he could accept the use of a man's house, he had no right to turf him out of his family home. The smaller villa that he chose to live in and work out of also possessed the virtue of not being able to accommodate an army of visitors, attendants and advisers. The most powerful man in the world wore a clean, plain tunic. His figure was devoid of jewellery. His hair and beard needed trimming. "I would much prefer to be Diogenes to Alexander the Great," the soldier had once heard his Emperor confess. Maximus had requested to see his commander-in-chief as soon as the party arrived at the town, to brief him on recent events. Aurelius admitted the praetorian immediately and calmly sat behind his desk as he listened to the centurion's revelations, showing little reaction and seldom interrupting the officer as he did so.

Maximus resisted telling his Emperor about Atticus' suspicions, in regards to his father, in his report. Not only did he not possess a shred of evidence to substantiate any accusation, but the centurion did not wish to further sour his optio's relationship with his father. Similarly, with one wrong word, he could jeopardise

Atticus' future career prospects, whether they rested in the military or in politics.

Marcus Aurelius pursed his full, unsmiling lips. His deep set, dark eyes seemed to look through Maximus for a moment or two. But his expression soon softened and he even appeared to shrug his shoulders at the officer's ominous report.

"We should remain conscious of there being some sort of a conspiracy afoot, but as Galen might say we cannot come to any conclusions without any evidence. We cannot even deduce whether our antagonists are from Rome or the north, or elsewhere. Ironically they may have helped rather than hindered us. I am even more determined now to ask the brother and sister to intercede with their father and win his support – seeing as how much our enemies fear the Arivisto becoming an ally. No, I will not allow the shadow of a threat to alter my plans, nor will I spend precious time on speculating where this threat might come from. Any conjecture will prove as substantial as idle gossip. I warrant that I am as likely to encounter an assassin as I am a sober Briton."

A rare joke and a rare smile lit up the Emperor's careworn features. Maximus smiled at witnessing the light and humour back in the sorrowful man's eyes.

"We must look forward rather than backwards, Maximus. Thank you for your report, but let us not dwell upon things which are unknown or things we cannot alter. We need to look to the present and future, to a victory. I do not believe I lack moral courage, but I am still to be tested in regards to physical courage. I am a commander yet to lead his army in a battle."

An Emperor was supposed to be semi-divine, but Aurelius was here admitting how he was all too human – and Maximus admired his general all the more for it. Maximus would have given his life for the noble man – his friend – in front of him even if he were a goat herder, instead of a Caesar.

"I do not doubt your moral or physical courage – the former will fuel the latter when the time comes."

"Thank you, Gaius. Your faith in me may help alleviate my doubts, but unfortunately you not have the power to dissolve my anxieties completely. Being guilty of thinking too much as a legislator is no great crime, but as a military leader I must be bolder in my actions. A year ago people spoke of the fruits of victory, but I fear this army may be beginning to wither on the vine. You have already heard the rumours about the extent of the desertions and disease in our army. Unfortunately many of the rumours are true. I worry that I have let enemy forces slip through my fingers. When the soldiers of Rome witnessed the sight of Caesar's cloak billow in the air at Alesia it was said to be worth another two cohorts. Should the armies of Rome now see my cloak billow they would but merely conclude that it was a windy day.

"I have recently won certain diplomatic battles, by bribing a number of tribes to fight on our side or remain neutral. But this war cannot be won through diplomacy alone. My sword has yet to see sunlight, let alone taste blood. The end to this conflict seems further away now than it did a year ago. And all the while the capital is lacking an Emperor. I even miss pretending to watch and enjoy the games at the Coliseum, whilst I work through correspondence. Commodus is growing up without his father. My wife says she misses me, though I suspect that she would miss Rome – and its shoe shops – more if she were here, by my side. Faustina was displeased with me when I left for the front, for auctioning off some of our valuables to help finance the war. I sold a diamond brooch of hers, which she still hasn't forgiven me for. You could say that the incident caused the sparkle to go out of our marriage."

Aurelius sighed, either in woe or indifference. He looked up at the dutiful praetorian and saw a model of stoicism, gaining strength from him. Earlier in the week he had written, "*Be like a headland of rock on which the waves crash upon incessantly. But the rock stands fast and the seething waters eventually settle.*" Perhaps he had been unconsciously thinking of Maximus whilst composing the meditation, Aurelius mused.

"But rather than lament the absence of my wife, I should be grateful for the presence of yourself. It's good to see you Gaius," the Emperor declared, rising to his feet and fraternally squeezing the centurion's shoulder. This was not the first time that the Emperor had shared some of his private thoughts with the praetorian, or been grateful to him for completing a mission. "I dare say that it has something to do with your sword arm, as opposed to the hand of a god, in keeping you and your party safe – but let us give thanks to the gods all the same. And how is Atticus? I trust he is in good health, too? Atticus is a world of a possibilities; I just wonder whether he has settled upon which possibility he wants to realise. He is a talented poet, a keen student of philosophy. He is also an accomplished soldier – and could flourish in politics too. Yet as much as he often appears contented when I see him I believe him to be far from satisfied with his life. There is a hole in his soul."

"I told him the other week that he needed the love of a good woman – and that he should take a wife. He replied that he preferred to have the love of several women. And he also said that he has already taken a wife – but she's married to someone else."

"It seems that Atticus has changed about as much as the position of our frontline over the past year. My only historic achievement so far in this conflict is to do what no other man has ever come close to doing before – unite the German tribes, against a common enemy."

"You should not be so hard on yourself," Maximus said, worried to see his Emperor appear so vulnerable and defeatist.

"I have to be hard on myself. I'm the Emperor, no one else will dare say anything to my face. Except perhaps you would be honest and brave enough to do so, Gaius. Certainly there has been plenty of talk behind my back. The people expect and demand an early, favourable end to the war. I am given to understand that some of the graffiti back in the capital has been quite witty and imaginative. The Senate has also been justified in some of its veiled, or unveiled, criticisms."

"You cannot please all of the people all of the time, even when at peace. Seldom can war be waged without any reverses. As you once told me, the acclamations of the multitude are akin to just the clapping of tongues."

"Who am I to ignore the wisdom of an Emperor?" Aurelius replied, half-smiling all too wistfully and briefly. "But I could use your counsel now, Gaius. Help me win this war." These last words come out as more of a plea than command.

"In the same way that Caesar crossed the Rubicon you must cross the Danube to defeat the Marcomanni," Maximus said with determination, looking up at the large map upon the wall.

"Everywhere we've tried to cross we've been repulsed, or defeated. Various generals change their minds each day as to the best strategy. Where would you attack?"

The seasoned soldier drew his knife, studied the map intently for a few seconds, and plunged the blade into the wall as if he were stabbing the enemy itself.

"There. Pannonia... Sometimes you've just got to get into the fight."

A silvery-grey haze, the colour of cobwebs, began to bleed into the night sky. Dawn would soon wash over Rome, as would a soupy brown acrid fog of smoke from furnaces, kilns, ovens and house fires. Pollio Atticus was in his study, his temper as hot as the coals burning in the braziers. His liver-spotted, claw-like hand screwed itself into a fist and he pounded the large cedar wood desk. Chen had just relayed the news from one of their agents that the attempted abduction of the Germans, by Bulla, had failed. This was now the second time that the brother and sister had slipped through the statesman's fingers. One of his agents had discovered that the Emperor had summoned for the children of the chief, in order to gain his support in the war. Pollio Atticus, to foil the Emperor's plans, had decided to abduct and murder the young Germans before they reached Aquileia. The chief of the Arivisto tribe would consequently withdraw any support for Aurelius. He may have also considered that blood was on the Emperor's hands and he would have sided with Balomar in the war. To add insult to injury it seemed that his own son had been instrumental in scuppering his plans.

"Damn Bulla, damn those half-wits from the tavern, damn Aurelius and damn my own son!"

The bust of Augustus shook as the senator continued to pound the desk. Spittle, along with motes of dust, peppered the air. Chen sneered in derision and sympathy, baring his sharp white teeth.

"At least the fool Bulla died in the ambush. Dead men tell no tales. Maximus and my son are no fools however – they may now consider that the original attack on the house wasn't a mere coincidence. Deal with that useless cretin Sinius," Atticus snarled, his usually well-oiled hair now out of shape.

"Dead men tell no tales," the Chinese bodyguard replied, his sneer transforming itself into a sly grin. He already pictured slitting the man's throat, the polished blade of his ivory handled dagger glinting in the moonlight. He would duly give Sinius the opportunity to fight for his life and draw his blade, too. His vain thrusts and appeals for mercy would amuse the sadistic assassin.

"We just have to hope that Aurelius proves to be the author of his own demise. Just one more defeat will turn the desertions into a full-blown mutiny. The Emperor has poetry in his heart – but Rome needs a leader with iron his soul."

Certain things are in place, the senator thought to himself with satisfaction. Significant members of the military and Senate had commenced a whispering campaign against the Emperor, doubting his suitability to lead Rome in such a crisis. They would raise their voices in earnest after one more setback. The likes of Cornelius Sulla and Marcus Dio were major players – and he could put words into their mouths at will. Atticus had the influence and money to put forward a candidate to fill the power vacuum, the commander Avidius Cassius. He had already secured the officer's loyalty – paying off his debts and promising him the hand of Claudia in marriage. She had duly bewitched Cassius, even before bedding him. But the wily senator had no desire to openly usurp the Emperor. He who wields the dagger never wears the crown. No, he would rather be a Sejanus than Tiberius – the power behind the throne. Pollio stepped forward out of the shadows when Pius had died and offered to mentor the inexperienced Aurelius – but the Emperor kept his own counsel. The senator retreated back into the shadows, nursing his wounded pride and will to revenge.

"Just one more defeat. And then I will make my bid for power. Vespasian, Claudius, Galba – soldiers crown Emperors, not gods.

Our fates lie in ourselves, not in the stars. The Praetorian Guard will not even be able to protect Aurelius should the legions turn against him. Indeed the Praetorian Guard may turn against him first," Atticus remarked, smirking at the prospect. Yet thinking upon the famed regiment forced the senator to think again about his irksome son. If he could not win the loyalty of just one optio, who was his own blood, how could he hope to win over the entire Guard? If only Rufus knew how instructions had been given to Bulla to spare all the soldiers during the ambush. The smirk fell from the old man's face, his crabby countenance heavy with bitterness and grief.

As if second guessing his master's thoughts Chen remarked, "And what of your son? When the time comes – and if he chooses to stand between you and the Emperor – what would you like me to do?"

"He's dead to me already. It will be of no matter to kill him again."

15.

"We defy augury," Atticus playfully argued, quoting a line from his favourite tragedy, when replying to the woman in bed next to him. Sabina had just told the soldier of the dream she had during the night, in which she had seen Atticus die in the forests of the north. It still wasn't too late to find someone else to volunteer for the mission of taking the Germans north. He shouldn't tempt the fate of her dream, she argued. Sabina would be lonely without him. Atticus suspected that the insatiable merchant's wife would not miss him for too long. She doubtless had a man in every fort, but the optio didn't think less of her for it. He had also met the woman's husband – and could not wholly blame the young, alluring wife for her infidelities. Galen should bottle the merchant's conversation and sell it as a sleeping potion, Atticus joked.

Sabina hooked her slender legs around his, her almond-shaped eyes smiled in sultriness. Her hand reached down underneath the sheets.

"Well I don't want you defying me, Rufus Atticus. And I don't want some barbarian woman taking your heart either."

"I'm much more concerned about some barbarian woman taking my life," he countered.

"You shouldn't joke," she replied admonishingly, hitting him on the chest too as a further rebuke.

The soldier thought how he had little choice but to deal with things through a sense of humour. One either laughed along with the joke of life, or fell victim to one of its punch lines.

*

"How do you think father will react when he sees us?" Aurelia asked, as she and her brother packed their saddle bags for the journey ahead.

"He will likely greet you with a hug and me with a scowl or grunt. I think Maximus and the Emperor overestimate the influence I might be able to bring to bear. But I do not want to let them down," Arrian replied, recalling the last exchange of letters between himself and his father. His father had sent him a letter explaining how he had recently acknowledged his illegitimate son, Balloc – and that he had announced him to the tribe as his heir. Whilst Tarbus may have believed that he was punishing his son, Arrian had breathed a sigh of relief upon reading the news. He could continue his studies and be free from the responsibility of returning to the north. He would rather be the thousandth man in Rome, as opposed to the first man with the Arivisto.

"What did you and the Emperor speak about at dinner? He seemed glad to give you his ear at the end of the table."

"We talked about literature, history, philosophy. He is remarkably well read. He recommended some philosophy tutors I should call on when we return to Rome. And he said he would provide some letters of introduction." Arrian remembered again the Emperor's words at the end of the evening. The philosophy student had asked; if the Emperor could impart one piece of wisdom gleaned from his studies and life what would it be? Aurelius had paused briefly in thought, equally amused and intrigued by the question, before replying, "While thou livest, while thou mayest, become good."

Rain drummed across the roof. Arrian rolled his eyes, realising how he was truly back in his sodden homeland. He scrunched his face up in vexation as he held aloft the pair of uncomfortable woollen trousers he would have to wear. Dressing in a Roman tunic could get him killed, once he crossed the Danube.

79

"But tell me, what were you and Maximus talking about at dinner? The rain in our homeland seems to have washed away your animus towards him."

Arrian smiled, as he recalled Atticus' whispered comment over dinner – that his sister was batting her eyelids at Maximus so much he was worried that she might blow out the candles on the table. Aurelia blushed, either from the embarrassment at being reminded of her previous attitude towards the centurion, or from something deeper. She had told herself that she would make an effort with the praetorian for Julia's sake, but it was more than that now. She liked him, for her sake.

*

Galen finished taking the Emperor's pulse. The stoical doctor reacted with neither concern nor contentment in regards to the prognosis. The patient similarly remained impassive – and enquired not as to whether all was satisfactory. The two friends merely carried on their conversation. They sat under an awning in the garden of the Emperor's villa. The worst of the rain had passed it seemed, but drizzle still misted up the air.

"The mission will provide Maximus with a distraction from his grief. Should he encounter the enemy then he may well be granted that which he perhaps desires most – his death," Marcus Aurelius posited. Maximus was his first choice to escort the brother and sister through enemy territory back to the Arivisto tribe – even before the centurion volunteered for the task and Arrian and Aurelia requested his presence.

"I dare say that, in Rome, in protecting you or fighting for his comrades, Maximus has something to die for. I'd just prefer that he had something to live for, too. Let us hope that the mission doesn't prove a suicidal one," Galen replied, watching a bird dart across his vision and wondering if he had encountered the species before.

"Maximus will not fail us. I cannot speak for Tarbus, the chief of the Arivisto, however. He could stand beside us like a lion, or his tribe could turn on us like a pack of wild dogs – smelling the blood of a weakened prey. Balomar may yet buy the support of the Arivisto before us also. My agents inform me that he has entered into the region, accompanied by a war chest to purchase loyalty and arms. The Marcomanni are growing in strength," the Emperor stated, sighing from a sense of tiredness or pessimism.

"You need to be mindful of your own strength, as well as worrying about the condition of your enemy. You need to sleep more and regain your appetite."

"I'll regain my appetite, my friend, once I've tasted victory."

*

Maximus spent most of the day on a run. He ran till his lungs burned and his feet bled, but still the centurion could not outrun his grief and memories. He might as well have tried to outrun his shadow. He remembered how he used to tell his son, Lucius, about his namesake: Lucius Oppius, the *Sword of Rome* – the standard bearer who led the invasion off the British coast. Oppius stood by Caesar as he crossed the Rubicon and fought at Pharsalus. He had also protected the young Octavius Caesar, as he travelled to Rome from Apollonia. Maximus pictured his son's face, bright-eyed and captivated by his stories. He tried his best to remember the sensation of Julia affectionately squeezing his hand. They held hands as if they were still teenage sweethearts, long after their wedding day. Foul as well as fond memories assaulted his thoughts though. Images of emaciated, sweat-glazed faces. A succession of funerals – for those who he lived for. Waking up in taverns, sick caked on his chin, from having drunk himself into oblivion, having been too frightened to go home to an empty house. Anger as well as sorrow swelled in his breast. Should a priest, or a God even, have tried to explain to him how the deaths of Lucius and Aemelia were part of a greater plan then he would have drawn his sword and run them through.

Maximus also ruminated upon his impending mission as he pounded along the woodland tracks and through the mountain passes. Unfortunately the intelligence was scant as to the number of enemy between them and the Arivisto tribe. Similarly, they couldn't be sure of the welcome they would receive when, or if, they reached their destination. The mission was hazardous; but it was also potentially vital to the war effort. The centurion found himself thinking about Aurelia during his run, too. He had enjoyed sitting next to her at dinner the previous evening. Maximus couldn't quite understand why the woman had softened towards him – he was just grateful for her apparent change of heart. He told himself that her new found amiability was welcome as it would make the coming mission easier, but maybe his gratitude was borne from something else.

*

When Maximus returned to camp he sought out Apollo. He found the young soldier in a tavern. The new recruit stood to attention when seeing his officer, but the centurion told him to sit, bought him a drink and gave him a gift.

"I can't really compete with the present Atticus gave you to unwrap in the tavern last week but, here, take this," Maximus said, giving Apollo a finely crafted dagger. "Think of it as a thank you present."

"What are you thanking me for, Sir?"

"You're about to accept an important assignment."

Apollo immediately felt a rush of excitement and pride at being chosen to carry out a special mission, but when he took in the grave expression on his commanding officer's face the archer began to realise that promotion to the Praetorian Guard could be the death – rather than the making – of him.

16.

The small size of the party (Maximus, Atticus, Arrian and Aurelia) meant that it could wend its way through the country nimbly and largely undetected. When they did encounter enemy soldiers or civilians Maximus and Atticus were pleasantly surprised with the young German's confidence and resourcefulness in dealing with his countrymen. He declared that he was the son of the chief of the Arivisto, on his way back home to join his father to fight the Roman invaders, and that he had employed a brace of deserters as bodyguards.

"I must confess Arrian, I've been impressed by the way you've handled yourself when we've encountered the enemy. You've lied so well that you might want to consider a career in politics," Atticus amiably conveyed to the student as he trotted beside him. They were riding abreast along a woodland track. Spindly branches, like bony fingers, hung over them. Plaintive birdsong blew through the trees, as did the stench of a nearby marsh. The air was damp, presaging rain. Hooves sloshed in the mud.

"I warrant that I still could not handle myself in the manner that you and Maximus did when we were attacked by bandits."

"There's more to being a hero than just carrying a sword, although women quite like a man who can use a gladius. Of course they are also attracted to those men who wear a purse full of gold on their belt. I try to carry both, in order to narrow down the odds further," the optio said with a conspiratorial wink to the awkward looking youth. The bookish adolescent had trouble looking most people in the eye at the best of times.

"Unfortunately I'm as good with women as I am with a blade. I'm married too much to my studies," Arrian replied, forcing a half-smile. The diffident teenager was all theory and no practice when it came to the subject of women.

"Then you need to have an affair. I know an actress in Rome who is comfortable in playing with any part. Or I could always break Apollo's heart and arrange a tryst with his barmaid back at the tavern on the road home. I'm sensing that you're not that enamoured with German women. I hear that on the whole husbands stay faithful to their wives here. But they may well stay faithful because there's no one worth having an affair with. Yet tell me, has your sister ever been married? She is certainly old enough to have been married – and divorced – twice over by now," Atticus half-joked, nodding up ahead towards where Aurelia rode alongside Maximus.

Arrian had once heard her sister declare that she would not marry because she wanted to remain "a bride of Christ", but he resisted, sharing this with the Roman soldier. He merely answered that Aurelia was still to marry – and then asked the optio if he had ever been wed, as he was old enough to have been divorced twice by now too.

"No, I've yet to embark upon that adventure, or suicide mission. It's also partly the reason why I've still gold in my purse, I warrant."

Arrian held out his palm and creased his face up in irritation as another shower broke out.

"You must not envy my homeland's weather."

"No, nor its fashions," Atticus quickly replied, creasing his face up in discomfort at having to wear Arrian's Germanic clothes. Aurelius needed to defeat the barbarians, if only for tunics to earn a victory over trousers for future generations, the soldier thought. "But all is context, as you may have realised in your studies. Germany is veritably arid compared to Britain, where I was once posted. I think the gods might cause it to rain so constantly there in order to help sober the natives up. Although sobering up a Briton may be a task too great for even a deity."

"And what are the women like over in Britain?" Arrian said, his curiosity overcoming his shyness.

"Somewhat closed-minded to Roman culture. But buy them a drink and they'll duly open up their hearts – and legs – to you," the soldier stated, smiling fondly as he recalled a pretty, bowlegged innkeeper's daughter from Londinium.

*

Maximus rode alongside Aurelia, but there were long periods where he did not utter a word to her, or indeed anyone. His strong jaw would clamp shut, as if a team of engineers would be needed to prize it open again. It was not the first time that Aurelia had witnessed the praetorian retreat into himself, inhabiting an internal forest far darker and more haunted than the one they were actually travelling through. Atticus had said how Maximus was never consciously being rude when he was taciturn. The optio told a story of how they had attended a dinner once in Rome. Maximus had sat towards the end of the table, silent, brooding. The wife of the host remarked how she had made a bet with her friend that the soldier would speak more than five words by the end of the meal. She hoped that she would win.

"You won't win your bet," Maximus laconically replied, remaining silent for the remainder of the dinner.

There had been instances of late, however, when the soldier had given himself over to talk to the German woman. Aurelia recalled how during the dinner the Emperor had hosted for them back at Aquileia she had subtly guided the conversation so Maximus spoke about his wife. At first he looked uncomfortable, even pained, talking about Julia, but he forced himself to carry on. Aurelia began to realise just how much Maximus was devoted to her friend, how they drew strength from each other. "She was kind and she was beautiful – and in a way she taught me how being kind and being beautiful are one and the same thing," the soldier confessed, with a mixture of fondness and sorrow in his expression. She thought she saw tears begin to well in the usually gruff looking praetorian's eyes. He quickly excused himself, saying that he needed some air.

Aurelia wanted to now tell Maximus that she had known his wife, been her companion. Perhaps it would bring him some consolation and contentment when she spoke of the Julia she knew. Or maybe he would miss her more. She didn't want to deceive him anymore though. Did he know about Julia's faith and devotion to Christianity?

Aurelia drew breath, as if to give voice to her thoughts, but she was cut short by Maximus raising his hand. Up ahead were a group of armed men next to a white stone marker. They had reached the territory of her tribe. Half a dozen barbarians walked forward, carrying spears. She recognised the lead barbarian as Balloc, her father's illegitimate son. Whether Balloc recognised Aurelia or not the scowl across his face bespoke of his perpetual hostility towards anything and everyone. Even the news of him being pronounced his father's heir did not bring a smile to his sour features. A jagged, lightning bolt shaped scar ran down his cheek and scythed through his beard. Long, lank brown hair half covered the warrior's face. He barked a few words in his native language – and Arrian responded. The atmosphere was far from warm or familial as Balloc led the brother and sister away from the soldiers to talk in private. Before doing so Balloc ordered his men to keep a watchful eye on the Romans.

Maximus was impervious, indifferent, to the antagonistic looks and snorts of derision from the swarthy warriors as they pointed their spear tips towards him. His focus was on Aurelia. Should things turn nasty Maximus was ready to draw his sword, kick his heels into the flanks of his horse and protect her. He had grown to like and admire the headstrong woman over the past week. She appeared calm and authoritative when speaking with the more animated Balloc. Her long black hair cascaded down her back. Her flattering figure even shone through the unflattering dress she was wearing. When Arrian had first spoken to Maximus during his recovery the German had praised his sister, describing her as intelligent, witty and kind. Finally the praetorian had reason to believe him.

"Do you think that we'll be welcomed with open arms when, or if, we reach the village? Or will they be up in arms?" Atticus remarked, eyeing the dour, hirsute figures around him with wariness and bemusement. Suddenly even the prospect of a dinner party with his father's friends seemed attractive, as opposed to the hospitality they might soon receive from the Arivisto.

17.

They reached the village within an hour or so. Balloc had ordered his men to walk either side of the Romans in order to guard, rather than protect, them. Occasionally he would turn and sneer at the soldiers – and Arrian – but otherwise he remained silent – making even Maximus appear garrulous.

There were a handful of stone cottages in the village but most dwellings were mud huts, or tents. Dozens of cooking pots bubbled away, filling the air with the smell of cabbage or onion soup. Occasionally a small, honey glazed boar turned upon a spit. The noise of a fast-flowing stream, as well as the bleating of livestock, could be heard in the background. The sound of laughter was conspicuous by its absence. When Atticus had set off from Aquileia he believed that he was dressed in little more than rags, but as he gazed around the village he felt veritably princely in his garb compared to the bedraggled natives. In some cases it seemed to be only the grime and mud that were still keeping the outfits together. Occasional flashes of colour could be seen though as some of the women – and men – wore braids, bangles and necklaces. Feral children played in the mud. Aside from the warrior class most people seemed malnourished and disease ridden. The smell of the onion soup couldn't quite overpower the ordure. The persistent drizzle raining down upon the village only added to the atmosphere of despondency and privation.

Maximus noted that there were plenty of well-armed men populating the settlement – and both the blacksmith and carpenter had queues forming around their places of business. Arrian had mentioned how the tribe were scattered throughout a number of villages. If other settlements possessed a similar quota of warriors then the Arivisto could indeed prove to be a significant ally, or enemy. The strangers attracted a variety of looks, ranging from the mildly curious to the openly hostile. Sensing the attitude of their masters a trio of dogs even bared their teeth and growled at the visitors.

A young boy ran up to Balloc and handed him a large cup of wine, which he downed in one (albeit as much wine ran down his beard as ran down his throat). Balloc nodded his head and grunted, conveying to the child to tell Tarbus that the hunting party had returned.

As Arrian looked around him he was struck by how little the village had changed in his absence. The earthy odours filling his nostrils prompted memories; few of them were pleasant. Ironically some villagers walked by him and looked down their noses at the youth, as if he were a bad smell. He had never quite fitted in, even before he had ventured to Rome. He had failed as a hunter. He had failed in embracing the tribe's traditions and gods. And he had failed as a son. But somehow Arrian instinctively knew that there was something different, better, beyond the lands of the Arivisto – and Rome, or rather philosophy, had saved his soul.

Arrian gulped, his mouth went dry and he felt his being shrivel up like a raisin in the sun as he spotted his father coming towards him. Tarbus would have been an imposing figure even without the large battle-axe which he carried in his hand as a king might carry a sceptre. He was a man used to being feared and revered (indeed the two were one and the same in his mind). Arrian had not inherited his father's tall, broad build. Indeed the student sometimes wondered if he had inherited anything from his father, to the point of believing that he may not even be his son. Bushy eyebrows hung over a pair of cunning, cruel eyes (as opposed to Balloc's aspect, which seemed solely concerned with cruelty). The other villagers gave their chieftain a wide birth as he strode forward, mud splashing up from his heavy gait. A sense of menace and brutality oozed out of him, like sweat. Maximus could barely work out where the chief's scraggly beard ended and equally where his scraggly fur coat began (should Galen have been present he could have informed the soldier that the belt fastened around the great coat was partly made of human bones). The barbarian's beard concealed a bull-neck and increasingly jowly face. Maximus briefly glanced at the huge axe, stained with blood and rust that Tarbus carried in his large, scarred right hand. The praetorian nodded his head in respect as the chief stood before him.

Tarbus grunted and knitted his brow at seeing his estranged son, but his craggy features softened as he took in his daughter. She smiled and bowed – and his demeanour softened even more. Father and daughter exchanged a few words and he clasped her hands in his. The re-union began to attract the attention of the whole village. To some, fuelled by the propaganda of Balloc, "Arrian" was a dirty word, or an insult. He had turned his back on the tribe and sold his soul to the enemy. He had even taken a Roman name, to add injury to the insult.

Tarbus looked on with stony indifference or boredom even as his son spoke. Arrian first remarked how glad he was to see his father and to have returned home – and then he reported on how he had been asked by the Emperor to discuss the prospect of an alliance between Rome and the Arivisto. The tribe could no longer afford to remain neutral in the war. Rome was willing to offer generous trade subsidies to the tribe, as well as arm and supply its warriors. At this point, conscious of all the suspicious faces glaring at him, Arrian asked his father if he wanted to retreat somewhere to discuss the terms of the alliance in private.

"I have no desire to discuss anything in private with you. I have no secrets from my tribe, as a father has no secrets from his children. It is strange that a son should keep things from his father, though. Do you think that we should be bowing before you and hailing your name for negotiating with the Romans on our behalf? You probably think you have been clever, no? Perhaps you were inspired by someone in a story in one of your precious books," Tarbus remarked, spitting out a gob of phlegm as he did so, as if the act represented what he thought of his son and his books.

Balloc sniggered, which in turn encouraged others around him to do so.

"Please, father, do not dismiss what he has to say. I believe the Emperor to be a good man," Aurelia said, stepping forward to do so. She cut short her speech however at seeing her father raise his hand, giving her a fierce look as he did so.

"I'm pleased to see you again, daughter. But women should be seen and not heard. Now hear this, both of you. You do not bet on the fighter who has been knocked down. You do not try to save an injured animal. You kill it – put it out of its misery. Rome has been wounded, bloodied. It will not and cannot win a significant battle against the Marcomanni and its allies. Your Caesar may be a good man, but he is not a good commander. You were a stupid, deluded boy when you left for Rome. You have returned a stupid, deluded man. But you were right in one regard. The Arivisto cannot remain neutral any longer. Everyone must choose a side. I have negotiated an alliance with Balomar – a strong commander rather than a good, weak man."

Aurelia's eyes widened in shock and peril and she immediately turned to Maximus. Her face conveyed an apology and also a plea for help. Although the soldier was unable to understand a word of the exchange between father and son he could intuit that all was not well. His suspicions were confirmed when, head downcast, Arrian remarked, "My father has made an alliance with Balomar."

91

Tarbus nodded at Balloc, at which point the young warrior growled out an order. Spear tips were raised. Maximus and Atticus struggled not as they were restrained and disarmed.

Aurelia's mouth was agape and a look of pity could now be seen on her pale face, as she gazed at the centurion. Her heart went out to him.

"I'm sorry," Arrian said, ashamed and saddened. Had the praetorian saved his life, twice, and journeyed halfway across the continent for things to come to this?

"Don't worry, it won't be you who'll be sorry," Maximus replied – speaking to Arrian but staring at Tarbus. Unflinching. Undefeated.

18.

"Looks like we're in the shit again," Rufus Atticus remarked, arching his eyebrow and looking down at the floor of the cage, which was littered with animal excrement. The soldiers had been placed in a cage, which the tribe usually used to store wild boars or livestock.

Darkness had fallen. A couple of torches, either side of the cage, still illuminated the scene. At least the villagers had now turned in for the night. They'd thankfully grown tired of firing off curses – and stones and mud – at the prisoners.

"Do you think they'll ransom us?" Atticus added. "If so then I fear my father may pay the tribe to keep me, rather than set me free. What do you make of our odds in getting out of this?"

"A one wheeled chariot has more chance of winning a race in the Circus Maximus," the centurion posited.

"So we've been in worse situations then?"

"Aye," Maximus replied, staring off into the distance. The praetorian was only half concentrating on his grim-humoured exchange with his optio. His thoughts had turned to Marcus Aurelius. The soldier had given his word to the Emperor that he would return before the army crossed the Danube at Pannonia. Not only had Maximus never broken his word to his Emperor before, but he worried for the army should Aurelius be given poor counsel. He did not want augurs and religious leaders getting their claws into his commander. Nero may have made his horse a member of the Senate, but not even he would have given control of his legions over to a priest.

"The omens are good," Salvidius, an oleaginous augur with a penchant for collecting fine pottery and young slave boys, had portentously remarked to the Emperor during a recent war council.

"More importantly, the troops are ready," Maximus stated, his manner as hard as iron.

"You will soon win a great victory Emperor, and after the battle we will praise and honour the gods," Salvidius later said, stroking his grey beard with his heavily ringed fingers.

"The first thing we will do, after winning any battle, will be to praise and honour the wounded and dead," Maximus countered. "Soldiers win battle, unless your gods want to don some armour and stand in a shield wall like the rest of us."

*

The night air chilled his sweat-soaked skin. Arrian trod as stealthily as he could over the glutinous ground. With every step he felt like he was sinking deeper into the mud – and deeper into trouble. Few who defied Tarbus of the Arivisto lived. He'd had little appetite over dinner – and not just because the food was about as palatable as his father's politics. Tarbus had sat Aurelia next to him – and also close to an ogling Balloc. Arrian however had been ordered to sit at the opposite end of the table, next to a couple of burly warriors who stank as much as the cage the Romans had been imprisoned in. The only time his father acknowledged him was when he ridiculed him. The rest of the table would then laugh, akin to the Chorus in a Greek tragedy. There had only been a brief moment during the evening when Arrian could speak freely with his sister.

"We need to save them. Tonight," he had whispered.

"Agreed," she replied.

Arrian saw his sister's silhouette melt into the night as she went to ready the horses. The cage was in sight. Thankfully the guard watching the prisoners appeared to be asleep. The key to the large

94

iron lock, which fastened the doors to the cage, sat away from the guard on a stool. The sentry would have to be silenced though.

Maximus gave a nod of thanks and encouragement to the young German as he approached. Arrian's hand trembled slightly, both with fear and from the cold, as he handed the knife to the praetorian through the bars of the cage. The student averted his eyes, not wishing to see what would follow. The centurion would cup his hand over the guard's mouth and cut his way through his windpipe and neck. But Maximus was stopped in his tracks, by the sound of booming laughter and slow clapping.

"Ha, finally you're of some use boy, and I'm grateful for you being alive. I had a bet with Balloc. He wagered that you would not help your friends because you'd be cowardly. I said that you would, because you were too stupid," Tarbus announced in a rough, contemptuous voice. Dozens of torches lit up, like giant fireflies, in the darkness. Shaggy, fur-clad figures came out from behind tents. The Arivisto formed a horseshoe around the prisoner – and traitor. Arrian pressed his back against the bars of the cage. Dread cut itself into his features. Atticus placed a consoling hand upon his shoulder.

"You did your best. We're grateful. And never mind your father, you proved me right. You don't have to carry a sword to be a hero."

Everyone's attention now turned to the sight of Balloc, dragging Aurelia by the arm. He grunted as he pushed the woman into the mud, in front of her brother. Arrian helped his sister up and they hugged. Tears began to stream down both of their cheeks. Fury and a sense of futility vied for the sovereignty of Maximus' being.

"Come here boy. You always were a cry baby. I remember you as a child, you used to water the crops more than the rain... Come here, I won't hurt you."

As if he were a child again Arrian obeyed. He hung his head and dutifully approached his father. All seemed lost. He would never be able to return to Rome, see his tutors or read his books again. He would never be able to attend the theatre, or baths. He would be condemned to live as an outcast within the tribe. A slave. Or his father would put him in a shield wall and sentence him to death. Yet death seemed a welcome fate, compared to the living death which was the alternative.

Tarbus viciously slapped his son across the face with the back of his hand, giving vent to his animus. The rings on his fingers sliced through Arrian's cheek and nose. The student fell to the ground. Blood rather than tears ran down his face. Aurelia let out a plea, to both God and her father, to spare her brother. She could barely be heard above the cheers and curses of the tribe however. Wine dulled their sense of compassion – and fuelled their ire.

"You've dedicated your miserable life to studying boy. Well I'm about to teach you your final lesson – show you what happens when you betray your own people," Tarbus proclaimed, as much for his tribe's benefit as for his son's ears.

The chieftain gave a solemn nod of his head. Even before Maximus heard the sound of Balloc's sword scrape out of its scabbard he knew Arrian's fate. There was a look of satisfaction, even glee, on his face as Balloc strode up to his half-brother and shoved the point of his sword into his victim's neck. Before, or as he did so however, Arrian remembered a quote from Epicurus:

Death does not concern us, because as long as we exist, death is not here. And when it does come, we no longer exist.

This time everyone heard Aurelia scream. She rushed to her brother. Blood gurgled out from the glistening wound. There was a look of shock, rather than the usual sweet expression, on Arrian's ashen face.

"You should not mourn a traitor, daughter. I hope that Rome has not turned your head – and poisoned your heart – as well. You can finally come back home. Your future is with the Arivisto," Tarbus announced. He had promised his daughter to Balloc, to secure the bloodline within the tribe, but he might also be able to strengthen his alliance with the Marcomanni by giving his daughter to Balomar.

Balloc turned to the cheering crowd, raising his arms and gore-stained blade as if he were a gladiator who had just won a great victory in the arena. The warrior bared his teeth and stuck his tongue out when he turned to Atticus – but the optio altered not his own expression. He merely gazed upon the bastard son of Tarbus as if he were already a corpse.

Aurelia rose to her feet and stared at her father as though he was already dead to her. It was not that she thought that he had changed during her time in Rome, but rather it was she who looked at him with new eyes. Aurelia felt she had nothing more to say to the chief of the Arivisto. She was too sad, shocked and angry.

Rain commenced to slap upon the muddy ground. The stars seemed to dim in mourning. The sister bent down, closed her brother's eyes and lovingly kissed him on the forehead. She squeezed his hand, as she used to do to bring him comfort and confidence when he was alive. The woman then wordlessly walked towards the cage. She retrieved the key from the stool, unlocked the door and entered. Aurelia felt safer and freer imprisoned with the Romans – more so than if she were queen of all the German tribes. She would share the fate of the captives and her brother. The crowd watched in part disbelief, part curiosity. Aurelia fell into the centurion's arms and buried her face into his chest.

Tarbus' disappointment in his daughter quickly turned to disdain. "So be it," he said with a snort. "But I expected better from you."

Aurelia heard her father's words and was tempted to reply that she expected better from him too, but she remained silent. She just clung to the praetorian – for if she let go of him Aurelia felt she might fall.

"If they decide to execute us tomorrow I'm taking a few of the bastards, or one bastard in particular, with me to meet the ferryman," Atticus remarked, still staring at a triumphant Balloc.

Maximus nodded in reply. If Tarbus came within an arm's reach he would break his neck.

"You can all stew in there until the morning. It could be the last dawn you see. As for the rest of you the show is over. Go back to your beds. Get some rest. For tomorrow we set off to join our German brothers – and we will wash our spears in the blood of the Roman imperialist scum," the chief shouted, over the increasing roar of the rain.

"I'm sorry," Aurelia murmured, looking up at Maximus – apologising for everything, for things that the soldier was unaware of. "We're damned."

"No. We can still be saved. Have faith," the praetorian whispered back, determined that his war wouldn't be over so soon.

19.

Atticus eventually drifted off to sleep, with thoughts of how he would get close to Balloc on his mind. He had sharpened a flat stone and would slice it across his enemy's neck. They would kill him for the crime – but they couldn't execute him twice, so it was a worthwhile venture, the optio reasoned. He was dead anyway. Tarbus would not ransom them now. Atticus wished that he could write to Claudia, or to give instructions to a friend in regards to publishing his poetry. But, as he confided to his centurion, "I don't have any regrets – aside from being captured and sentenced to die of course."

It was deep into the night. Even the owls and nightingales had gone to sleep. The sentry also slept, this time in earnest, occasionally snoring.

Maximus and Aurelia were still awake, however, sitting next to each other. The praetorian had given the woman his cloak to wrap around her. Yet her convulsions were from sobbing, rather than shivering from the cold. Aurelia turned her head to glance at the soldier. As usual his stony expression was unreadable. She knew not how he would react when she offered up her confession. But she was compelled to finally do so. Her voice, like her heart, cracked occasionally as she spoke. She stared straight ahead of her, fearful of breaking down should she look the widower in the eye.

"I need to tell you something. You might be tempted to interrupt, but please let me finish. I need to tell you things, while I still can. I knew Julia, she was my friend. We got to know each other while you were on campaign in Parthia. I loved her like a sister – an older, wiser sister. She made me laugh. She taught me the meaning of friendship."

Aurelia heard Maximus take a deep breath, as if he were about to speak, but she placed her hand upon his and carried on speaking, before he could interject.

"Julia became a Christian. I may have introduced her to my religion, but she gave herself to God freely. I think that God was in her life before she even met me. He had called out to her. Christianity just gave her a name to call back to... But you were important to her as well. She once told me that she loved you before she even met you. She loved the idea of you... I once believed that Julia had to choose between you and God. In some ways I was jealous of you, the hold you had over her. I was wrong to think such things. She argued that, in knowing you, she found love. And, in knowing love, she found God... We drifted apart, just before you returned to Rome. I never got to say goodbye or to apologise to her. When I met you I hated you, because you reminded me of her. I was also prejudiced against soldiers. The army captured and executed many of my friends. Not all Christians may be Christian, but most are. They were good people – and I wrongly held you responsible for their deaths. But yet I'm glad you're here with me now, partly because you remind me of Julia. You carry a part of her in you."

Aurelia felt Maximus squeeze her hand. His whole body seemed to tense up. The icy wind blew through the bars of the cage, sighing.

"Julia's still part of me – the best part of me. But there is also a hole in my life, where she once lived. I try to fill the emptiness with grief, work, drink and anger. Yet when it comes to the last thing at night, or the first thing in the morning, the emptiness is still there. It's like a wound – and the stitches keep bursting... Julia told me about her religion. She would often even read the Gospels and other texts to me. She also mentioned a friend that she wanted me to meet, who introduced her to your congregation. You made her laugh too... But Julia worried about you increasingly though, when she wrote to me. She thought that you were devoting yourself too much to religion, as opposed to God...Her faith brought to her a sense of comfort and contentment. In the end, she said that God was calling to her. I urged her to ignore his call though and stay with me. Heaven has enough angels, by all accounts. This world has fewer. If you were jealous of Julia's love for me, I grew jealous of her devotion to God... She said that she was at peace, when the end finally came. I'm still not at peace though. If your God exists, then he took my wife and children from me. If he wants me to give him service, over and above that which I owe to Caesar, then pray to him to give them back."

The soldier's tone was imbued with as much grief as it was resentment. He sighed again, as if Maximus wanted to expel all the life, as well as air, out of him too.

"I believe you to be a good man, Maximus. And in being good, you are already giving service to God."

"Julia often said that God works in mysterious ways. Just to see her again in the next life will be reward enough for any scrap of good I can do on earth."

"When the congregation disbanded and then Julia passed away there was a part of me that wanted to die, too. I feel like that again. I've got nothing, no one, to live for," Aurelia mournfully issued, her hand now limp in his.

Maximus wanted to say that she had him. Aurelia wanted him to say it, too. The lambent moon came out from behind the clouds and lit up their faces as they turned to each other. Maximus smiled and squeezed her hand – and she responded in kind. They shared a moment.

Their moment was cut short however by the sight of Apollo slitting the throat of the snoring sentry.

20.

Atticus rubbed the sleep – and disbelief – out of his eyes at seeing the young legionary open the door to their prison, wiping the bloody blade that his centurion had given him on his trousers.

"Hope for the best, plan for the worst," Maximus expressed by way of an explanation. The praetorian had instructed Apollo to track his party from the moment they left Aquileia. For the past few hours the archer had posted himself in a large oak tree, overlooking the village and his centurion, biding his time.

"You could've told me."

"I thought you liked surprises."

"I must confess, I'm enjoying this one," the optio said, his semblance filled with gratitude and respect for the new recruit. Apollo's boyish grin widened even more in reply. They moved with stealth and speed into the forest. It would be dawn soon however and their absence would quickly be discovered. There was a danger that Tarbus could use his hunting dogs to track the fugitives. Aurelia in particular would need a head start if she was to make it back across the Danube. Yet Maximus had already formed a plan to keep the Arivisto occupied.

"Did you bring the fire arrows?"

"Aye, it wouldn't very well be a party without them," Apollo answered, exhilarated rather than scared by the situation they were all in. Drills, marching and sentry duty were not half as much fun, or as meaningful, as the mission as he was on now.

"Atticus, I need you to take Aurelia and head back towards the nearest fort on the other side of the Danube. Get a message to the Emperor, brief him on the Arivisto's alliance with Balomar. I won't be too far behind."

"No, we won't leave you. We should stay together," Aurelia anxiously argued, not wishing the praetorian to sacrifice himself, or be parted from her.

"Neither you, nor your father, can get rid of me that easily, don't worry. I promise I'll be following close behind you both. Apollo and I just need to give the village a wake-up call."

"I can help the lad out if needs be," Atticus volunteered, not wanting his friend to potentially sacrifice himself either. He sensed that he was Aurelia's second choice in escorting her back to the fort.

"With your aim with a bow you'll more likely set fire to Pompeii from here. No, both of you, go now," Maximus said, with a blend of warmth and sternness. His gazed rested on the beautiful, Christian woman for a couple of extra, telling seconds – and the eerie atmosphere of the forest was fleetingly coloured by an air of romance. He hoped that he would see her once more. As much as they had recently shared, it felt like their story had only half been told.

Aurelia embraced the young legionary and thanked him for saving them all, with a kiss. Even in the dim light of the forest Atticus noticed Apollo crimson. He'd been kissed before – but never by a lady. The optio bid the recruit a fond farewell also.

"You're a god send, Apollo. When we next visit a tavern back in Rome I'll make sure you won't be able to stand the following morning, from the drink and women that I'll treat you to… Keep saving the life of your centurion, too. You never know, he might just put you on latrine duty only every other night as a thank you."

Aurelia embraced Maximus. She held onto him for a couple of extra, telling seconds, and whispered something in his ear.

*

The dawn light glowed in the distance, but the village burned brighter. Apollo had reported with relish how the Arivisto stored their hay and heating oil together in the barn. Each flaming arrow struck its intended target as the two accomplished archers rained havoc down upon their enemy. The air spat and crackled with fire. Plumes of smoke billowed up into the sky. For once the Arivisto would have welcomed the sight of grey clouds and rain. Flames devoured tents and wattle and daub houses in minutes. Villagers scattered themselves like ants, torn between saving their possessions and combating the blaze. The fate of the village duly eclipsed the fate of the escaped prisoners. Tarbus was as enflamed as his surroundings though, when he discovered the empty cage and the murdered sentry. He vowed to join his allies as soon as possible and take the fight to Rome. "There will be blood," he snarled.

As tempted as Maximus was to watch the settlement burn – and get Tarbus in his sights – he headed for home as soon as their fire arrows were all spent. The praetorian would keep his promise to his Emperor and join him when he crossed the Danube. The legions had little need to advance northwards however – for Balomar had marched south.

21.

A light drizzle hazed up the air and diluted the afternoon sun. The great turquoise river flowed on, blissfully ignorant of the dreams, actions and follies of the people scurrying about all along its banks. As a philosopher Marcus Aurelius gazed at the undulating water and was reminded of a meditation that he had recently composed: *Time is a river of passing events and its current is strong; no sooner is a thing brought to sight than it is swept by and another takes its place, and this too will be swept away.* Time, Life and Nature were all so much greater than the war with the Marcomanni, than Rome itself.

As a Caesar, however, he stared at the river and starkly thought to himself, *the Danube is my Rubicon.*

The Emperor sat astride his dapple grey horse and pensively looked out across at the opposing shore. The birch and willow trees looked the same on the other side, the bird song sounded the same and the sunlight would be no brighter or dimmer across the Danube – but everything would change when he reached the other side. History's pen hung over him, like the Sword of Damocles. Would he be the Emperor who saved, or damned, the Empire? The stoic in him bore the burden without complaint, but Marcus Aurelius the man felt frail, anxious, lonely – human. As Emperor he could have chosen to remain in Rome. He could have delegated his command to another. He could have been having lunch with his wife, Faustina, in the imperial palace right now, he mused. He would have been nodding incessantly, listening to her gossip and news about what she bought whilst out shopping during the morning (whilst in his head Aurelius would have attended to the business of the state). Or he could have been reading to his son right now and teaching him Euclid. Both of their faces would have lit up too as the wisdom of Socrates and poetry of Horace took root in his fledgling intellect and soul. But duty called. Would it be his Siren song?

Aurelius sat with his back to his advisers and army, concealing the anguish and indecision which lined his ageing face. The Emperor's cloak hung around him, disguising how he was doubled-over in discomfort (or rather pain) from a returning stomach complaint. Galen could help relieve some of the symptoms, but he could not remedy a cure. He suffered in silence.

His expression had remained as unmoved as one of his statues when a messenger had delivered the news that the Arivisto had formed an alliance with the Marcomanni. The Emperor could not help but emit a sigh of relief at hearing that Maximus had returned safely though. The sigh of relief turned to one of grief soon after however when he heard the news that Arrian had been murdered. He had liked the student. He had not held the blade, but was he not guilty of killing him?

Aurelius rode at the vanguard of his army. He was but accompanied by a few cohorts at present, as the rest of the army negotiated the marshes and forests of the province of Pannonia. His scouts had just reported that the enemy were making their way back north, from having executed a number of raids in Roman territory. The Marcomanni were in striking distance. The army were awaiting Caesar's orders.

His officers had advised caution. They should wait for the rest of the legions to form up, before engaging the enemy. By the time that would happen however there wouldn't be an enemy to engage. It remained unspoken how the legions had still to best the enemy in combat when the numbers had been equal – and from the scout's report the force of barbarians was even greater than that of their cohorts.

What would Maximus do? The Emperor knew the answer to the question he posed to himself, before even asking it. Maximus would take the fight to the enemy and believe in the courage and skill of the legions. He would argue that his officers were advising caution because they were more concerned with not losing a battle, as opposed to winning one.

Whether it was due to the cold air, or due to the fact that he had never drawn it before and the blade needed oiling, Aurelius struggled slightly to unsheathe his sword. But unsheathe it he did. The weapon felt heavy and alien in his hands – but he could and would get used to the sensation.

The die is cast.

The Emperor turned to face his council of war. Despite the pain he sat up straight on his horse. He instructed his senior centurions to form up the cohorts. They were marching eastwards. They were going to engage the enemy. He quickly dispatched messengers to order the legions to turn eastwards too.

"But, Caesar, should we not consult the auspices as to the merit of engaging the enemy? Surely the Emperor would want to know if he has the gods on his side?" Salvidius anxiously exclaimed, having no wish to be by his commander's side when he gave battle.

"Who needs the gods when you've got the Praetorian Guard," Maximus expressed, as he trotted up to the senior staff, alongside Atticus.

22.

The wooden bridge bowed a little as the first of the enemy commenced to cross over it. Aurelius and Maximus looked down upon the scene – and felt the ground murmur a little. It dawned on the Emperor how a few hundred Romans would soon face a few thousand barbarians. The bulk of his army was still half a day away, at best. Maximus had inserted into the orders to the commanding officers of the legions that there was plunder to be had from the enemy. "That should put more of a spring in their step in them getting to the party on time."

The ragged line of men snaking out from the woods, onto the road and then narrowing to cross the bridge, seemed endless to Aurelius. It was a river of men – that his forces could drown in. His doubts began to re-surface and he already had the expression of a man in mourning, as if honouring the dead already.

"Are you sure that we should not wait for the rest of the legions?"

"I'm sure," the praetorian replied, squinting to see who appeared to be commanding the Marcomanni army. Was it Balomar himself? Had the Arivisto had time to join with their new allies? He then turned his attention back to his Emperor. "I remember you once giving Commodus some advice. You were in the garden. It was after one of his lessons. You said that one should not waste time arguing about what a good man should be, but rather be one. You should not now think too much on how a good commander should act, but rather be one."

Maximus fleetingly thought of the Emperor's son, how a wise man's advice would likely be in vain. Commodus was over-privileged, conceited and, though young, already developing a cruel streak. "The apple that fell from the tree seems to have landed in a different orchard," Atticus had once slyly quipped.

"I should have you writing philosophy, as well as commanding my armies, Maximus. You are right, though. The God of War hates those who hesitate, as Euripides once wrote. Order the men to form up. We will advance down onto the plain. The enemy will look to stab through our shield walls with a column, but we will hold the line and cut off the head of the snake. Instruct what little number of archers we have to conceal themselves in the tree line – and attack the column from the side. Have one of the veteran cohorts join them. After blunting their frontal offensive we can attack their flank."

"And drive the bastards into the Danube," Maximus said, finishing off his Emperor's thought, if not quite using the language that he would have employed. "Hopefully the enemy will underestimate us and not commit all of their forces. Crossing back over the bridge will also delay any reinforcements. If we're lucky they'll also charge our lines early. The muddy ground will slow their momentum and sap their energy. But no matter what, our soldiers will stand."

"Because they'll fight for Rome?" the Emperor asked, his expression still creased in worry as he watched the line of enemy warriors continue to stream out of the forest.

"No. Because they'll fight for you."

*

"Are you nervous, lad? You wouldn't be alone if you are," Atticus remarked. The optio noticed how Apollo's hands trembled as he sharpened his arrowheads one last time. It dawned on him also just how young the new recruit looked – and was. He still possessed puppy fat. Years of drink, violence and privation had yet to age his features like other legionaries. Atticus had seen twenty-five year olds with grey hair and the vacant stares of fifty year old veterans.

Apollo shrugged his shoulders, though he could have answered more honestly if he just nodded his head and declared that he was nervous. Indeed, he was scared. The elation and encouragement from succeeding in his previous mission had subsided.

"Do you remember your first battle, Atticus?"

"Well, it's not the sort of thing you want to relive regularly. But I can recall some of it. Self-preservation, more than courage, compelled me to fight on. Just when you think that you can't hold up your shield any longer you discover that you can, as an axe may come down and cut you in two if you don't still hold it aloft. And just when you think that your arm is about to fall off from thrusting your sword forward again and again you'll find the will and strength to do so – again and again – else the enemy will stab your friend standing next to you in the shield wall. I remember my thoughts before the engagement too. I wanted to prove my father wrong, who believed that I wasn't cut out for the army. I ran through my drills and training in my head. I also pictured which one of my past girlfriends would look best in black at my funeral. But you're going to be fine, Apollo. It's just unfortunate that Aurelia is still back at the fort. You won't receive another kiss once it's all over."

A smile broke the tension in the legionary's face, amused and embarrassed as he was in equal measure. Apollo did not want to let Atticus and Maximus down. They believed that he was not just cut out for the army – they considered him good enough for the Praetorian Guard. He did not want to earn a promotion and then not live to see his first pay packet.

"Don't worry, lad. When we get back to Rome I'll introduce you to some women who'll do more than just kiss a war hero. Their husbands are far more interested in politics, or boys even younger than you. Or both. When you tell them that you were at the battle of Pannonia they'll devour you like a lioness would a lamb."

"That'd be one fight that I'd be happy to lose," the bright-eyed archer replied, his hands no longer shaking.

23.

The clouds parted to reveal a crisp blue sky, as if the Gods wanted a better view of the imminent contest. Three ranks of legionaries were lined across the plain, between the tree line and river bank. A mass of barbarians were similarly forming up – preparing to swarm. Some donned headbands to keep the hair out their eyes. Some smeared their faces with blue or red dye. Some jeered, or howled in intimidation and exhilaration. Most were seasoned warriors, buoyed by a number of successful raids in enemy territory. At the head of the formidable force stood Tangan, Balomar's brutal second in command. Tangan had a taste for raping women, in the sight of their husbands. He possessed the bulk of a wrestler, but the speed of a Thracian gladiator. His beard and long greasy hair billowed in the breeze as he repeatedly thrust his spear in the air, with its giant leaf-shaped blade, in time to spitting out a guttural war cry.

Maximus stood in the centre of the front rank of legionaries. He eyed the opposing force believing that discipline could overcome ferocity – method could triumph over madness.

"They bark and howl like dogs. So let us put them down like dogs... Remember how much Roman blood they have spilled. Let us now soak their lands in their blood... The Emperor has put his faith in us, so let us repay the compliment... Pannonia will be carved into the annals of our history. Immortal fame beckons. We are adding a verse into the song of swords. But you will not just be rewarded with a sense of pride and eternal fame... German food may be bland. German wine may be acidic. And according to Atticus their women taste sour. But victory against the Marcomanni will taste sweet. We will relieve them of their plunder

113

and be rewarded in this life, as well as the next… Do not break formation. Let them come to us, throw themselves on our spears and swords…,"

Maximus, after bolstering his men's courage, offered up a silent prayer, to Julia's God as well as Jupiter, that Rome, the Emperor, would be victorious – even if he had to sacrifice himself. He remembered Arrian. A part of the widower had envied his young friend. He had found peace.

*

Balomar, his expression as hard as flint, watched on from across the Danube. His body was taut with muscle – and expectation. Tangan, standing before his warriors, would serve as the tip to the blade which would scythe through the Roman lines. The great king of the Marcomanni wore short leather trousers and a studded leather jerkin. Small scars marked his bald head, from where it had crashed down upon various noses, cheek bones and jaws over the years. He wore a large gold torc around his neck, a prize stolen from a Dacian tribal chief who had dared to challenge him to a duel. He gazed intently, his aspect filled with either fire or ice, at his army forming up, preparing to advance. He smiled in satisfaction, revealing a pair of fangs for front teeth from where he had once chipped them in a fight – and filed them into shape afterwards. As a result the king often hissed as he spoke. Some of his warriors would, quite literally, eat the hearts of their vanquished foes. The ground would soon be awash with Roman blood, of the dead rather than just the wounded, too. Mercy was an indulgence – exercised by either the all-powerful or the weak. Was that the Emperor himself taking to the field, too? Aurelius had experienced Balomar's guile – now he would suffer his martial prowess. Should he capture Aurelius – he would then kill him. Like Achilles with Hector he would drag his body after his chariot and send his corpse back to Rome, looking all too mortal.

After today no one would have to live under the yoke of Rome. Balomar would show his enemies that the Germanic people were the master race.

*

Beer and wine fired their spirits, but they would also dull their wits and coordination Maximus thought to himself. The enemy advanced in the shape of an arrowhead, or wedge. Crows flew in and perched upon the trees, cawing in expectation of the feast to follow. The Marcomanni possessed few horsemen. Balomar would save his cavalry for when the Romans routed – and they could cut down the fleeing legionaries. A few of the troops started to shuffle nervously in the shield wall, but Maximus, Atticus and other veterans moved forward slightly, rather than back.

In an act of bravery, or lunacy, Tangan broke off from his army and ran forward as if to take on the enemy alone. Blood lust, or wine, spurred him on. He raised his shield (a Roman one, a spoil of war from a previous engagement). Perhaps his intention was to provoke the legionaries into firing their javelins at him. Still he ran forward, kicking up mud like a horse. The Marcomanni cheered their champion on. Maximus thought that he would give his own troops something to cheer about, though. He broke ranks from the shield wall and drew his gladius, running towards the hulking warrior. They closed upon each other in the open space between the two armies. Maximus feinted to the right and Tangan stabbed his spear forward with a roar. The praetorian quickly darted to the left however, as the leaf-shaped blade of his enemy sliced through thin air; Maximus span and buried his blade into the side of Tangan's head. The warrior fell to the ground immediately. Some paused in the ranks of the Marcomanni, aghast that their champion could be cut down so quickly. Others were enraged though, as if oil had just been poured onto a fire. They charged, earlier than the

115

aghast and furious Balomar, observing the engagement from across the river, would have liked.

Maximus took his place again in the centre of the shield wall. Men cheered and patted him on the back.

"If you live through this you might get a medal," Atticus said, tightening the chin strap on his helmet.

"The only thing I'll want to get, if we live through this, is drunk," the centurion replied, in earnest.

The line of Roman soldiers was slightly curved, so that the two wings had a better angle to fire their javelins from. The volley of spears from the rear rank skewered into flesh and shields; but still they came. The battle-cries grew in volume and ferocity. Many a legionary uttered a prayer beneath his breath, or pictured a loved one – before his thoughts turned to the business of killing. Some of the more experienced soldiers bucked backwards before transferring their weight forwards – thrusting their bodies and large scutums into the oncoming enemy. The human wave crashed into the human dam. It bent, but did not break. Yelling, howling, screaming, the crunch of shields against shields and the ring of blades upon blades erupted into the air, over and over again – separately, yet one continuous sound.

Blood soon flecked the faces of Romans and barbarians alike. The churned up muddy ground reddened. Legionaries stood behind their shields, relentlessly stabbing their swords out into shins and faces – tapping into the muscle memory of hundreds of drills. A few of the legionaries fell but the gap was immediately filled by the reserve ranks.

Some of the Marcomanni possessed mail or plate armour, but most didn't. The Romans were well-equipped, well-provisioned, well-trained. Although the Emperor had yet to win a major battle he had quickly mastered the art of logistics, in regards to his army. No detail escaped his judicious eye. The army was more loyal to

Marcus Aurelius than many in the Senate thought. Rations found themselves into the bellies of soldiers, rather than onto wagons belonging to bureaucrats or quartermasters. Discipline was maintained not just through a culture of corporal punishments.

Balomar watched on, his nostrils flared in rage. Although he could not quite make out which side was gaining the momentum, the Roman line had yet to break. But the sheer weight of numbers would surely tell, like a pack of hyenas bringing down a lion.

24.

Some of the barbarians called it "the Whisper of Death" – the sound of a Roman arrow swishing through the air. But the whisper grew louder as dozens of archers appeared from out of the tree line and fired missile after missile into the tightly packed ranks of the enemy. Apollo didn't even check to see whether his arrows hit the mark. Instead he just concentrated on firing off the next one. Every shaft which struck an enemy meant that there was one less barbarian capable of killing his friends.

"Keep firing, lad. Don't stop till you meet a Gaul who doesn't surrender, a Greek who pays his debts, or a Briton who's sober," a rough-voiced, grizzled comrade exclaimed.

The remaining cohort also appeared from out of the woods and launched their javelins, arcing them over the first line of barbarians (who had turned and raised their shields towards the new enemy) into the centre of the opposing force. Confusion and fear, as much as death, swept through the Marcomanni. Some of the enemy started to move backwards, whilst others still surged forward, looking to engage the Roman lines. Curse-spitting warriors commenced to trip over the living and the dead. The left side of Balomar's army started to buckle and thin out. The Roman cohort formed up from out of the trees and advanced. The flanking manoeuvre not only gave the main contingent of the Emperor's army time to pause and re-strengthen its ranks, but such was the loss of the Marcomanni's momentum that Maximus ordered a slow advance. The injured foes who they stepped over were methodically stabbed in the neck or groin.

*

Galen had recently tried to give encouragement to the Emperor by arguing, through a syllogism, that warfare was merely problem solving. Aurelius was adept at problem solving. Therefore he was adept at warfare. Aurelius sat upon his horse on the high ground behind his army and thought how warfare was more akin to conducting a group of musicians. He hoped that he had timed the introduction of his archers and reserve cohort well. He had marvelled at the way his soldiers had stood there during the initial onslaught – and he thought of Maximus, leading and representing the legionaries. *Be like a headland of rock on which the waves crash upon incessantly. But the rock stands fast and the seething waters eventually settle.* Hope began to triumph over worry as Aurelius saw his troops drive the enemy backwards – and also closer to the river.

*

Balomar cursed the Roman army – and then his own – as he saw sections of his forces begin to retreat. Many of them had little desire to fall during the final battle of their campaigning season. Dead men can't enjoy their spoils of war. Balomar realised that much of his own plunder was still loaded on wagons, on the wrong side of the bridge. One wagon in particular carried enough gold to finance his regiments of mercenaries for the coming year. He called for Tarbus. It was time to blood his new allies in battle.

*

Some shed their furs and dived into the Danube with the intention being to swim to the opposite bank. Some disappeared into the forest. Some ran back to the bridge and baggage train, looking to secure their valuables (as well as the valuables of their comrades). Some fought on, because they had to – or because they believed that they could still defeat the enemy.

Maximus continued to bellow out orders for the men around him to keep their shape. At the same time he also sent an order to his fellow centurions on his right to wheel the line around and envelop the left side of the enemy army. The wave that had once crashed about their shore was now a tide that was retreating.

Defeat for the Marcomanni turned into a rout when Maximus felt the ground shudder at the arrival of a cavalry detachment. After hearing about the possible spoils of war to be won a decurion had requested permission from his commanding officer to race ahead of the legion and join the Emperor. The legate acceded to the request (on condition he receive a cut of any possible plunder). The cheers – and sighs of relief – could just about be heard over the rolling thunder of their galloping hooves as horsemen streamed out onto the battlefield. They swarmed – and stung.

*

No one perhaps sighed in relief, or inwardly cheered, as much as Marcus Aurelius himself. Sweat soaked his reins from having gripped them so tightly.

"The gods have granted us victory," Salvidius remarked to the Emperor, shortly after sighing with relief also.

"Mortals have granted us victory today. Deities had nothing to do with it. Unfortunately too many have proved just how mortal they were," the Emperor mournfully replied. He hoped that Gaius Maximus was still alive. Not even the Emperor of Rome had the power within him to resurrect and thank a dead man.

*

Maximus finally had a chance to catch his breath and survey the battlefield. His arm, up to his elbow, was crimson (soldiering was sometimes little more than butchery, he sometimes thought). The Danube, which for so long had served as a protective moat for the northern tribes, was now a cause of their end as many fleeing warriors lost their fight with the strong currents and drowned. He saw Apollo, close to him, pull arrows out of corpses and re-fire them at the enemy. The praetorian glanced behind him to see if the

Emperor was still on the ridge but it appeared that he had, along with his bodyguards and the senior staff, repositioned himself. Maximus just hoped that Aurelius hadn't retreated just before he could have witnessed his hour of triumph. Partly due to the lure of the baggage train – and partly perhaps that they could have been isolated and counter-attacked if they crossed over the river alone, the cavalry concentrated on scything down the enemy on the southern side of the Danube. As such, realising that safety resided on the other side of the river, a tide of people surged across the bridge. Yet Maximus could not help but recognise a familiar figure swimming against the stream.

"Atticus, Apollo. Collect up as many arrows and archers to hand. We're going hunting."

25.

Tarbus looked like he had swallowed a wasp, which had been coated in vinegar, after Balomar ordered him to retrieve the strong box on the Roman side of the bridge. Partly the chief of the Arivisto was more used to giving than following commands. He took consolation from the fact however that at least his tribesmen had not been ordered to take part in the main offensive against the enemy. Yet Tarbus felt now an itch, as potent as the pox, that he had formed an alliance with the wrong side in the war.

Balloc and half a dozen other warriors joined their leader as they attempted to cross the bridge in the opposite direction to everyone else. Tarbus brandished his fearsome weapon, in hope that the waves of people ahead of him would be inclined to move asunder. He shoved and barked at the throng, his ire still burning from the fire in his settlement. The damage to the village would take months to fully repair. Tarbus yearned to swing his battle-axe at anything – and no matter who he slaughtered he would picture his enemy as the stone-faced praetorian.

Yet the vengeful chieftain stared across the battlefield to witness Maximus already moving towards him, though there was a line of Marcomanni warriors between them.

*

A giant horseshoe of barbarians attempted to cordon off the baggage train and allow time for others to escape. Due to the cavalry and the desire for several legionaries to win riches, rather than just honour, from the engagement there were increasing breaks in the line. Unfortunately a host of warriors still stood between Maximus and his target. They raised their shields and spears upon seeing the centurion and his optio approach. Just as

Maximus was about to issue the order for Apollo and his fellow few archers to start picking the enemy off, so he and Atticus could cut through the line, several Roman horsemen did the job for them. The warriors fortunate enough not to be cut down by razor sharp cavalry swords were skittled over by the horses.

"It is within the reach of every man to live nobly, but within no man's power to live long. Seneca. Or as another wise man once said, sometimes you've just got to get into the fight," Marcus Aurelius remarked with the hint of a smile, after turning his charger around to face the speechless centurion.

*

Due to the wealth of coin inside – and the fact that Balomar did not trust his warriors not to steal from him – the strongbox had been chained and padlocked to the wagon. Tarbus cursed his new ally, who had been keen to furnish him with orders rather than a key. The horses had long been commandeered so they could not ride the wagon back. Tarbus climbed on top of the vehicle though and brought down the heavy axe head upon a rusty section of the chain, roaring in frustration, hate and everything else as he did so.

Balloc and a dozen or so Arivisto warriors stood close by the wagon, acting as a last line of defence. They fidgeted with their weapons in their hands, either out of nervousness or from desire to use them. Their lips curled in up in disdain when they saw the two soldiers who had half burned down their village in front of them. A look of confidence and contempt was still visible behind the grime and dried blood on Rufus Atticus' face. Balloc, remembering his gesture after murdering Arrian, proceeded to raise his arms, open his mouth wide and waggle his tongue at the optio. Balloc briefly closed his eyes as he also let out a gargling battle cry, hoping to provoke the soldier into rushing into the fray. In a single fluid movement, however, Atticus drew one of his knives and threw it at the barbarian. The dagger smashed through his face, as if his open mouth had sucked in the polished blade. Balloc lifelessly fell to the ground, like a puppet whose strings had been cut.

"I never liked that bastard," Atticus drily remarked to his friend.

The Arivisto veterans had little time to be shocked, or to retaliate. Death whispered in their ears, as a flurry of arrows rained down on them from Apollo and his fellow archers. Some were killed immediately. Some retreated. A couple desperately jumped over the side of the bridge in an attempt to avoid the deadly missiles.

Maximus raised his hand to signal to cease firing.

Tarbus no longer had any thoughts for Balomar, the strongbox or even escaping. He just wanted to kill the Roman, cut down the man with his axe as if he were a tree that needed felling. His eyes bulged with rage, yet he walked towards the centurion as calmly as the centurion walked towards him.

"I am Tarbus of the Arivisto, a descendant of the Ariovistus, the *Scourge of Rome*," the barbarian proudly announced in Latin, thumping his chest, before swinging his giant battle-axe.

Tarbus cleverly lengthened the reach of his weapon by clasping the bottom of the shaft, but Maximus leaped out of the way in time. The chieftain wore a well-crafted, reinforced breastplate over his fur jacket. His bare upper arms, which appeared flabby but were also packed with muscle, each possessed a tattoo of his beloved battle-axe.

The barbarian grinned wolfishly beneath his thick beard, believing that he had the measure and beating of the short-sword carrying Roman. He swung his axe again and Maximus took cover behind the wagon. The centurion realised that it would be difficult for the point or edge of his gladius to penetrate his opponent's armour. So he altered his strategy.

124

When Tarbus swung his axe again Maximus quickly stepped inside, but rather than try to find a weak spot in his plate armour the centurion swiped his sword at the handle of the axe. Tarbus' low roar turned into a high pitched scream as the Roman cut off two fingers on his left hand. Blood pulsed out from the gruesome wound. Tarbus' eyes now bulged in shock, pain and grief as he gazed at the digits on the ground. It was now Maximus' turn to grin wolfishly. The weakened chieftain could no longer wield his heavy weapon effectively. When Tarbus next swung the weapon, with only one hand on the shaft, Maximus was able to easily avoid the blow – and then yank the axe away from his enemy. The soldier then slashed his sword across his opponent's left thigh, bringing the great chieftain to his knees.

"I'm Gaius Maximus, descendent of Lucius Oppius, the *Sword of Rome*. You murdered your son Junius Arrian – who was my friend," the praetorian coldly remarked, just before he stabbed his enemy through the neck.

Epilogue

Evening.

The breeze carried on it a strong scent of pine trees which could still, just, be recognised through the smell of smoke and the dead which stained the air. Maximus briefly looked to the clear, serene night sky - as a respite from the charnel house around him. Fires burned bodies. Wounded were being tended to. Wine soaked the throats for those who sung or talked of victory, or of fallen comrades.

The moon and stars seemed brighter to Maximus, as if they were new or closer. He recalled a phrase spoken by Julia the day before she passed away. "The light shines in the darkness, and the darkness comprehends it not." She said it was from one of the Gospels. Julia made Maximus promise that he would try and read the book after she had gone.

The centurion walked across the bridge with his Emperor. Both men felt mournful, yet also philosophical. The Danube shimmered in the moonlight.

"This is not the end, Maximus. It is not even the beginning of the end. But it is, perhaps, the end of the beginning," Marcus Aurelius uttered, giving voice to his thoughts in regards to the long war ahead. "Already I have received messages from a number of Balomar's allies, or should I say former allies, requesting peace talks. We may all talk of peace but behind such words we will all still plan for war."

"You've defeated them once. You can do it again. Indeed after today the sight of your red cloak may be worth as much as half a cohort," the centurion drily remarked.

The Emperor permitted himself to smile, briefly.

"There will be talk of a triumph, no doubt. You may have to accompany me on the chariot Maximus, whisper that I am mortal. Others may prove too sycophantic and pour praise into my ear instead, except perhaps my wife. But this is just as much your triumph as mine. Indeed the victory belongs to all of us – and I will endeavour to use any spoils of war – or of peace treaties – to reward those who fought here today. I will also send what we can to the families of the wounded and dead. But, tell me, how can I reward you?"

"I'd ask that you grant a pension to Aurelia. She will need to be supported when she returns to Rome. I'd also like to request to escort her back to the capital myself."

Aurelius agreed to his requests and was cheered on the inside. When his friend spoke about the young woman there was a light in his eyes. He would tell Galen that perhaps Maximus now had something, or rather someone, to live for.

"I believe that Aurelia should be thankfully free from harm, in regards to those that wished to abduct her. I'm not so sure that you and I will be so fortunate as to escape future plots by our enemies, however," the Emperor said. "Can you also escort Galen back to Rome? He is presently attending to the wounded. But his place is in the capital. Not only do I feel more at ease, knowing that he can take care of Commodus should he fall ill – but he has his own great war to wage, against the plague. The victory of a cure will do more to save the Empire than a thousand battles in Pannonia."

*

At first he thought that it was the sound of a woodpecker, but then Maximus realised the distant noise was that of legionaries hammering stakes into the ground to construct the fort. Aurelius had indeed crossed his Rubicon. The war would still be a long hard slog, but they were closer to victory now than they had been this morning. That was all one could ask for.

The centurion walked back to his tent, to find Atticus and young Apollo sharing a jug of wine. The legionary was listening to his optio talk about how he believed that the Empire was in decline. Apollo understood little – and maybe cared even less – but he nevertheless indulged his superior officer and pretended to be interested.

"...If the treasury keeps debasing the coinage then our currency will become worthless. And if the currency becomes worthless, everything will lose its value. Someone should tell the government that you cannot keep minting money as a cure-all to the problems of the economy... As both a state, and also as individuals, we have crippled ourselves with debt. We're like a man who, stuck in a hole, tries to dig deeper to get out. Sooner or later though, the hole becomes his grave... Or our end will come, Apollo, from being taxed to death... For reasons of efficiency – and indeed freedom – you should be able to choose what you do with your money, rather than let a government, made up of over-bloated, self-serving bureaucrats, decide. Tax is as much the enemy as the Marcomanni. High taxes have been implemented not just to pay for the war, but rather to pay for a client state, populated by those who work for the government and those who receive their dole from it. Such are those numbers now that too many can and are persuaded into voting certain politicians into power – who further fuel high taxes, indebtedness and a client state... And then we have the problem of China. Gold is flowing out of the Empire as fast as the Danube to pay for Chinese silk, for dresses. But China seems content in hording its wealth, like Crassus, rather than using it to pay for Roman goods. Trade needs to be encouraged... And finally we have the war and the plague."

Atticus here paused to take a drink, and come up for air. Maximus had heard his friend's arguments many times before and felt that Apollo might need saving.

"Cease fire. I fear that you're depressing the lad. Or, worse, boring him. Don't worry, the Empire's not on its knees yet. You too should have some faith, Atticus."

"Faith and wine are in short supply at the moment. The lights are going out all around the Empire," the optio replied. The usual glint in his eye had also dimmed, from talking about the possible decline and fall of Rome.

"It's never all doom and gloom though. The light shines in the darkness, and the darkness comprehends it not," Maximus said, quoting from a book that he had just started to read.

Sword of Empire: Centurion

1.

Rome. 174AD.

"How's the wine?" Gaius Oppius Maximus asked.

"Sharper than a satirist's, or harridan's, tongue," Rufus Atticus replied, draining the cup. He winced slightly as he did so. "But it's still better than the swill that the quartermaster gets his hands on back at the frontline."

The two officers in the Praetorian Guard were sitting in a tavern, having recently returned to Rome from the ongoing war with the northern tribes. It was late, but the night was still young for most of the patrons of *The White Bull*. The smell of stale wine – and even staler bread – hung in the air. Men laughed, belched and cursed with an almost religious observance. Serving girls expertly weaved their way through the crowd carrying jugs and plates, trying to avoid being groped. A number of patrons shouted out their food and drink orders, whilst others discreetly whispered into the ear of the owner. They enquired about the services they could order from the serving girls which were off the menu. A lone, stray dog howled outside in the street. Maybe he was pining to be let in. Or perhaps the mongrel's howls were caused from having tasted the wine, too. Cheers, jeers and the sound of dice being rolled across tables could also be heard at the back of the tavern. A couple of rival stonemason guilds sat in opposing corners. At best they eyed each other with suspicion, although looks of suspicion would likely turn more hostile after a few jugs of wine; there would be blood, rather than stale wine, staining the floor by the end of the night.

133

"And how's your meat?" Atticus asked, gazing without envy at the bowl of mud-brown stew in front of his friend.

"I'll let you know once I come across any," Maximus replied, with little humour. The war had cut a few more lines into the centurion's rugged features, adding to those borne from grief. The soldier's wife and two children had died from the plague. It had now been a few years since her passing but Maximus still remembered Julia, with a mixture of fondness and sorrow, every day.

"Most things taste better with wine, even this slop. Are you sure you don't want me to pour you some?"

"No, I need to keep a clear head tonight. I'm due to see the Emperor tomorrow morning. He returned to Rome this afternoon." Maximus reached again for his cup of barley water.

"I hear that Faustina has been keeping the marriage bed warm for him, through a succession of lovers. Show me a faithful wife and I'll show you an honest politician, a poor tax collector or, rarer still, a faithful husband," Atticus asserted, conveniently ignoring the irony that he himself had been the cause of many a wife proving unfaithful on a number of occasions. Indeed Atticus had not been back in Rome for even a week and he had now spent more than one night in the company of Senator Pollux's wife, Lavinia.

Before Maximus could reply a buxom serving girl, displaying both of her charms, appeared before the soldiers and addressed the younger, more amiable looking officer.

"Would you like anything else this evening?" the dusky-skinned girl, with a light in her eyes, asked as she bent over in front of Atticus and re-filled his cup. "I'm all yours," she added with a suggestive wink.

"That will be all for now, thank you," the charming, aristocratic officer replied. When he winked back her heart fluttered and her eyes lit up even more, envisioning both what was between the soldier's legs and also inside his purse. She headed back towards the kitchen, with the intention of warning off any rivals from attending to the two praetorian guards (or rather one of them in particular).

"It seems you've caught the girl's eye," Maximus remarked to his friend, unable to suppress his amusement. "Unfortunately that's the least that you may catch off her. The serving girls double-up as the whores here, I believe. It's just a shame that they can't add the ability to cook to the tricks of their trade," he added, pushing the bowl of stew away from him. Even the smattering of flies buzzing around the room stayed away from the house special, Maximus noted.

"Aye, food poisoning may be the least of someone's worries after spending the night here. We'd best not tell Apollo about this place. Not even he'd be able be shoot straight whilst scratching his balls at the same time from a pox. Where is the lad, anyway?" Atticus asked, referring to the young legionary and archer Cassius Bursus, or "Apollo" as he had been nicknamed.

"Keeping an eye out as usual. I told him that this trip would prove to be far from a holiday for him. He can eat at the barracks. We should get back ourselves. I've got an important meeting tomorrow."

Aye, but not with the Emperor, Rufus Atticus smilingly thought to himself. Maximus was due to meet someone far closer to his heart.

2.

Glinting stars studded a cloudless evening sky. A cooling breeze frequently took the sting out of the humid air. A film of grime coated the narrow streets. The fetid stench pervading the quarter the two soldiers walked through was even less appealing than the smell of *The White Bull's* famous, or rather infamous, stew. Occasionally Atticus noted the sound of a baby crying, or a husband and wife arguing, behind the shutters of the apartments he passed. Marriage was the greatest advertisement for the single life, he concluded.

"So has it all sunk in yet, being promoted to centurion?" Maximus asked his former optio. The officer furrowed his brow as he did so, noticing some graffiti on the wall which accused the Emperor Marcus Aurelius of being an "absent landlord". His tenants were dying from the plague – as he abandoned them to seek military glory. Unfortunately Maximus had witnessed similar, trite comments since he had returned to the capital.

Atticus had fought well during the recent wars with the Marcomanni and Iazyges. He had saved his centurion's life on more than one occasion too, most notably of late when Atticus had wounded himself from killing a Dacian mercenary who was looking to stab Maximus in the back. Though Maximus would miss him, on a personal *and* professional level, he recommended to the Emperor that his optio should be promoted to centurion and be given his own command. Atticus was a courageous and intelligent officer. His birth and breeding gifted him a natural authority over his men. Atticus' good humour and charm further enhanced the soldiers' loyalty towards him. The aristocratic Mark Antony had possessed a similar affinity with his men. He could drink, joke and fight with them with equal aplomb. Maximus recalled many a time on the parade ground when Atticus would merely raise his eyebrow, rather than his voice, to castigate one of their men and instil enough disappointment in the legionary to improve his performance for future drills.

"Has it been worth it, being promoted? I'll tell you once I receive the pay rise. The burden of paperwork is much more daunting than any burden of command though," the new centurion glibly replied. Despite his usual cynical and sarcastic humour, however, a certain amount of worry had begun to nag at Atticus since his promotion. He had commanded men before, but never his own. He had always been following Maximus' orders. Previously he had considered that his chief responsibility was to look after his centurion. Now he would be responsible for dozens of lives. He would have to give the order to attack or withdraw, although Maximus had once said leadership was not always a question of merely attacking or retreating. "Sometimes all you can do is just hold the line." Battles, lives, could be lost as a result of the decisions he made. Before enlisting in the army the son of the wealthy senator had spent his days counting syllables for the poetry he composed, or arranging dinners with his mistresses. As a centurion, however, it would be his duty to count the dead and arrange the rations for a hundred men. The former philosophy student, who had long concluded that life was a joke, no longer felt like laughing.

"Well if it's any consolation the paper cuts sting less than the spear tips of Dacian mercenaries."

"I'm pleased to hear it. Any other pearls of wisdom?"

"Aye. The wisest thing you can do is to pick a good optio... I know I did," Maximus expressed, with a rare fondness in his tone.

"Now usually I would think that a compliment from you meant that the drink was talking, but I know that you've not touched a drop this evening. Did you honestly think that I would make it this

137

far though? I'm not sure if I did. I knew more about Horace than Hannibal when I first stepped onto your parade ground."

"I was confident that you'd survive and flourish. To misquote a phrase – 'don't give me a great legionary, give me a lucky one,'" Maximus replied, his dry humour returning to replace the fondness in his voice.

But it seemed that Rufus Atticus' luck was about to finally run out.

Four rough-faced, well-built men appeared from out of the shadows as Maximus and Atticus neared the barracks. They seemed like former soldiers, or gladiators. Two carried spears with leaf-shaped blades, which Maximus recognised as coming from the arena, rather than being military issue. The remaining two held up wooden cudgels and sneered at the praetorians, looking to intimidate them. The largest of the thugs, his bare head gleaming in the moonlight, stepped forward, snorted and spat out a globule of phlegm at Maximus' feet.

"I'm afraid you're too late, gentlemen. The tavern has already relieved us of our money for the evening. Or, to quote Juvenal, 'The traveller with empty pockets will sing in the thief's face.' You'll have to turn somebody else over if you want to get paid tonight," Atticus amiably remarked.

"We've already been paid," the chief thug replied. His voice was unnaturally hoarse. The soldiers noticed a long, grey scar running across his neck like a smirk. Such was the gleeful, cruel look in the villain's eye that Maximus suspected that he would have taken the job for the sport alone.

"By whom?" Atticus asked, slightly bewildered by the encounter.

"By the man whose wife you slept with last night," a haughty voice emitted, as a small-set, weasel-faced man stepped forward from behind the four brigands. Both Maximus and Atticus recognised the man as being Marcus Pollux, a prominent senator who worked as a senior administrator for the purchasing and storing of Rome's grain supply. A neat, black beard covered a pointy chin. A black wig sat upon his head – with all the grace and attractiveness of a dead crow, Atticus thought. His eyebrows were painted on, which apparently was the latest style among the political classes. Stupidity never goes out of fashion it seems, the newly promoted centurion further mused. Pollux was also wearing a garish purple cloak, fastened with a large, bejewelled brooch which almost out-sparkled the night sky.

"Here I was thinking that we would need to guard against spies and enemies of the state, rather than jealous husbands, when we returned to Rome," Maximus said to his friend, rolling his eyes a little in exasperation. The soldier caught a whiff of the senator's perfume as he moved forward to address Atticus – and Maximus would have preferred the smell of the watery stew to that of the florid scent currently assaulting his nostrils.

"One of your fellow officers told me that you would be heading back this way. I'm here to teach you a lesson."

"Hopefully it won't be a lesson from you in how to dress." Atticus eyed up the four men who accompanied Pollux. He sensed that this was not the first time that the senator had used the men to help teach someone a lesson. Rufus would have fancied his chances with Maximus alongside him should there have just been two of them, but the extra numbers and the two spears gave Pollux an advantage. The squat but muscular figure to his left either possessed a pronounced sneer or hare-lip. Saliva seemed to be forming in the corner of his mouth. Perhaps he was salivating over the impending violence. The thug directly in front of him looked Egyptian. He gripped his spear tightly and kept switching his gaze between Atticus and Maximus, as if weighing up who he wanted to attack, or kill, first. He wore a chain around his bull-neck which appeared to be decorated with ivory – or human bones. The large, bald-headed brute in front of Maximus wore a grey tunic which was either stained with wine, or blood. He jutted out his chin and offered a challenging gaze at the stone-faced soldier before him.

Finally, to Maximus' right, Atticus took in a man with flat, porcine features. He tapped his cudgel against his thigh, impatient to get the beating over and done with – so he could spend his earnings on women and wine.

"If you turn back now and go home I won't cripple your men, or break your nose," Maximus flatly remarked, with all the raw contempt that a soldier should have for a politician.

"Either you're incredibly arrogant, or incredibly dumb. Or both," Pollux, his face screwed up in disdain, replied. The senator looked – and spoke – as if he had a permanent bad taste in his mouth. Perhaps his bitterness was borne from never being elected to the consulship. Marcus Pollux had never felt rich or respected enough for his liking. He had beaten his wife (or rather he had one of his attendants do so) to punish her for disrespecting him. For turning him into a cuckold. Now he would instil fear and respect into these two lowly soldiers. "Nobody touches my wife."

"That may well be the reason why she strayed," Atticus drily pronounced. He recalled how Lavinia had said that her husband slept in a separate bedroom to her. His tastes were for young boys and girls. Increasingly the senator would spend his nights at a high-class brothel for the political and merchant classes. The establishment both fed and satisfied his appetites. Atticus had seduced Lavinia at a party. Later that evening, when he climbed up the balcony and knocked on her shutters, she willingly let him in. Lavinia opened up her heart, and other bodily parts, during the remainder of the night.

The senator's face reddened in either anger or embarrassment. He was just about to give the order to unleash his human mastiffs upon the soldiers when Maximus' voice sounded out in the half-light.

"Apollo, take out the two spears."

A second or so after the centurion gave the order an arrow thudded into the thigh of the thug in front of Atticus. The arrowhead cracked the man's femur.

The archer had positioned himself on the balcony of a nearby house, having shadowed the officers since the tavern. Before entering the capital Maximus had warned the legionary that they might run into trouble at some point. Cassius Bursus had kept an eye on the situation and readied an arrow, awaiting an order from Maximus.

The Egyptian brigand let out a curse but Apollo barely registered the sound as he fired off his second arrow. The spear-wielding assailant in front of Maximus swung his head about, searching in bewilderment and fear for the enemy archer. The ambushers had been ambushed. The sound of the zipping shaft in his ear was quickly succeeded by a biting pain in his hip. The hoarse cry of pain the former gladiator let out was cut short through Maximus stepping forward and punching him in the throat.

The squat brigand's face with the hare-lip was now twisted in terror, rather than in a sneer, as he ran down the street, anxiously looking behind him for an arrowhead glinting in the moonlight. He melted into the darkness, nearly as quickly as his courage had disappeared.

The thug with the porcine expression had his features flattened even more as Atticus' fist crashed into his face. His cudgel clattered to the ground, shortly before he did.

The Egyptian whimpered on the cobble stones. The hulking, bald-headed brute who had led the assailants was also prostrate. He looked up at the impassive soldier, baring his teeth in either fury or agony.

Marcus Pollux's red face was now pale with fear as the centurion walked towards him. The senator's wig was comically askew. He thought about offering the soldier some money, in order not to harm him. He could also make a promise to Rufus Atticus that he would not stand in his way should he wish to continue to see his wife. Pollux opened his mouth, but for once the verbose senator lost the power of speech.

"If I ever see your face again you'll need a mortician rather than a surgeon. You understand?" Maximus said, or rather growled. Pollux nodded his head vigorously in reply. The fringe of his black wig now reached down over his painted-on left eyebrow. Without warning the soldier jabbed Pollux in the nose, breaking it in two places. The weasel yelped and did his best to remain conscious at the sight of his own blood. "That's just to prove to you that I'm a man of my word, which is more than can be said of most of our politicians."

4.

Morning.

The shimmering heat dried Maximus' throat and made his palms sweat even more as he strode up the Palatine Hill towards the Imperial Palace. Rome sprawled out beneath him, a great tapestry of wealth, poverty, vice and (to a lesser extent) virtue. His heart beat faster and he was filled with a sense of anxiety – and happiness – not because he was due to meet the Emperor, but rather he would soon be seeing *her*.

Aurelia.

They had first met three years ago. The Emperor had ordered Maximus to escort Aurelia and her brother Arrian to the front. Their father was a German tribal chief. Marcus Aurelius asked Arrian to petition his father to support Rome in the ongoing war with the Marcomanni. The tribal chief betrayed Maximus, but his son and daughter didn't. Arrian died helping Maximus and Atticus escape. Aurelia chose to leave with the Romans, rather than remain with her father. Initially she had borne resentment in her heart towards the soldier when they first met. Aurelia was a Christian and she had viewed Maximus as her enemy. During their time together Aurelia grew to admire him, however. And to love him. She had returned to Rome whilst he remained on the northern frontier but they regularly wrote to each other. Maximus thought her witty, compassionate and beautiful. He still thought about Julia, but did he now think even more about Aurelia? She didn't ask anything of him and he didn't promise her anything in return – but they both envisioned a future together. A rare daydreamer's smile lit up the praetorian's usually stony expression. The guards at the gates of the palace almost didn't recognise their superior officer, due to the strange grin on his face.

The Imperial Palace may have been considered two buildings in one, the Domus Flavia (which contained the state function rooms) and the Domus Augustana (which served as the Emperor's residence). The palace had originally been commissioned by the Emperor Domitian. Domitian was a ruler with few virtues, but at least he had the good sense to employ someone with good taste to oversee the project – the architect Rabirius. As Maximus walked through the gilded state rooms and corridors of the Domus Flavia he was as awestruck now as he had been when he had first been posted on guard duty at the palace. The decor was a perfect marriage of grandeur and taste. As Atticus had commented to his fellow centurion recently, "Too many people nowadays equate money with taste... They believe that the apogee of art is to shock, or be new or different... But there's nothing new under the sun, including vulgarity... Even Rabirius would fail today to create something memorable if directed by the wife of Rome's leading charioteer, for instance. Have you seen her? You can take the girl out of the subura, but you can't take the subura out of the girl it seems... If only the rest of Domitian's reign had been as impressive as the Imperial Palace, though. Even Martial didn't have a bad word to say about the design."

Maximus walked over polished marble floors of differing colours and geometric patterns, past gleaming black basalt statues of Aeneas, Scipio Africanus and Augustus – and more than one of Domitian himself. The centurion had long lost count of the number of dignitaries he had seen grow wide-eyed and slack-jawed as they took in the building's opulence and feats of construction. Many had been humbled into considering that the palace was home to a deity rather than man – indeed when sitting in his throne room Domitian would demand that he be referred to as "lord and god",

145

and the largest banqueting hall was named "Jupiter's dining room". Yet Domitian knew he was all too mortal, as evidenced by the number of white marble walls throughout the palace – which the Emperor had asked to be installed so that he would be able to see the reflection of any potential assassin behind him.

Domitian could often be found sitting in the Aulia Regia, his throne room, during his reign. Marcus Aurelius, however, spent more time in the adjacent hall of the basilica, where he heard and made judgements on legal disputes. Maximus recalled how the Imperial Palace would have once echoed with the sound of harems and feasting, yet during guard duty at the palace the praetorian had only ever heard raised voices during passionate philosophical debates, which were fuelled with watered down wine and fresh fruit.

*

The smell of freshly baked bread and freshly cut grass filled the nostrils of Galen, the Emperor's physician. The slightly grating sound of wooden practise swords clacking together on the lawn filled his ears, as two teenagers played soldiers. Galen pursed his lips and tried to stoically endure the disquieting noise. He concentrated on the peaceful sound of the fountain in the background and tried to lose himself in thought. He was due to give a lecture later on in the week. Galen began to compose mental notes on his subject – and also jokes, at the expense of his backward looking rivals in the medical profession.

"Thank you again for saving him," the Emperor remarked with heartfelt gratitude, as he fondly gazed upon his son fencing with a friend on the grass. Galen wordlessly nodded his head in acknowledgement of the comment and took in his friend, Marcus Aurelius. His beard was greyer and the crow's feet were more pronounced around his tired eyes. Yet still intelligence and nobility were enthroned in the Emperor's features, Galen judged.

If only he could say the same for Commodus, his unruly son. A month ago Galen had indeed arguably saved the boy's life. Commodus had returned from his afternoon at the wrestling school with a fever. The tonic that a respected physician prescribed only seemed to weaken the patient and Commodus' condition became critical. Thankfully Galen was able to treat the patient in time. He realised that the tonic was the cause of his weakened constitution, rather than a cure for it. Ignoring the protests of other physicians Galen ordered that the patient should be given a solution of honey and rosewater. By the end of the week Commodus had recovered his strength – and was even demanding that he should be allowed to commence wrestling again. Faustina had written to her husband with the news that Galen had saved their son.

In saving the boy though, have I damned an Empire?

The Emperor judged his son to be "spirited". The more objective physician, who had spent more time with the boy than his father, had other words to describe him. Commodus shared his birthday with Caligula. If only that were the only thing he had in common with the tyrant, Galen lamented. Commodus was a handsome boy, despite occasional bouts of sickliness. His bright eyes could flash with both charm and spite, depending on his mood. His hair was blond and curly. He had of late been given to sprinkling flecks of gold in his hair, to give off "an aura of the divine", as the teenager had pretentiously remarked. Galen could almost forgive the boy's wilfulness and vainglory – he was a young man after all – but what troubled him was the cruel streak which ran through the son of the Emperor. Commodus actively enjoyed bullying and humiliating playmates, staff and officials alike. He scolded people and encouraged any audience present to laugh at his victims. He was fond of decapitating animals – dogs, goats, ostriches – for sport. Alarmingly, for Galen, Commodus frequented the coliseum far

147

more than the lecture halls. He seemed obsessed with violence, particularly gladiatorial combat. He had recently taken to dressing himself up as a *secutor* gladiator. He would also stride about throughout the Imperial Palace carrying a club and wearing a lion skin. Galen recalled the incident a few days ago when an official had called him "Commodus, son of Marcus Aurelius" – to which the petulant youth replied that he wanted to be introduced as "Hercules, son of Zeus."

"Excuse me," Marcus Aurelius remarked to his friend, as he got up from his chair and left Galen in order to attend to a clerk who wanted the Emperor to glance over some documents.

Galen gently shook his head in disappointment, as he continued to think about Commodus – Rome's future. Galen was shaking his head in disappointment in relation to the Emperor, too. Few people knew Marcus Aurelius as well as Galen. The physician admired his friend as a ruler, philosopher and even warrior. But as a father he had failed, or was failing. Marcus professed love for his son – but love is blind, Galen judged. The Emperor had provided an abundance of good tutors for his son but, to use a Christian analogy, he had been throwing pearls before swine. Galen appreciated his friend's wisdom and insight on all manner of subjects, but Commodus was his Achilles heel. That very morning the Emperor had tried to convince Galen, or more so himself, that the youth was slowly but surely improving in regards to his studies. He quoted Hesiod, to bolster his belief.

"If even small upon the small you place

And do this oft, the whole will soon be great."

In his reply Galen was tempted to quote Plutarch, "One should not put good food into a slop-pail," but the usually forthright physician desisted.

A short, shrill yelp sliced through the air. The boy Commodus was playing with cradled his hand and ran off, whimpering, as the

Emperor's son crowed and lifted his wooden gladius aloft in triumph. Commodus had impetuously – and viciously – struck his opponent on the hand before the fencing bout had officially started. Galen shook his head, more vigorously, in disapproval and disappointment. The boy had, consciously or not, committed the offence while his father's back was turned.

The adolescent's eyes lit up on seeing the centurion Gaius Maximus walk towards him. Commodus preferred gladiators to soldiers, but Maximus' fame preceded him. The teenager had met the officer during one of his visits to the frontline. The visit had coincided with a number of victories and the army considered the boy a lucky mascot. Perhaps he would have the soldier serve as one of his bodyguards when he became Emperor, Commodus thought.

"Maximus! Did you see me fight just now? Did you see me win?" His voice was high-pitched, demanding, aristocratic. The centurion had heard such voices a hundred times before in the army, as scions from great families gave the order to attack whilst sitting upon their expensive horses behind the shield wall.

"I saw everything, Commodus."

"One day I will be proficient enough to fence with you and the finest gladiators in the arena," the youth proudly said, puffing out his chest as he did so.

"I look forward to it. I'll make sure to wear a gauntlet for protection, however," Maximus replied, looking at, or through, the figure in front of him. He recalled again the scene at which the Emperor and his son had attended the flogging of some legionaries on the northern frontier. Marcus Aurelius had looked on in sorrow, wincing slightly with each lash – whilst Commodus had taken everything in with a sense of glee in his eyes, wildly grinning with each crack of the whip.

Commodus felt a small shard of shame under the glare of the centurion, which he resented. And he resented the common soldier daring to talk to him in such a manner. He was the future Emperor. He was Hercules, the son of Zeus.

Gods should punish transgressions rather than show mercy.

Commodus thought how the praetorian would need more than just a gauntlet one day to protect him from his wrath.

Whoever's not for me is against me.

5.

As the Emperor attended to various officials and correspondence, Maximus spoke with Galen. The physician admired the soldier, for his loyalty and professionalism. Galen had been witness to how integral Maximus had been in helping Aurelius to contest and win the Battle of Pannonia. Pannonia had been a significant victory (the enemy hadn't crossed back over the Danube to attack Roman settlements since) but it had not ended the war. Indeed the battle had just been the beginning of the bloodletting. The Marcomanni and other northern tribes had learned the lesson of entering into large scale, pitched battles with the Roman army. Yet the conflict was still not devoid of bloodshed. Skirmishes and ambushes broke out in forests and marshlands as the Emperor pursued the enemy. Few days passed without Maximus having to draw his sword. Even the most visceral nightmares could not rival the horrific scenes the soldiers experienced during the day. Hands grew calloused from carrying shovels, as well as swords, as legionaries buried the dead – their friends. The wetlands were home to more diseases then even Galen could classify. But still the army advanced and won minor victories. The Emperor out-manoeuvred his enemies through both feats of arms and diplomacy. He proved ruthless in dealing with the Iazyges, a nomadic warrior tribe who sided against Rome. Although the Iazyges did not possess a homeland Marcus Aurelius vowed to wipe the barbarians off the map. The constant campaigning took its toll on the Emperor and Maximus however, both physically and emotionally. Maximus, like many a soldier before and after him, drank to take the edge off things. During the journey from the north to Rome the centurion could still taste a tang of blood in the air. The smell of burning settlements – and corpses – still filled his nostrils. Only the thought of Aurelia brought the weary soldier some genuine peace.

As important and welcome as the news was from the north that Rome was continuing to win the war, Maximus was more concerned with the battle that the Emperor had asked Galen to fight at home – against the plague. The scourge hung over Italy – and beyond – like a storm cloud. Some Christians preached that the disease was a punishment, sent by the one true God, for Rome's paganism and sins. Some critics and graffiti artists had also recently proclaimed that the plague was a punishment for the Emperor prolonging the war in Germania – albeit the plague pre-dated the start of the conflict by several years. Facts rarely got in the way of certain politicians and dissenters spouting nonsense, however. What was true was that the plague was decimating the Empire: farmers, soldiers, merchants, slaves, aristocrats, women and children. At its worst the soldier had heard that the disease had killed up to two thousand people a day in Rome alone. The storm cloud rained on one and all. The centurion had all too often passed through settlements along the Danube and Rhine where the dying outnumbered the living. More soldiers had fallen to the disease rather than to German spears. "Decimation" was underestimating the scale of the pandemic, for the scourge killed more than one in ten. But the one enemy that Maximus wished to defeat the most he couldn't even bring to battle. A cure wouldn't bring back his wife or children, but it might just bring him some consolation to know that the disease would no longer widow or orphan others.

The worry lines deepened, like scars, in Galen's brow when Maximus asked the physician about the pandemic. Over the years Galen had witnessed all manner of horrific injuries and diseases. He had dissected all manner of animals. Blood, pus and infections had been the meat and drink of his career. Yet the plague was different. The physician had found it increasingly difficult to remain objective in the face of the disease. Whereas many people had had their faith shaken in the gods in the face of the plague, the pandemic had shaken Galen's faith in the power of science – and himself. Science dictated that diseases should have cures, problems should have solutions. But the plague appeared to laugh, contemptuously, at such mantras.

Word had spread that the Emperor had charged the famous physician with finding a cure – and many people in Rome called the scourge "the Plague of Galen". Galen remembered a scene from many years ago when, after having dinner with the Emperor, Marcus Aurelius had ordered the scientist to find a remedy. Or rather his friend pleaded with him to do so, after cataloguing the extent of its destruction whilst burying his head in his hands. It was the only time that the physician had ever witnessed the stoical Emperor break down and cry. Ironically, to combat his sorrows, Galen threw himself into his work, following one of his own maxims: *employment is nature's physician, essential to human happiness*. He worked tirelessly, recording symptoms and experimenting with treatments – all the time exposing himself to the deadly disease.

When walking the streets in Rome now the physician, who had once basked in his notoriety, often wore a cloak and hood in order not to be recognised. Some had looked at him with pity in their eyes over the past year, appreciating the burden the doctor must have had to bear. Some stared at him and then averted their eyes in disappointment. But worst were the expressions of hope that the physician encountered from people and patients, when they believed that he would be their saviour.

It was in hope more than expectation when Maximus asked the physician if he had made any breakthroughs in finding a cure.

Galen's grief-filled sigh articulated his answer as much as the words he spoke.

"Unfortunately the only breakthrough I've made is that I believe we are dealing with not one, but two, plagues. And each disease is as fatal – and incurable – as the other... But let us not ruin this sunny afternoon with too much gloom, Maximus. Let us speak of other, better, things. Have you taken the opportunity to visit Aurelia since you have been back in Rome?" Galen remarked, eyeing him knowingly.

The usually stern looking soldier suddenly appeared a little surprised and awkward – with blushes even colouring his suntanned complexion. Maximus knew that Aurelia and Galen had kept in touch since their mission together in the north all those years ago. But how much did he know about Aurelia's feeling for the praetorian and, conversely, his feelings for her?

"How has she been?" Maximus asked, unable to suppress the light in his eyes when he thought of her.

"Aurelia keeps herself busy. She invested the money that the Emperor gave her wisely. Yet she ploughs most of her wealth back into the clinic and refuge she set up for the poor... I still occasionally see her, every few months or so. She is a remarkable woman Maximus, accomplished, well-read and good natured. But there's something missing in her life I think. Despite locking herself away she still has plenty of would-be suitors knocking on her door, admiring either her beauty or wealth..." Galen smiled inwardly, thinking of how, whenever he saw Aurelia, she would always steer the conversation towards asking after the soldier. Galen also hoped that the centurion would take the hint when he had said that there was something missing in the young woman's life.

I may not be able to find a remedy for the plague, but at least I can hopefully cure two people of their loneliness.

"Should *you* knock on her door, though, Maximus I'm sure that Aurelia would let you in."

6.

"Let us hope that we can draw out the fox from his burrow. Rufus' plan is sound and based on reliable intelligence. I'm not sure how triumphant he'll feel, however, if his plan works and his suspicions prove correct," Marcus Aurelius evenly remarked. He wore a plain, simple white tunic. Maximus thought he looked more like a school teacher than an Emperor, military leader or demigod. After bidding Galen farewell in the garden the Emperor had invited Maximus into his study to discuss their real purpose in returning to Rome. Events and intelligence reports suggested that the Emperor possessed a new enemy, one who lurked in the shadows rather than facing him on the battlefields of Germania. There was increasing evidence of someone spreading propaganda throughout the Empire, to soldiers and civilians alike, in the towns and in the countryside. It labelled Marcus Aurelius a warmonger, more concerned with personal glory than the welfare of the people. The pamphlets and graffiti also accused the Emperor of ignoring the plague, or even causing the scourge through his devotion to philosophy rather than religion. The gods were angry, they reasoned. Falsehoods, like weeds, grow quicker and are harder to eradicate than truths.

"Rufus will do his duty, even if it indeed turns out that his father sits at the centre of the spider's web," Maximus replied, still worried for his friend should it turn out that Pollio Atticus was the snake that Rome was clutching to its bosom.

The two men sat at the Emperor's large cedar wood desk. Copies of Plutarch's *Lives* and the teachings of Epictetus sat open on the desk. Various correspondence also covered the entire surface of the aged but still sturdy piece of furniture, which had once belonged to Augustus. Some letters were due to be read, some Aurelius was writing himself. Maximus also noticed that the Emperor was still composing his book of meditations, which he had worked on in an ongoing way whilst campaigning. Soldiers, ever conscious of how orders could get them killed, learned to read upside down and Maximus took in the lines the philosophical Emperor had recently written.

The soul becomes dyed with the colour of its thoughts.

"If I were a Tiberius or Nero I could execute Pollio on a mere suspicion or whim. Should Pollio be Emperor too and he suspected that I was conspiring against him I've little doubt that he would execute me in the blink of an eye. But I will need proof, the law should be adhered to, in regards to bringing any enemy of the state to justice. The best revenge is to be unlike him who performed the injury," the Emperor said sagely.

Maximus here less sententiously thought to himself how he would put the venerated statesman to the sword, rather than put him on trial, should he prove to be guilty. Weeds must be cut down.

"We should soon know how guilty or innocent Pollio Atticus is. Rufus and I will be attending a party he's hosting tomorrow evening. We also believe we have some strong enough bait to lure him out into the open."

"Be mindful you do not fall into any traps yourself, Maximus. There are more serpents in Rome than in any marshland back on the northern frontier. At least the Marcomanni line up in front of us in a shield wall, when trying to kill us. But in Rome you are more likely to perish through receiving a dagger in your back, by your best friend."

"How were things on the frontier when you left for Rome?"

"Our enemies are still drawing away from us, like a retreating tide. Yet there's wisdom in their cowardice. Our supply lines grow

157

ever longer – and thinner. We need to recruit more cavalry units. I have staff due to meet various horse dealers while in Rome. Horse dealers and quartermasters together in the same room, however, may make even politicians and tax collectors seem honest," Marcus Aurelius posited, sighing in exasperation. The increasingly grey-haired Emperor then looked up at the map of Germania on the wall and narrowed his eyes in concentration. "I fear, Maximus, that my reign will see more years of peace than war, despite our recent advances."

"History will treat you well," the centurion said, sincerely and determinedly. Maximus had spent enough time by his Emperor's side to consider him a good man. Marcus Aurelius had shared many of his soldiers' privations and led from the front. He was a just legislator and keenly felt the losses that the war and plague had had on Rome.

"It's not History that I have to look at in the mirror each morning though, unfortunately. History doesn't have to write letters to the families of fallen soldiers. Posterity and praise will not reduce the numbers dying from the plague this month. I've been unable to save so many, Maximus. Black thoughts blacken my soul."

"You have done your duty."

"But it's not been enough. We both know that Rome is dying. I sometimes feel that I've been more of an undertaker than an Emperor. But I have no wish to live to bury you Maximus. You too have done your duty by Rome. But you also owe a duty to yourself, to be happy. I do not want you to return to the frontier with me. Rather than soldiers, I will soon need more diplomats and bureaucrats on my staff, to draw up peace treaties. You should remain in the capital. My wife's collection of dresses and shoes is probably worth more than anything else in the Empire; I dare say I will have to build a new wing for the Imperial Palace in order to house her wardrobe. You can guard it by day and at night I want you to return to a wife and family... Find some peace Maximus, that's an order."

7.

The afternoon sun massaged rather than stung Maximus' skin. He heard the faint sound of birdsong in the background, behind the spluttering cacophony of curses and the other noises that Rome daily threw up. Even the smell of ordure, which usually stained the air of all but the Palatine Hill, was absent from the streets as Maximus made his way to Aurelia's house. He had had Apollo launder his best tunic. He had also paid Atticus' barber, rather than using "Chopper", the barrack's barber, to cut his hair.

Although the praetorian seemed half caught in a dream, with his mind's eye fixed on the woman he was visiting, Maximus couldn't help but notice the number of beggars and amputees – ex-soldiers – in Rome. The Empire often honoured the dead from wars and glorious battles, but too often the people forgot about the living, those who returned from conflicts. Ex-soldiers were often looked over for jobs. Few recognised a legionary's virtues and usefulness when he no longer wore his uniform. After reading Maximus' letter about soldiers who had been wounded and had returned to Rome, having taken up drink rather than employment, Aurelia had made a conscious effort to hire veterans and amputees for the businesses she had a share in. She did so out of reasons of productivity, as well as compassion.

*

Atticus regretted having eaten at the barracks, given the endless dishes of meat, fish and fresh fruit being offered to him by the slaves at his sister's house. Occasionally Claudia would sample a tiny amount from one of the plates but then with a wave of her hand she would dismiss the attractive looking slave boy or girl. The brother and sister sat in a richly furnished triclinium. Sunlight shone off various ornate marble statues. The newly promoted centurion sunk into one of the sofas, half swallowed up by the soft cushions. Although he had grown up in similarly opulent and privileged surroundings the scene now felt slightly unreal to the soldier.

"I'm pleased that you can attend the party tomorrow evening, mainly for selfish reasons of course. You can help keep me company, Rufus, as I look down on half of the guests in attendance. I'm joking – it'll be much more than just half the number of guests. But father will be happy to see you, too," Claudia remarked, popping a small cube of honey-glazed pork into her mouth. Her long legs were tucked beneath her as she sat on an adjoining sofa. She wore a shimmering turquoise wrap over an elegant, silk stola. The graceful woman would have to make sure that her lover, who would be visiting after her brother, did not crease her new dress in a clumsy show of passion.

"Hopefully he'll set aside for me just the few moments that he methodically apportions to all of his guests at his parties. If father sees me for any longer than that then I fear I'll start looking down on him – and him on me – again," Atticus replied, half-joking at best.

"Will we be seeing Maximus at the party too?" the woman asked, nonchalantly. She even sighed, as if already bored by the whole event. Claudia had long admired her brother's superior officer though, both for his physique and also his character. Maximus was unlike all the would-be suitors who had tried to court Claudia over the years. He neither sycophantically held her up to be a goddess, nor treated her like a high-class whore. She had known him when he was married and hoped that, after Maximus had mourned his wife, they could become friends – or something more.

"He would rather prefer engaging with a dozen German spearmen than engaging with some of father's friends, but yes he'll be attending. And what of Fronto? Will this be one of the few evenings in the year where you suffer his company?"

"No. Thankfully my darling husband is away, taking care of some business. He is no doubt taking care of his new mistress also. She is the wife of a tax collector, of all things," Claudia remarked bitterly, ashamed that her husband had chosen to have an affair with someone so lowly in rank. "She lacks wit, style and taste. She's a social climber, who will forever be stuck on the first rung. In short, they are perfectly matched and no doubt they make a happy couple." Claudia slyly smiled at her own joke – and from looking forward to seeing Maximus again, unencumbered by the chaperone of her husband.

*

Maximus' heart beat even faster than when he was about to advance into battle. He wiped his sweaty palms on his tunic, took a deep breath and knocked on the door. The house was tucked away in one of the nicer, quieter parts on the Aventine Hill. Fruit trees hung over the walls and vines and myrtle criss-crossed along the side of the property.

A shutter opened, and then, after the unlocking of several bolts, a fresh-faced maid opened the door and the visitor was welcomed in. The house was clean and modestly furnished. The centurion noticed a few landscapes on the wall, scenes from the *Aeneid*, which Arrian had painted years ago. Maximus was unsurprised to see a well-stocked library as he was led down a corridor to enter the triclinium, which opened out onto a pretty garden – where Aurelia was waiting for him.

It had been three years since the soldier had last seen her. Three long years. But the three years, through their letter writing, had been filled with hope, affection, friendship and – hopefully, now – love.

*

"I will duly pick out which women are available – and those who are married – at the party. Although the one can often still mean the other," Claudia said, smiling into her wine cup. She had missed talking to her brother these past few years, if nothing else because she thought him as equally immoral, or rather amoral, as herself. Most of the women she knew were either untrustworthy, or prudes. As for the men in her life they usually had only two things on their mind, sex and money. Yet with Atticus she could also discuss literature, politics and poetry. With Maximus too Claudia felt comfortable with being herself – that self who she wanted to be.

"How do you know that I have not fallen in love – and promised to be true to someone? Maybe now I'll go no more a-roving?"

Atticus broke into a grin before even finishing the sentence, unable to keep a straight face. His sister, having drunk a couple of cups of wine, let out a burst of unaffected laughter. It was the first time Claudia had laughed in such a way for a long time. For all of her lovers, she often felt desperately lonely and unhappy. The more women envied her, the more she wanted to be someone else.

"I know you as much as I know myself, brother. You get bored too easily to promise to be true. You're fated to be a Tantalus or Sisyphus – forever unfulfilled. I'm just surprised that you have been wedded to army life for so long."

"Maybe I'm no longer the epicure and wastrel that you once knew." Atticus grinned not as he spoke this time.

"I'm not against being proved wrong, but the older I get the more I sense than no one ever really changes. When you take off your uniform you're still you underneath, Rufus. No amount of Virgil or Horace, or being in the presence of our divine Emperor even, can edify some people. No one can outrun their shadow, even if

163

they run away and join the army to fight barbarians on the northern frontier. By the time we reach our twenties we are fully developed. I could not now grow a moral bone in my body, even if I tried to," the woman said, with as much sadness as satire in her voice.

"Maybe I'll get to surprise you. But more so, I hope you get to surprise yourself one day."

*

Although Aurelia had barely slept the evening before, thinking about her meeting with Maximus, there was life rather than tiredness in her expression. She rose from the bench she was sitting on to greet her visitor. Her long, glossy black hair was pinned up on her head. She wore a simple white linen dress that was fastened by a black belt. Her figure was demure and athletic at the same time.

"Hello," she said, beaming as warmly as the afternoon sun and tucking a couple of stray hairs behind her ears which had fallen down onto her face.

An array of flowers bordered a lush green lawn, brightening and perfuming the air. But for Maximus, they paled in comparison to Aurelia's gleaming jade eyes and fragrant scent. The birdsong sounded sweetly, but not as sweetly as her voice. If his heart had recently pounded like he was going into battle then Maximus now felt victorious – or defeated by her loveliness. Now, finally, he felt like he was home.

He stood and gazed at her, dumbly, for a moment or two. Making sure she wasn't a dream. Her sun-kissed features had softened, rather than hardened, with age.

She's even more beautiful now than she was three years ago...

She took him in, an alloy of honour and strength. The usually tough-looking soldier was smiling like a teenager. She sighed, in relief and pleasure. Her prayers had been answered. He had come back to her safely. Three years. His letters had been the highlight

164

of her weeks. Aurelia wondered again if Maximus had heard her whisper those words in his ear in the forest, when they were escaping from her village. She had said them because she feared she might never see him again. But she also said the words because she meant them. Maximus hadn't responded at the time, nor had he said anything when he had escorted her back to Rome.

Maybe I whispered the words too quietly.

"Have you come from your meeting with the Emperor?"

"Yes."

"How is he?"

"Tired, melancholy, overworked. But he's still good humoured and good natured. In short, he's the same as ever."

"He's the best of Emperors I think, but in the worst of times... I have seen some of the graffiti and read some of the propaganda attacking him... But the people are devoted to him."

Maximus was tempted to reply that the people may prove to be as faithful to the Emperor as Faustina, but desisted.

"I believe that they would love him all the more if they knew him," he loyally stated.

I fell in love with you, the more I grew to know you.

*

Claudia shooed away the slave girl approaching her with a plate of sliced, spiced apples. With the same gesture of her hand, however, she beckoned over the boy cradling a jug of wine.

"The frog-faced senator I'm about to see is unlikely to intoxicate me, so I may as well have another," the mistress of the house exclaimed, after seeing Rufus raise his eyebrow at her drinking. Wine helped her forget, lose herself. Her father had introduced Senator Piso to her a week ago. He had asked her to lunch with him the following day. The evening after that, when his wife was absent, the aged senator invited the attractive, urbane woman to dinner at his villa. Claudia left the following morning, while the

165

would-be consul remained snoring, or rather croaking, in his bed. Pollio Atticus sometimes used money or veiled threats to win influence, but at other times he employed other assets at his disposal. Claudia could not now remember a time when her father hadn't pimped her out to his friends – or enemies. The young girl had obeyed him all those years ago because she respected and loved her father. He had instilled in her the importance of family. She also enjoyed the attention she received from some men. Beauty was power. "You are worth a dozen cohorts my dear," her father had proudly exclaimed, after she seduced a wealthy merchant to help the family win a mining contract. Claudia had once felt that she was in competition with her brother to gain her father's attention and respect. But now she envied Rufus, for having escaped his baleful influence. Her eyes were red-rimmed with sleeplessness – and tearfulness – behind her make-up. She had suffered so many miscarriages that she could no longer bear children, she believed. Her gown hid the bruises on her arms from where Piso had roughly held her from behind.

Everyone has a uniform, or a role they must play.

Yet for once Claudia would willingly do her father's bidding. It wouldn't be business, but a pleasure. The previous evening Pollio Atticus had instructed his daughter to seduce Gaius Oppius Maximus.

*

Maximus and Aurelia sat on the bench together. A breeze rustled the leaves of the tree hanging over them. Sunlight melted the wisps of cloud overhead like snowflakes. Laughter entwined itself around the birdsong. A young slave girl watched her mistress as she stood by the door, ready to attend to her but at the same time giving the couple their space. The waifish teenager, Helena, had been orphaned by the plague. Aurelia had met the girl during a visit to the refuge for the poor she had set up and had decided to

166

employ her within her household. Helena smiled at seeing her mistress interact with the centurion. She had never seen her laugh or be so animated – and enamoured – with a man before. The smile on Aurelia's face reminded the slave girl of the expression she had worn when she had ventured out into the garden to read – and re-read – the letters the soldier sent her.

"Galen tells me that you have invested wisely with the money the Emperor gave you after the Battle of Pannonia," Maximus said. "You've earned the old physician's admiration it seems, which is easier said than done."

"Galen also told me that I have you, as much as the Emperor, to thank for the capital he gave me. I wanted to thank you in person, which is why I've not expressed my gratitude before. You could have kept the money for yourself, no?"

"Let's just say that I thought you were worth investing in. And I was right. The right people are seeing the fruits of your labour, from what Galen says."

Aurelia, glowing from having earned Maximus' admiration, was about to quote from the gospels to explain herself, but she suddenly thought of something the Emperor had said, whilst she had sat near him at a dinner one evening.

"The only wealth which you will keep forever will be the wealth you give away."

Their eyes were locked on one another as their hands crept forward, until they laced their fingers together. Three years. Three years thinking about the words she had whispered into his ear, in the forest. So much remained unsaid. When Maximus escorted Aurelia back to Rome all those years ago he believed the timing wasn't right in telling the young woman how he felt. Did he even know how he felt? She had been in mourning for her brother and he had still been in mourning for Julia. But three years had been a long enough wait. It was now time.

Maximus gently squeezed her responsive hand and leaned towards her. Aurelia's body trembled a little, but not in fear. A slight splash could be heard from the pond in the garden as a koi carp broke the surface of the water, fleetingly scanning the scene. Helena's eyes widened in shock, and happiness, as she saw Aurelia lean in towards the handsome centurion.

"I love you, too," Maximus whispered in her ear, finally responding to her words, three years after having first heard them.

She drank in the words and the sight of his contented face. He squinted in the sunlight, and at her beaming countenance.

"What do we do now?" Aurelia remarked, innocent, curious, excited. The virginal young woman had never been with a man before. Maximus had been worth waiting for though.

"Well, after I kiss you, I'm going to tell you how the Emperor has decided that I should remain in Rome, rather than journey back to the frontier. I'll also tell you how much I want to make a life with you...,"

Marry you.

8.

Evening.

Shadows danced upon the wall. The flames from the fire by Pollio Atticus' desk flickered in his cold eyes. He smoothed the sides of his oiled, silvery-grey hair and adjusted his toga. Too many politicians forsook the traditional garb of political office nowadays, but the would-be revolutionary was also a staunch traditionalist.

Finely crafted mosaics, depicting scenes from Rome's war against Carthage, decorated the walls and floor of his private chambers. Busts of Vespasian and Seneca sat either end of a large desk, which had once belonged to Marcus Crassus. The seller would not have dared lie to the buyer about its provenance. Pollio Atticus also wore a gold ring that once belonged to Pompey the Great, and carried a dagger within the folds of his toga that Marcus Brutus had reportedly used when assassinating Caesar. The statesman collected antiques, as well as people.

Atticus continued to finish off the sentence he was writing, not wishing to lose his train of thought, before looking up to address Chen. The powerfully built Chinaman served as Atticus' bodyguard, as well as an agent, enforcer and assassin. Chen had just returned from a visit to the gladiator school, situated just outside of Rome, which his master owned.

"How are the men? Has the delivery of arms and equipment arrived?" Atticus asked, scratching a speck of dirt off his toga. The senator had recently purchased the school as a cover to train a small force of mercenaries. Pollio Atticus intended to destroy the city's grain supplies by burning down the large wharf on the Tiber which stored the surplus.

169

"The fastest way to get to a man is through his stomach Chen... Aurelius once preached that poverty is the mother of crime, but more than poverty hunger will cause a man to despair and revolt... Rome will look to its Emperor to feed it, but he will be unable to do so," Atticus had slyly remarked to his agent several months ago. Through bribing, Marcus Pollux Atticus had also secretly been able to buy up the surplus of grain from the east. The crisis in the capital would quickly spread to the rest of the Empire – a plague of civil unrest. When the time was right, the senior statesman would step in as the saviour of Rome.

Cracks were already beginning to form. Atticus need only prize them open some more. There had recently been food riots in Capua and Ostia. Dockers had downed their tools in Brundisium. Atticus had composed most of the propaganda himself. He targeted mothers whose sons had been conscripted and farmers whose workers had been taken from them by the state to feed the Emperor's appetite for warmongering. Christians, those "great haters of the human race" as Tacitus had once described them, needed little encouragement to dissent. Atticus' pamphlets encouraged them not to pay their taxes and not to serve the false idol of the Emperor, quoting scripture to support his arguments. At the same time he criticised the state for not collecting taxes efficiently or fairly – the people should not suffer at the hands of a corrupt bureaucracy. After composing such propaganda and giving his agents their lines, to perform like travelling actors, Atticus would then meet with his fellow senators and remind them of how the Emperor demanded "contributions" from them at the beginning of the war – and then state that Aurelius was intending to tax the rich again to help pay for his vain-glorious campaign.

The people deserved strong leadership. When in power Atticus would put the whole of the northern frontier to the sword, as Caesar had put down the rebellion in Gaul. *Corpses can't revolt.*

Similarly, to deal with the plague, he would cut off any diseased limbs. He would quarantine and terminate the contagious without mercy. He would at first promise the people a cure though, to give them hope and gain their support, even though they knew none would be found. *The world wants to be deceived, so let it.*

Atticus believed he could garner the support of half the senate, when the time came. The other half would follow like sheep. Or he could win support through bribes and threats. If need be Chen would make a senator an offer that he couldn't refuse. Yet the wily statesman had no desire to challenge the Emperor openly. *He who wields the dagger never wears the crown.* Atticus intended to be the power behind the throne. *Real power.* He had selected his challenger to Aurelius years ago: Avidius Cassius – an ambitious, popular commander who possessed the support of numerous legions in the east. Atticus had paid off Cassius' debts years ago. The only debt he owed now was to the senator. Atticus had also introduced Cassius to Faustina a year ago – and nature had taken its course. The two were now lovers. Even the Emperor's wife would want to see an end to Aurelius' reign.

Pollio Atticus was sage enough, however, to know that the Emperor's reign was far from over. He still retained the loyalty of the majority of the army, especially the legions who had served under him in the north. The "Absent Landlord" had also returned to Rome. The food dole had increased to celebrate his homecoming – and games had been organised. *Bread and circuses.* Frustratingly Atticus was still in the dark as to the Emperor's true purpose in returning to the capital. Unofficially he was visiting his wife and family, during a break in the campaigning season. But something was amiss. Far more than Faustina and Commodus, Aurelius had been spending time with various senators, rebuilding his power base. Atticus' spies had also

171

reported that the Emperor was spending an inordinate amount of time with the scientist and self-regarding quack, Galen. *Why?*

His frustration boiled over the previous evening when the senator had dinner with his young mistress. He had raped her, as he had done to her mother a decade ago when she had served as his lover. The "Augur", as Atticus was sometimes called for predicting and shaping the political wind, needed to know what his enemy was up to. Yet he soon would know, he smilingly thought to himself. His agents had informed him about how close the centurion Gaius Maximus was to the Emperor – and that the praetorian had returned to Rome shortly before his master. And so Atticus had instructed Claudia to get close to the soldier. *She's Circe, Cleopatra and Calypso all rolled into one.* Men became as garrulous as Nestor in her company. Like so many others before him Maximus would be boastful and indiscreet, looking to impress his guileful daughter. *He'll talk – pillow talk.*

"The men are ready. The equipment has been delivered," the Chinaman said. Chen had often drilled – and disciplined – the small force personally. In order to cement his authority and "inspire" the mercenaries he had murdered half a dozen insubordinates, or slackers, during the course of their training. He had also culled the men for pleasure. The humourless Chinaman only felt amused, or alive, when killing.

"Have the other targets been finalised for the coming month?" Italy, not only just Rome, needed to bleed and burn for the people to rise up and the Emperor to fall. After destroying the grain supply in the capital Atticus would deploy his secret, private army elsewhere – in dozens of towns. They would incite violence, destroy food supplies and spread propaganda throughout the peninsula, motivating others to do so, too. The Emperor would be powerless to stop things – and a powerless Emperor is no Emperor at all.

"Yes. All is set." Chen smiled, revealing a set of sharp, blackened teeth. He smiled out of pride for fulfilling his orders – and in anticipation of bloodying his sword again.

9.

Dawn.

Steam wafted up from the plates of freshly baked bread and sizzling bacon on the table in the tavern, *The Trojan Pig*. Rufus Atticus and Cassius Bursus delved into their breakfasts, finally coming back to life after the long night beforehand. The centurion had treated his legionary to an evening in a high-end brothel.

"The night off will put a smile on his face," Atticus had explained to Maximus, back at the barracks.

"Just so long as it doesn't put a rash between his legs," the centurion had replied, before declining to join his friends.

The young archer grinned, wolfishly, from the taste of the fatty bacon and from the memories of the previous evening.

"The redhead told me that she wanted to see me again, that I was a good lover," the soldier eagerly exclaimed, still intoxicated by her beauty and still smelling her exotic perfume on his skin.

"Just be content to lose your money rather than your heart to her Apollo," the centurion said from experience, wryly smiling from recalling his own rakish teenage years and his first visit to the establishment.

Cassius Bursus nodded to convey he understood, but he still believed that he was special to her. She seemed genuinely impressed that he could be so young and yet serve in the Praetorian Guard... and she even told him her real name.

"Did you ever lose your heart to someone when you were my age?" Apollo was always keen to know more about the enigmatic officer's colourful past, although the more he got to know Atticus the more he seemed contradictory or unknowable. Perhaps there was a love affair in his past which explained everything.

"I used to be a poet. I lost my heart every week to a woman, especially to the ones who spurned me. There were some girls who lost their hearts to me however – especially when they saw the size of my purse."

"Your father is wealthy, no?"

"As wealthy as sin, as a Christian might say."

"And you chose the army over your inheritance? Never mind about losing your heart, did you lose your mind?" the legionary said in good humour, mopping up a pool of grease on his plate with his bread.

"I chose a life serving in the army rather than serving my father... Despite being a rake and gambler when I was young, I still felt I wasn't sufficiently morally depraved enough to go into politics."

Atticus' father loomed large in his thoughts again. More than anything he needed to know if he was guilty or innocent of crimes against the state, and if he was responsible for trying to kill Arrian – and himself – three years ago. As the Emperor had said, "I need evidence, rather than coincidences." Atticus thought that, if he had been all powerful, he probably would have also been all paranoid and looked to prosecute and punish his enemies on the basis of mere suspicion. Caesar's famed clemency was insincere, but astute, in the days of the Republic. The centurion hoped that Aurelius' genuine clemency wouldn't prove his undoing.

Atticus recalled how, as a child, saying the name "Marcus Aurelius" was tantamount to swearing in his house. "The imperial family are a bunch of bastards, illegitimate... All that should matter to you is this family... The blood which flows through our veins flows through the history of the Empire, as much as the waters of the Tiber flow through Rome," his father had drilled into him, on more than one occasion.

And so when Atticus had announced that he would be joining the army – and serving the Emperor – Pollio criticised his son for betraying the family, as well as for making an idiotic decision. The powerful statesman wasn't used to being defied. Nor did he wish to suffer the embarrassment of having a son serve in the army as a lowly infantryman.

"You are breaking your mother's heart by the way you are conducting your affairs."

"I rather think that mother's knowledge of your extra-marital affairs has broken her heart," Rufus had argued back.

It was at this point that Pollio Atticus, enraged that his son or anyone had dared speak back to him in such a way, raised his hand to Rufus. Yet the young man flinched not and, witnessing the formidable look in his eye, the senator struck his son not.

"I know you. You will soon come running back to Rome."

"It's because I know you – and that I don't wish to turn out like you – that I'm running away."

Honey-coloured sunlight poured into the tavern, as did a few other late night revellers and some market workers, grabbing themselves a hearty breakfast before starting their shifts. Atticus yawned and promised himself that he'd catch up on some sleep, as well as paperwork, before attending the party that evening.

"Rufus Atticus, as I live, breathe and shit," a rough voice called out. "I thought a vicious barbarian, or a jealous husband, would have caught up with you by now."

The centurion grinned and shook the hand of Milo, the landlord of the tavern which was situated close to the barracks. The praetorian had spent many a late night and early morning in *The Trojan Pig*. Atticus took in his old friend, a former legionary. His nose was still as red as the wine he served. He looked a little older, however, as his serving girls seemed a little younger, than he had when the soldier was last in the capital. Atticus introduced the infamous owner of the establishment to Apollo.

176

"Apollo, this is Milo... He's the best landlord in the district. His cups and jokes may not be clean, but his girls are...,"

"You'll do well to listen to this man here, lad. He'll keep you out of trouble, or if you're lucky he'll lead you into some," the sanguine veteran said, laughing at his own joke. "So what brings you back to Rome?"

"Family business," Atticus wryly replied, after a short pause.

10.

Dusk glowed like the orange embers of a dying brazier. A dry heat filled the summer evening. Lanterns, burning olive oil and a musky perfume hung upon trees all around the garden. The rustling of silk dresses competed with the sound of rustling leaves. Rome's senatorial and plutocratic elite strutted on the lawn like peacocks. Attractive slave girls and boys, wearing specially designed tunics braided with gold, carried endless silver trays of wine and food and served the guests. Couches, next to marble and bronze tables, were dotted about over the grass along with ornate sculptures. A juggler, a poet, a sword swallower, a fire eater and a brace of wrestlers entertained a small crowd towards the far end of the lawn.

Husbands and wives, or sometimes husbands and courtesans, conversed in hushed tones. Some laughed with their fellow guests – gossiping about those who were absent or uninvited. More business and policies would be enacted this evening, during whispered conversations, than would be during a month of discussions in the Forum. Pollio Atticus, his toga flowing in the wind, gracefully and purposefully moved amongst his guests (when people weren't forming a queue to catch a moment of his time), bestriding Roman society like a colossus. He remembered most people's names, although those who he got wrong were too scared to correct him. His eyes gleamed like the lanterns. He smiled as much as the courtesans. With the Emperor absent the former consul was the brightest star in the firmament for the guests to flutter around like moths.

"You look nervous," Atticus said with an amused, rather than worried, look on his face. He and Maximus walked out into the garden, dressed in their uniforms. Maximus surveyed the scene before him and took a deep breath, remembering how much he disliked attending such events. There was no one he wished to buy – or sell himself to. The only society he had needed in the past, when serving in Rome, was his wife and children. The people here didn't like him and he didn't like them. *But duty called.*

"I'd rather be a new recruit again, about to step out onto the parade ground for the first time," the centurion replied, exhaling in exasperation. The officers already drew a number of looks. Most of the aristocratic statesmen eyed them up, looking down their aquiline noses at the soldiers. A few of their wives, however, raised their eyebrows in appreciation – and smiled suggestively.

"You look more like an actor who's about to go on stage for the first time."

"Aye, unfortunately I've the urge to step out and throw rotten fruit at my audience though," Maximus said, scrunching his face up in annoyance as a flamboyantly dressed senator eyed him up too – and smiled suggestively.

"Well, like it or not, it's time to say your lines. Seize the day, to quote Horace."

"I'd rather seize a jug of wine."

"Well if it's any consolation I've reason to be nervous, too. I suspect that there are a dozen women in attendance that I've slept with over the years – and *they're* in attendance with their husbands."

"Duty calls."

Maximus looked forward to a time when Aurelia, rather than duty, would be calling out his name.

*

As Atticus went off to speak to his mother, Maximus fended for himself. People and trays of food swirled around the awkward looking centurion. He gripped the handle of his sword, either out

179

of habit or to intimidate anyone from approaching him. Maximus beckoned to a slave girl and asked her to fill his cup – again. He wished he could be back in Aurelia's garden, his head in her lap, as he lay on their bench. The afternoon sun and her fingers had caressed his face. She had read Virgil to him – the battle scenes, but her voice had still been soothing. They had spoken about the future, something the soldier hadn't dared to do for some years. Aurelia had mentioned how she had bought him a ring, a gold band, but she would give it to him after she had had it engraved.

"Centurion Maximus, it is an honour to have you here," Pollio Atticus remarked, parting the officer from his fond memories of his afternoon with Aurelia.

Maximus was tempted to reply that it was an honour to be in attendance, but he knew he wasn't that good an actor. Pollio was used to playing the part of the gracious host, however, and he smiled and made charming small talk. With the raising of a finger and nod of his head he also directed half a dozen attendants whilst giving the impression that the guest he was addressing was the most important person in the world to him.

"Have you met my daughter, Claudia?" the statesman asked, moving aside slightly to allow the soldier to take in his daughter in all her glory.

"I have." Maximus bowed his head slightly, but was unable to take his eyes off the captivating woman in front of him. Claudia was so alluring that it almost hurt some men to look at her and not possess her. Half her hair was pinned up, whilst the remainder hung down in delicate, shiny ringlets. An elegant satin dress, shimmering from the light of a nearby brazier, accentuated rather than disguised her lithe figure. Her eyes, lined with kohl, were fine and narrow and seemed to curl upwards in a smile.

The soldier had been long starved of such beauty, Pollio Atticus considered, as he watched Maximus feast his eyes on his daughter. She would render him speechless, until it was time for him to talk.

"It's nice to see you again, Gaius. Thank you for keeping your promise and taking care of Rufus on the frontier." Claudia's smile dazzled as much as her silver and pearl earrings. Maximus remembered the last time he had seen her, three years ago, when leaving to journey north. She had asked him to look after her brother. Maximus could also remember the first time he had met her. It was at a lunch. He could even remember some of her witticisms and what she had worn. The soldier may have been happily married at the time, but he wasn't blind or dumb.

"My family owes you a debt. If ever you need anything, my door will be open to you Maximus. Let me start by having my daughter take care of you, as you must please excuse me. My arm isn't nearly aching enough from shaking hands with people and my voice isn't nearly hoarse enough from thanking guests for attending. When you see Rufus could you please tell him that I would like to speak to him before the end of the evening? No matter how hoarse my voice becomes, I must congratulate him on his recent promotion."

Pollio Atticus grinned and briefly nodded his head at the centurion, before waving to another guest and walking over to shake his hand.

"Your father certainly knows how to put on a party," Maximus remarked, as another legion of slaves ushered past him, carrying trays of oysters, sliced melon, buttered asparagus, cured meats, spiced goose liver and various other foodstuffs that the soldier didn't even recognise.

"My father likes to project power, although given the choice of some of his decorations – and guests – I rather think he is sending out the message that money can't buy taste," Claudia replied, with an amused and askance expression, lingering a little on the sight of a woman with gold baubles in her hair like eggs in a bird's nest.

"You are your brother's sister, Claudia." Maximus thought how Rufus would have said something similar, with a similar look on his face.

"Usually people say that I am my father's daughter."

"No. You're funnier and kinder than your father," Maximus replied, in earnest, with a meaningful look on his face.

"Unfortunately that's not too difficult." Claudia inwardly – and outwardly – beamed at the soldier's comment. She recalled the first time she had met him, at a lunch. At the beginning she had been bored, or rather had looked unimpressed to affect a sense of boredom, but she had soon warmed to the good humoured praetorian who her brother had spoken so highly of. Every time she had seen him subsequently she had been tinged with a little frustration and sadness that he was (happily) married. But she had still enjoyed his company. They were friends. And how many people could she say that about?

"True. You'll have to forgive me. It's been some time since I've had the opportunity to compliment a woman. I'm out of practise."

A collected gasp sounded out towards the other end of the garden, where the juggler had set fire to the daggers he was throwing, but Maximus and Claudia ignored the sound and spectacle.

"Well, just to let you know I would be willing to let you practise on me some more, at any point. Flattery might get you everywhere with a woman."

Maximus laughed and Claudia thought how attractive the soldier was. There was a nobility, as well as ruggedness, to his features. There was a glow about him this evening, too. Maybe it was due to him being home again, away from the frontier. Maybe it was due to the wine. Or maybe it was due to her. She sensed he might genuinely like her – and not just for her name, looks or the fact that she was the sister of his best friend. She beamed, brighter. She put her father's instructions out of her mind. She was with Maximus because she wanted to be with him.

"I'm sure you're not short of men complimenting you, Claudia."

I am of real men – and real compliments.

"Well do not think that I am just idly complimenting you Gaius, but I'm glad to see you again. You're funnier and kinder than any other man present – although unfortunately that's not too difficult. Julia was fortunate to have you though. I never really knew you that well when she passed away – and I didn't really offer my condolences at the time. But you were in my thoughts. Did I ever tell you that I spent the afternoon with her once? We bumped into each other at the market and had lunch."

She was funnier and kinder than me. It's probably why he loved her so much.

"Julia mentioned it in a letter she sent me while I was serving in Egypt. She said that you made her laugh – and blush." Maximus recalled how his wife had also mentioned that Claudia seemed to be forever playing a part for others, whether she was dealing with her husband, father or other women. Yet behind the act there was a far more interesting and virtuous character trying to get out. "I felt that I was the more fortunate one between us though."

I still miss her.

"She was genuinely lovely. I liked her, although I also envied her a little for having married the only man in Rome that my brother could ever approve of, in terms of me marrying someone." Claudia's eyes flashed with warmth – and something else. "I'm not so sure my father would have approved of me marrying you, however."

"I'll take that as a compliment," Maximus replied, with warmth – and something else – in his tone too.

A couple of women, their faces pinched in disgust, walked away at the unseemliness of the barbaric and strange scene. Most remained wide-eyed and rooted to the spot, however, as the Chinaman took off his shirt and unsheathed his long, slightly curved sword. Pollio Atticus had instructed his bodyguard to give an exhibition of his skills, to entertain the guests at the party. His skin stretched over his face, like a reptile's. His body, marked by a number of gruesome scars, looked supple and muscular. A couple of the spectators gasped at the sight of the beastly looking foreigner.

Chen proceeded to run through a display of lightning quick and unorthodox sword drills, shouting out in his native language to add a further air of colour and ferocity. Large melons were placed on tripods, which his razor sharp blade sliced in two, without knocking them over. The Chinaman remained stone-faced, apart from his lip curling up slightly in contempt for the ignoble people who made up his audience, but he soon began to inwardly enjoy the attention of some of the women who applauded him.

"He's very skilled, isn't he?" a lissom teenage girl giddily proclaimed, whilst clutching the arm of an indifferent looking centurion.

"Yes. It must have taken him years to learn how to defeat a melon, or cut thin air in two," Rufus Atticus replied (loud enough for the Chinaman to hear) to the over-excited Lucilla.

As much as his father always encouraged Atticus to join the Senate when he spoke to him, his mother was constantly trying to get her son to marry. Although both institutions shared the same skill sets of lying and spending other peoples' money, the soldier wasn't ready to commit to either quite yet. His mother persisted, however, and, after catching up with her son, she had introduced him to Lucilla, the youngest daughter of a frontrunner for a consulship. The constant jangling from the various items of jewellery Lucilla wore (bangles, anklets, necklaces) nearly annoyed Atticus as much as the sound of her shrill voice. Her teeth were too large and her brain was too small, he judged.

She's more horse than woman.

Lucilla giggled, or rather whinnied, at the handsome officer's comment, having nervously laughed at every other joke Atticus had made since being introduced to him (he had just commented how he would rather swallow his sword than any further verses from the poet in residence at the party). The sound of her squealing laughter, as well as the praetorian's sarcastic comment, disturbed Chen's concentration and he knocked over the tripod when slicing the final melon in two. Atticus let out a burst of goading laughter, witnessing the Chinaman's mistake.

"We've had a juggler, now it seems my father has offered us up a clown for our amusement," the soldier loudly remarked whilst applauding, causing the audience around him to laugh with him.

The assassin's narrow eyes widened in rage. He snorted and glowered at the arrogant young officer. Chen tightly gripped the handle of his sword and his knuckles turned white as he envisioned slicing the praetorian's head off like a melon. Yet his antagonist was his master's son. The Chinaman believed the man to be disloyal and dishonourable. Rufus Atticus had helped to thwart his father's plans three years ago, when he had aided the German boy and his sister to reach the northern frontier. The soldier also served the Emperor, their enemy. But his master had given the assassin express orders to spare his son's life.

"I wish to first find out the reason why my son has come back to Rome. Dead men can't talk. Also, dead men can't fuck. I need my son to produce an heir. Claudia may well be barren... Rufus provides my best hope to carry on our name and bloodline... The needs of the family must even prove sovereign over my desire for revenge."

Atticus continued to wear an amused expression on his face as his father's bodyguard continued to glare at him as if he wanted to kill him. Atticus remembered how one of the Emperor's agents had reported that a Chinaman had been responsible for the distribution of negative propaganda. The praetorian had thought of his father's bodyguard when reading the document – and had grown suspicious.

"Chen, isn't it? That was a fine display. You must be of great use to my father, especially when he is in need of a fruit salad. Or do you have any other talents?" Atticus was keen to provoke his father's bodyguard, to either help ruin the party or substantiate his suspicions.

The assassin walked towards the soldier with fire in his eyes, muscles rippling along his sweat-glazed arms.

"I have other talents, too. You may even get to see them soon, close up. You may not be so willing to mock me then," Chen threatened, almost in a whisper. His hand wrapped itself around the ivory handle of his sword.

"Oh I'm not so sure about that. The more I get to know someone the more I usually find reason to mock them. It seems you want to teach me a lesson though, Chen. Did you hire the brigand Bulla to try and teach me a lesson all those years ago too?"

The simmering Chinaman's blood was about to boil over. He was about to confess his crime and answer yes. He would prove to the impudent Roman that he didn't need to hire Bulla or anyone else to teach him a lesson. He was superior to the white man in every way; indeed the Chinaman considered the Roman to be the barbarian out of the two of them. He belonged to the master race.

"Master Rufus, sorry to disturb you, but your father wishes to see you in the house. If you would like to accompany me," Sextus, one of Pollio Atticus' attendants, remarked. Sextus had served in the household for over a decade. The all-seeing Pollio had observed his bodyguard approach his son. The statesman quickly instructed his slave to part the two men, for fear of Chen doing or saying something out of turn.

The centurion sighed but agreed to see his father – and not just because he wanted to free himself from the cloying Lucilla.

*

Rufus Atticus sat in the triclinium, waiting for his father. He noticed how the marble floor had been retiled, again. Every five years the house was redecorated. Projecting wealth was as good as projecting power. The most expensive, as opposed to the best, works of art hung on the walls. It wasn't just the unfamiliar decor which made Atticus feel like he was a stranger in a strange house, though. The palatial property always felt more akin to a mausoleum than a home, a museum dedicated to affluence and the history of his family. The library – and tavern – had felt more like home to him when he had been a teenager.

The soldier looked out onto the party. All of his father's cronies were present. He saw Senator Antonius Reburrus snaking his arm around the Chinese wife of a wealthy silk merchant. His tan was as well-oiled as his hair. Antonius, a former consul, had manipulated the senate five years ago into invading a region in Persia, rich in natural resources. He now served as a special peace envoy to a neighbouring province in the area. Such had been his increase in wealth since he left office that no one could accurately judge the extent of his fortune. Atticus had also noticed Antonius' wife, Sabina, at the party earlier. She was equally self-serving and rapacious as her husband, if not more so. Sabina came from a family of distinguished advocates. It was perhaps no coincidence that during Antonius' consulship the number of laws which came onto the statute books had increased threefold compared to the previous year. As Atticus had once heard Sabina's father exclaim, "It's simple. The more laws we have the more money we can make." Sabina had been so concerned with making money over the past few years though that the glare of gold had blinded her to her husband's frequent affairs. And what did Antonius and his wife do with their wealth? Buy even more modish, vulgar works of art than his father, and spend money as if he were a consul still, or an Emperor. No matter how many expensive outfits Sabina bought, however, she would still be mutton dressed up as mutton, Atticus mused.

A guttural, wine-fuelled laugh drew the centurion's attention to Julius Porticus. His chin, or rather chins, swayed as he laughed. He was just about to tell a fellow guest how much of "a man of the people" he was, having once served as the head of a carpenter's gild. The former praetor was still under investigation for defrauding the treasury. Not only had he been accused of embezzling funds, which had been set aside in the budget for the maintenance of the city's aqueducts, but Porticus had also used public money to buy a house on the Palatine Hill. His argument was that if he lived and worked out of his villa, situated just outside the capital, then he wouldn't have been able to do his job to the best of his abilities. The tragedy was, Atticus thought, that Porticus *had* done his job to the best of his abilities. The aqueducts still needed repairing and the official inquiry into his crimes had gone on for so long that most people had forgotten about it. He was helped by being able to employ his uncle, Sabina's father, as his advocate. He also attended the same school as Antonius and was friends with a number of senators who had been asked to form the committee to oversee his case.

The sneer on Atticus' face betrayed the sneer in his thoughts as he saw Gnaeus Varro standing next to Porticus. Varro had spent the first two years of the war against the Marcomanni campaigning to reduce the rations and men that the Empire devoted to servicing the legions. For the past two years, however, after inheriting an estate which included property situated on the frontier and a foundry in Ravenna which manufactured arms, Varro had tirelessly petitioned the Senate to furnish the Emperor with more men and equipment. His slogan now was, "Let's finish the job." Suffice to say Varro was in the process of selling a number of shares in the foundry to his senatorial colleagues, in order to win the argument and give Marcus Aurelius "the tools to finish what the enemy started."

Even Hercules would be at pains to clean Rome's augean stables, Atticus thought. Perhaps it was now only corruption and hypocrisy holding everything together. In the days of the Republic many of his father's guests would have been sewn up in a sack with a wild animal and thrown into the Tiber for their crimes. Perhaps a greater punishment would be to throw them all into a sack and make them suffer each other's conversation for an eternity.

"Rufus, thank you for waiting and for meeting me," Pollio Atticus amiably said, the iciness having melted from the tone of their previous encounter. Rufus remained seated and silent. He decided that he would allow his father to do most of the talking when they met, partly in hope that he would say too much. The statesman offered his son a conciliatory expression, which seemed genuine.

"I want you to know that I haven't come back from the war to become embroiled in a different type of conflict," Rufus exclaimed, wary of his father but still willing to hear him out.

"I know. And I understand. It's unusual for me to apologise, as either a politician or father, but I want to say I'm sorry Rufus. I was wrong. I was wrong for trying to prevent you from joining the army. And I was wrong to doubt that you would succeed. I know you think that I do not have a high opinion of the Emperor, but we have shared a number of letters these past few years. He has been kind enough to apprise me of your wellbeing and advancement. And I understand congratulations are in order, in regards to your promotion... As a politician and father you have been a victim of listening to a countless number of my speeches, but please now hear me out. The Empire is divided enough for a father to be in dispute with his only son. I am asking you to forgive my pride – and stupidity... I will no longer ask you to give up your career in the army for a career in politics. You are your own man. And if the Emperor is happy having you fight by his side, who am I to argue with him? Yet I would like you to consider taking a wife, Rufus. Before I would have argued that you should be doing this for yourself, or that it would make your mother happy to see you married. But you know me better than that. I am asking for selfish reasons."

"Master, sorry to disturb you," Sextus remarked, entering the room and interrupting the senator. "But it is a matter of some importance."

"No, Sextus. *This* is a matter of some importance, talking to my son. Unless Nero is burning down Rome again, any other business can wait," the statesman said firmly, but not too harshly, to his attendant.

Sextus gave a brief nod of his head and retreated.

"Now, where was I?"

"I was about to get my new wife pregnant," Rufus said.

"I'm not asking you to give me a decision here and now. I would just like you to think about things. The old Pollio Atticus, as you know, would have demanded to select your wife for you. But I trust you will marry wisely. We both want you to be happy. I will also instruct your mother not to interfere either, as much as she may choose to burn down Rome at hearing such news. Do you know how long you will be back with us for? Has the Emperor said anything to you about why he has returned to the capital, and when he is planning to return to the north? It's just that it would be nice to arrange a family dinner while you are here... I now realise, Rufus, that for far too long I devoted myself to becoming the father of my country, as opposed to being the father of my children."

"I'm unsure how long I will be in the capital for. The Emperor is due to make an important announcement soon. I'm unable to say any more on the matter though. I hope you understand. I will also consider what you have just said. I've changed, I think. Maybe I am ready to marry. Of course that could just be the wine talking."

Pollio Atticus grinned at his son's jest and warmly clasped him on the shoulder.

"I understand, in regards to your need to be discreet, and I also understand how you have changed. I hope to prove to you how much I have changed, too."

Aye, but a snake which sheds its skin is still a snake.

11.

Marcus Aurelius stood up and walked around his desk in order to bid a farewell to Gaius Avidius Cassius, after their meeting together discussing the politics and strategy in the east.

Cassius cut an imposing figure and physically dwarfed Aurelius. Broad shouldered and strong jawed, a pair of dark, doubtless eyes hung over an aquiline nose. The military commander smiled, or rather smirked, as he firmly clasped the hand of the man he was cuckolding. Avidius Cassius was a descendant of the Seleucid King Antiochus IV – and some senators remarked that he was beginning to rule over the peoples in the east as if he were a monarch. He was a disciplinarian – in regards to both his own soldiers and also the civilian population – whose ambition and pride often clouded his judgement. His authoritarian behaviour was not the solution to the problem of increasing rebellion in the east, but rather the cause of it, some considered. Others argued that ruthless commanders such as Cassius were a necessary evil for running the Empire.

Cassius had cause to believe in himself, even if others didn't. The commander had been instrumental in winning a series of brilliant victories during the Parthian War, although the co-Emperor at the time, Lucius Verus, was unfairly given the credit for his triumphs. Marcus Aurelius had recognised the soldier's abilities, however, and proceeded to promote him, to the point where Cassius now held imperium over a number of provinces and legions in the east. Cassius had shown loyalty and gratitude towards his Emperor during the early part of his career, but he now believed he was worthy enough to usurp his place on the throne – as well as his place in his wife's bed. He recalled Pollio Atticus' remark, that he had more royal blood running through his veins than the Emperor. He had promised Pollio that if and when the time came he would do his duty and succeed Aurelius, "for Rome's sake." Cassius would concede that the Emperor had brought stability (and he thanked the Gods that Aurelius rather than the debauchee Lucius Verus had become sole Emperor) but stability wasn't progress. Cassius believed that he could win the war in the north, even if he had to burn down every tree that a barbarian could hide behind.

I am younger and stronger than him... and my bloodline is nobler. He is old, tired... I'm not even sure how much he still wishes to be Emperor.

Faustina had confessed to Cassius how Aurelius had sex with his wife out of duty, rather than desire.

One should enjoy, rather than just endure, being a Caesar. Pollio Atticus is right. It isn't just the plague weakening the Empire, it is the Emperor.

The soldier continued to smile and shake the Emperor's hand. Aurelius thanked the commander for meeting with him and for giving up his evening. Cassius sniggered to himself, however, thinking of the amount of late nights he had spent in the Imperial Palace attending to the Empress. Aurelius finally asked after his friend's family and wished them well, before the two men parted.

The Emperor sat in, or rather slumped into, his chair. He sighed – and nearly blew out a candle as he did so. The oak chair creaked as his bones cracked. He barely noticed, or cared, as one of the oil lamps in the chamber went out. Two different tonics, in purple ceramic phials, stood on his desk. Both were from Galen. One was concocted to help the Emperor sleep, the other to keep him awake so he could work through the night.

Cassius is a good soldier, but I'm not so sure that he is a good man.

Marcus Aurelius could not help but compare his commander in the east with Gaius Maximus. The Emperor recalled the quote from Juvenal, after re-reading the satirist yesterday afternoon; he thought about how apt the words were to describe the officer.

Many individuals have, like uncut diamonds, shining qualities beneath a rough exterior.

Marcus Aurelius reflected that Cassius' breastplate was polished, but his soul was besmirched – as much as Faustina spoke well of his character. The Emperor once again sighed – and then reached for one of the phials.

12.

Aurelia began to doubt whether the body was wholly separate from the soul, as both thrummed with happiness while she lay next to Maximus. She'd finally caught her breath back. Aurelia placed her palm on his chest and her racing heart slowed, attuning itself to the calm, contented, beat of his.

The morning after the party Maximus had visited Galen at his house, but then in the afternoon he had come to see Aurelia. They had had lunch in the garden and had spoken about their future.

"I don't want to wait any longer," Aurelia had said, sunlight gilding her soft features. Desire had (just about) overcome her nervousness. She wanted to be with Maximus. She had thought about little else the sleepless evening and morning before. Maximus had cradled her face in his hands and kissed her – before taking her hand and leading her up to the bedroom. She had felt awkward, passive, at first. Maximus had been gentle, as well as passionate. Something soon awoke in the woman though – a fire was lit – and Aurelia had given herself to him, body and soul. It was like nothing she had ever felt before. She had gasped and sighed. She had closed her eyes, arched her back in pleasure, and while many Christians might have deemed that she was living in sin, Aurelia had suddenly felt like she was in heaven.

Helena had nearly dropped the plate she was cleaning as she heard the floorboards – and her mistress – groan.

Aurelia now rested her head upon Maximus' chest, after making love for the third time. Motes of dust sparkled from the amber sunlight pouring through the window. Maximus breathed in her perfume and lovingly put his arm around her, his fingertips caressing her silken, tingling skin. He wanted as much of their bodies to touch as possible. Maximus hadn't been with another woman since his wife had passed away, although before Julia he had slept with any number of serving girls, whores, and women bored with their husbands.

"Thank you for waiting for me Gaius... Thank you for saving my life three years ago – and for saving me from a half-lived life now."

"You were worth the wait," Maximus replied, smiling as he recalled Galen's comment from earlier. "Aurelia needs a man in her life, other than Jesus Christ."

"I want to get married... I don't want to replace Julia though. I'm me... But I don't want you to think that I want you to forget about her. She's part of you."

Maximus had vigorously shaken his head as he had sat beside his wife on her deathbed, when Julia had said that he should find another wife after she was gone. The soldier had shaken his head to convey that he wouldn't, or couldn't, love again. And because his wife shouldn't say such things – because he had believed she was going to live. Julia was still with him, through his memories and dreams. For a couple of months or so during the past three years, Maximus had stopped writing to Aurelia, believing that he was somehow being unfaithful to Julia by having feelings for someone else. But Julia would have wanted him to be happy. He needed something in his life, besides death and duty. And so the centurion had commenced to write to Aurelia again... Maximus no longer felt guilty in wanting to be with Aurelia. He would still cherish his time with Julia, but he was ready to love and marry again.

The praetorian did feel guilty, however, in that, after leaving Aurelia's bed, he would be spending the evening with Claudia.

13.

The four men had just finished their shift on guard duty at Pollio Atticus' house. They squatted down in the courtyard under a sweltering sky and drew out a large circle in chalk. One of the men, Titus, a former lictor, retrieved his jar containing a number of large beetles. Each man proceeded to pick and mark an insect on its back. Money and banter were exchanged. A jug of sour wine was also passed around. The beetles were placed in the centre of the ring and the race commenced for the first one to cross the line of the circle. The men cheered their champions on as if the black bugs were charioteers in the arena. More bets were placed. One man started to plan what he would spend his winnings on as his beetle energetically scurried towards the chalk line – before energetically changing direction to head back to the centre of the circle. He swore enough to make a lady, or harlot, blush.

The cheers and excitement increased, nearly reaching a crescendo, as two of the insects neared the finishing line together. Titus, who had called his beetle "Fury", started to call out his name in order to spur it on to victory. Just as the insect was about to get chalk on its legs, as well as its back, a large boot squashed "Fury" in its moment of glory, as Chen callously ruined the men's sport and the atmosphere. The Chinaman grunted as he strode on towards the house, to meet with his master. Titus cursed the yellow-skinned barbarian beneath his breath, rather than out loud.

He's a dog… But every dog has its day.

Chen sneered-cum-smirked as he pictured the shocked and resentful expressions behind his back. The Chinaman considered the puny guards to be mere insects themselves – and their hatred of him fed his sense of amusement and power. He spared the guards little more thought, though, as he continued to walk towards the house where he was due to report to Atticus in his study. Chen's sneer turned into a fully-fledged smirk as he thought of how he would ask permission to possess his master's daughter again, as a reward once the mission was complete.

*

I must be Caesar, rather than Catiline… I cannot risk everything – and fail.

Pollio Atticus stood in front of three drawings on the wall. One was a map of the whole of Rome, another focused on the area around the grain warehouse on the river, and the final one was a plan of the warehouse itself. He noticed his fingers were stained with ink from composing more propaganda. Soon he would have blood on his hands. But he was doing what he was doing for Rome.

The ends justify the means... Tomorrow night will be the beginning of the end... You may be stoical enough in the face of impending starvation Aurelius, but the mob won't be… The first thing I'll do when you're gone is pay the army a donative, their full purses will fill the void of your absence… The people too can be bought off, as easily as a politician. Virgil wrote that "Fickle and changeable always is women." The line may be applied to the mob, too.

Chen stood attentive to his master as a determined Pollio Atticus ran through the plan again. The agent would lead his main force, carrying arms and barrels of highly flammable oil, up the street which ran alongside the river towards the grain warehouse. They would easily best the small number of men guarding the warehouse. Once inside, his men would douse the grain in the oil and set fire to the food supplies. A number of men also needed to be designated to cover the outside of the warehouse – and surrounding buildings – with graffiti, blaming the Emperor and the regime for being the cause of the desperate act. Pollio Atticus reiterated that it was important, however, that Chen did not let his men run riot. They should not set fire to any other buildings. They should not loot. When entering and exiting the city they should do so in small groups to avoid raising any suspicion. Although Chen's force would appear to be acting as an angry, desperate mob his men needed to conduct themselves with proficiency and professionalism.

The Praetorian Guard would be unable to muster a sufficient enough force in time to stop Chen's men, but if any opposition did arrive on the scene then he should deal with the enemy accordingly. *Dead men tell no tales.*

"You can enjoy yourself," Pollio Atticus said to the warrior, who would relish testing himself against the best that Rome had to offer in the form of the Emperor's elite soldiers.

Chen thought he would particularly enjoy himself if somehow Maximus or his master's son were on duty and ordered to deal with the disturbance. The agent felt he had unfinished business with the pair after failing in his mission three years ago. He would also be happy to provide Rufus Atticus with another close-up display of his abilities. Since their encounter at the party the assassin had imagined killing the centurion in more ways than one.

Pollio Atticus afforded himself a smile as he finally explained how he would provide men to help put out the fire later in the evening. The statesman also enjoyed the irony that the Emperor would soon be betrayed by one of his most loyal officers. Gaius Maximus had accepted his daughter's invitation to dinner.

His secrets will soon be hers – and mine.

14.

A bulbous moon swelled, ripe, in the night sky. The shutters were opened throughout the house to let in a cooling breeze and freshen up the oppressive, muggy air.

Desire – and something even nicer – fluttered inside Claudia as she prepared herself for her evening with Maximus. She remembered, from a conversation many years ago, what he liked to eat and asked her cook to produce a number of dishes accordingly. She wanted him to have what he wanted, rather than what she thought would impress him.

At first she tried on the outfit that she thought her father would have wanted her to wear – a low-cut stola, without her strophium, made from translucent red silk. A long, unsubtle slit ran up the sides of the garment – showing off her tawny legs. The cut of the stola hugged her figure, to the point of constricting her... But the outfit had looked, or felt, wrong.

Instead Claudia chose her favourite summer dress and she saw, for once, a smiling face staring back at her as she looked into the polished silver mirror. Her dresser thought, for once, that her mistress appeared happy – and all the prettier for it. She had a glow about her. Her hairdresser was given the evening off as Claudia decided to wear her long hair down, how she liked it, and how Julia used to wear it. Usually her hairdresser had to pin the lady's hair up and construct an edifice worthy of Archimedes. Claudia also, for a change, barely wore any make-up. She reddened not her lips with ochre, to make them appear fuller, nor thickened her eyebrows with soot. To finish off her outfit Claudia asked her dresser to fetch her gold and sapphire brooch, in the shape of a swan, which her grandmother had given to her when she was barely a teenager. As her dresser fastened the brooch on her left breast Claudia recalled the speech that the formidable – and funny – aristocratic woman had given to her, when she had first pinned the heirloom on her.

"You'll soon learn, my girl, that it isn't all that easy being a woman of your class in Rome. You have to play dumb more than an actress and smile more than a politician does around election time… And it only gets a little easier the older – and the more practised – you get. As much as you may change, unfortunately men and society won't… Just wake up every day and try to do more good than ill. And grow old gracefully, or disgracefully, depending on your mood… Try to marry a good, as well as a rich, man – and if he's neither then attempt to turn him into both… Failing that, take a lover who can put a smile on your face and money in your purse."

*

The breeze whispered into the murmuring braziers. Claudia had arranged for them to eat in the moonlit garden. The scent of summer flowers proved welcome to Maximus, after having breathed in certain other aromas over the past week that Rome had to offer, but the smell of grilled fish and meat was heavenly for the soldier.

He had been served with oysters for a first course and lobster claws for his second, but Maximus' eyes truly widened in satisfaction when he came eye to eye with the honey-glazed suckling pig. If the soldier had been in the presence of his men, rather than that of a lady, he might have even salivated. It made her happy to see him so happy. The look of surprise – and pleasure – on his face was akin to that of when he had seen her for the first time that evening, Claudia thought. He had never looked at her in such a revealing – and amorous – way before. Perhaps he had always thought of her as his friend's sister. Maybe it was because he had been happily married before, or he had thought her happily married. For a moment Maximus had been speechless, captivated. His heart had been in his mouth when she walked down the stairs to greet him. Before long though they had started to talk and laugh like old friends. Maximus revealed how the Emperor had asked him to remain in Rome, rather than return north with him. Claudia calmly replied that he might now get bored serving on guard duty, compared to the dangers of the frontier, but her heart sang at the news that the officer would be staying in the capital.

Oil lamps hung above them under an awning and shone upon her burnished skin. The light caught her brooch and silver earrings – and winked at him like the stars. Maximus drained his cup of wine again and openly admired his seductive host. He seemed equally as intoxicated by the wine as he was by her beauty.

In another world, in another life, I could and should be with her.
Father wants me to be Calypso. Perhaps I've played that part for so long I'm unable to be anyone else. But I want to be, for once, Penelope – faithful, loved and worth coming home to… I want him to see my goodness, rather than guile.

"So how did Rufus react to the news that you were having dinner with me this evening?" Claudia asked, with the hint of a smile on her face from picturing the shock on her brother's usually relaxed features.

"I'll let you know once I tell him. He may well be more upset with me for not sharing this suckling pig with him, than sharing the news that I had dinner with his sister."

"I'm sure that Rufus will forgive you on both counts. He's very fond of you Gaius, and my brother isn't fond of many people as you know, aside from other men's wives. But I'm very fond of you, too. I want you to know that I didn't just invite you to dinner because you are my brother's best friend. You mean more to me than that."

They shared a meaningful look, for a moment.

"It's also not just because I need a lady to practise my compliments on that I accepted your invitation Claudia. My compliments to your cook too, by the way."

Maximus gulped down another half-cup of fine wine. He drank to forget himself, or rather to forget about Aurelia. Yet he remembered her words – and the contentedness in her expression – when he had parted from her that afternoon.

"I'll let you say goodbye now. But when you come back, you'll be coming back to me for the rest of your life," she had said as he parted.

Maximus willed himself to concentrate on the woman in front of him, rather than the woman inside his head and heart.

"Well it's partly because you never showered me with cliché-ridden compliments that I noticed you all those years ago, Gaius. Most men used to put me on a pedestal only so that they could look up my skirt, I'm afraid. But you were, or are, different. You're the most honourable man I know. You've always been nice to me, even when I haven't always deserved such treatment."

They shared another meaningful look, for a longer, lasting, moment. Neither knew who held the other's hand across the table first.

"I wish we could have somehow done this in the past, Claudia. Have dinner. Spend the evening together. Talk. I had the right feelings, but it was never the right time. But it's the right time now."

Night time. Bedtime.

*

"Morning," Claudia purred. Her slender legs were coiled around Maximus'. A fragrant film of massage oil still glazed Claudia's body and shone in the honey-tinged sunlight. His head throbbed.

The night before hadn't felt like the first time for Claudia, but it had felt like the best time. She had first asked Maximus – but then almost ordered the soldier later in the night – to make love to her. She had wanted him inside her, so much for so long. She squeezed his hand as the pleasure increased, as he kissed her lips, thighs, breasts and… She wanted him to love her like Odysseus loved Penelope.

"Morning," Maximus replied. He felt fatigued, as though he had just spent the night in battle. Yet the centurion found the strength to kiss, deliciously, the remarkable woman again. His fingertips caressed and ran down her back, buttocks and legs. She hummed in satisfaction, breakfasting on the sensation.

"Hmmm, I could get used to waking up to you like this," Claudia smilingly remarked, hungrily kissing him on the chest and then on the mouth in reply, her hands swirling around his body beneath the silk sheets.

"I could too. I'm not so sure your husband could, though."

"Fronto is a joke, which I have to suffer the punch line to. We live separate lives already. He means nothing to me. We'd commit to divorcing each other with more passion to that of what we had when we married each other… I feel like my whole life has been plotted out for me by my father, social convention, and by the role I must play as an aristocratic woman and wife. I want for nothing, materially. On the outside my life may seem like a comedy, with the happiest of happy endings. But being adored is not the same as being loved. A palace can still be a prison. I want someone I can grow old, not bored, with."

My life is a tragedy. Yet you can write another act into it. Be the hero.

Maximus felt more sympathy, than love, for the woman but hoped his expression wasn't betraying mere pity.

"I'm not sure that I'll be able to keep pace with you."

204

"I'll wait for you – and if I fall behind, wait for me. Spend the day with me Gaius."

"Unfortunately I have to spend the day with the Emperor, as much as I'd rather attend to a goddess than a god. But Aurelius is due to deliver some important – and good – news soon. I need to ask you to keep this to yourself, but we may be about to defeat a greater enemy than boredom even – that of the plague. Galen believes that he has identified a cure. He has still to run some final tests at the laboratory at his house, but it seems that more people will now get the opportunity to grow old together."

"That's wonderful news," Claudia enthused, but her happiness was as much for her finding love as for Galen finding a cure. They embraced and kissed each other – and she didn't want to let him go. "We should celebrate, tonight."

Maximus agreed, sorrowfully thinking how he had also agreed to spend the evening with Aurelia. He was breaking his word – and his heart.

15.

Duty called. Shortly after Maximus left at midday to return to his barracks – and then see the Emperor – Claudia went to report to her father. A slither of her soul was tempted to keep her word to Maximus and keep the news of Galen's cure a secret. Yet the fear of her father finding out that she had kept intelligence from him shaped her thoughts – and she ordered her litter bearers to wend their way through Rome's busy streets even faster than usual. Her husband – and the law – could provide little protection should she earn her father's displeasure by betraying him (or "the family," as he would argue). Claudia had witnessed her father ruin the lives and reputations of his enemies many times before, indeed she had occasionally been involved in the process.

Chen led the slightly agitated and slightly perspiring woman through the house towards Pollio Atticus' study. Despite the sultry summer heat Claudia still felt a chill run down her spine in the Chinaman's presence. She shivered as she felt his lecherous eyes crawl over her. Every so often her father would order his daughter to spend the night with the Chinaman, as a reward for his agent's work and loyalty.

Pollio Atticus appeared pensive at best, saturnine at worst, when Claudia entered his study. The shutters were closed, yet still a little sunlight bled through. He looked at her both sternly and expectantly. His brow was as creased as the silk sheets on her bed, she thought fleetingly. Atticus had covered over two of the three maps on his wall (leaving only the general map of the city visible) out of precaution. Claudia, however, was already aware of her father's scheme to cause unrest by destroying the capital's grain supply. Some months ago, during the last time her father had rewarded his bodyguard, Chen had sought to impress Claudia by revealing how he had become her father's most trusted agent – and he spoke of their grand plans. Pillow talk.

"Did he talk?" the statesman asked, with little concern for the wellbeing of his daughter.

"They always talk. It seems that the Emperor has returned to Rome to make the announcement that he, or rather Galen, has found a cure for the plague. The doctor is currently running some final tests at his house, but Maximus is meeting with Aurelius today. The Emperor will make his proclamation soon, maybe even in a day or two."

Pollio Atticus remained impassive at hearing his daughter's brief report. Yet he subtly exhaled, flaring his nostrils – and he made a fist around the stylus he was holding. He cursed Aurelius – and Galen – beneath his breath. His blood coursed like lava around his body. The senator had had visions of late of the warehouse in flames, and now he felt like that his plans – dreams – could turn to ash. Should Aurelius prove responsible for delivering a cure to the plague – and saving the Empire – he would be hailed as a new Augustus. Any support that Atticus could currently count on in the Senate would drain away, like sand through his fingertips, should he or Avidius Cassius challenge Aurelius' authority. The Empire would soon be feasting, rather than starving, at hearing the good news. Agriculture and the economy would thrive again. The army would serve its Emperor with even greater fervour. Aurelius saving the Empire would condemn Atticus to being no more than a footnote in history.

He must be stopped. There is still time.

Aurelius could only announce that he was in possession of a cure, if it was true. It appeared that the remedy only resided in Galen's laboratory – and inside the scientist's head – at the present time. He could destroy both, tonight.

Desperate times call for desperate measures.

Chen still needed to command the mission at the warehouse. So he would personally lead a few men and pay a visit to the physician. He would need to interrogate Galen and assess the situation himself. He could make things look like a robbery and/or arson. He may need to abduct the doctor. He could leave the burnt corpse of a slave in the laboratory as a substitute for Galen. The secret of the cure would seemingly die with him. But when the time was right Pollio Atticus would make the announcement that he had discovered a remedy for the scourge – and be proclaimed the saviour of Rome. *Augustus. Caesar.*

No. All is not lost.

Claudia broke the silence as her father sat, slate-faced, deep in thought. She willed herself to bury her feelings for Maximus deep down inside her as she spoke about him.

"From what I could gather Maximus is close to the Emperor. I could continue to see him. He could prove a useful source of intelligence."

Atticus' hard eyes turned upon his daughter. He looked at first as if he were about to reprove her for speaking out of turn and disturbing his thoughts, but then he suddenly smiled.

"I agree. Yet sooner or later, or sooner rather than later, the irksome soldier will be sleeping underground rather than in your bed. He'll fall, along with Aurelius. Hopefully he won't need to put his oafish paws on you for much longer. Chen will take care of things, when the time comes. Won't you, Chen?"

The Chinaman nodded and grinned. There was a glint in his eye, like sunlight shining off the polished blade of his sword.

Claudia's heart cracked, but her face remained unchanged. Pollio Atticus had taught his daughter how to mask her emotions many years ago, to such an extent that it had become second nature. Ecstasy was feigned during agony. The dusting of make-up that Claudia wore cracked not, either in a smile or frown, as she appeared indifferent to the fate of the centurion. But she was far from indifferent. Something had broken inside of her – and in doing so something else had slotted into place.

He must be stopped.

"Continue to extract what intelligence you can out of the praetorian. Find out about his meeting with Aurelius today. Well done though, Claudia. I am pleased with you. See your mother's dressmaker on your way out. Treat yourself to a new outfit, on my account. Perhaps you may wish to arrange an outfit for Gaius Maximus' funeral. Something that you can wash the crocodile tears out from," the statesman drily remarked – and chuckled at his own joke.

Claudia smiled, serpent-like.

"I will order the dress."

But the funeral will be yours.

"Thank you. That will be all. Now please leave us."

As much as she wanted to be party to her father's intentions and plans, Claudia dutifully obeyed the order. She remained in earshot, however, to hear her father remark, "We will still proceed as planned tonight. I have a special task for you beforehand, though."

16.

Night time slowly but surely commenced to bleed into the horizon. The temperature dropped. The clinking of armour sounded over the cawing of the birds who circled over the barracks. A brawny centurion, who led a dozen of his men across the courtyard, barked out the order of "Eyes front" as an optio accompanied a finely dressed woman through the complex. Claudia did not notice the ogling looks, however, as she walked quickly, in order to meet with her brother. Her head was downcast – in thought, shame and worry.

He must be stopped.

Rufus Atticus stood up from behind his desk as his sister entered his small office. He looked at her neutrally, neither showing the surprise, anxiety nor pleasure which Claudia considered that he might, given that she had never visited him at the barracks before. Atticus did not say a word as she ran towards him and buried her head in his chest. The centurion soon felt tears on his shoulder.

"I've done something terrible. But I want to prevent something worse happening," Claudia confessed, her tears cutting scars through her make-up.

"I think that you had better sit down. Would you like some water, or wine, to help calm yourself?" Atticus remarked evenly, in stark contrast to his distressed sister.

"Water, please," the woman said quietly, struck by her brother's air of seriousness. She was used to him only being serious about his indifference – or enjoying himself. She briefly took in his desk, filled with correspondence and work.

Perhaps he has changed. Perhaps I have, or can, change too.

Rufus poured his sister a cup of water from the jug on the table. He then silently sat down and picked up his stylus, ready to make notes in regards to whatever Claudia was about to say – as if he would be interrogating her. Again Claudia was struck by her brother's cold, rather than concerned, demeanour. She also noted his lack of shock or curiosity at seeing her turn up at his barracks without notice. It was as if he had been expecting her.

"You mentioned the other afternoon, Rufus, how you hoped that I would someday surprise myself. I am going to surprise you also by what I have to say. Father asked me to seduce Gaius Maximus, in order to extract information out of him about the Emperor's intentions and his reasons for returning to the capital. I know that you are aware of how father has asked me to seduce other men in the past. In being a good daughter I have been a bad wife and person. You never judged me though in the past, Rufus. Please do not judge me now as well, at least until I finish what I have to say. I do not want to lose you, as well as everything else. If you have thought ill of some of the immoral things I've done, know that I have loathed myself more. But when father ordered me to get close to Gaius I did so willingly. I have always liked him. I've also surprised myself by the realisation that I think I might love him. We spent last night together."

Claudia let her confession hang in the air. A silence passed between the brother and sister. In the background they could hear the sound of clanging swords and cheering as soldiers wagered on a fencing bout. The centurion seemed unperturbed by his sister's revelation, however, indeed there was even a hint of a knowing smile on his face.

"I am going to surprise you by what I have to say, Claudia. The plan was not for you to seduce Gaius, but rather for Gaius to seduce you. Father may be powerful, but he's also predictable. I knew he would use you, like he's used you in the past. I'm just

211

sorry that I have used you as well. We've suspected him of being an enemy of the state for some time. We just needed some proof. For once you were the victim of a honey trap. Have you passed on to father the information about Galen finding a cure to the plague? Have you baited the hook?"

A dozen thoughts galloped around the stunned woman's mind, kicking up dust. All was, momentarily, a blur. Claudia felt like crying again, but she no longer would be able to embrace her brother. Her world was turned upside down. The huntress had become the prey. When, or if, she saw Maximus again she didn't know whether she would fall into his arms or slap him around the face. Perhaps she would do both. Her father had used her for years. But this was a new hurt, a new betrayal. Claudia merely nodded in reply, unable to look at her brother.

"Do you know what he is now planning to do? Is he going to attempt to kill Galen and steal the cure?" Atticus asked, raising his voice a little and losing his composure. The centurion leaned across the desk, his eyes burning with curiosity – and something else. Despite Claudia looking distraught the soldier still needed to question his sister. Duty called.

"Yes," Claudia murmured, her chin buried in her chest. She seemed in a stupor. Pale. Half dead.

"The more you can tell me, the better it will be for you. If you can help bring father to justice then I can petition the Emperor to grant you immunity from prosecution. I do not want you sharing father's fate," Atticus said in earnest – and also to encourage her to confess. "Do you know his plans in regards to Marcus Pollux? He's been paying the grain administrator a substantial sum of money over the past few months." Agents of the Emperor had provided intelligence that the administrator was operating outside of his remit. But Atticus had discovered Pollux's links to his father

212

– from both searching through papers in his office and sleeping with his wife.

"Father has recently recruited a force of mercenaries. He's intending to burn down the warehouse on the river which stores the city's grain surplus. He believes that starvation will feed civil unrest – and lead to a revolution. Chen will lead the attack tonight. Father has been paying Pollux to purchase private stores of grain from the east."

"Tonight?!"

For the first time in their meeting shock and condemnation could be traced in Atticus' expression as he glared at his sister. The bronze stylus bent in his hand as the officer made a fist.

"What time tonight?" he hurriedly asked, standing over his sister.

"I don't know," Claudia replied, with shame and fear in her voice.

"How many men does he have?" Atticus demanded, glowering.

"I don't know."

"The only thing I know is that you've either helped save or damn the Empire, depending on what happens this evening." Atticus shook his head, in disappointment at his sister and from experiencing a sense of doubt over whether he could manage the situation.

"I'm sorry, I'm sorry," Claudia tearfully repeated.

"Apollo!" the centurion shouted, calling in the young legionary who was standing to attention outside his office. The soldier entered, struck by a rare desperation in Atticus' voice and bearing.

"Yes, Sir," Apollo said, partly distracted by the sight of the officer's tearful, but still beautiful, sister sitting on the chair before him. Half of her pinned-up hair hung untidily down her face. Her usually fine eyes were puffy.

"Immediately muster as many men as you can on the parade ground – officers, legionaries, archers, even raw recruits. I'll need a couple of trusted messengers too – one to be despatched to the Emperor, another to Maximus."

Cassius Bursus nodded and departed.

"There is one more important thing, Rufus. It's why I'm here. Father has instructed Chen to murder Gaius. He will do so after tonight."

"Then the bastard won't see the dawn," the centurion replied determinedly, as he pulled his sword belt around his waist.

He must be stopped.

"I care about him, more than you know. Do you think he may have feelings for me?" Claudia said, looking up, wide-eyed, at her brother – almost pleading with him to say "yes".

"No. I've lied to you enough over the past week. I have no wish to lie to you now. Gaius is in love with Aurelia. He's going to live with her – and ask her to marry him. You mustn't now come between them, Claudia. If Aurelia finds out about what happened last night then I'll know that it came from you – and you will then lose me if you ruin Gaius' happiness. The gods know that he deserves some."

Claudia's heart cracked, again. Perhaps the gods also knew that she deserved to be unhappy, the woman thought to herself. Her life had been a series of sins, strung out like jewels upon a necklace. But she believed that last night could not have been all an act. It had been real for her. Yet she loved him enough to not stand in the way of his happiness.

He's too good for me…

"I understand. I don't want to hurt him. Can you give a message to him though?"

214

"Of course," Atticus answered, with an air of understanding – realising how much pain, as well as shame, his sister must be enduring.

"Tell him he's still the most honourable man I know," Claudia said with sincerity and sadness, feeling more than half dead.

17.

Silvery-grey clouds marbled the night sky. The murky waters of the Tiber slapped against the jetty. A chill wind blew off the river. Cassius Bursus was just about to board a barge, along with a dozen fellow archers, after receiving his orders from Atticus.

"This is either my Venus – or Vulture – throw of the dice Apollo," the officer quietly said to his friend, feeling the need to confide in someone in the absence of Maximus. Atticus' usually calm and confident countenance was flecked with distress. A fear of failure was eclipsing a desire to succeed. He expected his first command to be in the forests of Germany, not on the streets of Rome. The centurion had mustered as many men as he could, as quickly as he could, to lead an advance force and protect the warehouse. Most of the Praetorian Guard had been off duty or outside of the barracks when he had heard about his father's plans to destroy the capital's grain surplus. He had left instructions to form-up and send a relief force to secure the warehouse, but at present the newly promoted officer only commanded around a hundred men to ward off the imminent attack.

"You'll be fine. What was it Maximus once said? Don't give me a great general, give me a lucky one. And you're the luckiest man I've ever met, Sir."

"Thanks for the – I think – vote of confidence. Let's hope my luck lasts out until the morning. If you make your arrows count, though, Apollo I may not need to rely on good fortune."

The two men shook hands and Atticus went back to address his men. He forced himself to smile, to give off an air of confidence. Yet, inside, he was mired in anxiety. *The burden of command.* Atticus wryly thought back to when he had been a poet, rather than a soldier, and the only things that he had had to worry about were writer's block and a broken heart. Now he needed to worry about the lives of the men under him – and a city and empire perishing.

Atticus ordered a small portion of his men to keep watch over the two narrow streets which led towards the warehouse. He also posted men to guard the entrances to the grain supply. The bulk of his force, however, was assembled before him in two ranks, across the main street which ran parallel to the river. The centurion began to notice the air mist up in front of him from the soldiers' breath. A few had a gleam in their eyes, looking forward to tasting glory or blood. Most of the men, their faces pale in the moonlight, wore more wary expressions, though. The numbers and nature of the enemy were still unknown. Some doubtless hoped that it would all just prove to be a false alarm – and the only thing they would have to do battle with tonight would be a jug of wine back at the barracks.

Atticus thought about the many times he had lined up in a shield wall before – instead of facing it as he now was. He read the legionaries' faces and sympathised with how young he must have seemed, compared to other commanding officers. Gaius Maximus' optio was little substitute for Gaius Maximus. His reputation for conquests in the bedroom would mean nothing on the battlefield.

My first command could prove my last.

*

Blood marked the Chinaman's tunic from the task he had completed that night before meeting up with his small army of mercenaries. They were a force to be reckoned with, he judged with pride. Chen wanted to prove to his master that he could be a trusted leader of men, as well as a loyal lone assassin. The new regime would need new commanders. He hoped that Pollio Atticus would recognise what a feat of cunning and logistics it had been to smuggle all his soldiers, and their weapons, into the city. He had also smuggled several barrels of flammable oil through the city gates via a wine merchant.

The men congregated in a square, close by to the grain warehouse. Nigh on two hundred men, dressed in ordinary civilian clothes, which were concealing an array of cudgels and short swords, stood waiting to be unleashed. Many wished to just get on with the task, as the sooner they got their money the sooner they could spend it. Some of the men licked their lips at the prospect of committing an act of violence and terrorism. Rome, or the army, had made their lives a misery at some point. They would now take their revenge on the capital.

A few onlookers who lived around the square took in the ominous scene behind half-closed shutters. Others completely shut out the sight and sounds of the suspicious mob, not wanting any trouble. Calling on a force of vigils, or the Praetorian Guard even, could well lead to violence rather than prevent it.

Chen gave one last debrief to his six lieutenants, who were each responsible for a section of his army. He was confident that every man knew his purpose. Fear, as well as financial reward, would generate success, the Chinaman concluded. He reminded his officers that there should be no witnesses left at the warehouse. *Dead men tell no tales*. He also reminded his lieutenants of the plan to disperse the men throughout different districts in the capital, after the deed was done. *Nothing should be left to chance*. Chen pictured the warehouse ablaze – and also the Imperial Palace being stormed, after months of the capital facing starvation. Perhaps his master would let him take his daughter as his wife, as well as reward him with a generalship, when the dust settled. The Chinaman grinned, revealing a set of swollen gums and rotten teeth.

This command will be the first of many.

Silence and apprehension hung in the air, like the smell of a corpse. Spray from the river chilled the men's faces. Fear of the unknown chilled their hearts. Atticus was lost for words. He didn't know whether to tell a joke or warn his men of the seriousness of the situation. The newly promoted centurion thought that the usually laconic Maximus would have known what to say. A row of blank, or defeated, expressions stood before him – looking to him for direction and inspiration. Leadership.

I'm failing them… Losing them. And if I lose them, I'll lose the battle…

Atticus – and his men – were finally distracted from their mordant thoughts by the sound of distant voices and the low rumbling of footsteps. The centurion's ears pricked up and he raised his head and turned, as alert as a hunting dog.

The officer drew his sword – and the legionaries duly did the same. The metallic, scraping noise felt familiar, even comforting, to the centurion. Atticus squinted, trying to gauge the numbers and nature of the enemy appearing from around the end of the main avenue along the river. Atticus also recognised the sound of wagons trundling over cobblestones. Blades momentarily glinted in the moonlight. The oncoming force slowed, but halted not, as the front ranks took in the row of soldiers.

We're outnumbered. But we won't be out-fought.

Some veterans might have advised the centurion to attack – to seize the moment and the momentum. Others would have advised caution – to retreat and wait for reinforcements. Despite the gelid air a bead of sweat formed on the young officer's temple and ran down his jaw. His heart pounded like an army, either advancing or being routed.

Two options… Attack or retreat.

The number of the enemy continued to grow. Hydra-headed. Atticus began to discern the build and features of the front ranks of his father's mercenary force. They were well-built, with battle-hardened faces. As with his dinner parties, Pollio Atticus had spared no expense, Rufus thought. They were all former soldiers or gladiators, disciplined yet vicious.

Attack or retreat... Death or honour.

Atticus turned to observe dozens of legionaries staring at him, awaiting an order – any order. Their expressions faded into the background, however, as the centurion pictured his father, smiling in triumph at his failure.

Attack or retreat... There is no other option.

But there was. Instead of his father looming large in his mind's eye, Atticus pictured Maximus.

Sometimes it's not a question of attacking or retreating. Sometimes all you can do is just hold the line.

18.

"I worry that we may be spoiling the child. He's becoming too wilful and selfish," Marcus Aurelius remarked to his wife in their bedroom, furrowing his already wrinkled brow. He wrinkled his nose too, from the pungent smell of the jasmine and rose of his wife's perfume.

"And by 'we', I take it you mean me?" Faustina replied, arching her plucked eyebrows. She briefly stopped brushing her long, auburn hair to offer her husband both a questioning and accusing look. "An Empress should be beyond reproach, even from an Emperor," her mother had once told her. Even when looking haughty the Empress still appeared desirable. Age had not withered her. Childbirth had failed to ruin her figure. For once poets and fawning courtiers could be sincere when they complimented their Empress on her beauty. She had inherited her large, coquettish eyes from her mother – and could express attentiveness or boredom within the blink of an eye. All of her life Faustina had either been the daughter of an Emperor, or wife to one. She seldom believed she was playing a part, as she was seldom off stage. She was *Augusta*, far more even than her husband was an *Augustus*. He had been adopted, whereas she was noble.

As a young girl Faustina had loved her father dearly, and had taken instruction from her mother about being Empress. When duty called Faustina answered it. She had been married at fourteen, but quickly became at ease in the bedroom and at court. She had smiled when she needed to, praised the right gods on the right feast days, behaved with majesty or humility before the people

221

depending on the occasion, could say "Welcome" in over a dozen different languages, and had provided the Empire with heirs.

Early on in her marriage the people had praised Faustina for her fecundity. Coinage was also minted, honouring the Emperor's wife for her chastity (Rufus Atticus had nicknamed it "funny money" at the time, aware as he was of the Empress' infidelities). Once Rome's favourite daughter in her youth, Faustina was now called the "Mother of the People." And she loved her children in return – although she sometimes grew jealous and resentful, sensing that they loved their father more. But still she owed them a debt of duty, though she also possessed a sense of entitlement as Empress. And at present Faustina felt entitled to either disagree with, or ignore, her husband's dull moralising.

"It's not about assigning blame, but rather finding a solution to the problem," Aurelius replied, wishing to placate rather than provoke his wife. He wanted to be the voice of reason – but since when did people listen to reason, especially in regards to their children?

"Well I think we can both agree that your continued absence will do little to solve the problem, as you see it. Your letters to Commodus, extolling the virtues of Plato or instructing him to devote himself to geometry rather than fencing, are poor compensation for you actually being here, engaging with your son. He needs deeds, not words," the woman pronounced, somewhat relishing the scenario of being able to chastise her philosopher-husband. Faustina proceeded to turn to face her mirror, tossing her head in doing so, and continued to brush her hair.

"You know that I have duties as Emperor."

"You also have duties as a father," Faustina replied, this time raising her voice and losing her composure a little – although her outburst also coincided with her hairbrush becoming snagged, which may have increased her frustration. The Empress regained her poise, however. "We need not consider Commodus' behaviour as a problem, but rather as a prospective virtue. He will be Emperor one day. Wilfulness and selfishness are part of the job description. He is just growing accustomed to ruling and getting his own way."

Aurelius first sighed, as if wanting to release any anger or anxiety from his body, and then took a deep breath as if he were about to make a long speech. Yet he merely sighed again, too tired to argue.

Marriage is an endless campaign… And there are always more defeats than triumphs.

Faustina sighed to herself too as she looked up at the simmering, low-cut gown hanging above her dresser. It was made from the finest Chinese silks. She loved the feel of the material on her stomach, breasts and thighs – caressing her like fingertips. *He –* Avidius – had bought the dress for her last year (although unbeknownst to Faustina Pollio Atticus had given the soldier the garment to make a gift of it to his lover). She wanted to wear the dress for him this evening, to have him undress her with his eyes. Yet her lover had met with her husband tonight instead of her, to talk about politics.

As much as Faustina, as a mother, could criticise Aurelius for being an absent father, she was glad of being able to live a separate life from her husband as a wife. *Absence may make the heart grow fonder, but familiarity breeds contempt.* Living apart for most of the year had probably saved, rather than ruined, their marriage. Faustina recalled how they had had much to catch up on during her husband's first night back in the Imperial Palace. She had asked him about the war in the north and he had asked her about Commodus. They had slept together too, although she had considered that he had done so out of politeness. But by the following evening a familiar wall of silence had grown up between them both again. Neither was sure who had laid the first brick – and neither appeared to want to breach the wall now it was in place.

Aurelius climbed into bed. Perhaps he would pretend to fall asleep again before she joined him, Faustina thought – and hoped. The Empress finished brushing her hair and then began to clean the make-up off her face, before rubbing oil into her skin. Her back was turned to the bed but she occasionally glanced at her husband in the mirror, who had his back turned towards her. Occasionally she opened her legs slightly, tilted her head back and brushed her fingertips along and between her thighs. Her skin tingled as she imagined *him* touching her. She pictured his brooding looks, his strong jaw and cleft chin – which she would kiss and run her tongue over. They didn't make children in the bedroom, they made love. Faustina had taken many lovers over the years, but this affair was different. She believed that she loved Cassius. She remembered their last night together, how their sweat-glazed bodies had slotted against each other, and how Cassius had promised he would take care of her and Commodus if anything happened to Aurelius. And he had meant it.

Yet Faustina would never leave her husband. She was the wife of the Emperor over the mistress of a soldier. She was the First Lady of Rome – and the Mother of the People could not abandon her children. She admired and was devoted to Marcus, too – in her own way. She thought him intelligent, hard-working and just. He was a good man. *Too good.* His decency was construed as a weakness. Rome needs a Caesar, rather than Cicero, as its Emperor. She would sometimes shout and rail at him, but he would neither raise his hand nor voice in return. She occasionally wished he would – just to show some passion. *Be a man, rather than a statue…*

224

As well as tingling for Cassius, Faustina felt twinges of guilt in regards to her husband. *He should take a mistress, either out of desire or revenge... He is probably the only faithful Emperor in the history of Rome... I want him to feel what I feel when I'm with Cassius – love and happiness...* Faustina thought how over the years numerous courtesans, young men and young wives had batted their eyes at the stoical Emperor, but he had merely rolled his eyes in reply. He took in little wine and ate simply. The only things he devoured were his books. *He looks more like the grandfather of his people now. More than love him, I pity him... He's too good – for this world.*

Marcus Aurelius pretended to be asleep. Rather than worrying about the future of his marriage he was thinking about Rufus Atticus' news – and the future of Rome. He tried to remain stoical, but couldn't.

19.

"Hold the line!" Atticus bellowed over the roar of the approaching enemy. At first the mercenaries had walked towards the line of legionaries, spitting out curses and looking to intimidate the soldiers through the weight of their numbers. But, twenty yards from their enemy, the snarling pack were let off the leash and ordered to attack the praetorians.

Spear tips and sword points quickly poked out from the front rank of shield wall. The soldiers gritted their teeth and gripped the sweat-soaked straps of their scutums, ready to stand firm against the first wave of men who would crash against their human dam.

Chen stood on top of one of his wagons to survey his battlefield, his face twisted in malice. The Chinaman had been surprised by the presence of the soldiers but he judged that the small contingent of praetorians could but delay, rather than defeat, his purpose. His men would punch through part of the shield wall, pour through the breach and then attack them from all sides. They could either retreat now, or die.

The second rank of legionaries stood as a buttress behind the first. The second and third ranks of mercenaries spurred the first on. Their lack of shields gave the praetorian's a distinct advantage, however, as the two forces met, like two rows of butting stags or rams. Atticus pushed his shield forward and stabbed, furiously and ferociously, at his enemies. His gladius was slick with blood immediately as it sliced through hands, thighs, shins and necks. A familiar cacophony of sounds reverberated in his eardrums – the clang of swords, blood-curdling screams and thousands of curses being traded to create a crescendo of hatred. Cudgels and short swords thumped upon his scutum. His men, to the left and right of him, similarly worked themselves up into a frenzied rhythm of carnage. Sword arms glistened with blood and gore. When they felled their enemies they swiftly stabbed them in the chest or face. A wounded man can still fight on, but a dead man can't. Atticus killed and injured more than most, looking to lead by example as well as just survive.

But still the enemy advanced. Hydra-headed.

*

"Pollio Atticus? I thought that I was the only one who was supposed to make house calls in the middle of the night. Are you ill?"

The statesman, accompanied by a couple of (armed) attendants, had entered Galen's ground floor laboratory. The smell of sulphur, tar and garum (from the physician's evening meal) filled Atticus' nostrils. The aristocrat turned his nose up as much at the décor as the pungent smells, though. Instead of statues lining the walls Atticus took in all manner of ghastly looking stuffed animals. A half-eaten plate of food sat next to a half-dissected lamb. Various noxious liquids simmered away on a large table, which groaned under the weight of scientific apparatus.

"Politicians are not so different from doctors. I also stay up late and work tirelessly for the good of the people."

Galen couldn't quite tell in the half-light of the laboratory whether the senator's expression was unctuous or ironic.

"There are indeed perhaps a few similarities between our professions. Many politicians and doctors are overpaid – and many peddle false hope."

Galen remained seated at his desk at the end of the room, but stopped writing up his notes. He glanced nervously at the two menacing-looking attendants who had started to inspect and handle some of his equipment.

227

"You forgot to mention that we are also both akin to gods, doctor. When the people venture to the temple each day and pray for prosperity and good health are they not really supplicating us?"

"I'm not sure whether even *my* ego would permit me to call myself a god. Not even physicians live forever – and politicians more than most can suffer earthly changes in fortune."

"You are right, but changes in fortune can sometimes be for the better. As they have been today, when I heard that you had discovered a cure for the plague. You have saved the Empire, Galen. For once the peoples' praise might match the esteem which you hold yourself in. Do you have the cure in your possession? Who else knows about it?"

"I am afraid that I have been sworn to secrecy," Galen said, shifting uncomfortably in his seat, his eyes flitting back and forth between the statesman and his bodyguards.

"That's a shame. Fortunately you seem to possess the right instruments to make you open up to us though – and to extract any secrets," Atticus replied, smiling with equanimity, as he casually picked up a surgical clamp and bone saw from the table next to him. "I'd prefer for you to cooperate Galen, rather than have to say to you in the morning, 'Physician, heal thyself'."

"I'm grateful for you reminding me of a fundamental difference between our two professions. A doctor gives an oath that he 'will do no harm'. I'm not sure if a politician could give such an oath, let alone keep it."

"You think you have an answer for everything, doctor. But what would you say if I cut your tongue out?" The senator loomed over the physician at his desk. Cruelty gleamed in his eyes like two polished gold coins.

I'll extract the truth from him or he'll take his secrets – and the cure – to the grave.

"I'd answer for him," Gaius Maximus remarked, appearing from out of the doorway situated behind the physician. The centurion had listened from a storeroom whilst he heard the statesman incriminate himself – but decided to intervene when he felt that Galen might be in danger. From what Rufus Atticus' messenger had reported it seemed that Claudia's testimony would be enough to convict Pollio Atticus of treason, but his presence at Galen's laboratory cemented his guilt further. Unfortunately Rufus had been right about his father.

The esteemed politician was, for once, lost for words when he witnessed the fearsome soldier standing before him. His features dropped, as if he had just been told that someone had died – or that his fortune had been lost at sea.

"I am afraid that you have been wrongly informed, senator. I warrant that you will have more chance of finding the shield of Achilles, or the Golden Fleece, upon that dissected lamb over there, than the cure for the plague here tonight in this the laboratory. Much like the idea of an honest politician, the cure doesn't exist. There, see, and you didn't even have to torture me to discover the truth," Galen said, enjoying the moment. The enemy of his friend had been defeated.

Half a dozen stern-faced legionaries followed Maximus out of the storeroom, ready to apprehend their quarry. Pollio Atticus grimaced, baring his teeth like a cornered wild animal.

"It seems that the spider has been caught up in his own web," Maximus remarked, little masking the antagonism he felt towards the enemy of the state. "Or rather you've been caught up in a web of your own son's making. Rufus knew that you would be tempted by the prize of a cure to the plague. He also rightly judged that you would use your own daughter to glean information out of me. There are beasts which devour their own offspring that have treated their children better than you have yours. But Claudia has

229

finally taken her revenge and betrayed you. I've ordered a number of my men to search your study. I expect that they will uncover evidence of bribery and propaganda. No amount of dinner parties will be able to buy you favours and influence now."

Pollio Atticus glowered, unblinkingly, at the low-born but arrogant centurion. *Aurelius' lap-dog.* Resentment powered his heart and thoughts. He had been betrayed by his own family – the people who he had spent his life trying to protect and better. They could now burn and starve with the rest of Rome.

"You should take consolation from the fact that you will do that which even Cicero failed to do as a statesman, namely unite the classes. Senators, soldiers, merchants and plebs alike will all want to see you strung up for your crimes – and watch the crows feast upon you from the feet up. I may even request what's left of you, to dissect as a medical specimen. At least in death you may prove to be of some positive use to Rome."

"The crows will have plenty to feast on after this evening, doctor, don't worry. If you wish to do no harm to Rome, then you will have to do no harm to me. The Emperor will soon discover that I am of more use to the capital alive than dead," Pollio Atticus said, regaining some of his confidence, believing that he could still escape prosecution. *Aurelius is weak… He will need my grain reserves. He will negotiate…*

"I take it that you're referring to your plan to destroy the grain surplus? Rufus is in the process of dealing with your band of mercenaries as we speak. But even if your Chinaman succeeds in burning down the granary I'm sure that I can make Pollux open up, to use your phrase, and tell me where he is storing the grain that you have recently purchased from the east," Maximus said, thinking how, as much as he was enjoying apprehending the statesman, he would rather be fighting alongside his friend. *I am a soldier rather than spy.*

Pollio Atticus momentarily mused that if Chen encountered his son at the wharf, then he would kill him – and he knew not if he should feel pleasure or pain at the prospect of his son/enemy dying.

"You think that you have won – and thought of everything? Yet come the morning, centurion, you will feel a stronger sense of regret and remorse than I," Atticus announced, forebodingly.

Before Maximus had time to draw any meaning from the senator's words he was called upon to draw his sword. Pollio Atticus, realising that his capture would lead to his death, glanced at his two attendants and nodded his head – subtly commanding them to attack and aid his escape. *Desperate times call for desperate measures*. Atticus turned and ran towards the door at the other end of the laboratory, where he had originally entered. The two bodyguards filled the space he vacated and stood between their master and the praetorian.

Rather than just looking to stand guard and buy the statesman time to retreat, the larger of the attendants took the fight to his enemy. His muscular forearms were covered with a number of tattoos of small swords, signifying kills in the arena from his time as a gladiator. He charged forward like a bull with his large shoulders rolling – and his head down. Maximus reacted quickly and threw a ceramic beaker at his assailant. The beaker smashed against his forehead and a roar of anger swiftly turned into a howl of pain. The bovine, tattooed attendant lost concentration – without losing momentum – and when he regained his senses he found that the centurion was about to punch his gladius into his sternum. Even Galen winced as he heard the sound of the blade scrape against bone. The bull had been slain. Maximus raised his legs and kicked the body away from him, freeing his sword.

The second bodyguard, his wiry body twitching with unreleased energy and hatred, stood his ground rather than attacking the soldier. Two triangular bronze blades from the daggers he wielded glinted in the yellow light from the oil lamps hanging over him. In order to distract his opponent, to grant more time for his master to escape or to intimidate the centurion, the bodyguard commenced to skilfully twirl the knives around in his hands. Maximus merely rolled his eyes in response to the display, however, out of boredom and contempt. He turned his head, nodded to one of his legionaries to toss him the javelin he was holding – and a few moments later skewered his enemy.

Pollio Atticus walked around the corpse of his attendant as a brace of legionaries, who had been covering the front entrance to the house, led the statesman back towards Maximus.

"It looks like you'll have to now hire another couple of bodyguards, as well as a good advocate," the centurion drily remarked, whilst his thoughts turned again to how his former optio was faring at the wharf.

Hold the line.

20.

The tang of blood and sewerage from the river swirled around in the night air. Rufus Atticus' sword arm ached – and felt numb – as if it were one large bruise hanging from his shoulder. Although his throat felt increasing sore, Atticus still offered up words of encouragement to his men, in between trying to catch his breath. Thankfully, at last, there was a respite in the fighting. The front ranks of the enemy drew back. Once bitten, twice shy. Only half of the mercenaries facing them found the will to jeer at the legionaries now. A line of corpses was strewn across the street and acted as an effective barricade for the shield wall. They would have to step over their fallen comrades to get to their enemy now. Just surviving felt tantamount to a victory at the moment for the outnumbered soldiers, but Atticus knew that the only thing that he had won so far was time. But for now that was enough.

The centurion instructed his men in the second rank to trade places with the wounded in the first rank – and offered up a silent prayer to Apollo to save them all.

"Not one step back," Chen commanded, gnashing his teeth, but such was his frustration and ire that he did so, unconsciously, in his native language. Back in his homeland the first rank would have been ordered to fall upon the enemy's swords, in order for the subsequent ranks to advance. As if in sympathy with the Chinaman the mule, pulling the wagon he was standing on, screeched in complaint and confusion. Chen took consolation whilst he seethed, however. He would soon be rid of praetorian gadflies, having sent a contingent of men around the backstreets to come out and attack the shield wall from behind. They would be trapped in a press, but instead of olive oil, blood would ooze out. But there must be blood soon, he thought, conscious of the time. If these praetorians were aware of his force's presence then others were doubtless being mobilised – and Chen had no wish to be trapped between a burning warehouse and small army of legionaries once he had set the building alight.

The barge bobbed gently up and down on the river. Cassius Bursus attuned his body to its rhythms – and took account of its movements for when he would unleash his arrows… And at last a target had come into sight. A wagon carrying barrels of oil stopped close to the riverside, instead of being hidden among a group of the enemy. Apollo lovingly stroked his bow, strengthened and decorated with horn, out of habit and superstition. He nocked a shaft and ordered a young legionary to light him – and the rest of the archers – up.

Make every arrow count.

The fifty or so men that Chen had ordered to attack the irksome shield wall from behind finally appeared from the mouth of a street across the way from the soldiers – and began to form up. They launched into a united roar, or jeer, partly to intimidate the legionaries – but more so to announce to their comrades that they could soon coordinate their offensives. Somewhat out of breath though, from having raced through the backstreets, the small force slowly – but menacingly – marched towards the thin red line of Roman shields.

"Second rank, about face," Rufus Atticus commanded, making his voice heard above all manner of other sounds. "Nothing has changed. We still need to just hold the line. We can and will fight on two fights, as Caesar did at Alesia – and these bastards before us now seem about as courageous as Gauls too, no? A relief force is on its way." Or rather two relief forces, the centurion hoped. Atticus possessed more confidence in his tone than he did in his

234

heart, but that was part of the brief of being an officer, he considered.

Both groups of mercenaries, either side of the lines of legionaries, raised their weapons aloft to signal to each other that they were ready to attack and trap their enemy in a fatal vice.

Atticus wiped the blade of his gladius on the skirt of his tunic. Many of the soldiers looked more like butchers than praetorians. Fear froze a few jaws and knuckles cracked, as men gripped their shields and swords once more. They would fight on – and not just because retreating or surrendering were no longer options. They would fight on, for their own survival, for the man standing next to them, and for the glory of Rome – and in that order, Atticus judged. He had a letter that would go to Maximus, to help sort out his affairs, should he not survive the night. He told himself that he had been in more perilous situations and lived to tell the tale, but he was at pains to remember exactly when those situations were. He briefly remembered *her*. He always believed that he would see Sara again, in this world or the next. The philosophical soldier offered up a prayer to the gods to either let him live or let him find peace in the next life – and remembered his Socrates: *Death may be the greatest of all human blessings*.

*

Chen licked his lips in anticipation of the imminent massacre. His only regret was that his own sword would remain unbloodied, as he surveyed the encounter from the rear. The mercenaries lowered their arms as the signal to attack, but at the same time Apollo and his small force of a dozen or so archers launched their volley of fire arrows into the barrels of oil. Not all of the missiles hit their mark, but enough did. And the first volley was quickly followed up with a second. The large, sharpened, burning arrowheads cracked open the casks and set their contents alight. Bright yellow flames slashed through the inky night, covering the wagon and the men surrounding the vehicle. Globules of burning oil spat out in all directions. The rearing and charging mules did much to spread the fire and create chaos. A few of the mercenaries rightly hacked one of the animals to death, inspiring others to do so as well.

Panic and confusion ensued, each fuelling the other. The main attack on the line of legionaries stalled as the mercenaries turned their heads to look backwards rather than forwards. A few believed that fire was raining down upon them from the gods, protecting the capital. The fire sowed disorder, and as men scattered to avoid the flames another target opened up to Apollo's archers – and they targeted the wagon accordingly. The fire spread like a plague. The highly flammable oil set light to anything it came in contact with – timber, clothes and skin. Rivulets of flames ran in between the cobble stones. Another wagon erupted, spewing out flames like a mini volcano. A few of the mercenaries were trampled underfoot – and burned alive. Smoke began to belch out from the conflagration and choke the enemy, too. The fire arrows which missed the targets of the wagons hissed and thudded into necks, chests and faces. The smell of burning flesh, as well as burning oil, began to singe nostrils. Some, fearing that they could be trapped by the fire, retreated or jumped into the river.

Chen's eyes were ablaze and his rage burned as hotly as the fire. His mission, rather the grain warehouse, was turning into ash.

Atticus again ordered his men to hold the line. As tempted as some were to use the distraction and destruction of the fire as an opportunity to escape – or even counter-attack the enemy – the centurion realised that they should still just retain their defensive position.

Free from the threat of the fire – and the contingent of archers on the barge – the mercenaries positioned on the warehouse side of the battle decided to continue their attack. Their blood was up

– and the offensive might spur their comrades on to similarly engage the enemy. The Roman shield wall would break, as soon as it was pressured from both sides. Yet the encirclers were about to be encircled.

As well as sending messengers to the Emperor and Maximus earlier, Atticus had also sent a young legionary off to his old friend Milo, the landlord at *The Trojan Pig*. The tavern would be inhabited by various ex-soldiers, dockers, guild members and boisterous drunks. It was their city as much as his – and Atticus had asked Milo to mobilise as many men as he could to bolster his forces. They would be rewarded with gold, as well as a sense of pride.

Some looked as if they had already been in a fight that night – and had lost: scar-faced, haggard and glassy-eyed. Some were armed with short swords and clubs but others carried carpentry hammers, bread knives, rocks and clay jugs. They were all fuelled, however, with a belly full of wine and a sense of patriotism. They walked towards the line of mercenaries in a loose, but purposeful formation. Atticus offered up a salute to Milo. The landlord, who had recruited his rag-tag army from his own tavern and a couple of neighbouring establishments, gave a curse-filled order to attack. A handful of mercenaries at the end of the line escaped while they still could. But the would-be victors now became victims as they were caught between the praetorians and the tavern brawlers. Blood splattered the cobblestones. Legionaries stabbed, sliced and eviscerated. Retreat and surrender were not an option. Howls of rage and agony both spiralled up into the air, like the nearby tongues of fire. A skull was stoved in by a water jug. It was a massacre, but not the one Chen had envisioned. Soldiers and citizens out-swore and out-fought the band of cynical mercenaries.

By the time the legionaries and Milo's men had slaughtered the last of their opponents, over half of Chen's forces had retreated, routed by fire and fear. Atticus finally breathed out, believing the worst to be over. Sweat began to pour down his face from the furnace-like heat of the burning wagons – and corpses. He offered up a prayer of thanks to Apollo. He would have his men advance, in formation, but he would allow them to catch their breath first.

"Good job, Sir," Gneaus Casca, a grizzled veteran of campaigns in both Egypt and Germany, expressed whilst standing next to his centurion, nodding in appreciation at his officer. Casca was a descendant of the famous legionary Tiro Casca, who had fought alongside Julius Caesar and Maximus' antecedent, Lucius Oppius – the Sword of Rome. "You held the line."

"No, Gnaeus, we all held the line," Atticus replied, warmly clasping Casca on the shoulder – thinking how the veteran's approval meant more to him than a dozen medals.

*

"If I can see the weaknesses opening up throughout the Empire, you can be sure that our enemies can see them, too. If Aurelius cannot stem the tide against corruption, the tribes of the north, and the plague, then how do you think his wastrel son will fare when he comes to power? Rather than stem the tide we will all drown in a flood. The Empire will fall. A golden age will turn to rust…In restraining me, you are shackling progress." A proud, but defeated, Pollio Atticus carped on as a legionary bound his hands and feet with rope. Partly Maximus had wanted to restrain Atticus to prevent him from trying to escape again – but more so he wished to humiliate the self-important statesman and treat him like a common criminal. He envisioned him being locked up for years, like Vercingetorix – only seeing daylight on the day of his execution.

The centurion turned a deaf ear to the disgraced politician's protestations. He spoke instead to Galen, in order to convince the doctor that it may not be safe for him to remain in his house. It would be better for him to spend the night in the Imperial Palace, where Maximus could guarantee his safety. At first Galen was dismissive of the soldier's fears but eventually Maximus won the argument (it was perhaps the first time he, or anyone, had won an argument with the doctor).

After Galen had collected some things – and attended to a number of his experiments in his laboratory – they were ready to leave. Just as they were about to go, however, a breathless red-haired legionary, Horatius, rushed in. Maximus had sent the soldier to Aurelia's house earlier, in order to inform her that it was unlikely that he would be home that evening. Despite the strangeness of the scene – the restrained statesman and unfamiliar scientific equipment – the dutiful Horatius made a direct line for his centurion. His expression was pale, disturbed. He tried to compose himself before he spoke, but couldn't. He was unable to look his officer squarely in the eye, like he had been drilled to do when delivering a message or orders. Horatius leaned into the officer, gently laid a hand on his shoulder, and whispered something into his ear. As he did so Maximus looked like his legs might give way from underneath him. His fingers dug into the table like talons to prop himself up. The soldier's face first screwed itself up, as if it were about to collapse upon itself in grief – but then became a picture, a paragon, of anger. But anger was overthrown by sorrow again, as Horatius finished his whispered report. A couple of tears streamed down Maximus' cheek – and he seemed dead to the world.

All present were mystified by the exchange and intrigued by the news the centurion could have received from the young soldier, except Pollio Atticus – who now more than ever gave off the appearance of a condemned man. The politician attempted to look innocent when the centurion glanced in his direction, but for once he failed to do so.

239

Maximus calmly walked towards the prisoner, drew his sword and plunged the blade into Pollio Atticus' throat. Blood sprayed and gurgled from the fatal wound. Maximus grabbed the statesman's toga and briefly held him up, wanting to look him in the eye as the light, and life, was extinguished from his aspect. He then let the body slump to the ground. The centurion's expression seemed just as detached and lifeless as that of the corpse at his feet. Without a word, ignoring his duties and the people around him, the blood-strewn soldier proceeded to walk away. No one thought to try and apprehend the murderer of the prisoner. Galen, after recovering from the shock of what he had just witnessed, pursued his friend out of the house. But Maximus was nowhere to be seen. The night had already swallowed him up.

21.

There was a hypnotic beauty to the reflection of the swirling, amber blaze in the Tiber. But the reality, behind the reflection, was far uglier and deadlier. Timber from the wagons crackled and corpses sizzled. Smoke blackened all, a chorus of coughs sang out throughout the street and men shielded their faces from the intense heat. Blood and fire. The scene felt like Hades on earth, Rufus Atticus thought. The acrid smell – and gruesome sight – of a mule's eyeball burning whilst the rest of its head remained untouched, made a young legionary retch. Atticus heard Gnaeus Casca describe the aftermath as being like a "charred charnel house".

Atticus and his men moved forward, and were met with little resistance. The battle was won. The task was to secure the peace. Surrender was now an option for the enemy, although those uninjured preferred to retreat and escape. The centurion tasked Milo and his men to make sure that the fire did not spread to the buildings facing the river. The promise of more gold spurred them on in their civic duty. He also asked Milo to attend to the wounded. Some of his men were beyond saving, though. The next river they would be crossing would be the Styx, rather than Tiber. But they would mourn their fallen comrades later. There was work still to be done.

Earlier in the battle, after Chen had sensed that the tide was turning in the favour of the praetorians, he had raced towards the rear of his army in order to prevent the beginnings of a retreat. He had drawn his sword, bellowed out orders to advance and threatened his men – and he had even killed a couple of deserters to make an example of them – but not even the Chinaman could hold back the waters of defeat. The blaze had raged on and the mercenaries routed. One of his lieutenants had reported that the force, who were due to ambush the shield wall from behind, had themselves been ambushed and overwhelmed. Chen had again let out a curse in his native language and had vowed that he would hunt down and kill whoever had betrayed his master. If guarded by Hercules himself Chen would still torture and terminate the traitor. When his lieutenant reported that the centurion commanding the enemy was their master's son, the Chinaman was possessed by only one thought: *Kill him*.

Chen swam against the stream, heading in the opposite direction to the dishonourable curs of his men. His body firmed up beneath his blood and oil-soaked tunic. His skin glowed orange as he grew closer to the flames – and seemingly walked through them. He reached up and fingered a small piece of jade which hung around his neck. His father had given him the talisman as a reward for his first kill, at the age of fourteen. Out of superstition and habit he touched the stone every time he was about to kill someone.

The Chinaman drew his curved, polished sword and swiped the air with a flick of his wrist, cutting a path through the grey clouds of smoke.

Rufus Atticus was at the vanguard of his men. Flanked by two legionaries he moved forward, sidestepping corpses and puddles of flames. He passed a wagon, which had been turned sideways, half blocking the street. When he passed the vehicle flames spurted up and set light to a patch of oil, which ran along the other side of the street – causing a wall of fire which cut him off from the rest of his men. Atticus had little time to take in the situation, however, as the two legionaries beside him advanced to engage the solitary swordsman standing before them.

The Chinaman wore a deranged look on his face, as if drunk or drugged. He barked out something in a barbaric tongue and then spat out an insult, directed at the centurion, which the legionaries comprehended not, but seemed to contain the word "honour" or "dishonour".

The first legionary felt a rush of blood and ran and slashed at the enemy in one movement. Chen gracefully avoided the attack and deftly sliced his opponent's forearm, disarming him. The last thing the soldier heard was his gladius clang on the ground, before the tip of the Chinaman's sword sliced open his jugular vein.

The second legionary understandably approached the barbarian with more caution, crouching behind his large shield. Despite the leather-faced veteran's wealth of experience in combat he was unsure of his strategy in dealing with the mercenary, who had bested his comrade with such poise and savagery. Before the soldier had a chance to settle upon a plan of attack though, the assassin lunged forward with his body and sword in one motion and punctured both the legionary's shield and abdomen.

The centurion briefly closed his eyes in remorse – he had lost two more men, needlessly, after the battle was over. His eyes burned with scorn, however, when he opened them again.

Kill him.

Flames whipped up in the air behind the Chinaman. His face was streaked in sweat and spotted with blood. His cruel mouth twisted itself into a crueller smile as he glowered at the soldier. Atticus thought how Chen could have come from Hades, having been spat back out.

"Who betrayed our plans?" Chen demanded, rather than asked.

The centurion remained resolutely silent. *If I don't kill him, he'll kill Claudia.* He dropped his shield, believing that it could prove a cumbersome hindrance in combating the agile Chinaman, and swished his sword around in his hand, loosening up his wrist and arm. He was conscious of the throwing dagger he still possessed on the back of his belt – but was also conscious of how agile his father's bodyguard was.

"If you don't want to talk, that's fine. I'll be happy to cut the answers out of you."

Atticus approached his enemy; his men, shouting behind a wall of fire, spoke for him.

"Stick him, Sir… Kill the bastard…,"

The legionaries rated their officer as one of the best swordsman in the barracks, perhaps even quicker and more skilful than Maximus, but the foreign mercenary was an unknown quantity. A couple of soldiers readied their javelins to try and spear the enemy, should it look like their centurion was doomed. The shot would be difficult through all the flames and smoke, however.

Chen's speed – and the superior length of his blade – put Atticus on the back foot immediately. The best the soldier could do at present was just parry his opponent's attacks, which seemed to come from all angles; there wasn't any time to recover and launch counter-attacks. A song of swords rang out over the background of the snarling fire. Thankfully there were breaks in Chen's offensives. The assassin commenced to circle and prowl around his enemy before launching swift, brief sorties – a predator, toying with his prey. But Atticus hoped that confidence would breed over-confidence. If he could momentarily distract or decentre the Chinaman he might have a chance to make his throwing dagger count.

"Tell me, does my father house you with his slaves, or his pets? He spoke to me about you once. He says you were always eager to please, like a woman – or bitch…,"

Chen's next attack was more ferocious, but less clinical. He was also more breathless and less in control of himself when he spoke.

"I'm going to gut you like an animal – and make you scream like a woman."

"But you'll still be you and I'll still be me," Atticus replied, both unable and unwilling to mask his superiority and amusement in relation to his father's bodyguard.

Chen paused as a raw resentment welled up inside his chest – and a certain self-realisation dawned upon his face. Atticus sensed his opportunity. He would be throwing the knife with his weaker arm, but it had been strong enough in the past. His left hand crept behind his back but then unleashed itself like a ballista. The blade was aiming for Chen's right ribs but Chen quickly turned his body and brought his sword across, deflecting the dagger away. The assassin flared his nostrils and was angry at himself, as well as the soldier, for his opponent nearly besting him. There would be no respite now.

Kill him.

The flurry of lunges and slices came thicker and faster than before. He had felt safer earlier when being attacked by scores of mercenaries as he stood in the shield wall, compared to the threat of his current, solitary, opponent. Chen moved relentlessly forward, and Atticus retreated. His back was soon pressed against the plaster wall of the building which looked out onto the Tiber. The centurion flinched as his head nearly struck an arrow, still burning and lodged in a wooden shutter. Exhaustion – and the assassin's skill – told. Chen increased, rather than diminished, the power of his attacks. He eventually knocked the soldier's gladius from his hand. Atticus gazed at his enemy with a mixture of defeat and defiance. Rufus noted earlier that some of his men had their javelins still in their hands, ready to cut down the mercenary. But even if they had a will to do so, their view of Chen was now obscured by the burning wagon and haze of smoke.

"Feel free to come back and haunt me when you die, centurion. That way you can watch me when I cut off the head of your friend, Maximus."

Chen sniggered after speaking. The tip of his sword hung cruelly under Atticus' left eye. He could smell the garlic on the Chinaman's breath and the oil on his clothes.

"You'll see the fires of Hades before me," the Roman replied – and grabbed the flaming arrow next to him and tossed it against his enemy's chest. For a moment it looked like Chen wore a breastplate of gold. But it also looked like he would still run Atticus through, as he drew back his sword – ready to stab the centurion. But the Chinaman's tunic was too heavily doused in oil. Tongues of fire quickly licked his throat and then his face. For once the fearless assassin howled in fear and agony. His screams cut through the night air like a bolt of lightning. Atticus hurriedly gave the human torch a wide berth. Chen dropped his sword and attempted to beat the flames out with his hands – but his hands duly caught on fire. When he fell to the ground and rolled around in an attempt to extinguish the flames, he rolled around in oil. His skin blistered. The Chinaman writhed and stretched out his body – and then doubled-up into a ball. But the screaming didn't stop. The fire ate into his cheeks and eyes. The centurion was tempted to pick up his enemy's sword and put him out of his misery. But for once, Rufus Atticus refused to give into temptation.

*

Earlier in the evening Chen had cut through arteries and veins, so blood had both gushed and oozed out of Aurelia's body. Blood could be found on her bedclothes, the flowers on her desk, the tiled floor and the mosaics and paintings on the wall depicting scenes from Virgil's Idylls.

Pollio Atticus had ordered his bodyguard to murder the woman, in order to exact his revenge against Maximus. He would make him suffer – and then have him killed. An agent of the statesman had reported how close the officer was to Aurelia. Atticus not only wanted to pay the soldier back for thwarting his plans three years ago, before the Battle of Pannonia, but for stealing his son away from him. The officer had introduced his son to Aurelius – and Pollio considered him to be the reason why his son was now loyal to the Emperor rather than his own father. Pollio Atticus always settled his debts, in his favour.

Chen, accompanied by a quartet of trusted men, had forced his way into the house. No explanations were given, no words were uttered, as the staff were slaughtered. *Dead men tell no tales.* Aurelia and Helena had run up to Aurelia's bedroom and had tried to escape out of the window. But Chen had discovered them. He had been tempted to give the pretty serving girl to his men, as a prize. But time was precious, so he had stabbed her through the midriff and let her bleed to death. Chen had been more meticulous and imaginative when it came to killing Aurelia, however, as his master had ordered. He had first beat any resistance out of her. He had then clinically sliced open her hamstrings, breasts and face. "I want him to barely recognise her… Make her suffer, so he'll suffer," Pollio Atticus had remarked, whilst casually rearranging the folds in his toga.

Aurelia's last thoughts had been a prayer to God, for Maximus.

By the time Maximus had reached the house and found Aurelia her corpse had stiffened. He first properly covered up her naked, bloody body. Her face was horribly disfigured but he still held her in his arms and kissed her forehead, rocking her as if she, or he, were a distressed child. He frequently smeared himself in her blood, trying to wipe the tears from his eyes. Rage and remorse hammered upon his heart, alternating their blows.

As Maximus finally got up to leave, his hand now gripping his sword rather than cradling her head, he noticed the gold band on Aurelia's bedside table. It was the ring, back from the engravers, that she was intending to give him. He read the inscription, written on the inside of the band.

The light shines in the darkness.

*

The legionaries clapped the archers on the back and hailed them as heroes as they reached dry land again, though the archers felt the infantryman were the heroes for fighting in the shield wall against such superior numbers. Banter and roars of laughter could now be heard over the roar of the receding blaze. They would all be drinking and swapping stories long into the night – and morning. Milo would open the good stuff too, and either lower the prices of his wine or whores – but not both.

Spray still freckled Apollo's brow as he made his way through the crowd of jubilant soldiers. The tension only left his features, however, when he spied his centurion. The archer recognised a palpable relief in Atticus' expression too, little realising how much of that relief was due to being alive, rather than winning his first battle as a commander. The two friends met and shook hands.

"You've helped save Rome. They'll be a host of senators wanting to have dinner with you now, rather than just their wives," Apollo joked.

"I didn't save Rome alone," the centurion replied, looking on the men around him with a sense of pride and gratitude. "Thank you for making your arrows count."

"Well, if I'm honest, I didn't make them all count. One went wayward I think, and just struck some shutters on one of the buildings."

"That one counted too, don't worry," Atticus said, beaming with wry amusement. He also smiled due to the realisation that he had one less burdensome decision to make as a centurion – that of choosing his optio.

Epilogue

The afternoon sky was fretted with a lattice-work of snow-white clouds. The copper rays of the sun bleached the stone and plaster walls of the bustling, expansive city. The fires from the street battle had long died out, indeed there was little or no evidence of a battle ever having taken place a few nights ago. Rome was Rome again, normalcy reigned – for nearly everyone.

The roles were somewhat reversed when Galen encountered Rufus Atticus in the garden of the Imperial Palace. The usually po-faced doctor offered the centurion a consoling smile, while the often amused soldier remained disconsolate. The doctor was taking his leave from sitting with the Emperor, as Atticus arrived.

Marcus Aurelius sat on a chair on the lawn, wearing a sunhat akin to the kind that Octavius Caesar had worn as a boy and man. The Emperor took off the hat, however, to take in the centurion. His eyes were red-rimmed with drink and sleeplessness, or both. His mouth was uncharacteristically downturned. His gait was as heavy as his heart. Although Atticus had washed his tunic since the battle it was still stained with blood and smelled of smoke.

"Please Rufus, sit down. I take it that you haven't heard anything from Maximus?"

"No. No one has."

After saying goodbye to Aurelia, Maximus had gone back to the barracks, collected his personal belongings and disappeared. He had, however, left a letter each for Atticus and the Emperor, which largely expressed the same sentiments.

"The army and the Empire have had their pound of flesh out of me... Treat me like I'm a dead man. Don't try and look for me. All you'll find is the ghost of someone I used to be... I have valued

249

your friendship over the years; if you have valued mine then leave me be…,"

"And how are you, Rufus?"

"The art of living is more like wrestling than dancing," the centurion evenly replied, quoting a maxim that the Emperor had once shared with him.

"And how are you wrestling with the fact that you were right, in regards to your suspicions about your father?" Aurelius refrained from asking how Atticus felt about his best friend having killed his father.

"Galen may not have found a remedy to the plague, but Rome has at least been cured of another disease this week," Atticus answered, matter-of-factly.

"And how is your sister?"

The Emperor judged that Claudia's confession had helped prevent her father's mercenaries from burning down the grain warehouse. Atticus had failed to mention in his report how she had confessed not in order to save Rome, but to try and save Maximus. Aurelius had spared her from prosecution and, fearing for her safety from any of her father's agents who may wish to take their revenge, he offered her the use of one of his country estates to reside in. She had agreed to leave Rome, under the proviso that her husband would not be allowed to join her. Claudia had also insisted on paying for Aurelia's funeral. Her parting from her brother had been strained. Much had remained unsaid, on both sides.

"She will be fine," Atticus replied, lying. Claudia had discovered that she had a heart – only for it to be broken.

Aurelius was neither convinced by the centurion's words or by his demeanour. Atticus reminded Aurelius of himself, when he had mentioned to his wife that all would be well with Commodus.

"I'm pleased. You must feel free to take some leave and visit her, before we journey north again."

"Have you decided Maximus' fate?"

As seemingly abrupt as Atticus' question was, Aurelius had expected that the centurion would ask it, sooner rather than later. Maximus was now a deserter, one who had murdered a prisoner in cold blood – against the express wishes of his Emperor. Also, Aurelius had declined to tell Atticus that within two days of Maximus disappearing a number of his father's agents had been found brutally murdered. The Emperor had asked Galen to carry out autopsies on the bodies and concluded that the victims had been killed by an army issue gladius.

"As you may well have heard, Rufus, there are notable personages calling for me to condemn Maximus' actions, deem him a fugitive from justice and capture him. To make Maximus stand trial, and execute him. Occasionally politicians smell blood – whether mine or Maximus'. Antonius Reburrus, Julius Porticus and Gnaeus Varro – they are all getting on their moral high horses and calling for Maximus' head. I pray that sooner or later those self-same moral high horses trample them underfoot. They have been arguing that centurions, or friends of the Emperor, should not be above the law. I dare say that they would like politicians – and their friends – to remain above the law though.

'Should I give into their calls and prosecute Maximus, then I will earn the opprobrium of the Praetorian Guard, or indeed the entire army. Instead of preventing a riot the Guard may well cause one, should I hang Maximus out to dry. As you may well imagine, Rufus, I have been mulling over my options. I would rather have to answer the big philosophical problems, such as discern the nature of the gods or articulate what is the good life. I barely slept last night – not because I was worrying about my dilemma, but rather from trying to find a solution to it. Ironically, in such similar instances before, I would have consulted Maximus. Yet I realised that I still could – and that he had unwittingly provided me with a solution to square the circle and avoid upsetting either the Senate or the Guard – although neither may be entirely happy with the imminent outcome regarding Maximus' fate.

'Sometime in the near future Galen will discover a corpse and judge it to be that of the hero – and fugitive – Gaius Maximus. The face will be sufficiently disfigured, either from a flesh wound or fire, but Galen's word will be trusted. Maximus asked us to treat him like a dead man, so let us grant our friend his last request. I was reading Plutarch the other day, Rufus, and I came across the line, 'Nothing so befits a ruler as the work of justice'. I'm not sure that I am doing right by Maximus, in relation to the letter of Roman law, but I hope that I am being just. For true justice is mercy, I believe."

For the first time since finding out about Maximus, Aurelia and his father, Rufus Atticus' face lit up in a smile.

The light shines in the darkness, and the darkness comprehends it not.

Sword of Empire: Emperor

1.

Britain. 179AD.

Years of soldiering had marked his body and soul, but Rufus Atticus still retained his aristocratic bearing and handsome features. He turned the heads of not just the whores who worked at the inn, but some of the locals too. In particular he attracted the attention – and instant dislike – of Adminius Meriadoc, the son of the local chieftain. Adminius eyed the stranger with suspicion as he engaged Harbon, the mole-faced owner of the inn.

"Afternoon. I'm looking for an old friend of mine, who I believe lives in the area. His name is Quintus Verus," Atticus amiably remarked, despite being fatigued and soaked through. A young whore, Cordelia, gazed at the well-dressed and well-spoken newcomer with a suggestive expression. He looked like he might pay her double, though she would have gladly charged him half the fee should it have been in her power to do so. Jealousy now added fuel to the fire inside of the volatile Briton, Adminius. Before the stranger entered Cordelia had been eying him up. Adminius had had her last week – and he wanted her again.

"If he was any sort of friend wouldn't he have told you exactly where he lived?" Harbon replied, creasing his face up in scepticism. The stranger spoke the native language well but the innkeeper knew a Roman soldier when he saw one. But was he an officer or a deserter? Harbon was unsure whether to act with antagonism or deference towards the man who had just walked through his door.

"A fair point. But I can assure you I mean him no harm. Quintus will be pleased to see me, as I hope you're pleased to see me, too."

The hawk-eyed Harbon caught a glimpse of the gladius beneath the Roman's cloak as he extracted a couple of silver coins from his purse and placed them on the counter.

"You'll need to head west, along the road to the next village. Ask for him there. He lives in a house on the northern outskirts of the settlement, I believe. I hope that you don't mean him any harm, for your sake." Harbon had once seen Verus get into a fight and he still winced when picturing what had happened to his opponents – or victims rather.

Atticus nodded and grinned, more confident than ever that Quintus Verus was indeed the man he was searching for. Atticus then creased his face – and nose – up at the pungent smell of stale beer, sweat and boiled vegetables permeating the air of the grim establishment. At least the smell was better than that of the stench of horse, dog and human excrement outside. The room was dimly lit but what the owner saved on lamp oil he didn't invest back into the décor. The light of Roman civilisation hadn't quite reached into this dark, dank corner of Britain, the centurion considered.

But people seldom came to the *The Black Stag* for the décor. People came for the drink, women and food – invariably in that order. The inn was half full, populated by farmers and tradesmen who had finished their work for the day. Some were red-nosed from years of drinking. Others were as tanned as leather from having spent a lifetime working in the sun (what little sun there was to be had on the sodden island).

"Two beers and some food, please," Atticus said, removing another coin from his purse and glancing at the menu – a wooden board, filled with text and child-like drawings of animals.

"What would you like?" Harbon asked. Whether a deserter or officer the main thing was that the man's money was good.

"Whatever's fresh and tasty," the centurion replied, hoping that the establishment could at least meet one of those requirements.

Atticus decided that his optio, Cassius Bursus, could choose his own meal once he finished securing the horses with the stable master next door.

Above the hiss of the slanting rain outside Atticus heard the sagging ceiling above his head creak – repeatedly. It seemed that one of the whores had already started work for the day. The soldier also heard the abrupt sound of a chair scraping along the floor. Then came a jangling noise as Adminius, wearing dozens of metal bangles on his arms, walked towards Atticus. The nineteen year old possessed a lean build and spiteful expression. His long red hair needed washing and cutting. His red beard was slick with grease and redder in parts from wine stains. His cloak was made from a wolf's pelt and was fastened with a bronze brooch in the shape of a lion. A hunting knife hung down from his belt. Adminius Meriadoc looked like a man but too often behaved like a cruel, spoiled child.

"What's your business?" the Briton demanded. He slightly slurred his words and his eyes were glassy from drinking all afternoon. Adminius puffed out his chest, as best he could, and made sure that Cordelia was looking. He wanted to assert his manhood in front of the whore and also belittle the stranger. It was important that anyone new to the area realised the old order of things. Should the outsider have heard of the name of his powerful clan then he would rightly be intimidated by the son of the chieftain. If he hadn't heard of his family then it was about time that he did, having come into their territory.

"My business is just that – my business," Atticus replied evenly.

"I'm a Meriadoc. Adminius Meriadoc. Which means that any business this side of the river is also my business." Adminius swayed slightly as he spoke and poked himself in the chest. He had had too much to drink but Atticus suspected that the young Briton was just as unpleasant a character when sober.

257

"I'd advise you to sit down, before you fall down. Or before I knock you down." Atticus had walked into hundreds of inns similar to this one over the years – and nigh on all of them housed an Adminius Meriadoc in one form or another. It was best to put them in their place sooner rather than later.

"Ha, you and whose army?" The youth attempted to laugh off the insult.

The centurion was tempted to answer "Marcus Aurelius'" but he merely turned away from the Briton and perched himself upon a stool next to the counter.

"Are you ignoring me?" Spittle shot out from Adminius' mouth as he spoke. There was both bewilderment and anger in his voice – and the former fed the latter.

By ignoring him further the chieftain's son received his answer.

"Adminius, sit back down." The voice was gruff and authoritative and came from the corner where Adminius had been eating. A large plate of half-eaten dormice and chicken legs rested on the table in front of a fearsome looking Briton, as did a blood-stained short sword. Bardus Meriadoc was broader built and older than his companion, but due to his fiery red hair and flat features Atticus rightly judged the man to be Adminius' brother. The brute's eyes were narrowed in either self-satisfaction or drowsiness. The brat can't handle his drink or his temper, Bardus thought to himself. He was also more concerned with dealing with his thirst and indigestion than picking a fight with a stranger at present.

"This is a wolf's pelt. I killed it myself, stabbing it in the heart," the youth snarled, baring his blackened teeth and moving closer towards Atticus.

The insouciant Roman was now equally as bored as he was amused by Adminius. He was tempted to either laugh or yawn in response to the adolescent.

"It's a dog eat dog world," he drily replied, little disguising his contempt for the Briton. Atticus could little disguise his dislike for the beer that the innkeeper had just served him either.

"You think you're funny?" The would-be bully snorted as he exhaled. The Roman could smell the drink on his breath. Adminius' blood was about to boil over, rather than just simmer. Yet still the centurion remained seated – and remained calm.

"You are far more amusing than I am, trust me."

Adminius was about to spit out a curse in the insolent newcomer's face when he was cut off.

"Sit down!" Bardus commanded. Instead of acting as one of the family's enforcers, Adminius was behaving like a laughing stock. The stranger also had an air of danger, as well as calm, about him. His younger brother was liable to take a beating, as much as that might do him some good. But should the man raise a hand to his kin then he would have to step in.

"He's insulting the family, Bardus," Adminius shouted back, whilst not taking his eyes off his antagonist. He knew that the locals were too scared of his clan to come to the outsider's aid – and if he somehow got into trouble, then his brother would defend him. Bardus could swat the stranger like a fly, he believed.

"I'm not insulting your family, I'm insulting you. You're the one insulting your family." Before returning to the continent, Atticus decided that he would recommend that the army should post a presence in the area. The Meriadoc clan needed to learn that they were not the law of the land. Rome was.

"How would you like it if I stabbed you in the heart?" A rictus of hatred formed itself across Adminius' face.

"You could try boy, but I worry that you'd end up blunting your knife. According to my ex-wife I've got a heart of stone." Atticus smiled, which only fuelled the Briton's ire – as the soldier knew it would.

Atticus couldn't be sure whether it was from someone nearby laughing at his joke or whether it was due to him calling the would-be warrior a "boy" – but the youth's blood finally boiled over. The Briton reached for his hunting knife, but no sooner did he clasp its cold bone handle then Atticus swivelled around on his stool and punched the youth in the throat. Adminius fell to the floor and gasped for air. He gazed up at the stranger with an expression of shock and fear.

The next thing to fall to the floor was Bardus' chair. He grunted, stood up and grasped his "lucky" short sword, as he called it. Atticus also noted the hand-axe tucked into his belt. *The people here are as hospitable as the weather*. The centurion drew his gleaming, sharpened gladius. *Kill or be killed*.

Customers moved out the way to give the two men a wide berth. If not for the spectacle of the prospective fight – and the attraction of seeing another Meriadoc being floored – the patrons of the *The Black Stag* would have retreated out of the door. Cordelia sighed and rolled her eyes, thinking how she had little chance of bedding either the handsome stranger or Adminius now. Silence ensued as the two men sized each other up. Patches of grey infected the Briton's red hair and beard, like mould, but Atticus judged Bardus to be a veteran warrior as opposed to a has-been.

The creaking sound which broke the eerie silence came, this time, from a bow rather than the ceiling or floorboards. The optio's arms were as muscular as a blacksmith's. Cassius Bursus, who upon joining the Praetorian Guard had been nicknamed Apollo due to his prowess with a bow, had entered the inn unnoticed when all eyes had been on Atticus and Adminius. Bardus took in the archer and recognised that the man knew his business. He'd killed before and could – would – easily kill again. The Briton reckoned that even if he were five times the distance away then the archer could still comfortably hit his mark. The brutal warrior hadn't survived this long without knowing when not to fight.

"You should realise that you've got more chance of having a whole week of sunshine than my friend here has of missing his target. I'd be more than happy for you to call my bluff, however. We'll take our leave. You can have a drink on me, though I suggest you have your kinsman sober up. He'll find it difficult to talk for the next few days but people will doubtless consider that a blessing as opposed to a curse. You're welcome to have the food I ordered too, as a punishment rather than a reward."

Bardus gripped the handle of his short sword tightly – and his face twitched in anger – but he nodded his head and conceded to the stranger's terms. He may have lost this battle but he would win the war, he vowed.

"Ride fast and hard. Because if I see you again, I'll kill you."

"Funnily enough, those were the last words my ex-wife said to me as well," Rufus Atticus wryly replied. The praetorian was tired, hungry and yet smiling – believing that he would soon be seeing his old friend again.

2.

A watery light trickled through the clouds. The rain, thankfully, had abated but a chill wind still scythed through their clothes and bones. Atticus and Cassius Bursus had now come off the main Roman road and were heading north along an inhospitable trail towards Quintus Verus' house. Carts had cut ruts into the narrow track. The mud sloshed beneath the hooves of their horses. An unpleasant, gaseous stench from a nearby bog assaulted their nostrils.

Rome, under Emperor Claudius, had invaded Britain in 43AD with the intention of mining vast deposits of gold and silver. Instead they had found rain and rebellion. Too much blood had been spilt and too much money had been invested in the campaign for it to fail, however. Horace called the inhabitants of Briton the "furthest of earth's peoples" but they were eventually brought into the fold of the Empire. Although it became apparent that the country was better suited for mining lead than gold, Rome encouraged other industries such as pottery, glass-making, textiles and the production of salt. Animal husbandry also increased, albeit in some parts of the west of the country there were rumours that farmers had taken their love of animals a little too far. Industry encouraged trade – and trade brought cultural exchanges, as well as the exchange of goods. The island grew more prosperous and diverse. Many leading Britons were conscious of educating their children in Latin and promoting the virtues of Roman civilisation. Some even wore togas. Roman baths and theatres sprung up across the country. But a civilising force was still an occupying force. As increasingly civilised as Briton was becoming, it had also been conquered. Rome constructed roads to transport goods and foodstuffs – and also troops and tax officials. Yet Britain was not just ill at odds due to its level of governance from Rome. Atticus had noticed how people from Londinium and the south-east of the island tended to look down their noses at the northern territories. The self-titled "elite" claimed to rule the rest of the country but they didn't always represent it.

"What sort of welcome do you think we'll get from Maximus?" Cassius Bursus asked. The archer had served under Gaius Oppius Maximus ever since the centurion had promoted him to the ranks of the Praetorian Guard nine years ago. The loyal soldier held his old commanding officer in high esteem – and wanted to keep things that way.

"Well hopefully we'll receive a better reception than we did back at the inn – although that won't be too difficult."

The truth was that Atticus didn't know how Maximus would react in response to encountering his old friends again. It had been five years since Maximus had disappeared. It had been five years since Maximus had found Aurelia, his wife to be, butchered in her own home. It had been five years since Maximus had killed the senator Pollio Atticus, Rufus' father – the man behind Aurelia's murder and also behind a plot to destroy the capital's grain supplies. It had been five years since the Emperor, supported by the physician Galen, had pronounced the centurion dead (in order not to condemn him as being a fugitive). *A lot can happen to a man in five years.*

And much had happened to Atticus during the past five years. He had been married, twice. His first wife had been Annia, the daughter of a prominent senator. Annia was uncommonly pretty but also uncommonly dull. Her conversation had been as stimulating as her lovemaking. He had tried to make things work – but failed. Atticus had partly chosen to marry her to make his mother happy, who had been devastated by the death of her husband.

"Some men are not cut out for soldiering, some men are not cut out for politics. I'm not cut out to be a good husband... Marriage is either a stage or a battlefield," he had confided in Cassius Bursus over a jug of Falernian one evening. Shortly afterwards Atticus divorced Annia – only to marry his mistress at the time, Valeria, a few months later. A wife and a family still seemed to provide the best solution for filling the hole in the praetorian's soul. Valeria made a better mistress than wife. As a mistress she had been fun, as a wife she was formidable. Valeria was cruel to his slaves, vain and ambitious (both for herself and for her husband, who she kept pushing to sacrifice his military career in order to go into politics). "She was good in the bedroom but terrible in the kitchen... The only thing that I could trust her to cook up was an argument."

Valeria was also a drain on his finances, to such an extent that Atticus nicknamed her "the taxman" when he complained about her to his optio. "Her shopping trips are as long and costly as a military campaign." Over another jug of Falernian with his friend Atticus unburdened himself and resolved to get a divorce. "More than to my wife, I have to be true to myself... She's better off without me and I'll be better off, financially and otherwise, without her... I should just go back to doing what I do best and spend my nights in the company of other men's wives rather than my own."

During the past five years much had changed in the centurion's professional, as well as personal, life. Atticus had proved himself to be a trusted adviser and effective military commander to the Emperor. He was seldom absent from Marcus Aurelius' side on the battlefield or when negotiating diplomatic agreements. Atticus had also been instrumental in defeating Avidius Cassius in his bid to become Emperor.

"Do you think that this Quintus Verus will turn out to be Maximus, then?" the optio asked. There had been false reports before. The Emperor always followed up on any rumour however, whether there was a sighting reported of him in Gaul or Alexandria, and sent one of his agents to investigate. The most recent report added up to more than just rumour, though. A former legionary, who had set himself up as a wine merchant, had spotted Maximus at *The Black Stag*. The veteran, who had served in the same legion as Maximus, had sent a message to Atticus. The centurion passed the information onto the Emperor. The intelligence was up to date and from a trusted source. Marcus Aurelius had instructed Atticus and Cassius Bursus to journey to Britain.

"You're the only person who can bring him back, Rufus. I would like to see Maximus again – before I die."

As famished as the centurion felt, the rumbling noise came from the distant thunder rather than Atticus' stomach. His horse moved its head from side to side, as if shaking his head in disbelief, like its rider, that the sky would be filled with rain again. The evening was drawing in, like a surgeon drawing a blanket across a corpse. The chill wind sang in the air with even greater spite. The soldier also heard the faint evening song of a thrush. Instead of being flanked by weeds and hedgerow, Atticus noticed blackberry bushes and wild, winter flowers spring up along the track.

"We're about to now find out the answer to your question Cassius," Atticus replied, after a moment of silence. Both men stared into the distance and saw a house with its lights on. Their long journey was about to end – and another one was about to begin.

3.

The well-constructed two storey stone house was topped off with a wooden roof. Wisps of smoke spiralled out of the chimney. An out building of stables stood to the right of the property. Atticus also took in a vegetable garden and various animal pens which were home to chickens, pigs and goats (the latter of which bleated as the riders approached). He recalled how, around a campfire, Maximus had once declared that he wanted to own a farm – should he ever leave the army, and live the quiet – peaceful – life. But the centurion conceded that the second act to his life would probably live in the shadow of the first. His dreams as a farmer would be eclipsed by the nightmarish scenes he had witnessed during his career as a soldier. Nothing would be able to compete with the blood-pumping highs and lows of battle. "You can't help but feel alive, when life is a series of near-death experiences," Atticus had replied to his friend many years ago. "Drink will have to liven our spirits, or dull the ache, if we ever become farmers."

A figure, Dann, came out of the stables, carrying a rake, and walked towards Atticus and Cassius Bursus. The wizened old servant, wearing a moth-eaten woollen cloak over his tunic, was gap-toothed and bald. He eyed the strangers with a certain amount of chariness and moved his jaws, like a cow chewing upon cud.

"Evening. We're looking for Quintus Verus," Atticus said.

The servant tilted his head and scrutinised the two men even more stringently, hoping to divine their intentions in relation to his master. Before the Briton had a chance to open his mouth and respond though his master appeared before them, standing in the doorway to the main house.

"No, you're not. You're looking for Gaius Oppius Maximus. But you won't find him. Because he's dead," Gaius Oppius Maximus said, flatly. It had been five years since the soldier had last said or heard his name.

Atticus smiled on seeing his former commanding officer. He thought that Maximus' voice sounded distinctly rougher compared to when he had last heard it. Grey hair coloured his temples, like the markings of an old wolf. His face was lined with age or sorrow – or more likely both. A black, bristling beard covered his jaw and neck. The farmer still retained a soldier's build, although Atticus could discern a slight pot-belly beneath Maximus' tunic. His down-turned mouth managed a half-smile on taking in his former comrades. His eyes smiled not, however. Cassius Bursus was surprised by Maximus' lack of surprise. Atticus had once considered the centurion as being akin to a block of iron. But the iron was now flecked – infected – with rust. Maximus' careworn, bloodshot eyes revealed how much drink was dulling the ache too.

Maximus asked Dann to attend to his guest's horses and invited them into the house. Atticus surveyed the clean but austere interior. The furniture was simple but sturdy. The only nod towards his homeland was a painting on the wall, depicting a scene from the Battle of Pharsalus where Maximus' antecedent, Lucius Oppius (the "Sword of Rome"), had fought for Caesar against Pompey in the civil war. But the ex-soldier's wants were few and his possessions even fewer, it seemed. Atticus recalled a comment by Marcus Aurelius, in reference to Maximus: "He's an even greater stoic than myself. And perhaps more Spartan than Roman." Atticus couldn't work out if his Emperor had spoken in jest, admiration or pity.

Despite having questions, despite not having seen his closest friend in five years, Maximus remained silent as he tossed a couple more logs onto the fire and lit an extra couple of the lamps hanging from the oak beams criss-crossing the ceiling. Atticus couldn't be sure if his old friend was glowering in the half light. Was there despondency, disbelief or indifference on his face?

"Would you like a beer?" their host asked, finally turning towards his guests.

Cassius Bursus nodded his head enthusiastically, puffing his cheeks out in relief and prospective pleasure.

"When in Briton, do as the Britons do," Atticus replied.

Maximus poured out three large cups of the local brew. He also served his famished guests some ham and cheese. Cassius commented that he was so hungry that he would even eat the cuisine north of Hadrian's Wall.

"I'm afraid it doesn't quite look and taste as good as the stuff we drank in Egypt, but we've had worse."

The three comrades clinked cups, as they had done so a thousand times around campfires when campaigning against the northern tribes. Atticus peered over the rim of his cup. The liquid was about as transparent as a tax collector's accounts and he remembered, with even more fondness, the beers he had sampled when posted in Alexandria. They had been as golden as the inside of Cleopatra's jewellery box and as intoxicating as her perfume. The three men quickly gulped down the murky brew, however, as if it were the elixir of life, and the host brought over the jug to keep their cups re-filled.

They sat in a horseshoe around the fireplace. The beer helped warm the atmosphere too, although the air was still rife with shards of awkwardness. Maximus often looked at his two old friends but then said nothing. Rain began to spit across the wooden roof. The fire was bright but eerily silent. Atticus noticed how, when Maximus wasn't clasping his cup, he would fidget with the gold band he wore on the fourth finger of his right hand. The ring had been a gift from Aurelia. The inscription on the inside of the band read, "The light shines in the darkness." Maximus would often obsessively turn the ring on his finger, when in company or alone. The sensation reminded the praetorian of Aurelia – of her beauty, goodness and violent death. Maximus' soul had been blackened by so much grief over the years it was now incapable of letting light in or out. He had lost his first love to the plague, the second to politics. His heart was a small lump of coal, soaked in beer.

"So how did you find me?"

"Aelius Scaevola, an old quartermaster from the legion, spotted you in a nearby tavern and wrote to me," Atticus replied. *He's like a corpse that doesn't want to be dug up.*

"I always knew that my drinking would be the end of me," Maximus said, neither wholly joking nor wholly serious, as he thrust a poker into the fire and shifted the logs, to let the air in. "Did you come here for yourself, or were you sent?"

"Both. I wanted to see you. But the Emperor instructed me to find you. He wants to see you again Gaius. Before he dies."

Maximus paused but then spoke. "I've long since ceased giving or receiving orders, Rufus. Aurelius would be the first one to appreciate that we're all due to die. We've got more chance of civilising a tribe of Picts than changing that fact. Besides, the Emperor's a god. What does he need a mere mortal for? No. I won't be leaving here. He needs to let me live and die in peace. Tell him that I'm glad he'll finally find some peace, too. Tell him also that I never blamed him for not pardoning me."

Maximus got up and threw another brace of logs onto the fire, which now started to crackle. The rain slapped upon the roof. Maximus had often thought of his Emperor – friend – during the past five years. He had left without saying goodbye or thank you. When news came through that Avidius Cassius was challenging Aurelius for the throne the centurion had been tempted to come back from the dead and fight by his general's side, one last time.

"You can tell him yourself. You can always return here afterwards, should you want to. But the Emperor and army would welcome you back. My father's influence in the Senate has died out. You'll be a hero, not a fugitive."

"I don't much feel like a hero. I'm content to remain here. I live comfortably. I'm seeing a return on my investment in a local mine and Dann looks after the farm. The wine and weather may be disagreeable, but you can get used to both after a while. How has Aurelius been over the past five years though?" Maximus asked. Concern shaped his features.

"I suspect that five years has felt like five lifetimes. His health has been as fragile as the peace with the northern tribes. For all of the endless victories we've won, the war still rages on. It's a forest fire that keeps flaring up in different places. A piece of Aurelius died when Avidius Cassius looked to wear the purple, I think."

"His robes ended up red though, I understand. A centurion in his army assassinated him, before he could cause a civil war in earnest."

"Aye. But that's another story," Atticus answered, sharing a look with his optio as Cassius Bursus briefly paused whilst wolfing down his plate of salted ham and goat's cheese. "A greater piece of him died, however, when Faustina passed away. I must confess, I neither liked nor trusted the Empress. I've little doubt that she was Avidius' lover at some point. Yet Aurelius was still devoted to her, in his own way. When he honoured her, in his oration, Aurelius described Faustina as being "So submissive, so loving and so artless". Either he was being sarcastic, or blind. He was certainly wilfully blind before she died, refusing to read the correspondence she shared with Avidius. It probably would have incriminated her. Instead, he deified her. Aurelius also minted special coins with Faustina's image on, to commemorate her. She always did like to get into a man's pockets."

Maximus half-smiled at his friend's wit, but also sadly remembered the Emperor's lack of judgement where his wife and son had been concerned.

"And what of Commodus?" Maximus asked, hoping that the boy had become a man – a good man.

Atticus shook his head in disappointment and disparagement. "I think of him as the son of Nero and Domitian rather than Aurelius, unfortunately. He plays the dutiful heir in front of his father but he's religiously cruel, vain and depraved behind his back. Aurelius invited Commodus on campaign and to accompany him during a tour of the east. He introduced him to scientists and philosophers, hoping to inspire and edify the youth. But he has more chance of edifying a Pict. Once his face appears on our coins the currency will instantly depreciate. He was given a consulship aged fifteen, the youngest ever. But should he live to fifty he would not merit such an honour. The argument is that he is the worst option in regards to wearing the purple, but he is also the only option. A bad Emperor is preferable to a civil war and power vacuum. I admire Aurelius deeply but instead of passing more powers onto his son – in preparation for his death – he should have passed them to the Senate for safekeeping. Commodus will turn the marble of Rome into mere rubble, I fear."

"This country's weather will prove a blessing, if it prevents Commodus from visiting this corner of the Empire. He'll try and burn bright – and then burn out. But I'd rather turn my attention to this boy, who became a man," Maximus remarked, proudly looking at Cassius Bursus. "You look older Apollo – but you still annoyingly appear less than half my age. How have you been? Has the archer been struck by Cupid's arrow yet? Are you married?"

"He's unfortunately been struck down with a few diseases from women over the years, but not that of love," Atticus said, smiling at his own joke.

The optio blushed and grinned at the same time, perhaps fondly remembering the encounters with the aforementioned women, regretting not a minute he had spent with them.

"I've been too busy attending Atticus' weddings to attend my own."

Maximus widened his eyes in astonishment. His mouth was agape too, though he was lost for words.

"It's true, believe it or not. I've been married and divorced – twice – in the past five years." Atticus smiled, imagining how surprised and amused his old friend would be at the news.

"I thought that you might be dead by now, but never married. What was it you used to say? Hades will freeze over before you shackle yourself to a wife, ruining your life and hers. Cupid must have an even better aim than you, Cassius, to have hit such a fleet-footed target. Divorced twice I can believe, but not married twice," Atticus said, smirking and shaking his head in disbelief. "So tell me, who did Rome's most eligible bachelor lose his heart to?"

"Well my second wife was called Valeria. And I lost my savings to her, as opposed to heart. For her part she called me conceited, flippant and unfaithful. I should have never let her get to know me so well."

Maximus laughed. It felt like it was the first time he had done so in five years.

*

Maximus' cheeks were flushed from sitting next to the fire but his eyes were red-rimmed from years of heavy drinking, Atticus noticed. He considered that his friend was cocooning himself in a permanent drunken stupor. He had observed politicians do it before, ones who were bitter at never having attained the high office that they thought they merited. Or he had known veterans to consciously drink themselves unconscious, in an attempt to help blot out the various atrocities they had witnessed or committed.

272

Cassius Bursus had turned in for the night. The optio was exhausted and he had been instructed by his centurion earlier to leave him and Maximus alone for part of the evening.

The occasional flame darted upwards from the low-burning, smouldering fire. A stale silence hung in the air between the two old friends. It was a silence encompassing both five seconds and five years. How much of Maximus was there left in the semi-retired farmer – the man who had just wearily declared that he was just killing time, before time killed him? Maximus sat, his head bowed down as if too heavy to lift up. Finally he spoke, after pouring the dregs of the jug of beer into his cup.

"I'm sorry that I lost your friendship, Rufus. But I'm not sorry that I killed your father, all those years ago." Sober or drunk, Atticus could always count on Maximus to be honest – sometimes brutally so.

"I grieved the loss of my friend rather than my father. He was willing to see Rome starve to feed his ambitions. He ruined my mother's life. He nearly ruined my sister's life. He might have ruined my life, if a certain centurion didn't take me under his wing. You never lost me as a friend. You gave me a second chance, Gaius – and for that I'll always be thankful. I just want to now give you a second chance. Come back with me. The army – and Aurelius – are in Sirmium. You're slowly dying here."

I'm already dead. "It's not possible. Not even Galen could furnish me with a cure, a pick-me-up, for the way I feel. It's good to see you again, though, Rufus."

"Anything's possible. If I can marry, twice, then you can come back from the dead."

Maximus half-smiled. He recalled Aurelia reading her bible to him – about the story of Lazarus. Sometimes her ghost haunted him, sometimes it saved him.

"If I could bring anyone back from the dead, it wouldn't be me." Maximus thought of both Julia and Aurelia. Of Arrian, too. They deserved to live far more than him.

Atticus bowed his head as well, weighed down by his friend's sadness. But he raised it again. "There's another reason why you need to come back with me."

"What is it?" Maximus replied, his voice weakened with tiredness and sorrow.

"You need to see your son."

*

Maximus and Atticus continued to stay up long into the night as the centurion told his friend about the baby that Claudia – Atticus' sister – had given birth to five years ago – nine months after Maximus had spent the night with her. Claudia had named the baby Marius, after her grandfather.

"He's good-natured and healthy. He has his father's eyes, but thankfully not his grey hair… Claudia divorced Fronto whilst pregnant but Aurelius has made sure that mother and baby have wanted for nothing. My sister has changed these past five years. She's a good mother. Her better nature has been given room to flourish, from having come out of the shadow of our father. By killing him, you let her live."

There were tears in his eyes as Maximus tried to take everything in. Some of the tears were borne from remembering Lucius and Aemelia, his children from his first marriage who he had lost to the plague. But more so his tears were borne from the news that he had a son. Maximus felt guilty too, for not being there for his son and his mother. But he had not considered that Claudia would have had a child from their one night together. She had been instructed by Pollio Atticus to seduce Maximus. Maximus had in turn seduced Claudia, in order to pass on false intelligence back to her father.

274

"For years doctors told Claudia that she was unable to bear children. Galen delivered the baby. He called Marius a minor miracle. I know that he wasn't conceived in the most conventional circumstances, but something good came of something corrupt. It just goes to show you, anything's possible," Atticus remarked, placing a fraternal hand on his friend's shoulder.

The rain stopped but the fire burned on. Maximus would see Aurelius once more. He would see his son, for the first time. He would even draw his sword again, if he had to...

Anything was possible.

4.

Maximus slept fitfully that evening. But rather than being kept awake by spectres from the past his thoughts turned to the hazy image of his young son. He found himself smiling, uplifted. He had been absent from his life for five years. He had a lot of catching up to do. That night Maximus also prayed to God. For years he had cursed his name, or denied his existence. But a chink of light shone through the clouds and Maximus asked God to keep him – and Marius – safe. He just wanted the chance to see his son (even just once) and to provide for him.

Despite going to bed late he still woke up with the dawn. A dapple grey fog encircled the farm. The chilly air misted up his breath as well. The ground was dusted with frost. Maximus called Dann in to speak to him, after the Briton had given out his orders to the three farmhands for the day. After a couple of years of service Maximus had rewarded his land manager with a share of his estate's holdings. He could be trusted to keep his business affairs in order. Maximus told the leather-faced Briton that he would be returning to the continent and the army again. The old man nodded, masticated, and looked impassive for the most part – but then grinned, gummily, when he heard the news that his master had a son.

"You are a man with a mission again," Dann croakily remarked. Maximus wasn't sure if he was referring to fatherhood or his prospective military service.

"Thank you. Should you encounter any trouble or difficulties you should see Algar. I'm about to write him a letter now."

Algar was the chief of a nearby tribe. He had made the Roman an honorary member of the tribe when he had first come to the region, many years ago. Algar was a descendant of Adiminus, a former chieftain of their tribe who had served with Lucius Oppius at the battles of Alesia and Pharsalus.

"Will you be returning before the spring?"

"Anything's possible," Maximus replied, after a thoughtful pause whilst surveying the landscape.

*

Atticus and Cassius Bursus slept in. When they woke Maximus said that he was keen to leave for the continent that day. They would ride to the nearest port and charter a ship to take them to Gaul. The optio sighed a little inside. His trip to the famous – or infamous – island was going to be all too brief. He had hoped that he could sample some of the women of Briton. He had heard good things about the busty serving girls. It was rumoured that they were happy to be taken advantage of, after a few drinks. So too he would be happy for them to take advantage of him, drunk or sober. But the itch would have to remain unscratched for now, unfortunately (the soldier was so desperate for the arms of a woman that he would have even taken one from north of Hadrian's Wall, he considered). They were homeward bound.

By midday the three companions were ready to leave. They were just waiting on one of the farmhands to finish saddling Maximus' horse. Such was the cacophony of noises from the livestock that maybe the animals intuited that their owner was going away. Maximus knew that he was as much leaving home as journeying towards one. After escaping from Rome he had felt that the best place to isolate himself from the world would be on the distant island. He would miss his drinking sessions with Algar, although he would not miss how he felt during the mornings afterwards. His days of being Quintus Verus hadn't been all bad.

But the farmer would have to become a soldier again. Maximus' sword felt heavy in his hand when he strapped it on, after five years. Dann had kept the blade oiled and sharpened, thinking that his master might have cause to use it again one day.

As the wizened land manager stared across the horizon – and saw over half a dozen armed horsemen approaching the house – he suddenly thought how that day might be today.

5.

The midday sun had evaporated the fog and melted the frost. Maximus counted eight riders, trotting in a row. He could also just about make out the swords and axes popping out over their shoulders from being strapped to their backs.

"Friends of yours?" Atticus asked, squinting in an attempt to better make out the figures in the distance.

"Doubtful. I'm not exactly renowned in these parts for throwing dinner parties."

Maximus noted his land manager jutting out his chin next to him and firmly grasping his pitch fork. No matter who his visitors were, however, it wouldn't be the old man's fight. Maximus instructed Dann to fetch his pair of hunting spears – and then head back inside. He also instructed one of his farmhands to lead the horses back into the stables. He didn't want the animals getting spooked or injured, should trouble ensue.

"I'll take care of our guests Dann, don't worry. Apollo – post yourself up on the roof. Stay out of sight until I give the order."

The optio nodded and nimbly climbed up the side of the house, stationing himself behind the stone chimney.

"Unfortunately they're friends of mine," Atticus remarked, as he gradually discerned the frame and features of one of the horsemen. *Bardus Meriadoc.* "I recognise two of them, Bardus and Adminius Meriadoc. I suspect that their companions are family members. We had a slight altercation at the tavern yesterday. I knocked Adminius on his arse and Cassius nearly had to put an arrow in Bardus. In my defence I did buy them a round of drinks afterwards to try and take the sting out of things."

279

"Well, at least you didn't sleep with someone's wife. That's progress I suppose," Maximus said, as he planted the two hunting spears in the ground between himself and Atticus.

He had thankfully had few dealings with the Meriadoc clan over the years. They had perhaps left him alone because of his affiliation with Algar – and he lived just beyond what they deemed was their territory. Their reputation preceded them, however. They had started – and ended – more blood feuds than Maximus could recall. The head of the family was Ammius. The self-proclaimed chief had carved out his position in the region through violence, theft and intimidation. He routinely paid off corrupt tax collectors and military officials – otherwise people paid him, through rent money, interest on loans or his own form of taxation. Cruelty was a source of amusement to Ammius, as well as part of his business plan. He possessed four wives and had fifteen children (most of them sons, as daughters were less of an asset to him). He would have possessed five wives, but his last wife had died a year ago. Some said that Ammius had murdered her for being unfaithful, while others claimed he had disposed of her because she was barren. As well as a cruel streak Ammius also liked to display his sense of munificence every now and then – and on certain feast days he would arrange large dinners and tournaments (which members of his own family invariably won). It was a chance for Ammius Meriadoc to give something back to the community, which he regularly extorted money from throughout the remainder of the year.

The stolidly built chief rode at the centre of the line of horsemen on a large, snorting black charger. He also rode slightly ahead of his men. The default position of his mouth was a sneer. The polished bronze torc around his neck reminded Maximus of the one which Ballomar, the leader of the Marcomanni, had worn at the Battle of Pannonia. Maximus also took in the rest of his unwelcome guests. They shared similar features: red hair, beetling brows, flat noses and dark eyes. The family resemblance (Ammius' "wolf pack", as he called them, were made up of his brothers, sons and nephews) was accentuated through bedraggled beards and the equally bedraggled furs they wore.

Ammius Meriadoc stopped and looked Maximus up and down, his lip curled in an even more pronounced sneer. At the same time Bardus took in Atticus. He bared his yellow teeth and blood-red gums in a goading, self-satisfied smirk. Adminius Meriadoc, wearing a scarf to cover the bruising on his neck, was also bright-eyed with spite. He was keen to say something to Atticus, to show that he was having the last laugh, but his throat was still sore and he was unable to talk properly.

"You know who I am. You know why I'm here," Ammius stated bluntly in a guttural voice. "This man before you is a fugitive. He attacked a member of my family – and if you attack one Meriadoc, you attack every Meriadoc. I will have recompense, Quintus Verus, either in gold or blood. I'll leave that choice to you. But either way I will not be leaving your farm empty-handed. Forgiveness is not an option. Mercy isn't a Meriadoc family trait."

"Neither is intelligence, it seems," Maximus said as an aside to Atticus.

"Or a sense of style, judging by what they're wearing," the centurion added. "Although, from the look of them, a love of incest may well run in the family."

Before replying to the brutal looking Briton, Maximus was briefly distracted by a quartet of crows cawing to each other on a skeletal birch tree to the right of his house. Perhaps they were calling to one another – anticipating some entertainment, or a prospective feast. He also noted a couple of the men dismount and twirl their axes in their hands, in a bid to intimidate their quarry. One had a long neck like a giraffe and spat like a camel. The other

281

had a broken nose, which seem to zig-zag and defy Euclidean geometry, Atticus fancied.

"I've got a counter proposal. How about I let you leave here with your life, instead of my friend or my gold?"

The Briton let out a laugh, or rather a cackle. But then he snorted, in the manner of his horse, and glowered at the Roman. Nobody spoke to Ammius Meriadoc in such a disrespectful manner. He would now take their lives and take their valuables. He could make a gift of the property to his soon to be married nephew.

"I thought that you Romans were accomplished mathematicians. I see eight of us and only two of you."

"Should you want to even the odds and make it a fairer fight, we'd be happy to have you go back and collect more men," Atticus exclaimed, as his hand reached around his back to check that his pair of throwing knives were easily accessible beneath his layers of clothing.

Ammius was not the only Meriadoc to laugh this time.

"You're funny," Ammius remarked, slapping his hand across his leather-clad thigh. "Maybe I should enslave you, instead of kill you, and employ you as a clown to amuse my young children."

"Is his aim and arm still good?" Maximus quietly asked the centurion, referring to his optio.

"Aye, he's good. The kind of diseases he picks up only affect him below the waist. Should I be more worried about you? Do you still remember how to use that sword?" Atticus replied, not entirely in jest.

"I suspect that we're both about to find out."

The chief wiped the smile from his face and signalled to his two dismounted men (his younger brother and nephew) to attack the Romans. Bardus had asked his father that morning if he could be the one to kill the stranger who had disrespected the family, but Ammius had replied that if he was so keen to kill the man, he would have done so on the evening before, without the support of the rest of the clan. Also, it had been some time since his brother and nephew had killed someone. Their axes needed to taste blood.

Cassius Bursus covertly surveyed the scene from behind the chimney. He controlled his breathing, nocked an arrow and waited for the order.

The Briton with the long neck and fondness for spitting let out a battle-cry and closed in on Atticus. He was fearsome and heavy-set, but the centurion was willing to bet he was also slow. The axe swished through the air with little accuracy. Atticus stepped backwards.

The warrior with the broken nose attacked Maximus. His axe was modified and topped off with a spear point, which he jabbed forward at the Roman. Maximus sidestepped one of the thrusts, however, and moved inside. He whipped his elbow around to smash against his opponent's face – and shattered his left cheekbone. The dazed Briton was then easily despatched as Maximus jabbed his sword through his stomach.

The Briton grinned in pleasure, believing that he had the beating of his opponent. He soon grimaced in agony, however, as Atticus darted forward unexpectedly and sliced open his enemy's hand, which was gripping the weapon. The axe fell to the ground, as did the man shortly after.

"Apollo! Make it rain."

Maximus barely had the time to draw breath again, after bellowing his order, when the first arrow zipped through the air and punctured the lung of the man on the horse to the right of Ammius, who was about to launch his spear at Atticus. The shock for the Britons from witnessing their kin fall to the strangers was compounded by the appearance of the archer on the roof. Such was the speed with which the second shaft was released that for a moment it seemed that there may be more of the enemy raining death from above.

Ammius Meriadoc quickly unhooked the round shield on his saddle and placed it in front of him, just before an arrow thudded into the wood. Unfortunately his brother, to the left of him, was unable to retrieve his shield quickly enough to avoid the spear, which Maximus threw into his sternum. Adminius emitted a hoarse cry – or squeak – of despair. His plan was to dismount and take cover behind his mare, but he panicked and fell from his mount, spraining his ankle in the process.

Bardus decided that attack was the best form of defence. He kicked his heels into the flanks of his horse and aimed to mow down Atticus. The first of the centurion's throwing knives lodged itself into the Briton's shoulder. Atticus then leapt to his right to avoid the oncoming horse. He swiftly gained his footing and threw his second knife into Bardus' back, before he had the opportunity to wheel his mount around and attack again. The brawny warrior lost consciousness – and never woke up – as he slumped forward, and his colt galloped on into the distance.

Ammius surveyed the battlefield. His sneer morphed into a snarl. He was tempted to flee. He would lose his pride and honour, but not his life. He had more sons at home, who could help replenish his forces in a dozen years or so. He could hire mercenaries in the interim to retain his power base in the region. All would not be lost. But a red mist descended before the Briton's eyes. The Roman must die, even if he was injured or killed in the attempt.

He yelled and rode towards Maximus with his shield in one hand and his axe in the other. The charger's hooves churched up mud. At first Maximus looked to retrieve his second hunting spear but Ammius anticipated his intention. All he could do was dive out the way, to the side where his opponent held his shield rather than his razor-sharp axe.

Cassius Bursus spotted the danger to Maximus and nocked an arrow. The experienced warrior skilfully wheeled his horse around whilst his enemy was still on the ground. The Briton observed the archer target him however, and he raised his shield accordingly to fend off the missile. But by concentrating on the archer and raising his shield, Ammius exposed his mid-riff. Maximus firmly gripped his gladius but then let it fly out of his hand as he threw the sword at the warrior chief. The blade sheathed itself through Ammius' ribcage – piercing his heart.

Atticus stood over a pale, trembling Adminius. The slight but familiar metallic tang of flesh and blood began to lace the air, along with the smell of horses.

"You caused all this," the centurion remarked, unable to mask the contempt and melancholy in his voice.

"I promise, I won't cause any trouble again," the youth replied, his voice trembling as much as his body.

"I know you won't," Atticus said coldly, before plunging and twisting the blade of his gladius into the Briton's throat.

The crows cawed in the background even louder, as if applauding the spectacle.

Atticus watched his friend use the furs of his enemy to wipe the blood off his sword. The farmer had fought well. *Maybe he isn't that rusty after all.*

Cassius retrieved his arrows – and relieved the corpses of any valuables, too.

Maximus sighed in exasperation at the waste of it all and the fact that, even before they had set off, they had encountered delays. *I just want to see my son.*

"What do we do now?" Dann asked his master, grinding his teeth and thinking. He gazed at their chief and bid good riddance to the Meriadocs. Life would go on, for the better, without them.

"They're dead. We bury them and act as if they were never here," Maximus said flatly – although he was tempted to feed some of the corpses to his pigs as a goodbye present to them.

6.

Sirmium.

Galen had seen enough death in his lifetime to know that his patient – and friend – was dying. The famed physician didn't need to check the Emperor's pulse to know that it was weak, but he did so anyway. How much was his exhaustion physical and how much was it spiritual? Only the gods knew – and they would remain mute.

The room was populated by various desks, stacked high with books, scrolls, maps and all manner of documents pertaining to up-and-coming legal disputes and diplomatic treaties. On a bedside table to his left stood several empty phials, which had contained a special theriac Galen had concocted to ease the Emperor's pain and help him sleep. The physician had increasingly added more opiates to the mixture, which had the effect of sometimes dulling his patient's wits, as well as his pain.

Marcus Aurelius was sitting up in bed, supported by several cushions. He had been offered the billet of the finest residence in the area but the commander was determined to remain with his men in an army camp on the outskirts of town. The engineers had constructed a house for their beloved general within a week. Galen forced a smile, in reaction to taking his friend's pulse. The physician noted how his ailing patient's beard was now more white than grey. His skin seemed so ashen and powdery Galen fancied that a strong gust of wind might blow the tired expression from the Emperor's face.

But the divine spark hadn't been completely extinguished. Death, or life, had not broken him quite yet. The stoic was determined to endure the world for a little longer. Aurelius wanted to expand the borders of the Empire to the Carpathian Mountains. The Germanic tribes needed to be subdued, once and for all. He wanted to see Maximus again. He also wanted to make sure that Commodus was ready and worthy to inherit the throne. In regards to the latter, Galen thought that Aurelius would have to live another lifetime, however. An eternity. Far more than the campaign against the northern tribes his son was a lost cause. The physician had seen the youth in the camp earlier, cavorting with a courtesan and her brother. The brother and sister were rumoured to cavort with each other, too. *Caligula might even blush in the face of the boy's wicked and depraved temperament.*

"It looks like that the doctor will outlive the demi-god, no? I wouldn't want it any other way," Marcus Aurelius fondly remarked to his old friend. His voice was stronger than his pulse, but not by much.

"I'm sure that your name will outlive mine – and many others. Your book sales will doubtless eclipse mine, too," Galen said, noting how his patient had barely touched his food – some cereal sweetened with honey – which sat on a table next to his bed.

"I might be tempted to lay a wager on the opposite being true, if I thought that I'd be around to collect on the bet. Plato posited that states flourish under rulers who are philosophers. I'm not entirely convinced. My reign may prove to be synonymous with an endless, unwinnable war and a plague which decimated the Empire. Or, for better or worse, I will merely be forgotten. But that's as it should be. Everything fades away and quickly becomes a myth; soon complete oblivion covers us over," Aurelius said. He appeared to be at ease, rather than despairing, at the bleak thought.

"You are being too harsh on yourself. I'm not usually one to agree with 'the people' as such, but they are right to speak well of your reign. Let us hope that you still have a future. The Empire needs you."

"The Empire needs an Emperor – and one who can fulfil his duties better than I can at present. I have had my time, Galen. Commodus will soon have his. I know that you have not always approved of him. He has his faults but some of them may be delivered at my door. I was an absent father for most of his life. His mother indulged him, which is a mother's prerogative. Since Faustina passed away I have tried to do too much too quickly," Marcus Aurelius said, his head bowed down in pensiveness, shame and fatigue. *But it's proved too little and too late.*

"I will at this rate remember you as a ruler who was too hard on himself," the sage physician warmly replied.

"Commodus was more concerned with visiting the arena than the lecture halls during our tour of the east unfortunately." *And visiting the brothels at night.*

"You did your best, Caesar." *But your best wasn't good enough, for once.*

"He fulfilled his duty and sat in on numerous legislative cases that I presided over, which is something." *And was more interested in metering out punishments, than justice.*

Galen could not bring himself to openly disagree with his Emperor. But he could not bring himself to openly support his misplaced judgements either. His silence said it all.

"I am optimistic that the throne will ennoble him. He may prove to be more of a warrior than a philosopher – but a warrior is what Rome may well need."

He will prove to be more of a tyrant and sybarite than a warrior. "What will be will be," Galen said, philosophically.

"Indeed. We cannot alter the past or future. Commodus will be an Emperor of his own making. I have learned that it is impossible to make a man exactly how one wishes him to be. If it were

289

possible I would have created an army of men akin to Maximus and Atticus. If Atticus is able to locate Maximus then I believe that he will return. How is Claudia and their son?"

"She has settled in well at the house in town you organised and sends her regards. The boy is in fine health too," Galen replied, retrieving several phials of theriac from his bag and putting them on the bedside table to his patient's right.

"Claudia is much changed from the woman she used to be, isn't she? And changed for the better. The responsibility of motherhood has made her see the world – and herself – in a different light. Perhaps the responsibility of office will change Commodus for the better. Where there's life there's hope, as Cicero used to say."

It was now the Emperor's turn to force a weak smile.

7.

Sunlight sliced through the gaps of the shutters, as did the smell of pine.

Cassius Bursus washed down the grapes he was eating with a fine Massic vintage. He was, along with Maximus and Atticus, riding in an imperial coach through Gaul. The son of a village farrier had come a long way, he thought to himself. Cassius had long appreciated his father for forcing him to practise archery as a boy all those years ago – but the soldier duly appreciated him again, and more.

The ride was one of the most agreeable experiences he had ever had travelling, due to the construction of both the road and the coach. He admired the gold leaf scroll work which decorated the inside of the coach. He also pocketed a gold coin he found in between two cushions – and called it a tax rebate. It was a welcome change, travelling in such style. He was used to being the escort, rather than the one being escorted – in this case by the squadron of cavalry accompanying them. Cassius idly wondered if Caesar had ever travelled along the same road he was on, when campaigning in Gaul. He promised himself that he would one day visit the town of Alesia, to take in the scene of Caesar's greatest victory.

Although the shutters were closed to keep out the wintery chill, Maximus wore the expression of a day-dreamer and fixed his gaze at the window as if it were open. For the first hour or so of sitting in the carriage Maximus had sat on the opposing seat, as if looking back to Britain or the past. But he then wordlessly moved seats and Maximus now looked to Sirmium and the future. Occasionally his stony face would crack – and the hint of a smile would animate his expression.

"I instructed one of the cavalry to ride ahead and secure us rooms at an inn for the evening. Dinner will be on me too, or rather on the Emperor. It's refreshing to have some money in my pocket that my ex-wives don't feel entitled to," Atticus remarked in good humour, looking forward to a hot meal and warm bed.

"Despite the money they extracted from you Rufus, I can't help but think of your ex-wives as 'poor women' for being married to you," Maximus said, in equal good humour. "What prompted you to wed in the first place?"

"It made my mother happy. I also thought that I was in love, or told myself I was. And not in love in the poetical sense. Real love. But I was still as deluded as a poet. In the end, in regards to both wives, we were fonder of each other when we were apart. I guess I gave both of them handsome settlements out of guilt, for being unfaithful. I tell myself that I'm cursed with boredom. But really I'm just selfish. It could be worse, though. I could be boring. I also married out of a desire to have a family. I may well have the odd child out there already, being brought up by the husband to the wife I slept with. But I wanted a family of my own. You need to be a good husband before you can be a good father though, unfortunately."

"I'm just hoping that you're a good map reader and we don't stray into enemy territory," Maximus said. He wanted to get to Sirmium quickly, but safely.

"The lines of the map have been redrawn over the past five years. There are fewer bandits and raiding parties along the border now. Many of our enemies are now friends, out of fear rather than love. My worry is for the plans to redraw the lines of the map even more. The Emperor is intending to expand the frontiers of the Empire to the Carpathian Mountains. The Goths may not prove to be the most amiable of neighbours. I'd trust them to keep the peace about as much as I'd trust a Gaul in a shield wall to advance."

"So why does Aurelius want to redraw the map?"

"You may want to ask him yourself. But I believe that he is trying to give his son one last gift, before he passes away. He wants to occupy the territory so Commodus will never have to refight his battles – although eventually we may have to fight new ones, against the Goths. Rather than sow salt into the land, as Rome did with Carthage, Aurelius plans to plant forts and soldiers across the province. But the plague has weakened the army and its recruiting pool. His imperial overreach will exceed his grasp. To garrison the northern territories the army will have to transfer soldiers from the likes of Britain and Egypt, which could destabilise those regions. The army cannot fight on multiple fronts. Not even the gods can be in two places at once. The army needs more men," Atticus posited, apprising his friend of the situation.

I just want to see my son.

8.

"You look a picture of happiness there Cassius, with that girl sitting on your knee," Atticus shouted across the table at the inn.

"Aye, but the reason why I'm happy is because she *isn't* sitting on my knee," the optio responded jovially, before giving the dimpled, raven-haired whore a sloppy kiss. Wine stained his chin. He breathed in her cheap perfume. The avuncular owner of the establishment had boasted that his girls were the cleanest in the province, but also the most filthy-minded. *The Golden Plough* possessed "the finest whores in all of Gaul, at a competitive price".

A large, stoked fireplace heated a room filled with travellers, merchants and officials. Lamps hung from the ceiling, as did a collection of various tankards. Colourfully dressed women, their eyes darkened with kohl and their faces red with mulberry juice, led men off to private rooms where they would make good on the claims written by satisfied customers on the toilet walls.

Many a woman tried to catch Maximus' eye – and even more of them wished to capture the attention and purse of his handsome companion. But the two friends were content just to talk to each other – and allow Cassius Bursus to have their share of any fun.

"So tell me more about Avidius' attempted coup," Maximus said, pouring himself another cup of wine. "I never had much regard for him, although I'm sure he didn't much care as he had plenty of regard for himself. He lost my respect when I heard that he punished a number of looting soldiers by crucifying them. He also mutilated deserters to serve as adverse advertisements for others who might be tempted to desert."

"Well in some respects he deserted his own post, by challenging rather than serving the Emperor. After receiving a report that

Aurelius had died Cassius declared himself regent and Emperor. It's still unclear whether Faustina knew for sure or not that her husband was still alive, but initially she supported Cassius' bid to seize power. It was rumoured that she was willing to marry him to further strengthen his claim. On hearing the news of his friend's treachery Aurelius offered to pardon him. Cassius considered that it would have been un-imperial to abandon his claim. The self-titled demi-god wasn't keen on returning to being a humble soldier again, after pronouncing himself Emperor. He also proudly boasted that he was a second Catiline. Whilst looking to mobilize his legions in the east he also reached out to the Senate. Suffice to say they also didn't hold him in the high regard that he thought they should have. Soldiers, senators and the populace supported Aurelius. The would-be Emperor was armed with ambition, but little else. A friend wrote to Cassius and summed things up in just one statement, 'You are mad'. Aurelius prepared for war, although he was wary of dividing his forces too much and leaving the northern territories weakened. Thankfully he didn't have to."

"I heard that two of his own soldiers murdered him."

"They may have been two soldiers, but they were not his men," Atticus said knowingly, lowering his voice.

"Who were they?"

"Well one of them is sitting over there – with a girl on his lap – and the other one is sitting opposite to you."

Maximus' eyes were stapled wide. He shook his head in disbelief but then nodded it in approval. The praetorians clinked their cups and grinned.

"Well, anything is possible it seems. How many people know it was you?"

"Five. The Emperor, the agent who helped us infiltrate the legion, Apollo, myself – and now you. The agent insisted that we present the severed head of the enemy to the Emperor. To

Aurelius' credit he refused to look. The Emperor punished a few conspirators who sided with Cassius, but most he pardoned."

Maximus inwardly recalled something Aurelius had said to him many years ago, after acquitting a servant accused of murdering his master. "There is nothing which endears an Emperor of Rome to mankind as much as the quality of mercy."

The two friends were interrupted in their conversation by the front door to *The Golden Plough* opening, bringing in a gust of cold air and Quintus Perennis, the officer in charge of their detachment of cavalry. Perennis briskly walked over to the centurion and stood to attention, his polished helmet, topped with a distinctive red plume, cradled under his arm.

"Our horses have been watered and fed, sir. Would you like me to assign you any men to act as guards for the evening?"

"Thank you Quintus, but we'll be fine. Although I fear, perhaps, that Cassius over there may have to fight off all the women at some point tonight, if he's not careful. Consider yourself off duty. Make sure your men are watered and fed – and that you turn some of the water into wine," Atticus remarked, whilst tossing the officer a small bag of coins to cover the expenses for the evening.

"Thank you, sir," the officer replied, unable to suppress a grateful smile. Perennis then turned to Maximus. "I just wanted to say to you, sir, that my men and I are pleased to see you back with us. It's an honour to serve alongside you again. I was there at the Battle of Pannonia."

Maximus was unsure what to say in response so he merely nodded and half-smiled.

My war's over... I just want to see my son.

9.

Commodus' chest glistened with oil. Titus and Sabine, brother and sister, lay either side of the soon to be Emperor. Commodus had claimed the villa that his father had declined to stay in. The property, in the centre of town, was far away from the prying eyes of gossiping soldiers or the judgmental looks of his father. Commodus idly thought to himself how he might paint his chest hairs gold, to match his fair hair (which he often decorated with flecks of gold dust). *The people like majesty.*

Braziers surrounding the large bed glowed and illuminated the painted figures on the walls of the bed chamber, who were looking on like voyeurs. There was a light in Titus' eyes too as he gazed at his lover with undisguised adoration. Commodus smiled back, pleased and recently pleasured. Titus' hair was slicked back and fragrant with myrrh. He was a former artist's model, praised for his beauty. His features – his almond eyes and pronounced cheek bones – were almost as feminine as his sister's.

Titus was twenty years old. Commodus was the first lover he had taken (or who he had let himself be taken by) who was older than him. Usually he shared the beds (and secrets) of senators, plutocrats and other powerful men. Titus enjoyed being desired. He was attractive, charming and ambitious. "We have to use every asset we have," the son of a stonemason often said to his sister.

Titus had wormed his way into the affections of the Emperor's son after catching his eye at a party. Commodus had bedded him that night and Titus had proved his worth as a lover and also as someone his companion could confide in and receive advice from. He told Commodus what he wanted to hear and, although no great wit himself, Titus knew when to laugh at other peoples' jokes. When they all eventually travelled back to the capital Titus would serve as the young Emperor's chamberlain. He would stand in the shadows by day and lie in his bed at night. His greatest ambition was to be the Second Man of Rome. He would be master over all those grey-beards who had once looked down on him and treated him like a slave or whore.

Commodus stroked Titus' face with his fingertips and bestowed a kiss upon his "Ganymede", as he sometimes affectionately called him. Commodus then turned to bestow his attention on the woman. His leg was hooked around hers beneath the covers. Sabine smouldered more than any brazier. Lovers drunk in the courtesan's perfume and alluring looks. Her sphinx-like pout could signify a hundred things – but most men only thought about one thing when they saw her. Sabine was five years older than her brother and an even more experienced lover and consort than her sibling. She could dress elegantly or provocatively, with equal accomplishment. She could act demurely or play the wanton. Different performances could be tailored to different audiences. Sabine knew what men wanted – and gave it to them. Desire was all about supply and demand; it was a commodity that could be manufactured and traded. She had been married twice, to men who had plenty of money but little time left to spend it. A piece of graffiti in Rome commented about the lauded beauty saying that, although she had never bored her husbands, she had eventually worn them out.

Commodus ran his hand through her long, luxuriant auburn hair. She rubbed her head against his palm, almost purring with pleasure. To amuse himself though, Commodus suddenly and spitefully pulled a few strands of hair out of her head. The woman yelped in pain and was about to curse the perverted teenager but she wisely reined herself in. Sabine knew she could ultimately lose her head, as opposed to just a few strands of hair, if she displeased the vindictive boy. She smiled and allowed him and her brother to laugh (giggle) at the joke. Sabine had seen Commodus' aspect both glow with sensual pleasure and flash with ire in the past. He had been violent with her before. Frustrated with not being able to climax one evening he had blamed the woman and slapped her, repeatedly. He drank too much, especially for one who couldn't hold his drink. Drink made his temper even more erratic. He would slur his words, vomit and grow glassy-eyed. The courtesan pouted and smiled but thought to herself how the incident was another reminder to her that she had to leave her current life behind. Her wealth could buy her freedom and independence. She had no wish to belong to anyone anymore – and that included being part of Titus' schemes. He behaved more like a pimp than brother nowadays.

I don't want to be a trophy to be competed for anymore… I don't want to be the Emperor's wife or his mistress… I may even suffer blisters soon, from having to applaud everything the "young Hercules" does.

Sabine was tired of pretending to love someone. She wanted to love and care for someone for real – whatever that meant. She had recently met someone who was different. He made her laugh and she felt freer, alive, when she was with him. But should that affair prove chimerical too, then she was content to retreat from the world. Sabine may have been half as ambitious as her younger brother, but she was more than twice as intelligent. She painted, read voraciously and spoke three languages. She had recently started to translate *The Aeneid* into Greek and had purchased a villa in Puteoli that was rumoured to have once belonged to Cicero.

My life could be good.

Commodus knew he would soon grow tired of the sister. She was a proficient rather than passionate lover. He was as fond of her as he was a pet dog, peacock or ostrich (all of which he had executed for his sport and amusement in the past). A courtesan is still just a tavern whore – but with a larger collection of shoes, he thought to himself. Her brother, however, would be a different story. Commodus valued the young man, who would soon be in his prime, for his eagerness to please and his counsel. He would need such devotees when he ruled the Empire: men who would wake up early for him and stay up late with him. Keep him entertained. His chamberlain could sign documents for him and sit in on legal disputes, but Commodus would sit in on sentencing hearings and pass judgement. He enjoyed witnessing the extreme reactions on the faces of the guilty and innocent alike. Most people he would punish, severely. But in order to keep things interesting – and keep people guessing – he would pardon one in every ten defendants.

Already Titus acted as Commodus' agent, keeping him informed about who was an ally or potential enemy. He corresponded with senators on his behalf, procured suitable women and boys for his enjoyment, and collected donations and bribes from clients who wished to benefit from the Emperor-in-waiting's favour.

Unfortunately Commodus had mostly received mere trinkets and promises over the past six months. He knew, however, that the real donations – and ability to extort funds – would come once he was Emperor in earnest. He needed money for both his coronation and his father's funeral – suffice to say he would devote more expenditure to the former rather than the latter. Commodus had been planning the gladiatorial games in his honour upon ascending the throne for the past five years. His one regret was that he hadn't written his ideas down and most he had now forgotten. Yes, he would definitely employ Titus as a chamberlain and secretary when he became Emperor.

There had been false dawns before but finally his father would meet his end. Commodus would allow him two coins for the ferryman, but the rest of the imperial treasury would be his. The wait would soon be over. But for Galen's miracle cures, his father would have died years ago. Commodus inwardly cursed the priggish doctor, whilst conveniently forgetting that Galen had also saved his own life on more than one occasion.

Such was the Emperor's perilous state of health that the physician had warned Commodus, on his previous visit, that it might be his last opportunity to speak to his father. Aurelius had mustered his strength. He had first apologised again for not being as devoted a parent as he would have liked. Commodus had heard such words before though. When his father wasn't looking he had yawned.

Aurelius had then attempted to give his son one last lecture. He had quoted Epictetus, Augustus and, more so anyone else, himself: "Take care not to be too Caesarified and drowned in the purple. The first chapter of your life has been dedicated to pleasure. This next chapter that you are about to embark upon needs to be dedicated to duty, my son."

Commodus had nodded his head and looked dutiful – whilst vowing to himself that the next chapter of his life would be dedicated to tasting even more pleasures, carnal and otherwise.

The Emperor had also asked his heir to fulfil his father's last wish: "Promise me you will annexe and occupy this land. Finish off this war, in order to secure the peace."

"I will try, father. But I now have a duty to the state, which must supersede my wishes. Should I lose my life or health while on campaign, how will I best be serving the Empire then? Even a good man can but change the world for the better gradually. But a dead man can achieve nothing. In order to truly do my duty I must return to the capital."

Commodus enjoyed the spectacle of a gruesome battle, as he also enjoyed the bloody combat between two gladiators, but he would rather not routinely spend his days ankle-deep in mud, surrounded by grunting soldiers. He would not eat second-rate delicacies, nor expose himself unnecessarily to injury or contracting the plague.

An Emperor should sit upon a gilded throne in the Eternal City, not perch upon a wooden stool in a dingy tent.

Rome was calling Commodus back home, as surely as death was summoning his father.

"Leave us," the adolescent suddenly said to Sabine, callousness replacing the surface charm he had exhibited the evening before. His capriciousness was his most consistent characteristic, the woman considered. She submitted to his request, glad to be out of his company. It was often an act of will for the courtesan not to shudder in revulsion or fear when he touched her. There was something abhorrent, rather than just depraved, about the youth. Sabine climbed out of bed, put on her robe and retreated to the room next door to the bedchamber.

"Stay," Commodus then ordered, turning to Titus. He wanted to discuss business and political matters with his chamberlain – matters which were not meant for a woman's ears, be she a whore or an empress. "Anything to report?" Commodus asked, as soon as he heard the door close behind the woman.

Titus' features quickly tightened in seriousness, as if he were a soldier standing to attention. He was the Emperor's agent as well as lover – and he would do well to remember that fact. Commodus had struck him with a centurion's vine stick the previous week for not remembering his place correctly.

"Aside from the issues we discussed before dinner, I have heard a rumour that Rufus Atticus disappeared in order to locate one Gaius Maximus. Your father is apparently keen to see him. Whether for personal or political reasons, it remains unclear at present. Have you ever encountered this Maximus before?"

"I thought he was dead. At the very least he should be considered a condemned man. He was a centurion, one of my father's favourites – he trusted and admired the soldier. But five years ago Maximus murdered Pollio Atticus. It is likely that he also killed a number of the influential senator's agents, out of revenge for the death of his Christian bride-to-be. She met her god sooner that she had expected. Maximus was labelled a fugitive but was soon after pronounced dead by Galen, after a body was found in a fire. If Maximus does return then he will be given a hero's welcome by the army. My father will pardon him, too. Certain factions in the Senate, particularly those who seek to prolong the war, may try to recruit Maximus to their cause in order to win support throughout the rest of the army. This cannot be allowed to happen."

As a child Commodus had lionised the centurion, too. Maximus was the hero of the Battle of Pannonia and the boy would avidly listen to his father's stories about the officer's exploits, fighting the northern tribes. But Commodus also remembered how the praetorian often looked at him in disapproval. The lowly soldier also once dared to call into question his conduct during a fencing bout. The Emperor's son considered himself descended from Hercules, whilst the soldier's bloodline could probably be traced back to a pig farmer and a drab. Commodus had neither forgiven nor forgotten the transgression.

I will not pardon him, like my weak father… Treat him as an enemy. Am I being paranoid? No. Or yes – but paranoia is a virtue in an Emperor. Better to be safe than sorry. History is littered with the corpses of trusting people. History will also be littered with the corpse of Gaius Maximus.

303

10.

One of the Emperor's agents had arranged for fresh horses at designated towns to speed up the journey. They were making good time, traveling across the continent to Sirmium.

When and where he could, Maximus conditioned himself; slowly but surely his paunch flattened out and turned into muscle. He also looked to sharpen his reflexes and skills by fencing with Atticus and practising on the bow with Cassius Bursus.

After fencing practise one afternoon, whilst their horses were rested and fed, Maximus and Atticus caught their breath in a clearing by a stream. The air was crisp. Woodland surrounded them but the bare trees let in a watery light. The sound of the fast running stream at their feet hissed, or shushed, them.

"What will you do with your pardon? Return to Rome? Live near Claudia and Marius?" Atticus asked his friend.

"I'm not sure yet. Rome doesn't feel like home anymore." The capital held too many bad smells and bad memories.

"I've been granted a pardon too, of sorts. I asked Aurelius if I could be granted an honourable discharge. My new life, so to speak, will start as soon as he passes away. He tried to talk me out of it but my mind was made up. I have no desire to serve under Commodus. Cassius will also be leaving the army. Aurelius has granted us all handsome donatives by the way. I should have no problem attracting a future ex-wife," Atticus joked.

"Do you have anyone special in your life at the moment, whether in Rome or Sirmium?"

"Maybe. It is winter after all. I need someone to keep my bed warm. But what about you? Did you leave anyone behind?" A smile softened Atticus' features as he thought about the enigmatic woman he was seeing. He couldn't altogether work her out, unlike most women, which made him want to get to know her all the more. At first their relationship had been professional and based on a mutual sexual attraction. But now it meant something more to him.

Does it mean something more to her as well? Or are we just playing games, with ourselves and each other?

"There's been no one since Aurelia." Maximus' voice was as cold as the icy wind which blew through the skeletal trees. He again fingered the gold band upon his finger, as he looked off into the distance, or into the past.

Flakes of snow began to gently fall and twirl in the gelid air. There was both a harshness and beauty to the scene before them. Either the world was due to freeze and die – or be renewed.

"You haven't asked, but there's been no one since you in regards to Claudia."

Maximus thought again about his friend's sister, the mother of his child. Claudia was startlingly beautiful. A siren. The soldier, or spy, hadn't needed to pretend to like her all those years ago when seducing her. There had been plenty of men before him. *What do I say to her?* He had used her that night. The fact that she was trying to use him at the same time brought little consolation. *She must hate me.*

"I was in love once, I think," Atticus said wistfully, breaking the silence between them. It was his turn to stare off into the distance. "It was before I joined the army and met you. I was just a teenager. Her name was Sara. She was a Jewess. We'd meet in secret. She was worth getting up in the morning for… She never bored me. I even had faith in the gods back then, believing that they must exist. Because she existed."

Maximus nodded, thinking about Aurelia and his first wife Julia. "What happened?"

"Our parents found out. My father forbade me from seeing her – and Sara's father prevented her from seeing me. Shortly afterwards her family moved away from the capital. I always suspected that my father had threated their family, or paid them off, in order to get them to leave Rome. The son of Pollio Atticus couldn't be allowed to marry a Jewess, after all. It must have been a love story I was involved in, because it was tragic. We still wrote to one another but life ended up getting in the way of love. Her letters lost their perfume. Happy ever afters are like these snowflakes. If you try and grab one it'll just melt in your hand."

"You should watch yourself. You're turning into a poet again," Maximus wryly said, in an attempt to lighten the mood.

"There's no fear of that. A poet's pay is worse than a soldier's. The critics can also inflict wounds that not even Galen has remedies for."

Their conversation was interrupted by the sound of bracken snapping beneath Quintus Perennis' boots as he approached.

"We're ready to head off again," the cavalry officer said. "We should reach Sirmium by this time tomorrow."

"That means we've only got a day to work our way through the remaining wine," Atticus remarked to his friend, raising his eyebrows suggestively.

"Some battles are worth fighting, even when the odds are against you," Maximus replied.

11.

He's coming.

The messenger had said that her brother – and Maximus – would reach Sirmium by the end of tomorrow. Claudia's heart quickened and she took a deep breath. She fixed her hair and straightened out her dress as if he were about to knock on her door within the hour. She had just put her son to bed. Claudia had thought it wise not to tell Marius that he would soon be seeing his father for the first time, for fear of Maximus somehow not turning up. The woman was no stranger to the unexpected, or to tragedy.

Claudia walked into the triclinium of the house that the Emperor had rented for her from Publius Aponius, a local merchant who spent his winters in Athens. The villa was homely as opposed to overtly opulent. She sat down on the sofa and clutched one of the cushions to her chest, desiring something to hold. The oil lamps illuminated the striking murals on the walls. One depicted Cleopatra encountering Caesar for the first time, dripping with gold and sensuality. The second painting she recognised as a scene from The Odyssey, when Odysseus reveals himself to Penelope. Claudia had been Cleopatra in the past. Her father had turned her into a spy and trophy at an early age. But she yearned to be Penelope. Faithful. Good.

Flecks of snow, akin to white ash, continued to fall outside. Marius had eagerly asked his mother if the snow would settle.

"I don't know," Claudia replied. The boy had more questions than she had answers for – and not just in relation to his father.

There is so much I need to explain. To both of them. But not right away. Marius is too young – and he may not even want to speak to me. Does he still consider me an enemy of the state? Please don't let things be too awkward.

She felt like praying. But instead memories eclipsed the will to pray.

Claudia thought again about those two nights, half a decade ago. The night they had made love and the following evening when he had betrayed her, and she him. And when he had murdered her father. That blissful night, when they had been together, had it all just been an act? Had she lied to herself, as well as him, when she told Maximus how she felt? When she had woken up next to him, the morning after, she had thought that it might be the first day of the rest of her life. But happy endings exist only in books or on stage, Claudia considered. But maybe she had found a portion of happiness. Marius made her happy, gave her purpose. Galen had warned her when pregnant that there was a risk to her own health, should she choose not to terminate her unborn child. "You may not survive the birth." But she was willing to sacrifice herself. "I want something good to come from my life," she had said determinedly.

Claudia tucked her legs beneath her and made a shopping list for her housemaid that she would give to her in the morning. Claudia would cook dinner for him. She remembered Maximus' favourite foods. The Emperor had provided a house for her and a number of staff, although Claudia declined some members of a retinue, including a cook and a tutor for her son. Claudia had taken charge of her son's education from the start. The so-called "best" tutors were often the strictest – and the cruellest. She preferred to adhere to the writings of Quintilian. *I disapprove of flogging. We must take care that the child, who is not yet old enough to love his studies, does not come to resent them. Studying should be filled with pleasures.*

308

There had been no one else since Maximus. Claudia had told her brother that she had not remarried because she already had a man in her life, Marius. But partly it was because she still had feelings for the centurion, even if he could never return them. *He had loved his wife, Julia. And then Aurelia... I was just the sister of his best friend. Or something more monstrous...* Claudia occasionally envisioned him returning to Rome or meeting him by accident, for Rufus had long ago told his sister that his friend's death had been a ruse. Even if their night together had been founded on lies everything, everyone, seemed unreal compared to what she felt for Maximus. Men now just wanted her as a mistress rather than wife. She was the infamous daughter – and agent – of the treacherous Pollio Atticus. An enemy of the state. A piece of graffiti on the side of a tavern in the Subura described Claudia as "Ulysses in a frock", the name that Caligula had given to Livia, the scheming wife of Augustus.

As well as sparing Maximus five years ago, Marcus Aurelius also resisted the calls to punish Claudia. He saw her as a victim, not an agent, of her power-hungry father. The Emperor had invited her to dinner shortly after Pollio Atticus had died and Maximus had disappeared. "The difference between wisdom and intelligence is the difference between compassion and cynicism. There is nothing wrong with you mourning your father, Claudia, but his death may prove to be a turning point in your life. A moment when Androcles removes the thorn from the lion's paw... I know that you may not think you should have much faith in yourself at the moment, but I know that Rufus has faith in you. I do, too. Waste no more time arguing about what a good woman should be. Be one."

I've changed. Has he changed too? I just want him to see Marius.

The snow continued to swirl about in the air, like petals in spring. On the one hand Claudia wanted the snow to settle, as her son would enjoy waking up to such a scene. But at the same time, if the snow settled, he might be delayed.

But he's coming. What will happen when he gets here? I don't know.

12.

The following day.

Via the power of the gods, or due to the Emperor's religious stubbornness, Marcus Aurelius willed himself to leave his bed. His two attendants had helped him rise – and they also propped him up as he shuffled across the room. The Emperor now leaned on the table and peered over a number of maps. Galen had tried to dissuade his patient from overexerting himself but the demi-god had his way. The doctor suspected that Aurelius didn't want to appear too weak in front of his leading commanders and officials. At least the Emperor had deferred to his doctor's wishes in wearing a fur cloak to keep him warm. Galen also insisted that the Emperor wear the garment as it disguised his emaciated figure. With a subtle nod of his head Galen had a slave move a couple of braziers closer to the Emperor.

The physician barely registered what his friend said, as he addressed his men. Anxiety lined Galen's features, like lines scored into one of the maps on the table, fearing that his patient might collapse at any moment. Galen noted the worry lines creep into Commodus' expression too, though his anxiety stemmed from the fear that his father may have been displaying signs of a recovery. The observant doctor also saw that Commodus had invited his favourite into his father's inner circle.

If Commodus will be Caligula reborn, then this Titus may prove to be a new Sejanus. History seldom repeats itself in a good way.

Galen sighed. He then turned his attention to the Emperor. Aurelius was mustering his bodily and vocal strength, speaking more forcefully now than he had done over the past two months.

311

"It's been confirmed through two separate pieces of intelligence. We know the location of Balomar. He is staying with one of his kinsfolk here, just behind enemy lines. Come the spring he will tour the territory to form another alliance of tribes against us. We must not allow him to do so," the Emperor exclaimed, pounding his fist on the table. He sighed (or wheezed) immediately afterwards, from exhaustion and from disappointment at displaying such frustration and anger.

"Balomar" was the one name which could test the equanimity of the devout stoic. The leader of the Marcomanni had been a thorn in the side of Rome for over a decade. He was behind the initial raids on the Empire, which had started the war with the northern tribes. Balomar was a clever – and brutal – commander; he had been the author of too many Roman deaths – soldiers and civilians alike. Balomar had also been the architect of numerous enemy alliances. The wars with the Iazyges, Quadi and Chatti – Balomar had blood on his hands in regards to all of them. Whether through threats or promises he was the only man who could unite the Germanic tribes against Rome.

The bloodletting will only end once we let his *blood.*

"Just give me the order, Caesar, and I will wipe him off the map," Helvius Pertinax remarked, glaring at the mark on the parchment where it was reported the barbarian was staying. Pertinax spoke from a loyalty towards his Emperor – and personal enmity towards the leader of the Marcomanni. Balomar had been responsible for the raid at which his nephew had been killed – eviscerated.

Whilst the other soldiers in the room sympathised with Pertinax's sentiments, Commodus eyed the senior commander with suspicion. The son of a freedman, Pertinax had risen through the ranks (Commodus preferred officers to be high born). Pertinax was a popular and accomplished officer, to such an extent that

Commodus needed to keep a close eye on him, or else certain factions in the capital could recruit him to their cause when his father finally died.

"If we send a large force then Balomar's spies will alert him to our presence and purpose. He will disappear again and we will have more chance of finding a satisfied Pict. He knows the terrain and he has too many allies in the region. No, less will prove more. We need to employ stealth, not might. The plan will be to just send a handful of men behind enemy lines with orders to assassinate Balomar by any means necessary. It may not be the most honourable death for a king, but Balomar would slit all of your throats in the night in a blink of an eye should the tables be turned."

Heads around the table nodded in agreement. The Marcomanni had proved themselves to be as trustworthy as Carthaginians over the past ten years. They could sign a peace treaty with one hand whilst clasping a dagger behind their back with the other.

"Do you have anyone in mind for the mission, Caesar? Few in our ranks could be sure of recognising Balomar," Pertinax said, worrying that the wily Marcomanni chief might even employ a double to escape capture and death.

"I do indeed have someone in mind, Helvius," Aurelius replied, mustering his strength to raise an enigmatic smile. "An old friend."

13.

Claudia straightened her dress again and took a deep breath. She tucked her hair behind her ear and squeezed Marius' hand, from nervousness and out of affection. She had washed her son herself that morning. Marius had already been excited by the blanket of snow outside, but there had been wonder in the boy's eyes as she told him that his father was coming to see him that day. He asked a hundred questions, of which Claudia could only answer a dozen or so satisfactorily.

A freshly shaven Maximus came into the triclinium, accompanied by her brother and Martina, her young housemaid, who had greeted her guests at the door. Firstly Claudia was struck by how much Maximus had aged. She had always pictured him as his younger self, stuck in time, for so long. Still he possessed his strong jaw, and appeared tough. But Claudia had experienced the tenderness underneath, too.

Is he still the most honourable man I know?

"Thank you, Martina. That will be all."

The maid bowed her head and scurried off towards the kitchen, turning her head to take in the handsome brother of her mistress one last time before disappearing.

Age has not withered her, Maximus thought. Her full length woollen dress could not disguise the lithe figure beneath. A pair of violet coloured silk slippers poked out below the hem of the garment. Claudia also wore a silver brooch, in the shape of a deer, which the Emperor had given her. Unlike before, when she had been a celebrated beauty and shaper of fashion in Rome, Claudia now wore little or no make-up. Maximus recalled a phrase from

314

Ovid that Rufus had often parroted many years ago: *The best make-up remains unobtrusive.*

Both Claudia and Maximus stared at each other somewhat sheepishly. But their mutual awkwardness brought them together. The air was free from enmity. Maximus couldn't tell if his heart or head (from his hangover) was throbbing more. He half-smiled at the attractive woman from his past, the mother of his child. She smiled back, kindly – unaffectedly. Maximus had long forgiven her, to the point where he couldn't remember if he had ever had reason to condemn her. Her sins had belonged to her father.

And Claudia had long forgiven him. The centurion had been doing his duty – and had saved the city through his actions. Her father had been her jailor; Maximus had set her free. Claudia had rehearsed the scene of encountering Maximus again a thousand times before. But she couldn't now remember her lines.

A welcoming fire crackled in the hearth. Maximus' nostrils were filled with the smell of fresh bread and honey-glazed pork, roasting on a spit in the adjacent kitchen. His half-smile transformed itself into something more fulsome when he took in the child by Claudia's side, clutching her hand and skirt. He was sweet-faced and blue-eyed. Healthy and happy looking. Despite repeatedly planning what he intended to say to his son when seeing him for the first time, Maximus was lost for words. Something swelled up in his chest. Pride. Happiness. Love. A combination of all three and more. Cicero needed to add another word to the Latin vocabulary to articulate how he felt. Tears moistened his once sorrowful eyes.

"Marius, this is your father, Gaius Maximus," Claudia said, fondly, as she let go of her son's hand. Tears moistened her eyes as well, for reasons that the woman would be at pains to wholly explain.

315

Maximus dropped to his knees. Partly he was overwhelmed and partly he wanted to come down to his son's level. Look him in the eye. The boy tentatively walked towards the stranger. Marius' unblinking expression and the tint of his hair reminded Maximus of his own father. The child glanced at his uncle, who smiled back at him for reassurance. Rufus nodded at his nephew, encouraging him to approach his father. Marius looked back at his mother and she too signalled to keep walking. The child scrunched his face up in slight confusion, endearingly and adorably. Claudia smiled – and commenced to laugh and sob.

At first the nervous child slowed to a standstill – but then his sweet nature vanquished his shyness and Marius suddenly ran the final few steps and launched himself into the chest of his father. His tiny arms barely stretched across the soldier's broad chest but he grabbed Maximus' tunic and clung on. And Maximus wrapped his arms around the precious child in return, clinging on for dear life, as if he were embracing his future. Meaning. Hope. And partly Maximus thought of Lucius and imagined he was embracing his dead son, come to life.

"I should leave you all to catch up," Rufus remarked. "I need to catch up on some sleep." The centurion also thought about the woman whom he wanted to join him in bed. *I've missed her.*

"Are you sure you would not like to join us for lunch?" Claudia asked, thinking how it might be too premature to spend time with Maximus alone.

"I'm sure," Rufus replied, thinking how he wanted to skip straight to his dessert. "I'll call on you later. We still have to meet with the Emperor. He's expecting us. Duty calls."

14.

The snow gave way to sunshine.

Cheers stabbed skywards, along with spears, as Maximus entered the camp, accompanied by Atticus and Cassius Bursus. Word had spread throughout the legion faster than a pox that Maximus was returning. Legionaries who had served under him chanted his name and thumped their swords upon scutums to salute the centurion. Those who knew Maximus – or just knew of the legendary soldier – joined the throng around him. Jokes were traded, jugs of wine were shared.

"You look good, for a dead man," one veteran called out to Maximus, who had served with him in Egypt.

"We both know that the only thing that could ever kill me is your cooking," Maximus replied.

He was invited by half a dozen old comrades to join them around the campfire later for a drink and meal. But mainly a drink. The most frequent thing asked was whether the officer was coming back to lead them again.

"We'll see," Maximus replied, suggestively. His mind was closed to the idea of re-enlisting however. *No more.* He just didn't want to ruin the celebratory mood.

Titus was in the camp at the time and took in the scene and atmosphere. He knew that it was his job to report the news of the popular centurion's return to Commodus – and the army's reaction to it – but he feared he would put his master and lover in a foul and petulant mood if he did.

"Hail the conquering hero," Atticus remarked in sardonic good humour, not begrudging his friend his moment in the sun.

"Wouldn't you hail him too? He has, after all, conquered death," Maximus replied, winking, grinning and clinking cups with the centurion.

The air was soon clogged up with snow again, however, and Maximus' jubilant mood turned into mournfulness, as he turned his attention to visiting his ailing Emperor.

*

Sawdust was strewn across the floor to soak up the snow that visitors brought in with them. Braziers glowed and hummed. Maximus stood before the Emperor, who again was propped up in a seated position in his bed, as grey and white as a statue. For a moment or two Aurelius stared vacantly, listlessly, into the opposite corner of the room to where Maximus was. Oblivious to the soldier – and the world. Such was the stillness and pallor of the Emperor's expression that Maximus briefly considered that Aurelius was already wearing his death mask. Maximus also noticed the numerous empty phials of theriac scattered across the bedside table. His brow creased in worry at seeing his friend so frail, so diminished. During his time in Briton the praetorian had always pictured his commander at his best.

Age has withered him… But it withers us all.

"Thank you for coming Maximus," the Emperor said kindly, his expression softening into fondness and a smile as he turned to take in his old friend. "Britain's loss is our gain. What are your thoughts on the island and its people? I've heard conflicting reports."

"If Rome is concerned with bread and circuses, Britain concerns itself with beer and cockfights."

"Everywhere is different and everywhere is the same," the philosopher proclaimed, although he decided that that particular phrase would not be included in his book of meditations. "Please Maximus, come closer. Step into the light. My eyesight is growing as weak as my voice. Have you been able to see Marius yet?"

It was not just the oil lamps hanging overhead which caused Maximus' face to light up, as he beamed and thought of his son. After Rufus had departed Maximus had spent the afternoon with Marius. He had asked the boy about his studies and his home back in Campania. Then they had gone outside into the garden and Maximus had taught his son how to make and throw a snowball. "You should twist and use your whole body, it's like throwing a javelin." Marius had cheered and laughed with delight when he got one throw right and the missile soared over the garden wall. On subsequent throws he had imagined himself throwing a javelin and felling Rome's enemies. He wanted to be a soldier, like his father. Maximus had explained that he was now back, from a special mission that the Emperor had sent him on. He would explain more when Marius was old enough to understand. In the meantime he intended to live near his son and catch up on the time he had missed with him.

"Yes. He is a fine boy and in good health."

"And how is Claudia?"

"She is well."

Maximus refrained from giving voice to his thoughts about how well she looked. He had continually stolen glances at her across the table as they had eaten their lunch. He had forgotten just how beautiful she was. Maximus was taken aback too by how accomplished a cook she had become. Regardless of his heart, she captured the soldier's stomach. After the child's exhausting afternoon and a filling lunch Martina had taken Marius upstairs and the boy had quickly fallen asleep. Once alone Maximus and Claudia had spoken to one another in earnest.

"He's a credit to you. He reads his letters better at five than I did at fifteen."

"He wants to be a soldier, like his father."

"I'd prefer him to be smart and kind, like his mother."

319

Claudia had blushed – adding to her radiant expression.

"He still needs his father," she had replied, resisting from voicing the thought that she needed – wanted – him too. "Can you stay?"

"Yes. Now I've found him, I'm not about to lose him. I've been dead long enough for one lifetime."

"He'll be happy to know that you're staying."

I'm happy too. "I'm sorry that I've been absent, Claudia."

"You didn't know. I don't blame you. I should be the one apologising to you for what happened five years ago. For who I was. I need you to know though, that I didn't have any part in what happened to Aurelia."

"I know. I do not blame you. But let us not talk about what happened five years ago. Let's look to the future and the next five years. Although I cannot quite get over Rufus' change of heart. He was married, twice!"

"Perhaps he realised that he wasn't getting any younger. He no longer had the energy to jump out of the bed – and the window – when the husbands came home earlier than expected."

Maximus smiled to himself, recalling Claudia's joke. He also recalled her comments about how supportive the Emperor had been.

"I am grateful for you having provided for Marius and his mother in my absence. Rufus and Claudia told me what you have done for them."

"I publicly condemned you and pronounced you dead – I felt that it was the least I could do. I regret my decision in not pardoning you immediately, Maximus. In engineering your death however, I helped to spare your life I hope. I was caught between the Scylla and Charybdis of the army and various senators, loyal to Pollio Atticus. His allies are now weakened or dead, his influence non-existent."

After he spoke Aurelius winced in pain – and Maximus was reminded again of his imminent fate. The soldier had spoken to Galen, before meeting with the Emperor.

"He will be fortunate to see the summer. Or rather, given the bouts of torment he increasingly endures, he will be unfortunate to live till the summer," the physician had explained.

Maximus saw the Emperor's armour and weaponry on the wall opposite his bed. His attendant dutifully polished the set every day, full knowing that his master would never be able to wear it again.

"I am a dying man, Maximus. No matter how poor my eyesight gets, I see that. Even demi-gods cannot live forever. But to study human life over forty years is the same as to study it over ten thousand. Dying is but a sleep, to which one never wakes up. I do not fear death, but I do worry about what might happen in this life to my friends, Commodus, and the Empire."

The aged Emperor took rasping breaths, from anxiety and exhaustion.

"Would you like something to ease the pain?" Maximus asked, tempted to call for Galen.

"Yes. Kill Balomar. It's the only way to end this prolonged war. He's the keystone. Take him out and the edifice of any opposition will fall. He's been behind every broken peace treaty. I also believe he has encouraged some tribes to sign alliances with us, only to have them break the treaty at an opportune moment. I have recently received reports of his whereabouts, not far into enemy territory. His aim is to form a grand alliance against us in the spring. I believe that you can succeed, Maximus, where successive armies have failed. You are one of the few men who can recognise him – and kill him."

Maximus pictured the barbarian leader, as he had seen him across the river at the Battle of Pannonia. Muscular. Square-faced and bald-headed. Gesticulating and bellowing orders. The enemy claimed that Rome was guilty of telling scare stories for propaganda reasons, but Maximus had witnessed the results of Balomar's barbarism first-hand. Captured legionaries were decapitated or tortured for his amusement. Women and children were burned alive, under his direct orders. Maximus had had to cut free some of the charred corpses from the stakes himself in one village. Balomar was not even averse to butchering his own people, should they show any signs of colluding with the enemy. The warlord had been responsible for the deaths of countless friends and comrades. He was in some way responsible for the death of Arrian, Aurelia's brother. Should he form his grand alliance then he would be responsible for thousands upon thousands of other people dying.

But this is now somebody else's fight. I just want to see my son.

"I came back to be a father, not a soldier."

Maximus pictured Claudia, as she asked him about his plans earlier. She would rather him remain a farmer than enlist again. It would not be fair on her or Marius if every time Maximus left the house they worried about him not returning.

"I've no intention of rejoining the army, Claudia. I've served my time, done my duty. I owe a duty to my son and you now. Besides, the cook at the camp doesn't have your recipe for honey-glazed pork."

Aurelius sympathised with Maximus' plight, but still implored him.

"I can but ask rather than order you to accept this mission. It's a dying man's last request. I will reward you handsomely. You and your family will be provided for, for the rest of your lives… But you must kill him. Cut the head off the snake. Cut out the cancer in our lives."

The Emperor's rheumy eyes fixed themselves upon Maximus' face – and soul. For once, the stoic had briefly bared his teeth and snarled. He noticed the old man clasp the sheets of his bed. He was clinging to life, perhaps solely to hear from Maximus that he would fulfil his mission, as death clung to him too from the other side. There was delirium as well as desperation in his demeanour. The wisest person Maximus had ever known was, for once, being governed as much by hatred as reason.

He recalled his first real encounter with his Emperor, mentor and friend. Neither of them had grey hair back then. Maximus was a young praetorian, serving as a guard at the imperial palace. He would often observe Aurelius out of the corner of his eye, or strain to catch whatever he said. Aurelius would walk around the palace late at night, seemingly in a world of his own – wistful or amused by a private thought or joke. Or sad, for reasons that only he understood. Yet when he would speak to anyone, whether it be an official or to a lowly slave, he would treat the person as if they were the most important thing in the world to him at that moment. Maximus admired his judicial judgements. Aurelius was free from being corrupted by wealth, or the malign influence of powerful politicians calling in favours. "Let justice be done though the heavens fall."

Maximus was walking through the palace one evening, on his way home from his shift on sentry duty, when he saw the Emperor walking towards him along the marble-tiled, lamp-lit passage. Maximus stopped and stood to attention as the seemingly oblivious man strolled past him. Yet Aurelius was not four steps away from the praetorian when he stopped and turned towards the soldier.

"You are Gaius Maximus, are you not?"

"Yes, Caesar," he had replied, his rod-straight spine straightening up even more. Although Aurelius had worn a calm, equitable expression on his face, the young soldier had still feared he may have done something wrong.

"I have heard good reports about you, Maximus. Of course, everyone has a divine spark within them but yours may burn brighter than most. I have noticed you, standing at the back at the occasional judicial hearing and philosophy lecture I give. Did I say anything mildly interesting or memorable? I must confess I often forget myself what I say or meditate upon. I suppose I should start writing things down. Indeed, I will commence to do so from this evening onwards," he had remarked, pleased by his new found resolution.

The praetorian's palms had sweated, his heart had raced and his mind had initially drawn a blank in attempting to remember something he had heard his Emperor say. But, whether borne from a divine spark or not, a light had shone out in the darkness and Maximus had remembered a line from a lecture Aurelius had recently given.

"Each hour decide firmly – like a Roman and a man – to do what is at hand."

The following day Maximus had plucked up the courage to ask his future wife, Julia, out to dinner.

*

After visiting Aurelius and downing a few drinks around a campfire with some former comrades in arms, Maximus rode back to Claudia's house. He saw his son again and tucked him in, telling him stories about his time spent with the Emperor over the years. After Marius fell asleep his father shed a quiet tear in private, as he remembered his other children, Lucius and Aemelia, who had been victims of the plague.

Sunt lacrimae rerum.

The sound of a distant shutter slamming against its frame could just about be heard over the howling wind as Maximus, Atticus and Claudia sat in the triclinium. Maximus waited until after dinner to tell them about his meeting with the Emperor and his decision.

"But why does it have to be you? The Emperor should know, more than anyone else, how much you have sacrificed in the name of doing your duty." Claudia wrung her hands as she spoke. Anger eclipsed her exasperation.

Maximus had tried to explain that he owed the Emperor for providing for Marius, for pardoning him, and that their financial future would be secure if he took on the mission. In the end, however, Maximus told the truth, as to why he had acceded to the dying man's last request.

"Because he would do the same for me if our positions were reversed."

I owe him a duty, as a son does to his father.

Claudia pursed her lips, for fear of raising her voice even more and waking her son, and merely shook her head. She then stood up. First Maximus and Atticus heard the sound of rustling silk as the woman walked out of the room (her brother had noted how his sister had put on her best dress for the night, or rather for his friend). Then they heard the sound of a slammed door, as opposed to shutter.

"If I closed my eyes I might well have imagined myself back home, being married to my second wife," Atticus said, trying to ease any tension in the room. "As long as you make sure you come back alive, Claudia will forgive you. When do we leave?"

"I'll be leaving the day after tomorrow, with Cassius. I need you to remain here, Rufus. If something happens to me then you'll still be around to take care of Claudia and Marius. Besides, you've got more chance of cutting Balomar down with an insult than you have with a bow. Unless your aim has improved dramatically over the past five years."

"Just make sure you assassinate the bastard rather than try to be an emissary. The last diplomat we sent to talk to the Marcomanni was skewered by a captured ballista."

"Balomar's already dead. He just doesn't know it yet," Maximus said, with a determined look in his eye. Consciously or unconsciously, the soldier gripped his sword.

Atticus had witnessed that look in his friend's eye before – and believed him.

15.

Marcus Aurelius gazed on vacantly, glassy-eyed, for having taken Galen's ever more potent theriac. He was sat on a chair at the head of the table. Occasionally the eyes of the people in the room would flit towards the atrophied Emperor, but most squarely looked forward and focused on the task at hand.

The two agents who had composed the intelligence reports, confirming Balomar's location, briefed Maximus and Cassius Bursus. They provided maps and other useful nuggets of information. One of the agents, Vibius Nepos, would accompany the soldiers most of the way, as he was heading in the same direction into enemy territory on a separate mission. Vibius had served as one of the Emperor's chief intelligence officers since the beginning of the war. Despite his naturally duplicitous occupation, Maximus trusted his character and information. Vibius was a Roman aristocrat with a talent for playing the role of a German merchant or Greek diplomat. The spy was renowned for his ruthlessness and sartorial elegance. He had a narrow face with eyebrows that seemed perpetually arched, in a state of scepticism or accusation. A charming smile nestled itself within a neatly trimmed beard. Maximus also noted the large signet ring on his middle finger, which was rumoured to contain a poisoned needle.

"We will travel by horse up until this village, but then it'll be wiser to travel by foot and avoid the main roads. You both have a rudimentary knowledge of the local language, I believe?" the agent asked the soldiers.

Cassius Bursus nodded. He knew how to order a meal, drink and whore. To learn anything else seemed superfluous in the eyes of the optio.

"I know enough to get us out of any trouble, I hope. Though it may be the case that I know enough to get us *into* trouble. But the plan will be to avoid any locals where possible. And if need be, this will do the talking," Maximus remarked, clasping the handle of his sword. He also made a mental note to have Atticus teach him a few more phrases that might come in useful. His friend picked up languages as easily as he seemed to be able to pick up married women.

"I'm happy for you to kill as many locals as you see fit, just so long as it means you kill your principle target. We may not get another chance. *Carpe diem*. Balomar will be travelling with a personal bodyguard of around twenty men. But he will be away from the rest of his army – and those veterans with him will be rotated into three shifts. Once you do the deed then your best route back will be via these tracks and roads. I will arrange for men with horses to be posted here."

Commodus leaned forward and paid close attention to the map and briefing as the agent discussed Maximus' route back to the camp.

*

After the briefing – Aurelius gave a slow nod of his head to communicate that he was content – Vibius instructed an attendant to tell the slaves to start bringing out food and to pour the wine.

Lunch was a veritable feast – a non-stop procession of moreish delicacies: large cubes of ham dipped in honey and poppy seeds; wild boar sausages seasoned with pepper; pickled snails; red mullet on a bed of cabbage, lettuce and radishes; spiced figs; local and imported cheeses; honey-glazed game pie with pine nuts. A few keen gourmets stood near to the door where the slaves entered with their large pewter plates of foodstuffs, in order not to miss out on anything (and to secure second helpings before the servers disappeared back into the kitchen). The Emperor had made a special effort. Atticus later grimly joked that "it was like the last meal, of a condemned man."

Beer, as well as wine, was served. Toasts were made to Nemesis (the goddess of vengeance) and Victoria (the goddess of victory) to speed Maximus and Cassius Bursus on their way.

"The gods go with you," Pertinax warmly exclaimed, raising his cup to the soldiers.

Maximus lifted his cup up in reply but thought how he would have preferred the less ethereal figure of Atticus to accompany him on the mission.

Shortly after Maximus exchanged a few private words with Pertinax he was approached by Commodus. The young man was wearing an ornate breastplate covered in gold leaf and decorated with various medals and honours (which had been bestowed rather than earned). Suffice to say the uniform had seen more polish than blood. His build was sinewy rather than athletic. Maximus recalled how Atticus had once said that Commodus often had a "lean and hungry look about him", quoting Julius Caesar's comment about Cassius Longinus. Maximus had never been fond of the Emperor's son – Commodus had regularly questioned the centurion about what it felt like to kill a man or torture a prisoner, but when Commodus visited the frontline it would often coincide with a Roman victory, and many in the army considered the child to be a talisman. Over the years Aurelius would give his son various titles, to compensate for the lack of affection and attention he gave him.

"I wish you every good fortune for your mission, Maximus. For we know how fickle a mistress' fortune can be. A man can be a hero one day and a villain come the morning. Or even, in your case, a man can be dead one moment and alive the next. But I am preaching to the converted. You have experienced more triumph and tragedy than most," Commodus remarked, overly gesticulating with his hands as he spoke, his fingers tickling the air as if he were a bad actor. Maximus could smell the wine on his breath – and also perfume on his skin. "I fear that we will soon experience the tragedy of my father passing away. But my grief will be tempered slightly, and my father will feel better, knowing that you will serve me as you served him. You are re-joining the ranks of the army, are you not?"

"I am afraid that I am just enlisting for this mission. I have no doubt that you will be able to find enough suitable men to serve your ends."

"You should never say never, Maximus. Who knows how fortune may smile on you when I become Emperor. I am but asking for your loyalty now. As Emperor, I may demand it – for the good of Rome, of course. Remember that I have the right to do anything to anybody, to quote Caligula," Commodus said. His smile turned into a self-satisfied sneer. A sense of mischief and malice gleamed in his eye. The problem was that Commodus couldn't differentiate between the two.

"You would do better to quote your father – and learn from his reign – than you would Caligula when you become Emperor," Maximus replied, wishing that the young man would heed his advice, but believing that his words would ultimately be in vain.

"I will be conscious of being my own man when I commence to rule – and absorb the lessons of all the Caesars who reigned before me. Your loyalty to my father is noted, though. In some ways you were the son he never had. And I imagine that in some ways he was the father you never had. Does a part of you wish we could swap places, Maximus?"

"I am about to venture into enemy territory, nigh on alone, in order to kill one of Rome's most formidable enemies. Most might call it a suicide mission. So, in answer to your question, I wouldn't mind swapping places with anyone right now."

*

330

After lunch Maximus spent his time saying various farewells. In some instances comrades looked him in the eye and firmly shook his hand or hugged him as if it would be the last time that they would see the soldier. Maximus also called upon Galen, partly to hear his latest prognosis regarding the Emperor and partly to say goodbye. The physician was in the middle of preparing a poultice for an injured legionary but, once finished, he sat his old friend down and spoke to him in earnest. Age and fretfulness bedraggled his appearance but there was still a kernel of vigour and conviction in his aspect and voice.

"Should the choice be between fulfilling your duty and dying in the process, or failing in your mission but living to tell the tale, I want you to choose life, Maximus. You have a duty to yourself – and your family – over that of some noble idea you have in regards to the Empire. The Empire will still be the Empire whether Balomar's head is on a spike or sleeping on a pillow the following morning. You are in credit with Rome, you don't owe it anything. And make sure you bring Cassius Bursus back with you in one piece. He shouldn't fall in battle – but rather he should die from a pox in old age, as nature intended. You should return for Claudia as well as Marius," Galen expressed firmly, remembering what the woman had said to him shortly before Maximus was due to return: *He hurt me. But he's still the only one who can cure that hurt.*

As the crimson sun sunk into the horizon, Maximus looked in on the Emperor, to say goodbye. Aurelius was in bed, sleeping. He seemed at peace and Maximus didn't want to wake him. He gazed at the old man in sorrow and fondness, as if he were already starting to mourn him. Perhaps sensing a presence in the room, Aurelius woke and turned his head towards the door, but Maximus was already leaving and his lungs were not strong enough to call the soldier back.

Maximus had said his most important farewell that morning to his son, however. He had hugged Marius for what seemed like an age, and there had been tears in his eyes. The boy had sensed that something was amiss and had asked again about where his father was going.

"I'm going on a mission – to buy you a pony," Maximus had replied. "I'll be back in a few days, don't worry."

Shortly afterwards, outside in the frost-tinged garden, Maximus had met with Claudia in private. The wind had blown her hair across her face but it disguised her tear-soaked cheeks. She had tightened the woollen cloak around her shoulders, but shivered also in fear. In fear of losing him – and of telling him and not telling him how she felt. The woman's manner had been as frosty as the morning air, however, as Maximus tried again to convince her of the virtue of his decision.

Claudia had refused to say goodbye to the too dutiful soldier, having experienced a presentiment that, should she do so, she would never see him again.

*

That evening Maximus dined with Rufus Atticus, in a cottage close by to the camp which the centurion had rented. Maximus cast his eye around the place. The main room served as both a kitchen and dining area. An oil lamp above them squeaked, swaying from the breeze which whistled through the shutters. Shelves, bulging with books, lined the walls – interspersed with some freshly painted murals of Italian pastorals. A marble bust of Virgil (a gift from Atticus' latest lover) sat on the table, next to a bronze stylus. The officer had started to write again, inspired by something – or rather someone.

Atticus poured out two cups of wine and sat down opposite his friend.

"Aurelius gave me this vintage, on the condition that I should save it for a special occasion."

"Well it could well be our last drink together."

"I was rather thinking that it was special due to it being our retirement party," Atticus wryly said.

Maximus duly smiled and clinked his cup, thinking how he shouldn't get too drunk as he needed a clear head for his early start in the morning.

"I'll drink to that. Aurelius may well pass away before I return, Rufus. I need you to be ready to leave as soon as that happens. Claudia and Marius need to be ready as well. Commodus is not to be trusted. He may well view us as possible threats to his regime when he gains power. Or he may prove equally delusional and consider us allies – and we'll never be able to retire. I have no intention of being his friend or enemy. I owe Aurelius much, but I owe his son nothing."

"I've already placed most of our money with a trusted banker, if that's not a too oxymoronic title. I agree that we cannot entirely predict how Commodus will behave, so we need to be out of the reach of his sword arm, so to speak, when the time comes."

"I'll drink to that too," Maximus replied, holding his cup aloft again and thinking now that he didn't need *too* clear a head for the morning.

16.

The trio of Maximus, Cassius and Vibius Nepos had ridden hard for the first part of the day. A light shower in the morning had kept the ground soft but then the sun was on their back and the temperature rose to take the sting out of the chill wind.

Nepos was dressed as a merchant, but he had dressed the soldiers up to look like a couple of German hunters. They wore thick woollen tunics, which had been re-dyed and patched-up from different pieces of cloth to look authentic. They also wore woollen stockings and hooded brown cloaks which could double-up as blankets. The hoods would also cover their Roman faces and haircuts.

"Better to be warm and uncomfortable than cold and dead," Vibius said to Cassius when the optio complained about the coarse goat-hair undergarment he was given to wear.

As they neared enemy territory Vibius took them off the main roads. Although the journey would take longer he led them through a narrow woodland trail. The branches of tall oak trees criss-crossed above the riders. Cassius took point and scouted ahead while Maximus and the agent followed behind.

"So how good a shot is our optio?" Vibius asked, conscious that the success of the mission might ultimately rely on the archer's aim.

"He's the best I've ever seen. He'll be able to hit his target from fifty paces."

"It will need to be a kill shot, a head shot."

"I know. And Cassius will be able to hit his target from fifty paces. Or more."

The agent raised his thin eyebrows in scepticism.

"You may yet accomplish your mission – and live to tell the tale – Maximus," Vibius expressed, although not entirely convinced by his words. Balomar had slipped through the net many times before – and there were more outcomes related to failure than success.

"Even if we succeed, do you think that it will mean an end to the war?" Maximus asked.

"No. The war won't end but the act may prevent the war from getting worse. Balomar can be seen as a German Mithridates. Not only is he an inspirational figure for those who wish to defy Rome, but the Marcomanni chief also has the power to rally other tribes against us," Vibius posited, sending another small prayer up into the ether that Maximus would succeed in his mission and rid Rome of the thorn in its side. The agent was as keen to retire as the soldier – and spend the rest of his days with his young wife at his villa just outside of Massilia. Friends suggested that the aristocrat should live in the capital and go into politics but the agent had experienced enough back-stabbing and bribery to last him a lifetime.

"Do you really think that one man can make such a difference?"

"Aurelius thinks so, given how much he used to praise you for the difference you made at Pannonia, and also for saving Rome from the machinations of Pollio Atticus. You have made a name for yourself, Maximus. I've even heard you called the 'Sword of Empire'. But names can be targets – and swords double-edged. When Aurelius passes away Commodus may see you as someone he needs to court, or eliminate, given your popularity within the army," the agent remarked, his eyebrows raised in a warning to the soldier. He was worried by Commodus' imminent coronation, for himself, as well as others. Vibius envisioned being summoned to Rome in order to compose false intelligence reports and extract confessions from prospective opponents of the new Emperor.

Those who possessed various properties which Commodus desired would, of course, be most at risk at being labelled a traitor.

Before Maximus had a chance to respond to the agent, Cassius Bursus came back down the track, his brow wrinkled in concern and his hand clasping his bow.

*

Four seasoned warriors, armed with an array of weapons (short swords, hand axes and bows), were positioned at a crossroads on the trail. Two stood beside a well whilst the other two were starting a fire. Their four horses were loosely tethered to a post in the clearing. The Romans watched the barbarians through the dense woodland as they pulled out some ham, bread and a jug of wine.

"It appears they may be stopping for some time," Vibius said, shaking his head and pursing his lips. "We do not have the time to go around them. It's doubtful we'll be able to bluff our way past them, either. If just one of those men escapes then he could alert the nearest village. And they'll hunt us down like a pack of hounds, as well as have word sent to Balomar about our presence."

"Is this your diplomatic way of saying make sure you kill them all?" Cassius Bursus asked, retrieving an arrow from his quiver as he did so.

Vibius nodded.

"How good are you with that knife?" Maximus asked, referring to the dagger hanging from the agent's belt.

"About as effective as you would be drafting a peace treaty, unfortunately. But I've had some experience knowing where to put the pointy end."

"Let's consider it two against four then, Cassius. They're still better odds than usual. We've also got surprise on our side."

Shortly afterwards Maximus and Vibius were walking towards the crossroads. Maximus swung a jug of wine back and forth and swayed a little, pretending to be drunk. Vibius too sparked a light in his eyes and smiled serenely, as if half intoxicated.

Most barbarians from the northern tribes looked the same to a Roman: long greasy hair and beard; dull or ferocious eyes; dressed in furs, leather and adorned with crudely crafted pieces of jewellery. The four men that Maximus and Vibius were about to address did little to challenge their prejudices.

The warriors harboured their own distrust and prejudices too when it came to strangers, and they rose to the feet, their hands resting on their weapons, as the two travellers approached.

"Afternoon friends, would you care to share your fire and some food in exchange for some wine?" Vibius asked amiably in their native language, slurring his words slightly.

Maximus grinned and held aloft his jug of wine as the largest of the barbarians stepped towards him. The heavy-set German nodded at the strangers and licked his lips at the thought of more wine. Hands retreated from weapons.

There was a dull thud, and a slight clink, as Maximus whipped his arm around and struck the barbarian around the side of the head with the ceramic jug.

No sooner did Maximus hear the sound of his enemy slumping to the ground than an arrow whistled past his ear. The shaft struck the barbarian to the right of him. Cassius had targeted the man's upper chest, to kill him quickly and puncture his lung, silencing any scream.

The barbarian to Maximus' left was rooted to the spot, in either shock or fear. The Roman drew his short sword from beneath his cloak, as the German struggled to free his hand-axe from his belt. But just when Maximus believed it was going to be an easy kill, the barbarian suddenly launched himself forward, butting his chest like a ram.

In the meantime the remaining German had reacted quickly. The young, agile warrior had chosen flight over fight. He turned and sped towards his horse. Just as Julius Caesar used to mount his horse by leaping onto it from the hind quarters, so did the barbarian spring into position. He swiftly wheeled the black mare around, kicked his heels into its flanks, and galloped down the muddy track towards the nearest village.

Maximus was knocked to the floor. Winded. His sword fell out of his hand and he was unable to reach it as the growling barbarian straddled his chest and pinned him down. A pungent smell of sweat and rancid cheese filled the Roman's nostrils. The barbarian's bearded face was contorted in rage.

Cassius Bursus let out a curse beneath his breath. Vibius stood between the archer and his target. He was also conscious of the fact that one of their enemy had reached his horse.

The barbarian had now liberated his rust-spotted axe from his belt. The warrior clasped one hand around his opponent's throat, choking him, whilst his other was raised – about to deliver the killing blow.

Death would swallow another victim (one victim meant as much as the next). But perhaps death should be seen as more of a release – salvation rather than damnation.

The blade buried itself between two ribs, and slashed open his heart. Blood drenched his hand. The agent was as clinical as Galen in inserting his knife into the barbarian. Maximus gave Vibius a brief – but sincere – nod of thanks.

The rage was extinguished from the German's eyes immediately and Maximus pushed the odorous corpse off him.

The centurion didn't need to give the order. Cassius had already run out from the treeline and raced to set the fleeing horseman in his sights. Vibius bit his lip in anxiety, knowing that if the barbarian escaped the mission might as well be over. With every

338

moment that passed doubt took a chip out of the hope that the praetorian would be able to make the shot. The plan would have to be now to give chase and pray that their horses were up to the task.

The bow creaked under the strain and, for once, the archer's arm twitched slightly. Cassius gently breathed out however, and the arrow whished into the air. He had aimed upwards, in order for the shaft to arc back downwards into the target. He was unable to aim too high however, for fear of snagging one of the branches which hung over the track.

Hearts stopped and an expectant silence filled the air for a second or two whilst the arrow was in flight. But hearts then started up again, beating fast in triumph, as the missile stabbed itself into the horseman's back. The warrior arched his spine and then fell from his mount.

Vibius slit the throats of all the barbarians. Maximus noted how the urbane agent seemed to perform the duty with a sense of relish as well as ruthlessness. The mask slipped and the soldier took in the wild animal, or rather man, behind it. The spy's plan was to make things appear as if bandits had slaughtered the warriors. Vibius took what little valuables he found on the corpses. He also asked Cassius if he was carrying any dice with him.

"Yes, why?" the archer asked.

"There's a group of brigands who operate in the region – and after each raid they leave dice on one of the bodies, to mark their territory."

Vibius left the dice on one of the corpse's chests – a Dog throw, as opposed to a Venus throw, showing.

*

The three men rode hard through the forest. By dusk they reached a fork in the trail, where Vibius would have to go his separate way. Maximus and Cassius would now have to travel through dense woodland to remain off the map, so the agent took all the horses with him. He would be able to play his part and blend in more easily, without being hampered by the soldiers.

"What's your mission?" the archer asked as they were parting, intrigued.

"There are some affairs – not just extra marital ones – that are best left secret. If I told you I could compromise both of us, should you be captured. I know from experience, people always talk. Especially when I ask the questions," the agent remarked, his mouth turned upwards in a smile, like a curved blade, as he remembered his last torture session.

"Well good fortune go with you," Cassius replied, thinking that he never wanted to get on the wrong side of the cold-blooded intelligence officer.

"Good luck to you, too," Vibius said, thinking that, given the skill of the archer's aim, they had something even better to rely on than good fortune.

They may yet complete their mission and live to tell the tale. But if I were a betting man…

17.

Evening.

Lamps, braziers and candles were lit all around the bedchamber. Commodus' blond hair glowed in the light and he more than once admired himself in one of the full-length mirrors in the room.

Give me excess.

There were a couple of instances during the night when the wine-fuelled Commodus had believed that the figures in the murals decorating the walls were moving, swirling in a bacchanalian dance. Just after making love to Titus, however, his sense of revelry turned to paranoia. The figures were watching him, judging him. He blamed his headache on the painting rather than the wine. The classical figures, dressed in traditional Roman garb, represented propriety, virtue and his father. He was tempted to order his attendants to paint over all the faces, or just the eyes, in the morning. Or he would commission new pictures – of Dionysus, Hercules and Priapus.

I have the right to do anything to anybody.

Commodus and Titus lay on the bed, still a little breathless. Commodus wore a silk nightshirt dyed purple, inlaid with gold thread and studded with precious stones. He liked the feel of the material on his skin – and it amused him when the gems would scratch and cut his lovers as he writhed upon them. Titus was naked, marked with such scratches and cuts. Commodus had been rough with him earlier in other ways – but the would-be chamberlain did not dare complain.

Commodus had dismissed Sabine earlier in the evening. "I'm not in the mood for you tonight," the haughty adolescent explained, affecting a yawn. *She now bores me, like my wife does.*

The courtesan had bowed her head and gone into the next room. She would return if called for, as Commodus had instructed her not to leave the house.

The Emperor-in-waiting blindly reached over to the bedside table, knocking a half-eaten plate of oysters onto the floor, and grasped a golden goblet of wine. Some of the ruby-red vintage ran down his chin as he gulped it down.

His eyelids were half-closed and he lazily dreamt of the gladiatorial games he would soon put on.

I will mint new coins for the occasion, proclaiming a new golden age. Already I am called Germanicus and Augustus. But I will add to my titles, to add to my majesty: Pacifier of the Whole Earth, Invincible, the Roman Hercules… Lions will fight tigers, bears will fight drugged-up elephants. I'll order Galen to publicly dissect any exotic beasts afterwards, what's left of them. Blood will flow and cheers will rise up, alerting the gods to the earthly spectacle too. Dancing girls will fill up the arena between bouts… I will even fight myself – and break all records for a left-handed gladiator. I will fight as a dimacharerus – compelled to attack. And my enemies shall play the part of Hannibal, Spartacus and Catiline… People will remember the games. They will remember me. And love me.

"Have you recruited the necessary men and briefed them, to deal with the great hero Maximus?"

"It's done, Caesar," Titus replied. Commodus nodded – in approval and because he liked it when people called him Caesar.

"My father will have some company when he meets the ferryman."

"Two dozen mercenaries will ride out and post themselves at the ambush point. If Maximus and the archer somehow complete their mission and make it back through enemy territory, then Flavius

Ducenius and his men will be waiting for them. Yet it may be the case that Balomar – and the enemy – will do our work for us."

"Indeed. But I must confess that I am slightly in favour of Maximus completing his mission and assassinating the barbarian king. I have no desire for Balomar to prove as irksome to me as he has been to my father. Have you instructed the men to make it look like bandits? Should there be an investigation, or should the bodies be recovered, Caesar must be above suspicion. But mercenaries are not the most loyal and trusted creatures. Word, or rumour, may get out one day. We may have to also deal with Atticus at some point," Commodus remarked, nodding to signify that Titus should rub oil onto his chest, stomach and elsewhere.

"And what of Claudia and his child? Sons have been known to avenge their fathers," Titus said, thinking that he would slit the throats of the family himself if asked, to prove his loyalty – and love.

"It's only natural my friend – and to be admired. Though I must confess should someone now usher my father from the stage I would feel a sense of gratitude rather than vengeance. But we should just sharpen our blades, rather than use them, in relation to Atticus and the woman and child at present. We need to turn our thoughts to Rome, rather than this barbaric backwater. The fourteenth labour of Hercules must be to strangle out any dissenting voices in the Senate. My father compromised with the brood of prattling women too much. He listened to too many voices – and the Empire has been overstretched and pulled in too many different directions. I will listen to just one voice when I wear the purple: my own. Let them hate me, so long as they fear me. Caesar must be Caesar."

*

343

Darkness was legion in the forest. The sound of wildlife occasionally murmured in the background. The chill wind whispered too, between the trees, as if gossiping.

Vibius had provided the soldiers with extra blankets before departing – and both men slept near to the fire – but the cold winter night still bit into the bones of Maximus. Yet his thoughts, rather than the gelid air, kept him awake.

You were fortunate today. The German was faster and stronger than you. Five years ago you would have seen his attack coming and avoided it… Instead of retiring yourself someone else may well retire you… No man has unlimited reservoirs of courage and good luck. There are only so many battles a soldier can fight – and live through. You can't beat the odds all the time… The main thing is that I have provided for them. It's the least, or best, you could have done. Rufus will keep an eye on them when I'm gone. Claudia has managed admirably so far in bringing up the boy. What can I add? How much love have you got left in your heart, after Julia and Aurelia?

Maximus pulled his blankets around him even more, after tossing another couple of logs onto the fire. Tongues of flames darted out into the night with renewed vigour. He envied Cassius' ability to fall asleep at will. He envied the fact that the optio had nothing, and no one, to lose. But then Maximus recalled an encounter with Aurelius. The Emperor had asked Maximus to join him in the garden of the imperial palace. It had been night time, but a balmy summer's evening. He had just received his orders: he would be posted to Egypt. Maximus had been in two minds about whether to ask Julia to marry him. He loved her but was worried that he might make her a widow within a month.

"I fear death, Caesar. For both myself and for her," the young soldier had confessed, confiding in the man he had increasingly considered to be a friend and father-figure.

"It is not death that a man should fear, but he should fear never beginning to live," Aurelius had sagely replied, serenely taking in the divinity of the star-filled firmament.

The following day, Maximus had proposed.

18.

A blanket of mist still hung over the scene at midday, enshrouding the forest, large stone cottage and rippling stream. The atmosphere was damp and would soon be filled with rain. Similar to Maximus' own cottage, back in Britain, the secluded property had an outbuilding which served as a stable and a number of wooden pens which contained livestock. Maximus briefly thought of his own farm again and wondered if it would be part of his future, rather than just his past. Would Claudia like to live there? *We would be out of sight and out of mind in Britain, in regards to Commodus.*

Maximus soon shook such thoughts out of his head however, and refocused on his mission. Along with Cassius he peered through the trees on the other side of the stream. Two burly, fur-clad barbarians sat outside the cottage and played knucklebones. *Sentries.* Maximus had yet to confirm Balomar's presence but he was confident that the chieftain was residing at the house.

"What are the chances of you making the shot should the bastard poke his head outside of the door?" the centurion asked his archer.

"I'm too far away, this side of the stream. The wind and rain look like they're going to get worse, too. We may only get one shot – and I need to make sure I can make it count."

"Then we'll bide our time and wait for the right moment."

And so the two soldiers waited patiently. A shower came and went, dissipating the mist. Cassius occasionally gazed up at the serpentine plume of smoke emanating from the chimney, imagining a roaring fire and hot meal. To help kill time Maximus asked his friend about what he wanted to do, after leaving the army.

346

"So what's your happy ever after?"

"I wouldn't mind opening a tavern somewhere. I'd spend my days asleep and my nights in the arms of different serving girls. I'd fill the menu with my favourite foods and bar tax collectors and politicians. I'd rather have lepers, plague victims and even Christians frequent my establishment over those cretins. Of course you and the rest of my friends wouldn't be allowed to pay for any drinks," Cassius said, with a keen and impish gleam in his aspect.

"I think I'd prefer being a patron to an investor. Do you not picture yourself being married?"

"I thought that we were discussing my happy ever after?"

"You shouldn't let Atticus' experiences colour your thoughts too much. If you find someone who makes you laugh – or fulfils you in a way that a serving girl doesn't – then you might want to share your happy ever after with her. You should consider being a father too. Children are worth living for – and dying for," Maximus said. His expression softened in fondness, thinking of Claudia and Marius. He also thought of Julia, Lucius and Aemelia.

"It seems like you may have already found your happy ever after."

Before the centurion had a chance to reply he was disturbed by the noise of half a dozen warriors filing out of the cottage. The long-haired, swarthy looking Germans carried spears, bows and jugs of wine. It was a hunting party – hunting both for sport and for an evening meal of wood pigeon or wild boar.

Maximus recognised the large, bejewelled gold torc which hung around the man's neck. The Marcomanni king had obtained the unique piece of jewellery through defeating a Dacian tribal chief in a duel. The distinctive, bald-headed figure standing on the other side of the stream was indeed the same man Maximus had seen all those years ago, standing on the other side of the Danube at the Battle of Pannonia. The warrior king had aged but his features seemed no less stern and brutal. Deep-set, cold, calculating eyes looked out beneath a pronounced, bony brow. A cavalry sword, with a silver pommel, hung from his leather trousers. The sword had once belonged to a captured Roman officer. Balomar had used the weapon to skin the man alive. Under the banner of a religious rite the chief had then cooked the heart of his enemy – and consumed it. The Marcomanni king had been the author behind too many Roman deaths. It was now time to erase his name from the land of the living.

"It's him," Maximus said to Cassius. The usually stoical soldier's face was twisted in a sneer of contempt. *He's already dead. He just doesn't know it yet.*

The two men playing knucklebones were ordered to remain at the cottage. Maximus spotted another five warriors – and a couple of women – still inside the house.

The six men – and their chief – walked over the narrow wooden bridge. They were now on Maximus' side of the stream. Some of the men joked and clapped each other on their backs, taking swigs from a jug of wine. One or two looked to attach their bowstrings, only succeeding on their second or third attempt.

"They're going hunting. It looks like they're half drunk, which will hopefully make our job half as easy. The plan is to kill them all. There won't then be anyone who can come back, sound the alarm, and give pursuit. We may just yet get to live happily ever after."

*

The men were now deep into the sodden forest. Shards of sunlight cut through the canopy of trees, chequering the ground in patches of shade and light. The sweet smell of dew and pine laced the air. The ground was thick with ferns and shrubs, some waist high. The rain-soaked ground was also littered with weeds, mushrooms and spongy mosses.

The hunting party were about to split up, in order to cover more ground to locate their quarry. But the hunters were being hunted.

Maximus and Cassius had kept their distance. The carousing warriors had made enough noise – laughing, singing, shouting – to be able to be tracked by a blind man. The soldiers covered their faces and clothes in dirt to further camouflage themselves. Cassius' bow would be next to useless in the forest, so the centurion briefed the archer on taking their enemy out at close quarters.

"Come up behind the bastards, cover their mouths and hack through their throats as if you were starving and their neck were a joint of ham. Don't be put off by the blood that gushes out. Take it as a sign that you're doing your job properly. Just keep on cutting."

Cassius nodded in reply and drew his recently sharpened knife.

The hunting party split off into pairs, with Balomar making a threesome for one of the groups. They now concentrated more on their spears and bows than their jugs of wine. The laughing and ribald conversations ceased. The Marcomanni were now hunting in earnest. But so were the Romans.

Maximus decided to work his way left to right. There was now plenty of distance between the groups of barbarians, although they were still in yelling distance to each other. As it was most likely that the group of three would be able to sound the alarm to the others, they would dispense with them last. By then there would be no one left to call out to.

Maximus and Cassius moved stealthily towards their targets. They kept low, beneath the eye-line of their enemy should they unexpectedly turn around. The focus of the warriors was to look ahead of them, but their ears were pricked for any sounds of birds or rustling through the undergrowth. Thankfully the soft ground suppressed the sound of their footsteps. Despite the cold air

Cassius tasted sweat on his upper lip. He tried to control his breathing and move forward in unison with Maximus. They closed in and stood behind two trees. Their prospective victims were just a few steps away. The centurion communicated to the optio with a couple of simple hand signals that they should strike. The barbarians didn't even have time to turn around. Their eyes widened in shock and terror and they emitted muffled noises as hands covered their mouths. But then it was over. Blood splattered over the leaves of a fern and the bark of a tree. Blood warmed the numb hands of their attackers, too. The bodies slumped to the ground, their faces already ashen.

Maximus and Cassius crouched down, silently nodded to each other, and wiped the blades of their knives on the corpses.

Two down. Five to go.

The soldiers were soon stalking their next brace of barbarians. One of the Germans, Adalbern, walked with a limp, caused by an old war wound which ached even more in the winter chill and damp. Whereas his thick-bearded companion scanned for any movement ahead of him, Adalbern often cast his eyes downwards, possessing a fear, irrational or not, of being gored by a charging wild boar. He attuned his hearing, far more than anyone else, to the sound of rustling leaves and bushes. As such he turned towards his attacker before Maximus had the opportunity to creep up behind him. Yet the centurion was still too quick for the barbarian. Adalbern's warning shout to his comrades got stuck in his throat, along with the praetorian's knife. At the same time Cassius came up behind his opponent, cutting through his beard and then skin. Blood, sinew and wiry hairs matted the optio's blade.

Four down. Three to go.

Whilst the two warriors who accompanied Balomar were focused on the task of hunting – one stood poised with a spear whilst the other readied his bow – the Marcomanni chief turned his attention towards the quarry he had been stalking for the last decade: Rome. As much as Balomar had dreamed of Marcus Aurelius falling in battle, flesh dripping from his own axe, he was still content for old age and disease to kill off his enemy. Balomar permitted himself a smile, as he thought of Aurelius' successor.

The whelp will want to run back to his whores and pampered life back in Rome. He will welcome the peace settlement that I will offer him – and he can even call it a victory if he likes. The cease-fire will allow us time to re-arm and recruit. The Quadi and Iazyges will also know that Commodus is no Caesar, or Aurelius. The philosopher learned quickly, as a general and diplomat. Before Pannonia he hadn't won a major engagement, but afterwards he didn't lose one. But once I have united the Germanic tribes I will purge our lands of the Roman disease. Like Arminius at the Battle of Teutoburg Forest I will ambush and slaughter the enemy. I will force them back over the Danube – and the Rubicon. Should the gods be willing they'll drown in the Tiber, too.

I will flay Rome's arrogant and decadent senators myself. They derisorily call the people parasites. But the politicians are the true parasites, feeding off the labour and taxes of the populace. When the time comes the slaves will turn on their masters. I will but light the touch paper… Any society where the men perfume and oil their hair – and where husbands own bigger wardrobes than their wives – deserves to be conquered. But should Commodus dare to carry out his father's wishes of extending the boundaries of the Empire, then let him. Let them overstretch themselves, thin their ranks and extend their supply lines. Let them also reach the Carpathian Mountains and disturb the hornet's nest of the Goths. They will die a death of a thousand cuts. Once Aurelius' light is extinguished the Empire will decline and fall.

The Marcomanni chief knew he would be willing to give his life for the cause, though, to date he had been more efficient at laying down the lives of others in the name of freedom and victory. Balomar was distracted from his thoughts, however, as a pair of startled wood pigeons darted out from the trees and he, along with his fellow hunters, tracked their flight. Balomar was further distracted from his thoughts by the sight of two men standing before him, carrying knives, purposed to attack.

For a moment time seemed to stand still – for the time it takes a man's breath to mist up and disappear in front of his face – as the combatants took in the scene and assessed whether to fight or flee. Eyes widened, then narrowed, and glances were exchanged. Hearts stopped and then pulsated faster than ever.

The barbarian archer decided that he would fight. His bow, with an arrow already nocked upon it, creaked back. The shaft was lined up with Maximus' chest but just before the German could unleash his arrow, the Roman launched his knife into his enemy's throat.

Witnessing his comrade fall the Marcomanni warrior, carry a hunting spear, decided that flight was preferable to fight. He turned and fled through the forest, abandoning his chieftain to his fate – with the intention of raising reinforcements back at the cottage. Cassius looked to Maximus, who signified for his optio to pursue the enemy.

Five down. Two to go.

They drew their swords. The afternoon sun fell from above, slashing the scene in light.

Balomar snorted and spat out a gob of phlegm. He sneered at his enemy to reveal two fang-like front teeth. He raised his cavalry sword, admiring its polished blade and highlighting its length, compared to his opponent's gladius.

"Do you know who I am?" the Marcomanni chief asked in Latin, rightly believing his attacker to be Roman. He surveyed Maximus, not recognising the ghost from his past. "You should be scared."

"I'm too excited about the prospect of killing you to have time to be scared," the centurion replied, taking in his opponent. Scars, like scratches, marked his bald head. Despite his age he was still in a state of good condition. *Don't underestimate his speed or strength. Let him underestimate you.* Despite a burgeoning beer belly Maximus suspected that there was plenty of muscle as well as flab beneath his furs. Maximus had heard rumours about the prowess and ferocity of his enemy. Balomar had, on more than one occasion, defeated rival tribal leaders in single combat. A merchant once told him that the accomplished warrior even kept body parts from his defeated opponents as trophies.

"Do you think you're the first Roman to try and put me down? I've chewed up and spat out more of your countrymen than your Subura has whores," the barbarian proclaimed, grinning at his own insult, hoping to goad his enemy into making a mistake. "I'm even tempted to take you alive, to have the pleasure of torturing you. I'll snap your toes off one by one and eat your comrade's heart in front of your face. I'll even stuff his balls down your throat. As a Roman, you may even enjoy that."

"You certainly talk more than any woman in the Subura. But if you're playing for time, in hope that one of your men will come to your aid, you will be waiting quite a while. You're men are currently all rifling through their pockets, looking for coins to pay the ferryman."

The leer fell from the barbarian's face and he raised his weapon. Balomar stepped forward and swung his sword in one swift, fluid movement – taking the tip off a fern as he did so. Maximus just about blocked the attack in time – and those that followed – before taking a few steps back, out of the range of the long cavalry blade. The German's eyes were ablaze with hatred.

"Your time will soon be over. Rome's time will soon be over, too. We are now the master race."

Maximus continued to move backwards, as he formed a plan. It was unlikely that he would be able to get close to his opponent, given the chieftain' skill, experience and the superior length of his blade. The praetorian parried the next couple of attacks, but when Balomar swung his blade horizontally, Maximus deftly moved out of the way of the blow, instead of blocking it.

The freshly sharpened blade lodged itself into the hardwood tree behind the centurion. The German's eyes were now ablaze with terror. Balomar looked to butt his opponent, in an attempt to buy time to retrieve his weapon, but Maximus saw the attack coming – and the result was that the Marcomanni king shoved his head downwards onto the point of the soldier's gladius. The blood-curdling scream emitted by the barbarian, as the blade sliced through the jelly of his eye into his brain, frightened the two spectating birds away.

"Master race, my arse."

Six down.

But was there still one more to go?

*

Wet leaves slapped against Cassius' body and face. His damp furs weighed him down, but still he raced as fast as he could, ducking below low branches and leaping over exposed tree roots, in an attempt to close in on his enemy. He carried his bow, having sheathed his knife, just in case a shot presented itself. The optio spared a brief thought for his centurion, hoping that he would best the Marcomanni king, but then he refocused. His lungs burned and he felt the blisters on his feet burst open. He would indeed leave the army with an honourable discharge once this mission was over. The only thing he wanted to chase from now on were barmaids. The foliage thickened and Cassius lost sight of the German's head bobbing up and down through the gaps in the trees. But he would soon be coming to a clearing – a make-shift campsite in the forest – where he hoped he could spy the German again. He could not let him return to the cottage and alert his comrades.

The barbarian jabbed his spear forward, slicing through the Roman's hip. He had concealed himself behind a tree, just before the clearing, waiting for his enemy to come past him. The soldier barely felt the initial sting of the wound but he soon realised its seriousness. Blood began to soak his goat hair undershirt. He felt woozy, weakened. His legs nearly gave way.

Both men panted, attempting to catch their breath, after their long sprint. The squat, pig-faced barbarian grinned at the would-be assassin, savouring the moment. He would have a trophy from the day's hunt after all. His countenance was slick with sweat and grime. A dog-tooth jutted out from his mouth. He spat out a curse in his native language.

Cassius moved backwards, gingerly. He was unable to run. A wounded animal. There would be no escape. He still wanted to put as much distance between himself and his opponent as he could, though. Where there's life there's hope. Cassius mustered what strength and concentration he had left and reached behind him to retrieve an arrow. The smile fell from the barbarian's face, his eyes widened in surprise and alarm, as he read the archer's intention. He thrust his spear forward and charged at his opponent, looking to skewer Cassius before he had the time to nock the arrow and pull the bowstring back. The optio ignored the sight of his enemy

– and crimson spear tip – rushing towards him. He just had to get his arrow away – and firing his bow came as naturally as breathing to the archer. He did not panic. *The harder you practise, the luckier you get.*

The shaft sprang from his bow just in time and stuck into the barbarian's sternum. With what little energy he had left Cassius drew his knife and finished off the Marcomanni warrior by slitting his throat.

Cassius collapsed next to the corpse. Death was beckoning the soldier, too. Darkness closed in on him, as if he were wearing a cowl. The impish gleam in his eyes dimmed. His bloodless face began to shiver in the cold. The optio pictured his mother and father and thought how they would be proud of him. He had died in service to the Emperor. "It is sweet and honourable to die for one's country", his father had once told him, quoting Horace. Rufus would also send what gold he had accumulated back to his family, so they could live comfortably in their old age. Cassius, with the help of his centurion, had written a number of letters to his parents over the years, keeping them abreast of what was happening in his life. The soldier had consciously kept some things back however, not wishing them to worry too much about him. *I'll have time to tell them everything in the next life, though.* Cassius also drowsily hoped that there would be taverns in the afterlife.

20.

"I deposited half the money with your agent this afternoon – and you will receive the remaining half on completion of your mission. We are paying you a premium to buy your silence, as well as purchase your services," Titus remarked to the mercenary, Flavius Ducenius. The two men, sat on their horses, were in a field a couple of miles north of the army camp. Ducenius' squadron of cavalry were encamped in a neighbouring field. Night was drawing in. Black and grey clouds marbled the sky.

"Don't worry, I've no intention of boasting about the fact that I've assassinated Gaius Maximus. Even my closest friends in the army might crucify me for such a crime," the mercenary replied. Ducenius was a former legionary who had served out his twenty-five years and – along with a number of other veterans in their mid-forties who had retired – was a soldier for hire. Ducenius was tall, formidable looking and dressed in a fine fur coat. His armour and weaponry were custom made. His line of work as a mercenary was dangerous, but profitable. He provisioned and paid his men well, and in return they were proficient and loyal. Ducenius allowed them their fun – looting and taking women as spoils of war – but they always completed the job at hand first. None of them would hesitate if he gave the order to cut down the lauded centurion. His narrow, brooding, dark eyes took in everything but gave little away. "I met him once, years ago. He bought my men a round of drinks." *He's a good man.*

"With the money that we're paying you can buy your own vineyard when this is over. Don't let sentiment cloud your judgement when it comes to doing the deed." Titus viewed military personnel with a mixture of snobbery and fear. Yet he believed that people – soldiers and civilians alike – should start fearing him, given his closeness to the future Emperor.

Flavius Ducenius flashed a baleful look at the lackey, as he deemed Titus. He snorted and a globule of phlegm shot out of his nose and across the perfume-wearing agent, just missing him. The soldier had come across Titus' kind before, all too often. *Preening, conceited and cowardly.* Just because they spoke for important men, they believed they were equally as important as them. The decorated praetorian was worth a thousand of his ilk. But the fee that Titus' employer was paying was worth even more to the mercenary.

"Maximus may be a good man. But he's also a dead man."

*

"You didn't think that I was going to pass on the promise of free drinks when you open up your tavern, did you?" Maximus said, as the optio opened his eyes.

The centurion had tracked Cassius' path through the forest and found him – wounded and unconscious. He quickly lit a fire to keep his patient warm. With supplies and knowledge gleaned from Galen over the years Maximus sutured and bandaged the cut.

Whilst Cassius remained unconscious Maximus concealed the bodies of the enemy, just in case their comrades came looking for them. They would now smell, rather than see, the corpses first if they sent out a search party, he fancied. Before hiding the body of Balomar, though, Maximus pulled off the gold torc from around his neck. At first he would show it to Aurelius, as a trophy and evidence of his death. But then he would sell the valuable piece of jewellery and use the money to buy Marius the pony he had promised him.

Cassius' right side was stiff and sore with pain, as if his hip was on fire, but the archer had endured worse over the years.

"Balomar?" Cassius said, asking after the fate of the Marcomanni king.

"Not even Galen could bring him back to life. But how are you feeling?" The centurion was fashioning a make-shift crutch for his friend as he spoke.

"I'll live. You should see the other guy though," Cassius replied, part smiling and part wincing in pain.

"I did. If we weren't about to retire I'd give you training on how to use a sword and spear, though. Are you fit to walk?"

"Yes, just about, I think. Although it may be some time before I'll be ready to chase barmaids again."

"With the war wound you've just received – and the reward Aurelius will give us for killing an enemy of Rome – the barmaids will be chasing you from now on."

"Now there's a happy ever after I can definitely relate to."

21.

Sentiment wouldn't cloud his judgement, Flavius Ducenius thought to himself, recalling the lackey's comment, as he peered through the treeline, waiting for his target. Indeed the chief sentiment the mercenary was governed by was a love of money. Ducenius pictured Titus again, his haughty demeanour and hair slick with myrrh. Perhaps the young lackey would one day climb the greasy pole of politics and be able to make policy. Ducenius had every confidence in Titus' ability to give an incompetent order to advance when an army should withdraw, or vice-versa. Titus was also more than capable of offering or receiving a bribe too, to further his self-interest at the expense of soldiers' lives. *Politicians are politicians.* But hopefully Titus would make enemies during his career – and one day someone would come to the mercenary and pay him to assassinate the lackey. Ducenius considered that he may even offer a discount for his services, for once. The soldier gave little consideration, however, as to who wanted the centurion dead. Past experience told him that it could be a rival officer, a jealous husband, a scheming senator or a woman scorned. *Just so long as their money is good.*

Ducenius' men had made it to the ambush point mid-morning, having camped in the forest overnight. It was now late afternoon. The lackey had mentioned how the enemy might do the mercenary's job for him and kill Maximus (and the archer he was travelling with). If so then he would still retain half of the payment. The plan was to wait as long as three days for his target to appear. Ducenius divided his squadron into two watches, just in case the soldiers travelled down the road at night. And so half his force was back at the make-shift camp in the woods, nearby. They would be sleeping, drinking some watered-down wine around the campfire, or sharpening their weapons.

Sleet filled the air. The chill bit hard into any piece of exposed skin. Unfortunately the squadron were fated to follow where war, rather than good weather, broke out. The track was narrow and isolated, perfect for an ambush. They kept watch in the shadows, inside the treeline. Occasionally, on rotation, men would retreat further into the forest to warm themselves by a campfire and down a cup of heated wine. During the afternoon a number of locals and merchants had used the road. A few carried provisions that might have helped to shorten the prospective long days ahead but, as Ducenius reminded his lieutenant, Otho, they were soldiers, not common thieves. Rome and the Marcomanni had made the lives of the local people miserable enough. The mercenary had no desire to add to their privation.

"What will you spend your share on?" the hulking, bushy-eyed lieutenant asked his commander. Otho planned to use his bounty to pay off his debts, caused by his love of gambling and investing in risky business ventures.

"After my wife and mistress spend their shares I might well be able to afford to buy a jar of the army's finest acetum," Ducenius drily replied.

"That's funny."

I only wish I was joking.

"Although I may now be able to purchase two jars of acetum," Ducenius said, his narrow eyes widening and gleaming like two silver coins as he spied Maximus and the archer slowly making their way towards them. The mercenary gave the order for his men to ready themselves and surround their targets, when he gave the word. They were not to engage Maximus and the optio though, until he said so. Ducenius also instructed one of his men to race back to camp and have the other watch come to him and bring all the horses. Their mission would soon be over and he wanted to ride back to Sirmium as soon as he could – and collect the second half of his fee.

Maximus quickly drew his gladius and his body became alert at seeing the first couple of figures appear from out of the forest. His shoulders slumped, however, when the number of men grew to over ten. Neither flight nor fight were realistic options.

Ducenius, his sword drawn, approached the centurion. He briefly took in the injured archer: his pale face and black eyes. Cassius grimaced in pain as he turned his body to take in Otho, who stood by the side of him with his spear raised. He was half-dead already, it seemed.

"I don't suppose that you're here to provide us with an escort back to the camp?" Maximus asked, as he surveyed the band of mercenaries who surrounded him. Some carried swords, some axes and some spears. They had the grizzled look of veterans about them. They would all know how to handle themselves. They had all killed before – more times than some of them had bathed.

"If I said yes, would you believe me? I want you to know that this isn't personal, Maximus. In fact, I would much prefer to kill the person who hired me, whoever that is, instead of a fellow soldier. But business is business. You won't be able to talk or fight your way out of this one. There appears to be little fight left in you anyway, by the looks of things."

"You might be unpleasantly surprised by how much fight there is still left in me," Maximus replied, sword in hand, mettle in his voice. Although it appeared that a strong gust of wind might blow Cassius over he still firmly held his knife as well as his crutch. The optio cursed the mercenaries under his breath – and equally cursed the unknown treacherous bastard who had ordered their executions.

362

Ducenius nodded at the centurion, in acknowledgement and respect. The mercenary had little doubt Maximus had the skill and nerve to go down fighting. It wouldn't be good for morale, or business, if he needlessly lost men.

"You have fought with honour throughout your life, Maximus. It is only fair that I offer you a good death. If you die like a Roman and submit, then I give my word that we will take your bodies back with us so your families will be able to observe proper funeral rites and grieve you. Should you wish to pass on any messages to loved ones I will see that they are anonymously, but safely, delivered."

Cassius thought of his parents. He didn't want them not knowing what had happened to him. He wanted them to be able to say goodbye. The soldier was also sufficiently superstitious enough to want to die with funeral rites, rather than die like a dog in a ditch.

Maximus thought of Claudia and Marius... The centurion had experienced a presentiment before setting off that it would be one mission too many. He knew his story wouldn't end back in Sirmium, Britain or Rome. Poets and philosophers may claim that life is a journey – but death is the destination. After Julia and Aurelia passed away Maximus frequently thought about killing himself, when the light didn't shine in the darkness. He bought a vial of poison, which he kept in a draw by his bed. There was nothing to live for. He also knew that death was the only way to find out whether there was a God and Heaven. And he could endure Hell if he knew that the people he loved were in Heaven. He had been either too brave, or too cowardly, to end things before. But he would now submit – as much as dying like a Roman meant fighting like one. Perhaps he was fated to meet the ferryman at the same time as Aurelius, seeing as their lives had been so intertwined. He would live on though, through Marius. The soldier wistfully recalled something Rufus had once said, quoting Cicero, and hoped that there was some grain of truth in it: "The life of the dead is placed in the memory of the living."

"This is one fight we can't win, sir. I would like my body to go back to my family, if that's alright with you?" Cassius dolefully remarked, as if already in a state of mourning himself. *Some battles are not worth fighting.*

"I understand. You can buy me that drink in the afterlife." The officer clasped a hand on his friend's shoulder and offered him a meaningful look that communicated more than anything words could say.

The sleet turned to snow, misting up the air. Plaintive birdsong warbled out from the whitening forest. Part of Maximus felt guilty, for being responsible for Cassius' death. Part of him was scared: he was about to die. Part of him felt angry: he wanted to kill the man in front of him. Yet the soldier was also slightly and strangely at peace. Finally, it would all be over.

Ducenius smiled, but not too overtly, realising that the men would accept his offer. He would duly honour his promise and deliver their bodies – and any messages – to their families. He had given his word – and a deal was a deal.

"Happy ever afters only really exist in books anyway." The optio tried to muster a smile to accompany his comment, but couldn't.

"I'd ask you to grant me one last request as well," Maximus said to the mercenary. "I need you to get a message to the Emperor that Balomar is dead."

"I will do so," Ducenius promised, as he heard the sound of horses galloping towards him from behind. His men were keen to get back home too, he thought. *It's time to finish the job.*

"Any last words?" Ducenius asked. He planned to execute the centurion mercifully, efficiently, by stabbing him through the heart. Out of respect for the centurion's loved ones he didn't want to cut his throat or disfigure him. He would nod to Otho – and the lieutenant would similarly dispatch the optio.

The hour of departure has arrived and we go our ways; I to die, and you to live. Which is better? Only God knows. – Socrates.

"Yes," Maximus said, as a sphinx-like grin unexpectedly replaced the scowl on his face. "Here comes the cavalry."

The centurion recognised the distinctive polished helmet and red plume of Quintus Perennis through the wintry haze. His nostrils seemed to flare as widely as his large, sorrel charger's as the decurion rode at the head of his squadron. The mercenaries barely had a chance to recognise that the twenty strong horsemen were the enemy, as opposed to the comrades they were expecting. The battle could little be described as such; rather, it was a slaughter. Quintus cut down the first man he came to, slashing him across the chest (the gash ran from his right shoulder to his left hip). The next horseman, riding just behind Quintus, swung his sword low and sliced open a mercenary's stomach. His intestines spilled out onto the road as he fell to the ground. A high-pitched scream spewed into the air – to be closely followed by another, and another.

Maximus first attacked the axe-wielding enemy to the right of him. The pinched-faced mercenary at first squinted at the indistinct group of horsemen galloping towards him – but then his jaw dropped when the decurion finally came into focus. At that point the tip of Maximus' gladius whistled through the air and sliced through his chin, lips and cheek.

Given the shock he must have felt at the surprise attack, Ducenius reacted quickly. He realised he still had a chance to kill the centurion, flee into the woods and collect his fee. He lunged forward at Maximus but the centurion managed to parry the blow, having just felled the axe-man. With his opponent over-extended and slightly off-balance, Maximus counter-attacked. With a flick of his wrist the praetorian cut through the tendons of Ducenius' sword arm. His weapon fell to the ground and the mercenary let out a roar that must have shook the snow from the branches over his head. With his uninjured arm Ducenius looked to unsheathe his dagger, which hung from his belt. As he clasped the ivory handle, however, Maximus jabbed his sword point through the back of the mercenary's hand and into his abdomen. The centurion stood over the defeated Ducenius, gore dripping from his blade.

It was nothing personal.

Otho watched his comrades fall or flee, as they looked to escape the horsemen by disappearing into the safety of the forest. The pay was good, but not so good that it was worth sacrificing one's life for. It was every mercenary for himself. A sense of violence and vengeance welled in Otho's stomach, however. He would at least bloody his spear by skewering the wounded archer, who stood immobile in front of him. Cassius witnessed the intent in Otho's eyes. The only thing the optio seemed to have time to do was close his eyes and resign himself to his fate. Yet Cassius failed to feel the leaf-shaped blade of the mercenary's spear plunge into him. When he opened his eyes he saw one of Rufus Atticus' throwing knives protruding out of his enemy's shoulder. Before Cassius had time to then blink the flank of Atticus' horse slammed into the brawny mercenary – winding him and snapping his neck.

*

The enemy were slain or scattered to the four winds. Quintus Perennis still gave orders, however, to set up sentries and a defensive perimeter. Corpses littered the ground and ribbons of blood scarred the freshly settled snow. The cavalry officer dismounted and approached Maximus.

"It's now my honour to say I served with you, Quintus Perennis," the centurion said. "You have my deepest thanks. Perhaps you could fill me in."

"I think it's best if Atticus does so, sir, as I'm still in the dark as to some things."

22.

Evening.

A pair of owls, seemingly flirting, hooted to one another in the background. Tethered horses snorted, whinnied and swished their tails. A few of the cavalry remained awake and traded stories about the afternoon's skirmish. There had been a few injuries but thankfully they hadn't lost anyone during the fight.

Maximus and Atticus sat apart from the main part of the camp, around their own crackling fire, sharing a jug of wine. Maximus stared intently into the flames, perhaps wishing that the tongues of fire could speak and offer him counsel. And consolation. His body and soul ached as if he had been placed upon a wrack throughout the past few days – or decades. Atticus had just provided his friend with an explanation of events – and asked the question: "What do you want to do? Kill him?"

For once Commodus had had reason to be paranoid about the paintings on the wall staring at him, judging him. They had been. Or at least one had been, as Sabine had stood behind the mural and spied on the Emperor to be. The room in the house next to the large bedchamber which Sabine had retreated into was not, as Commodus thought, along the hall. But rather it was a secret passage running parallel to the wall of the bedroom. It was not uncommon for some husbands to install such chambers into their properties, in order to spy on their wives. Or, as Sabine knew all too well, some people just liked to watch.

The courtesan worked as an informant for Vibius Nepos, but she had recently reported to Atticus (who passed any relevant intelligence onto the spymaster, who was always conscious of thinking a few moves ahead in the game). The two agents became lovers – and then something more: friends. They shared a similar sense of humour and love of literature. Both parties harboured doubts – that somehow the other was just acting out a role (or that they were lying to themselves) – but both also nurtured a hope that what they had was real. When Sabine had heard Commodus and her brother discuss the fate of Maximus – and potentially Atticus – she knew she needed to pick a side and act. The following day the agent had located Atticus, although it took a frustratingly long time to do so, and Sabine had recounted what she had overheard the previous evening. Atticus in turn had tracked down Quintus Perennis.

Atticus' question to his friend, whether to murder Commodus or not, seemed to hang in the air like a coin toss. Maximus twisted the ring on his finger and thought of Aurelia. She was the reason why his soul ached so much. In her letters to him she had often quoted the Bible.

Man is born to trouble, as the sparks fly upwards.

The fire sent cinders spiralling into the night air.

Is this the light shining in the darkness?

"I feel like I've killed enough for one lifetime, Rufus. It's not that I consider that Commodus is any type of brother, but I do consider Aurelius to have been akin to a father to me. What was it you also recently said to me? It's preferable to have a bad Emperor than a worse civil war. The misery may well begin, rather than cease, at his murder. I've got enough blood on my hands. Like Cincinnatus, I should go back to being a farmer. It seems you have may have found someone worth spending your retirement with, too."

"That I have," Atticus replied, smiling. The expression upon his face, as he thought of Sabine, was one that his friend hadn't seen before. It mirrored that of when a younger Maximus had thought about his wife Julia, many years ago. "I'm using the logic of third

369

time lucky and thinking of making her an honest woman – if that's not too oxymoronic a title."

The two soldiers continued to talk, laugh and finish off their jug of wine. They also finished off discussing their plans for leaving. They would ride hard for Sirmium at first light. Rufus would collect Claudia and Marius, whom he had moved into hiding the day before lest Commodus' enmity towards Maximus extended to his family. Rufus would also meet with Sabine – and ask her to come with him. "If she says no then at least I can use my broken heart to start writing poetry again. But I need her to say yes. I love her," Atticus declared. It was only after saying the words that he realised how much he meant them. The plan would then be for them all to convene at the crossroads, west of the town. Before he could leave, however, Maximus would need to say goodbye to an old friend.

Epilogue

Galen was under orders to admit no one, except the Emperor's attendant, Commodus and Maximus. Commodus had already left the camp before the centurion arrived.

Maximus entered the room. Lamps, candles and braziers lit the chamber yet there was an air of gloom which couldn't be totally expunged.

The Emperor lay in bed. His hair was brittle. Maximus remembered how Aurelius' once glossy curls, which had hung down over his forehead, had inspired a fashion in the capital for others to demand a similar haircut. Liver-spots covered his snow-white brow and the back of his claw-like hands. The light flickered in and out of his milky, rheumy eyes – like the oil lamp hanging over the door, which flickered on and off.

The Emperor had decided to starve himself, to end things. "I want to turn the last page. I'm no longer going to fight death. Indeed, that may be the best way to combat it."

Galen had still protested, arguing that his patient should still eat something. But the Emperor wryly replied, "I may soon be feasting on ambrosia with the gods. I wouldn't want to spoil my appetite by eating mere cereal and honey."

That morning Aurelius summoned his senior advisers and Commodus. The stoical Emperor asked them not to mourn too him too much, and to do their best to advise and support his son.

"Here is my son, whom you brought up, who has just reached the age of adolescence and stands in need of guides through the storm of life. You must be many fathers to him, in place of just me alone...,"

Both Commodus and the advisers had dutifully nodded their heads, but ultimately the Emperor's words would fall on deaf ears.

"It's done," Maximus declared, deciding that he would not divulge his mission in its entirety.

The Emperor raised a smile, pleased that his centurion had survived and that his enemy had, finally, been defeated. Aurelius briefly closed his eyes – in repose, pain, exhaustion or peace. "Thank you. And Cassius made it back, too?" His voice was little more than a whisper, as weak as the rest of his body. The Roman moved closer to his all-too-mortal Emperor, to hear him better.

"He was wounded, but Galen says he will recover. The real pain will come from him not being able to exert himself in the tavern for some time."

Aurelius raised the corner of one side of his mouth, to offer up a smile. "Regardless of whether this conflict ends or not you must go back home, Gaius. Make a home, with your new family."

Maximus sat by his friend, clasped his hand and cried.

"I hope those are tears of happiness. For I'm going home. No one knows whether death, which people fear as being the greatest evil, may not be the greatest good," Aurelius said, quoting Plato, in an attempt to console his companion.

The centurion thought him the best of Emperors and the best of men. They spoke for a little while longer, as they reminisced and Aurelius asked Maximus about his son and his plans. Sensing the patient's fatigue, however, Maximus brought a close to their conversation. The praetorian's final duty was to ask his general about the watchword for the day.

He wistfully replied, "Go to the rising son. For I am already setting."

*

372

After leaving the Emperor Maximus encountered Galen in the adjacent room. Both men somehow knew they would never see each other again.

"You've proved to be the greatest physician of the age."

"Tell me something I don't know. My incompetent contemporaries have done their bit to grant me such a title, as much as I have earned it, however. But thank you… It is a curse and a blessing that I see most things through the prism of science and logic, Maximus. Like Aristotle, I'm compelled to classify. Yet it would be wrong of me to judge you as being just a former patient or colleague. I consider you a friend. You have also proved yourself to be the greatest soldier of the age, though I say this with the proviso that you must still retire. Find some peace."

Maximus at first clasped a hand on the old man's shoulder, but then he embraced the haughty doctor. Galen, a stranger to displays of affection, screwed his face up a little and felt decidedly awkward. But he also found himself wrapping an arm around the soldier, to return his embrace. He couldn't bring himself to hug the soldier with both of his arms, though. *No, that would have been too much. Much too much.*

*

Commodus spent the afternoon planning his gladiatorial games and going through designs and fabrics for his coronation robes. His good mood was punctured, however, by the news that Maximus had survived. He petulantly ordered for all of his attendants, bar one, to leave his chamber. He screamed rather than bellowed. Titus stood before his master. He put on his best contrite expression, whilst cursing Ducenius and Maximus underneath his breath.

"I do not know how he escaped, Caesar."

"An adviser should come to me with answers, not mysteries. Now get out of my sight, while I decide your fate." *I'll spare his life. But I will not reward failure. The whore can find another patron… Yet I will still need a suitable chamberlain and lover when I return to the capital.*

The soon-to-be Emperor smiled lasciviously and licked his lips as he recalled a young Greek freedman he had encountered – Saoterus. *A very suitable candidate… I'll take him. I have the right to do anything to anybody… He will love me, as much as the people and history.*

*

Sunlight poked through the clouds. The snow had melted. Buds were beginning to flower on the trees. Colourful songbirds darted through the air in a courtship dance – or a game of kiss-chase.

Maximus stood at the crossroads, outside of Sirmium, with Atticus.

"She said yes, would you believe?" Atticus said, grinning like a teenager.

"I hope she makes an honest man out of you, if that's not too oxymoronic an idea," Maximus replied, pleased for his friend.

Whilst Marius showed his new pony off to Cassius in the background Claudia approached the two centurions.

"We should leave soon. Are you sure you're fine about coming to Britain? The weather's bad and the food's worse," Maximus remarked.

"I'm sure. I'll be able to endure the rain and the cuisine, just so long as we all remain together. Marius is looking forward to it as well. He's treating it as his first campaign with his father." Sunlight – and something else – radiated in the woman's eyes as she spoke. Claudia had wept in private, in relief and joy, on hearing of Maximus' return.

"Cassius will be joining us too. He says he has an itch to visit the island again. And if he can make money anywhere from opening a tavern, it'll be in Britain."

Claudia kissed her brother goodbye and wished him well, before returning to her son and offering him some riding tips.

"Don't wait too long before visiting. Among other things I need to thank your wife-to-be for saving my life."

"Don't worry, I'll visit soon enough. You may be interested in having me as a business partner by then – and also as a brother-in-law," Atticus said, with a suggestive gleam in his eye, as he noticed his friend gazing lovingly at his sister.

Maximus smiled, blushed and nodded. "Anything's possible."

End Note

In some ways the sun set on the Roman Empire after the death of Marcus Aurelius. After the five "good" Emperors, as they are deemed, Commodus was a terrible leader and turned the clock back to the dark days of Tiberius and Caligula. Aurelius' greatest failing was choosing his son as his successor, one may argue. Others would argue that Commodus was, unfortunately, the only choice.

I have now written books on Caesar, Augustus and Aurelius. I hold the latter in the greatest esteem. It has been both a pleasure and a privilege to write about his life – and quote him.

As always thank you for your emails and letters. Please do get in touch if you have enjoyed reading the *Sword of Empire* books. I can be reached via @rforemanauthor and richardforemanauthor.com.

For those of you who enjoyed *Augustus: Son of Rome* you may be pleased to know that I have finally started working on the sequel, *Augustus: Son of Caesar*.

Richard Foreman.

For submissions to Sharpe Books please contact Richard Foreman richard@sharpebooks.com

Also by Richard Foreman

Warsaw

A Hero of Our Time

Sword of Rome Series

Sword of Rome: Standard Bearer

Sword of Rome: Alesia

Sword of Rome: Gladiator

Sword of Rome: Rubicon

Sword of Rome: Pharsalus

Sword of Rome: The Complete Campaigns

Swords of Rome: Omnibus of the Historical Series Books 1-3

Sword of Empire Series

Sword of Empire: Praetorian

Sword of Empire: Centurion

Sword of Empire: The Complete Campaigns

Sword of Empire: Omnibus

Raffles Series

Raffles: The Gentleman Thief

Raffles: Bowled Over

Raffles: A Perfect Wicket

Raffles: Caught Out

Raffles: Stumped

Raffles: Playing On

Raffles: Omnibus of Books 1 - 3

Raffles: The Complete Innings

Band of Brothers Series

Band of Brothers: The Complete Campaigns

Band of Brothers: Agincourt

Band of Brothers: The Game's Afoot

Band of Brothers: Omnibus

Band of Brothers: Harfleur

Augustus Series

Augustus: Son of Rome

Augustus: Son of Caesar

Pat Hobby Series

Pat Hobby's Last Shot

The Complete Pat Hobby

The Great Pat Hobby

The Return of Pat Hobby

Printed in Great Britain
by Amazon